UNIKORN

CREATED AND WRITTEN BY
DON HANDFIELD
& JOSHUA MALKIN

ARTIST
RAFAEL LOUREIRO

LETTERER
DC HOPKINS

COLORISTS
DIJJO LIMA
DANIEL DA SILVA RODRIGUES

COVER ARTIST
NICHOLAS ELY

FOR SCOUT COMICS

CEO
BRENDAN DENEEN

CMO
DON HANDFIELD

CCO
JAMES PRUETT

CO–PUBLISHER
DAVID BYRNE

CSO
TENNESSEE EDWARDS

CO–PUBLISHER
CHARLIE STICKNEY

PRESIDENT
JAMES HAICK III

ASSOCIATE PUBLISHER
RICHARD RIVERA

HEAD OF DESIGN
JOEL RODRIGUEZ

PIN UP ARTISTS

**RAFAEL LOUREIRO   RALF SINGH   LENO CARVALHO
POP MHAN   JOSEPH SCHMALKE**

EDITORS

**JORDAN MOORE   LILLIANA WINKWORTH   KATIE ARTHURS
SANDY SMITH   ANNA WEINSTEIN   DUFFY ASTRIAB**

FOR ARMORY FILMS

CHRIS LEMOLE   TIM ZAJAROS

FOR MOTOR CONTENT

JORDAN MOORE

UNIKORN, December 2021. First printing. Published by Scout Comics & Entertainment, Inc. 12541 Metro Parkway Unit 20, Fort Myers, FL 33966. ©2021 Don Handfield, Joshua Malkin & Armory Films. All Rights Reserved. Unikorn, the Unikorn logo, and all characters, likeness and situations featured herein are trademarks and/or registered trademarks of Don Handfield, Joshua Malkin and Armory Films. Except for review purposes, no portion of this publication may be reproduced or transmitted, in any form or by any means, without the express written permission of Don Handfield, Joshua Malkin and Armory Films. Pringles is a trademark of Pringles LLC, used with permission. All names, characters, locations and events in this publication are fictional. Any resemblance to actual persons (living or dead), events, institutions, or locales, without satiric intent, is coincidental. For more information on Scout Comics, visit the website at scoutcomics.com. For more information on Motor Content, visit motor.ink. Printed in the United States of America.

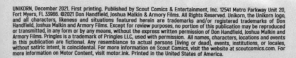

IN MEMORY OF
HARRY JEROME SEAMEN
ROBERT PATRICK KELLY
WANDA MARTIN
AMANDA GRAMP

"AND ABOVE ALL, WATCH WITH
GLITTERING EYES THE WHOLE
WORLD AROUND YOU BECAUSE
THE GREATEST SECRETS ARE
ALWAYS HIDDEN IN THE MOST
UNLIKELY PLACES. THOSE WHO
DON'T BELIEVE IN **MAGIC** WILL
NEVER FIND IT."

ROALD DAHL

FOR
ROBINSON & DEACON
– DH

FOR
CALEB & MIRANDA
– JM

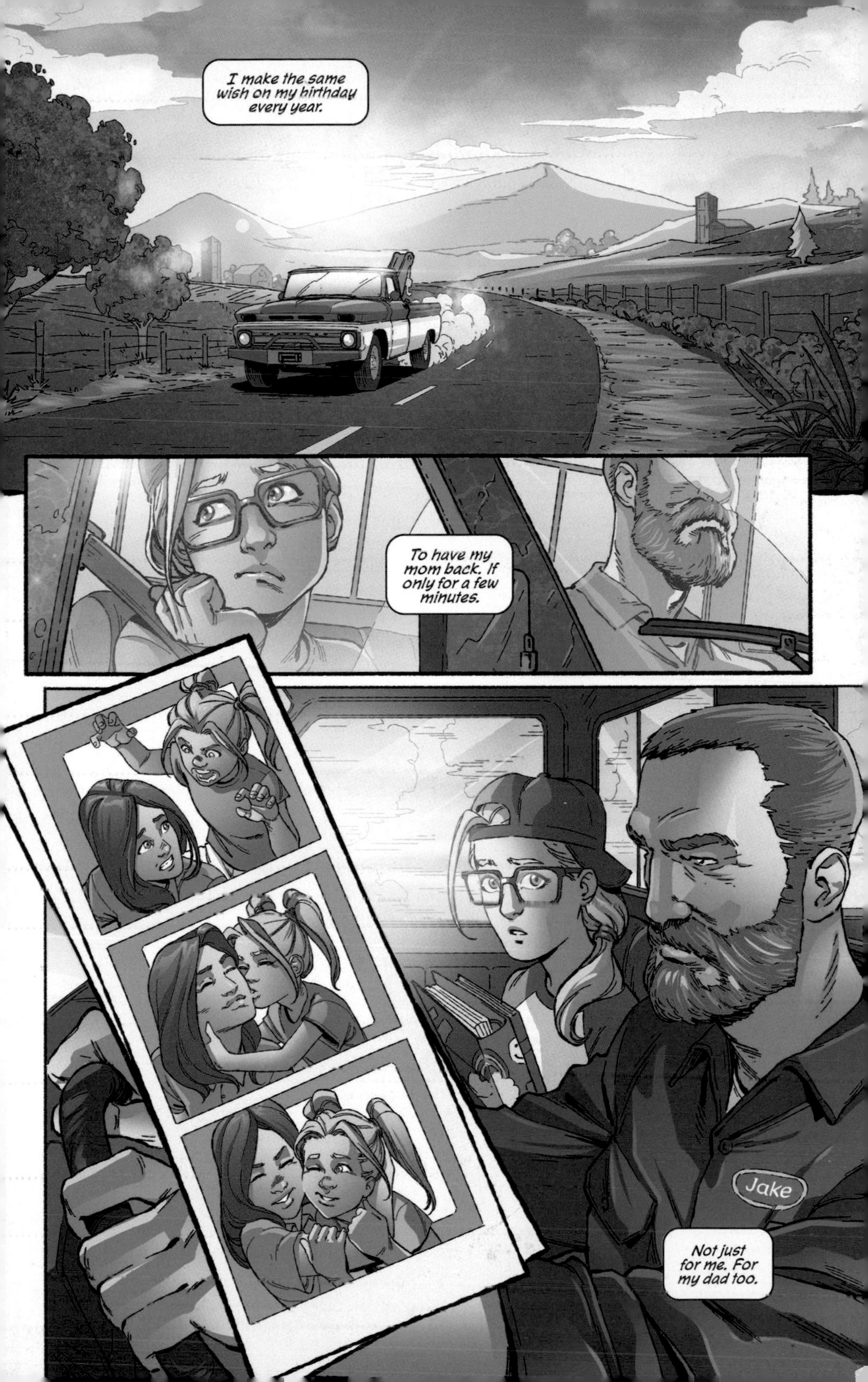
I make the same wish on my birthday every year.
To have my mom back. If only for a few minutes.
Jake
Not just for me. For my dad too.

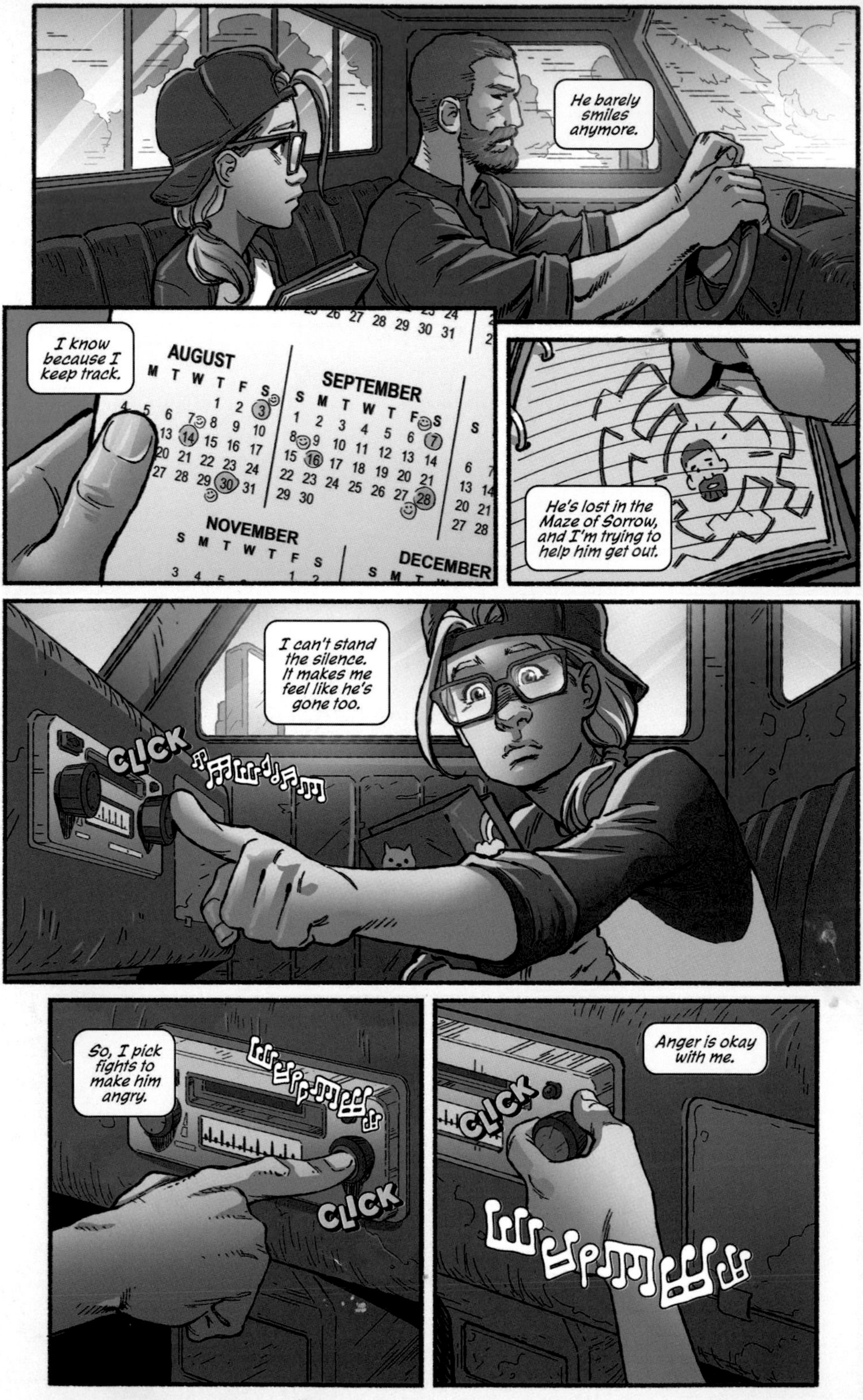
He barely smiles anymore.
I know because I keep track.
AUGUST
SEPTEMBER
NOVEMBER
DECEMBER
He's lost in the Maze of Sorrow, and I'm trying to help him get out.
I can't stand the silence. It makes me feel like he's gone too.
CLICK
So, I pick fights to make him angry.
CLICK
Anger is okay with me.
CLICK

Knock it off, Mae.

♩♪♫♬~*
CLICK

Anger means he still cares.

I don't remember the accident. But I know the bridge we went off. We drive over it every day.

Somehow, I wound up on the riverbank.

But they never found my mom.

I overheard the firemen say the currents probably carried her away.

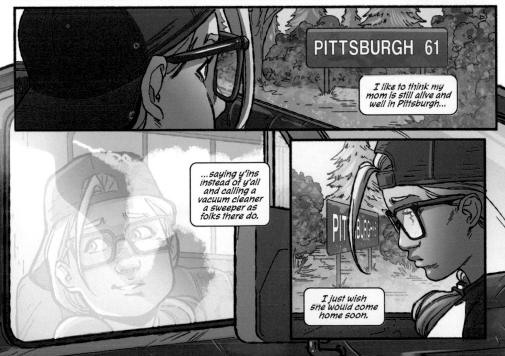

PITTSBURGH 61

I like to think my mom is still alive and well in Pittsburgh...

...saying y'ins instead of y'all and calling a vacuum cleaner a sweeper as folks there do.

PIT BURGH 61

I just wish she would come home soon.

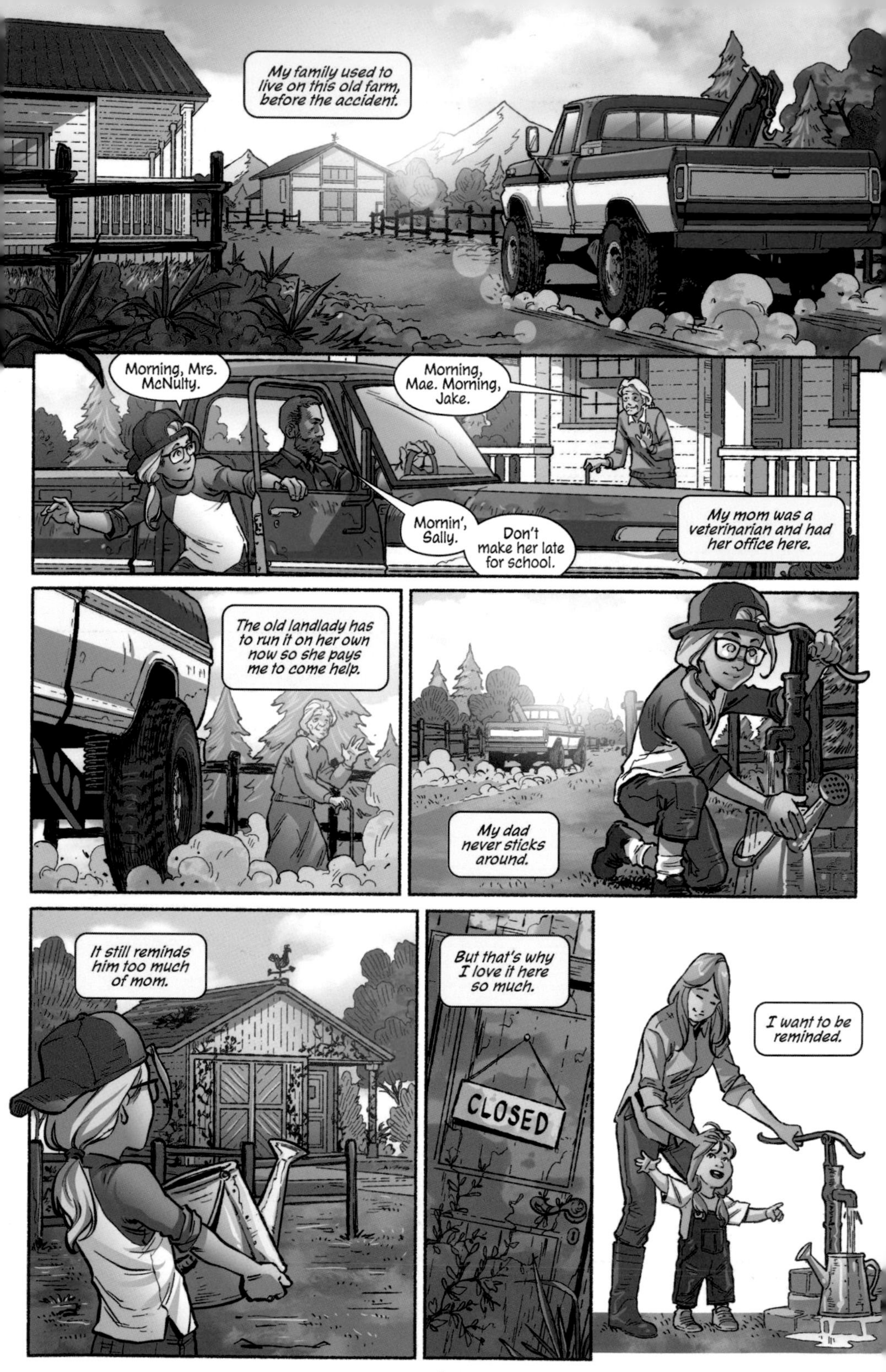
My family used to live on this old farm, before the accident.
Morning, Mrs. McNulty.
Morning, Mae. Morning, Jake.
Mornin', Sally.
Don't make her late for school.
My mom was a veterinarian and had her office here.
The old landlady has to run it on her own now so she pays me to come help.
My dad never sticks around.
It still reminds him too much of mom.
But that's why I love it here so much.
CLOSED
I want to be reminded.

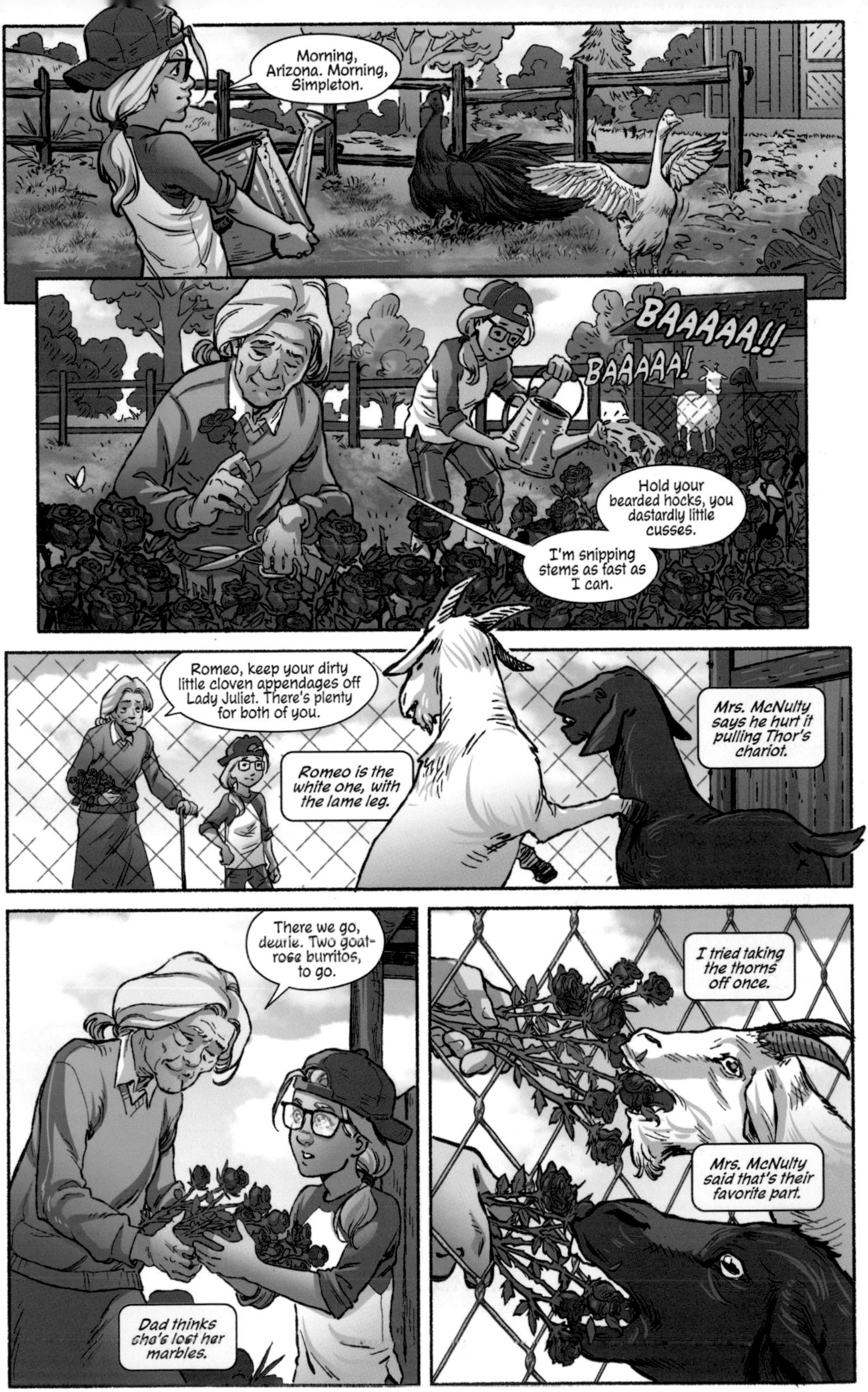

Morning, Arizona. Morning, Simpleton.
BAAAAA!!
BAAAAA!
Hold your bearded hocks, you dastardly little cusses.
I'm snipping stems as fast as I can.
Romeo, keep your dirty little cloven appendages off Lady Juliet. There's plenty for both of you.
Romeo is the white one, with the lame leg.
Mrs. McNulty says he hurt it pulling Thor's chariot.
There we go, dearie. Two goat-rose burritos, to go.
Dad thinks she's lost her marbles.
I tried taking the thorns off once.
Mrs. McNulty said that's their favorite part.

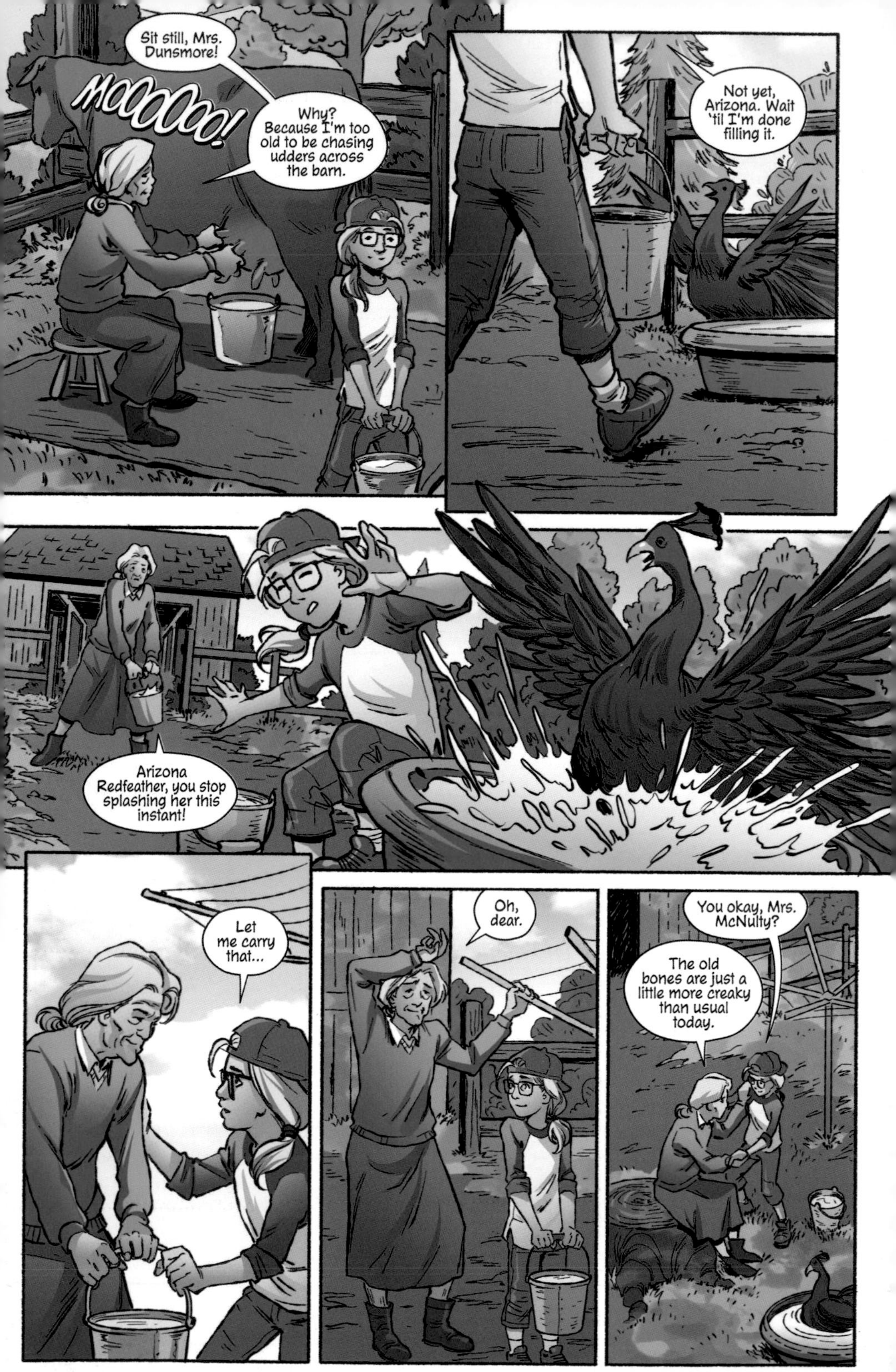
Sit still, Mrs. Dunsmore!
MOOOOOOO!
Why? Because I'm too old to be chasing udders across the barn.
Not yet, Arizona. Wait 'til I'm done filling it.
Arizona Redfeather, you stop splashing her this instant!
Let me carry that...
Oh, dear.
You okay, Mrs. McNulty?
The old bones are just a little more creaky than usual today.

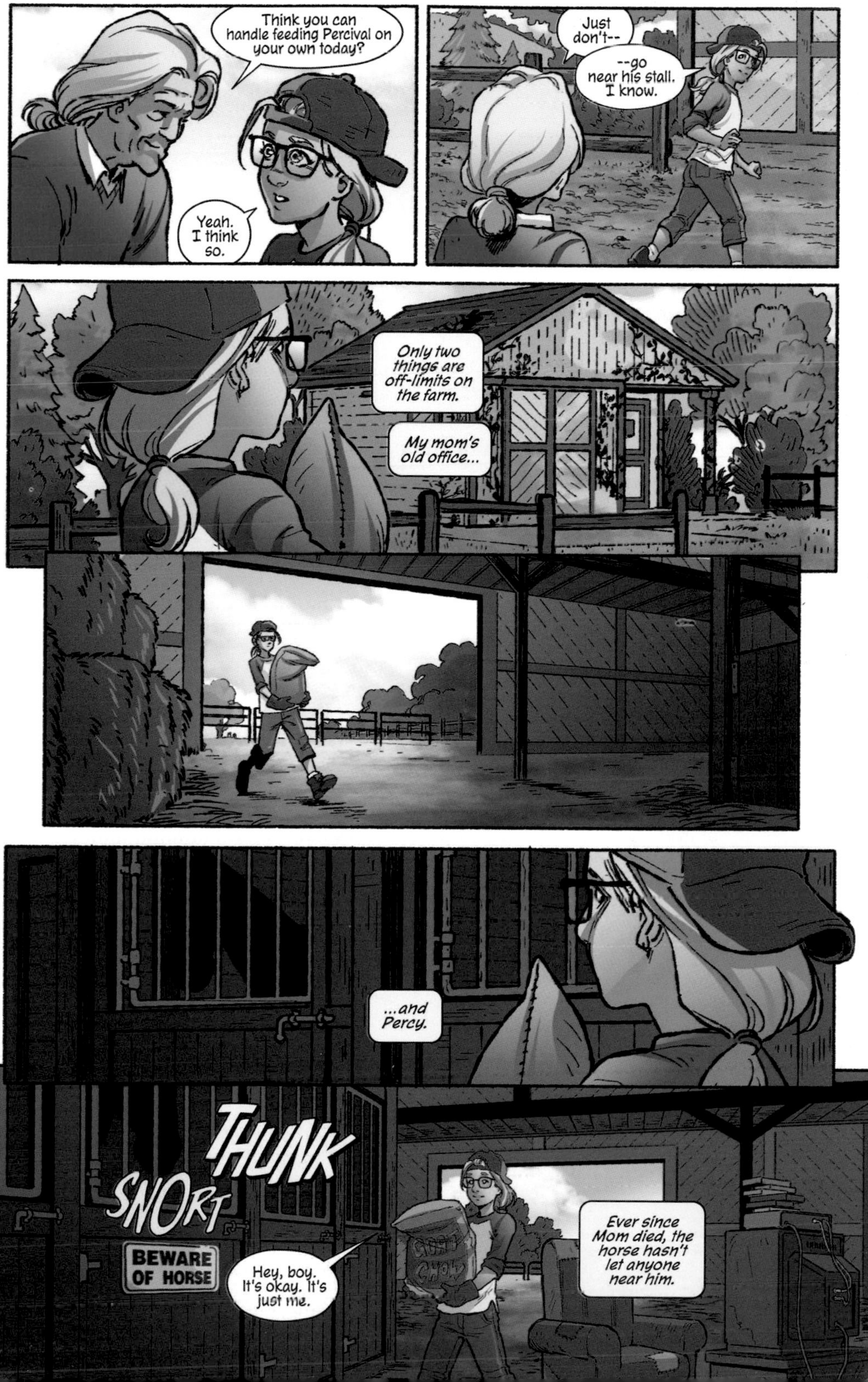
Think you can handle feeding Percival on your own today?
Yeah. I think so.
Just don't--
--go near his stall. I know.
Only two things are off-limits on the farm.
My mom's old office...
...and Percy.
THUNK
SNORT
BEWARE OF HORSE
Hey, boy. It's okay. It's just me.
Ever since Mom died, the horse hasn't let anyone near him.

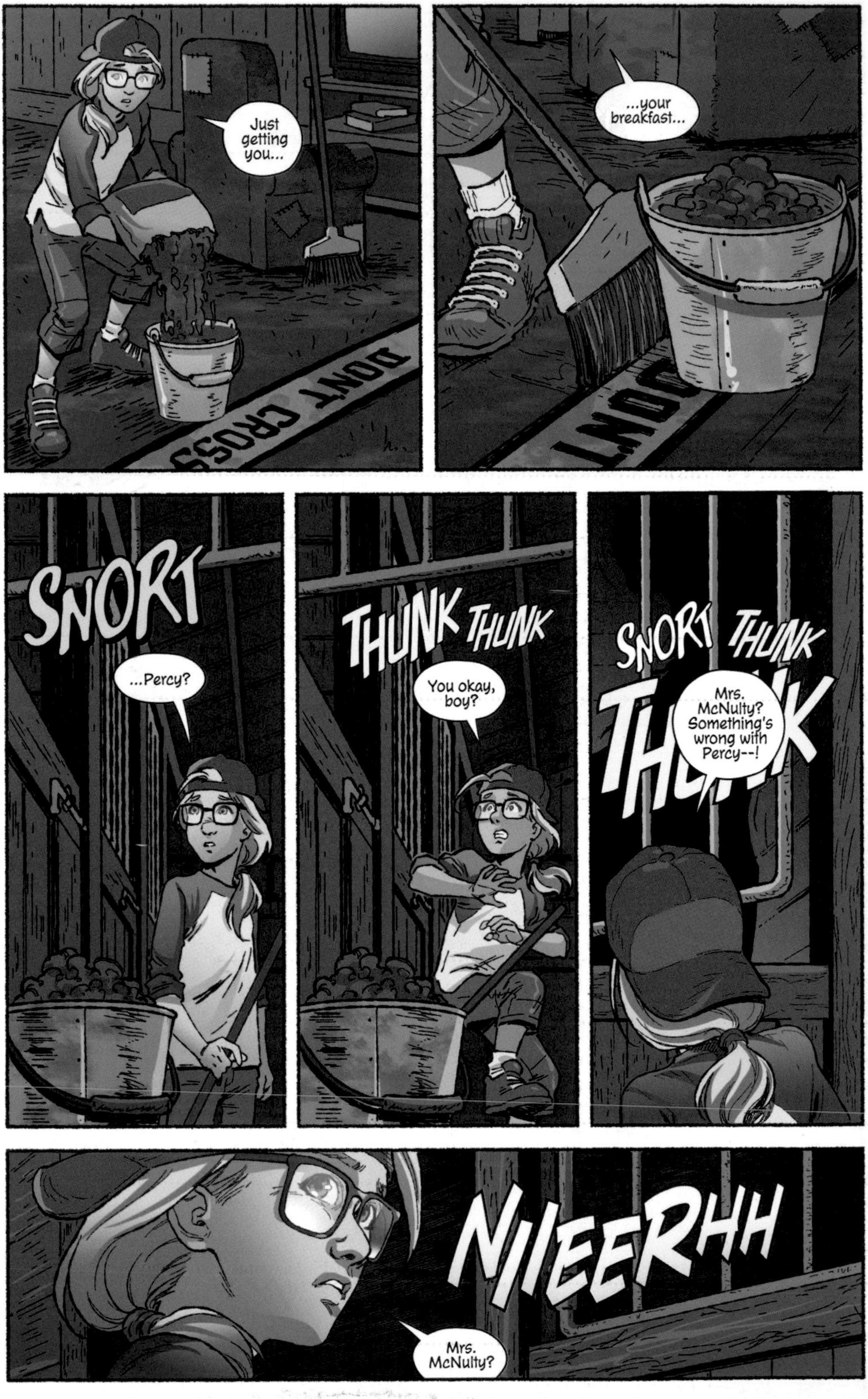
Just getting you...
DON'T CROSS
...your breakfast...
DON'T
SNORT
...Percy?
THUNK THUNK
You okay, boy?
SNORT THUNK
Mrs. McNulty? Something's wrong with Percy--!
NIIEERHH
Mrs. McNulty?

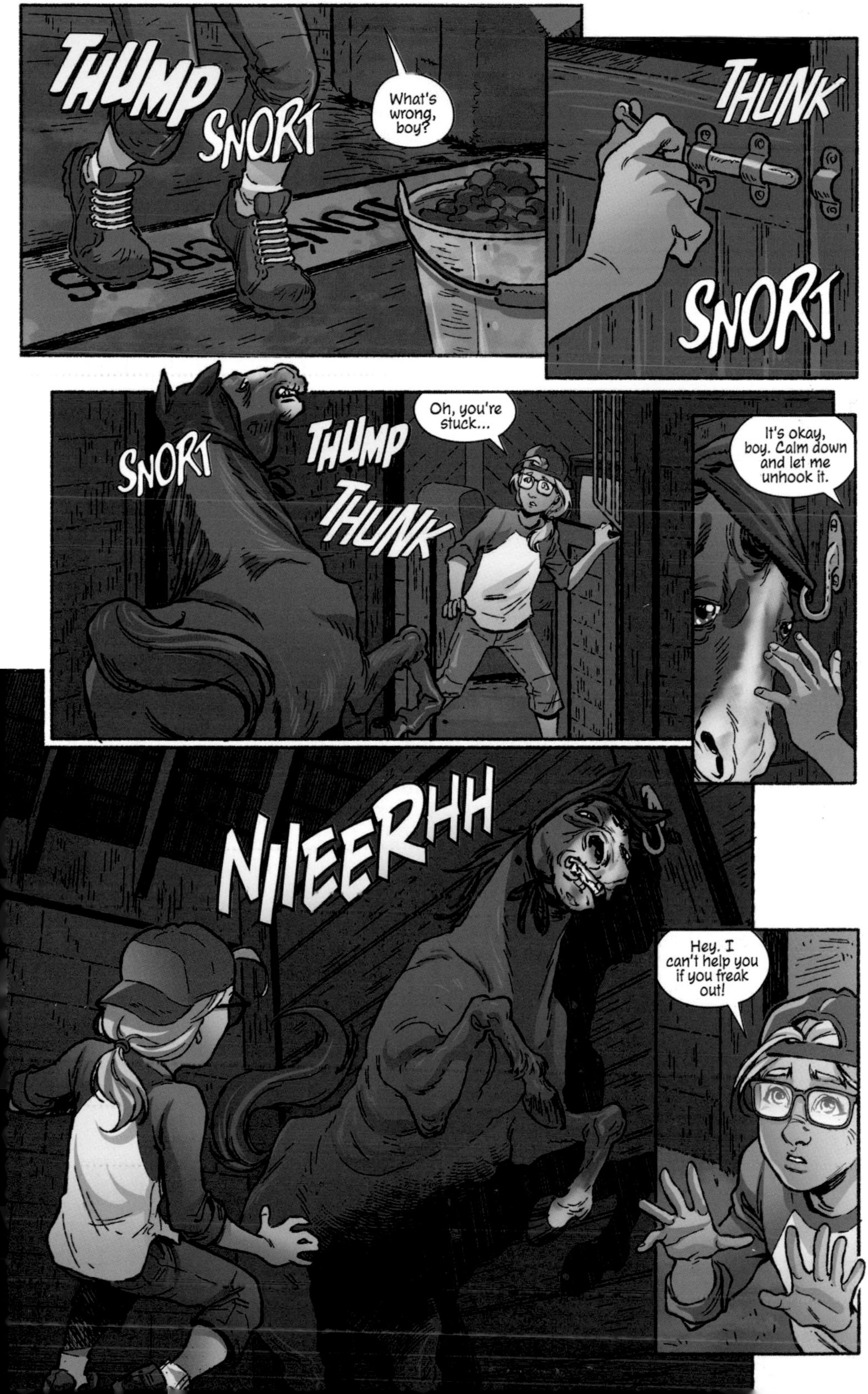
THUMP
SNORT
What's wrong, boy?
THUNK
SNORT
SNORT
THUMP
THUNK
Oh, you're stuck...
It's okay, boy. Calm down and let me unhook it.
NIIEERHH
Hey. I can't help you if you freak out!

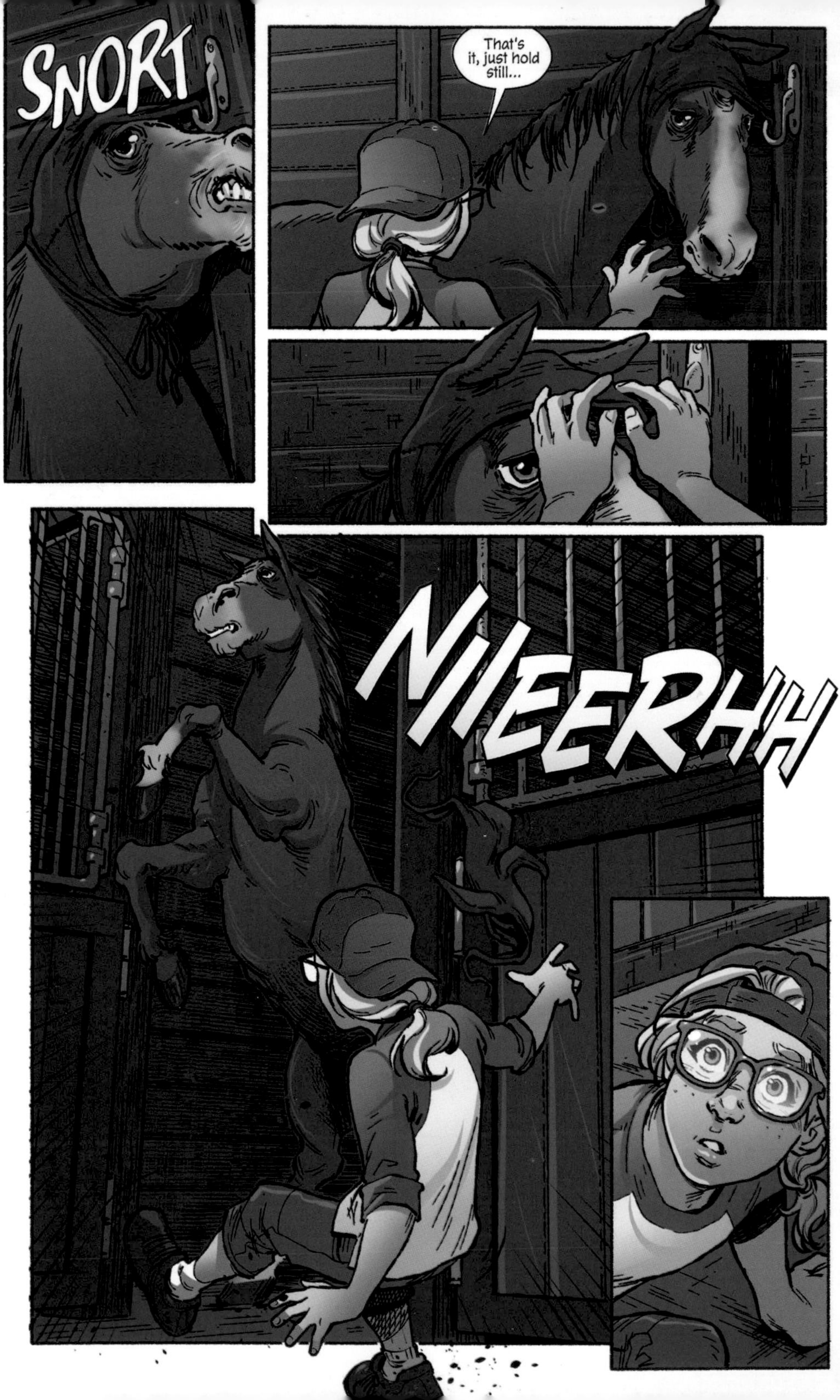
SNORT
That's it, just hold still...
NIEERHH

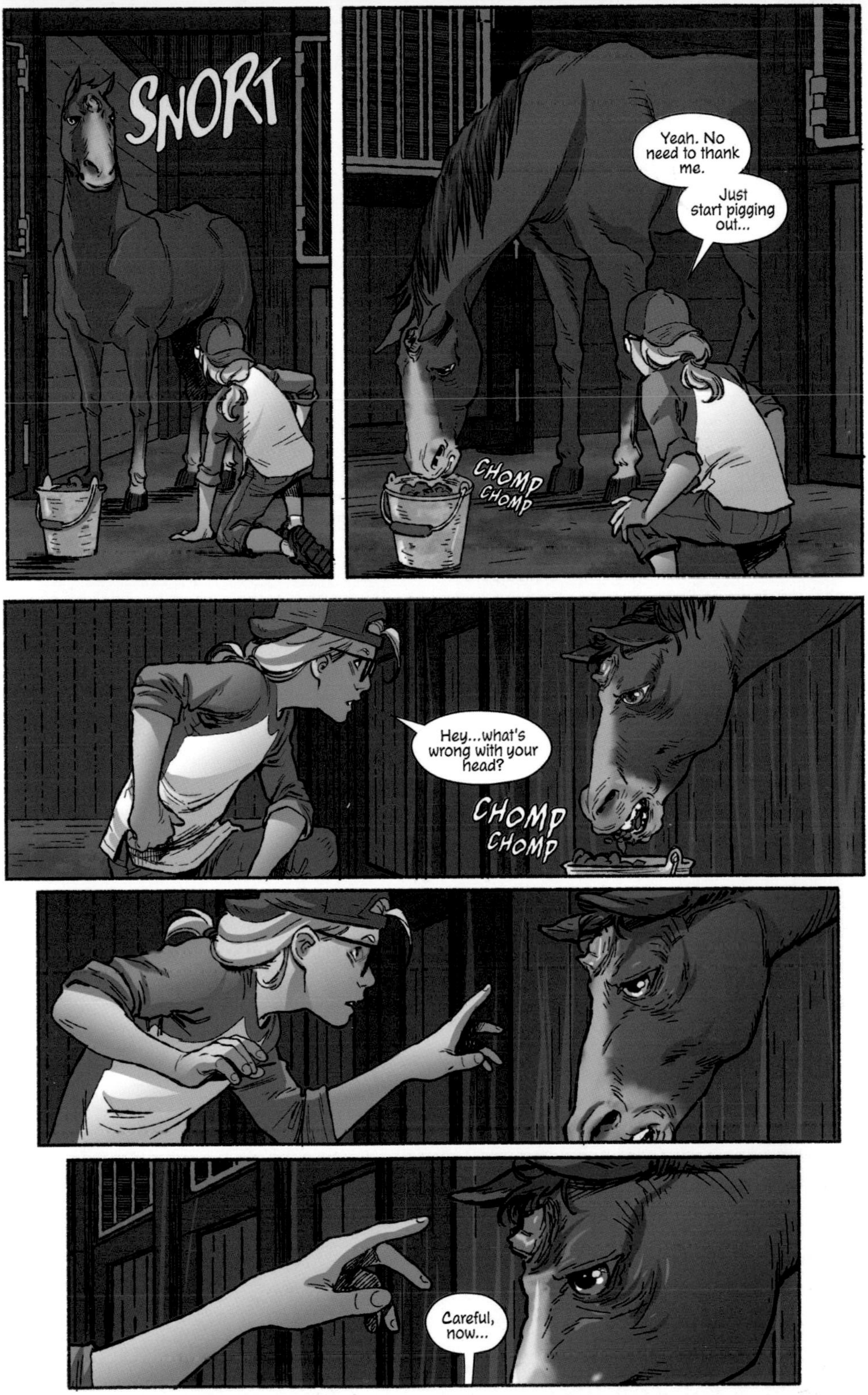
SNORT
Yeah. No need to thank me.
Just start pigging out...
CHOMP CHOMP
Hey...what's wrong with your head?
CHOMP CHOMP
Careful, now...

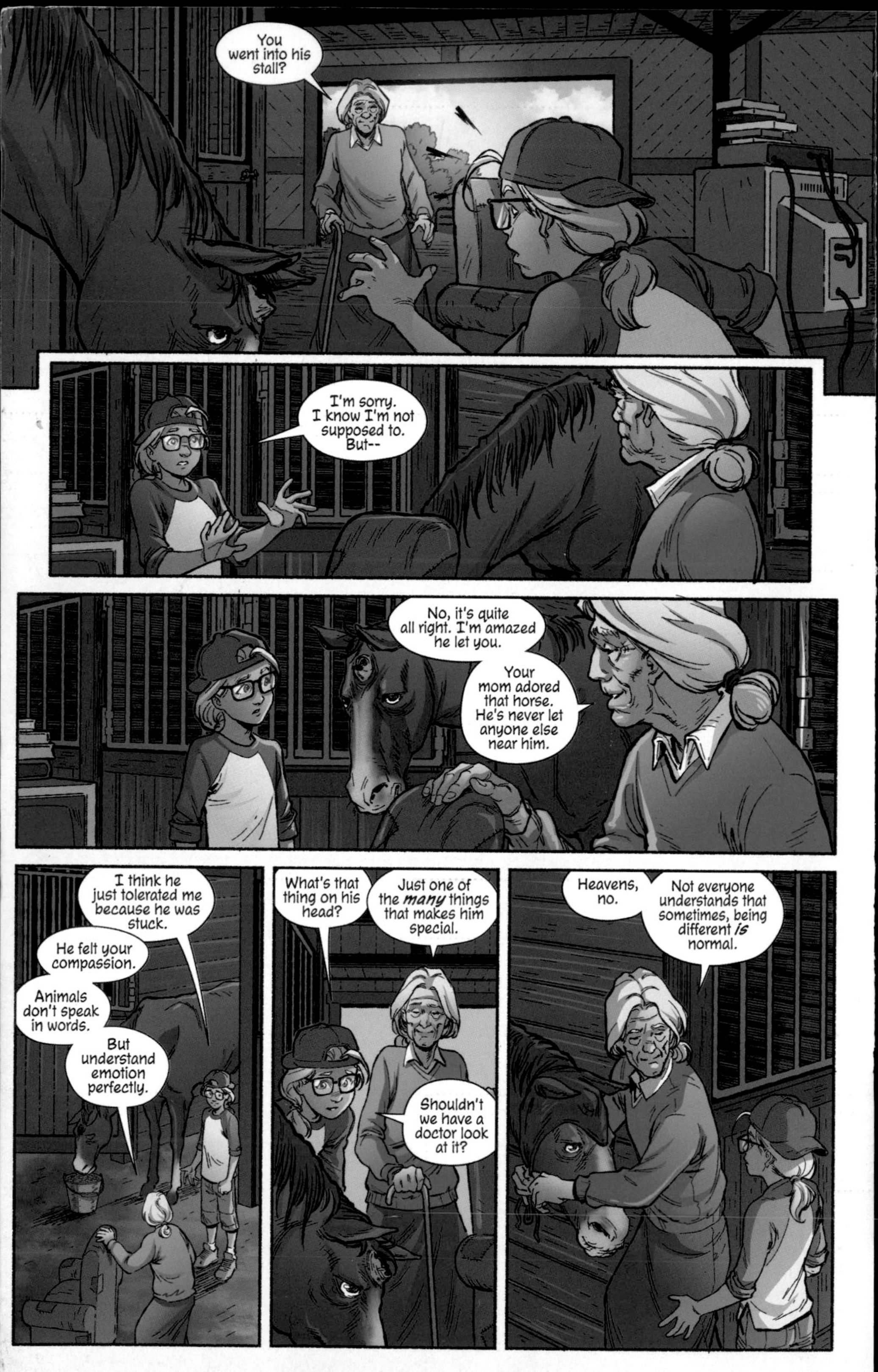
You went into his stall?
I'm sorry. I know I'm not supposed to. But--
No, it's quite all right. I'm amazed he let you.
Your mom adored that horse. He's never let anyone else near him.
I think he just tolerated me because he was stuck.
He felt your compassion.
Animals don't speak in words.
But understand emotion perfectly.
What's that thing on his head?
Just one of the *many* things that makes him special.
Shouldn't we have a doctor look at it?
Heavens, no.
Not everyone understands that sometimes, being different *is* normal.

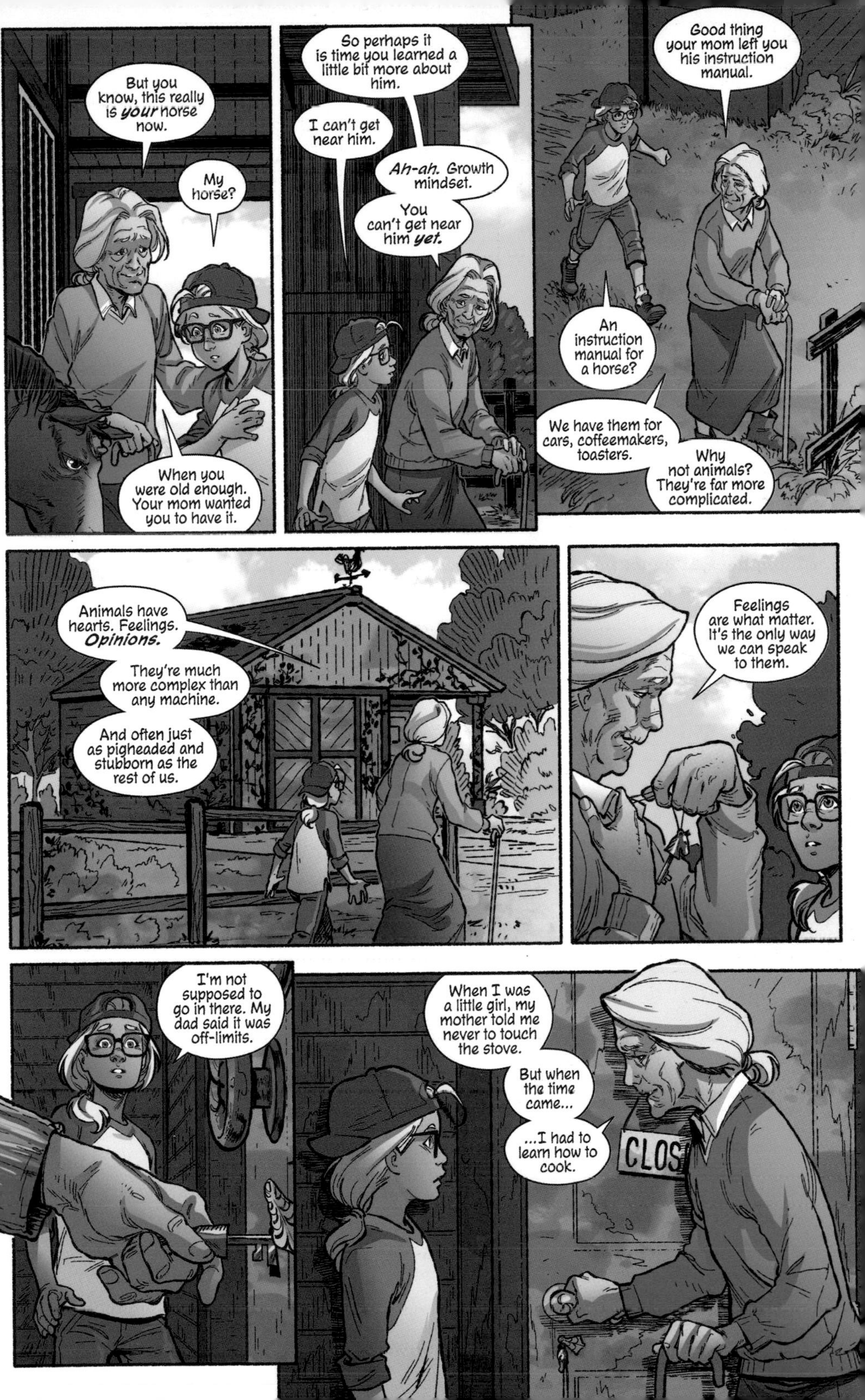
But you know, this really is *your* horse now.
My horse?
When you were old enough. Your mom wanted you to have it.
So perhaps it is time you learned a little bit more about him.
I can't get near him.
Ah-ah. Growth mindset.
You can't get near him *yet.*
Good thing your mom left you his instruction manual.
An instruction manual for a horse?
We have them for cars, coffeemakers, toasters.
Why not animals? They're far more complicated.
Animals have hearts. Feelings. ***Opinions.***
They're much more complex than any machine.
And often just as pigheaded and stubborn as the rest of us.
Feelings are what matter. It's the only way we can speak to them.
I'm not supposed to go in there. My dad said it was off-limits.
When I was a little girl, my mother told me never to touch the stove.
But when the time came...
...I had to learn how to cook.
CLOS

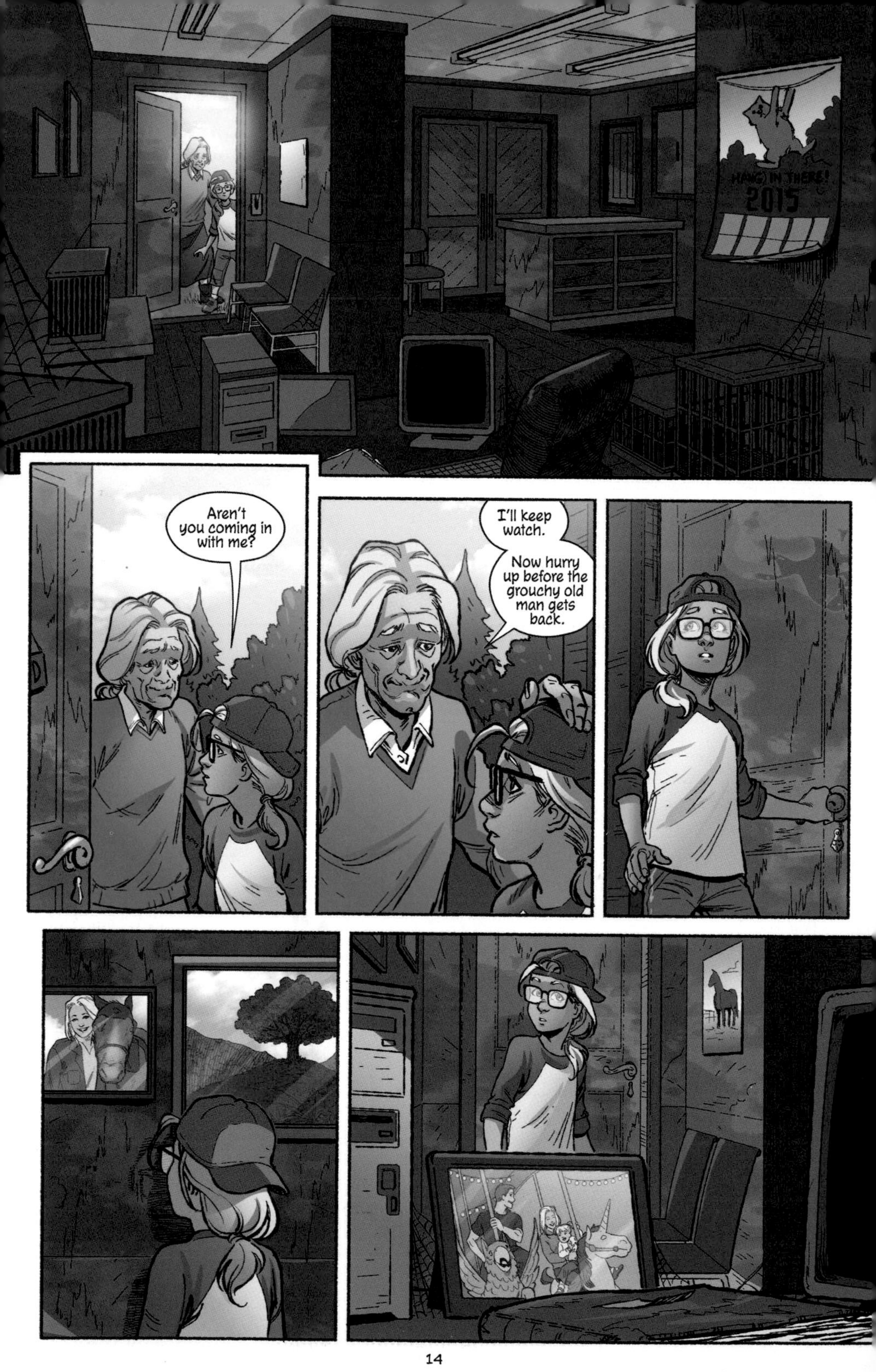
HANG IN THERE!
2015
Aren't you coming in with me?
I'll keep watch.
Now hurry up before the grouchy old man gets back.

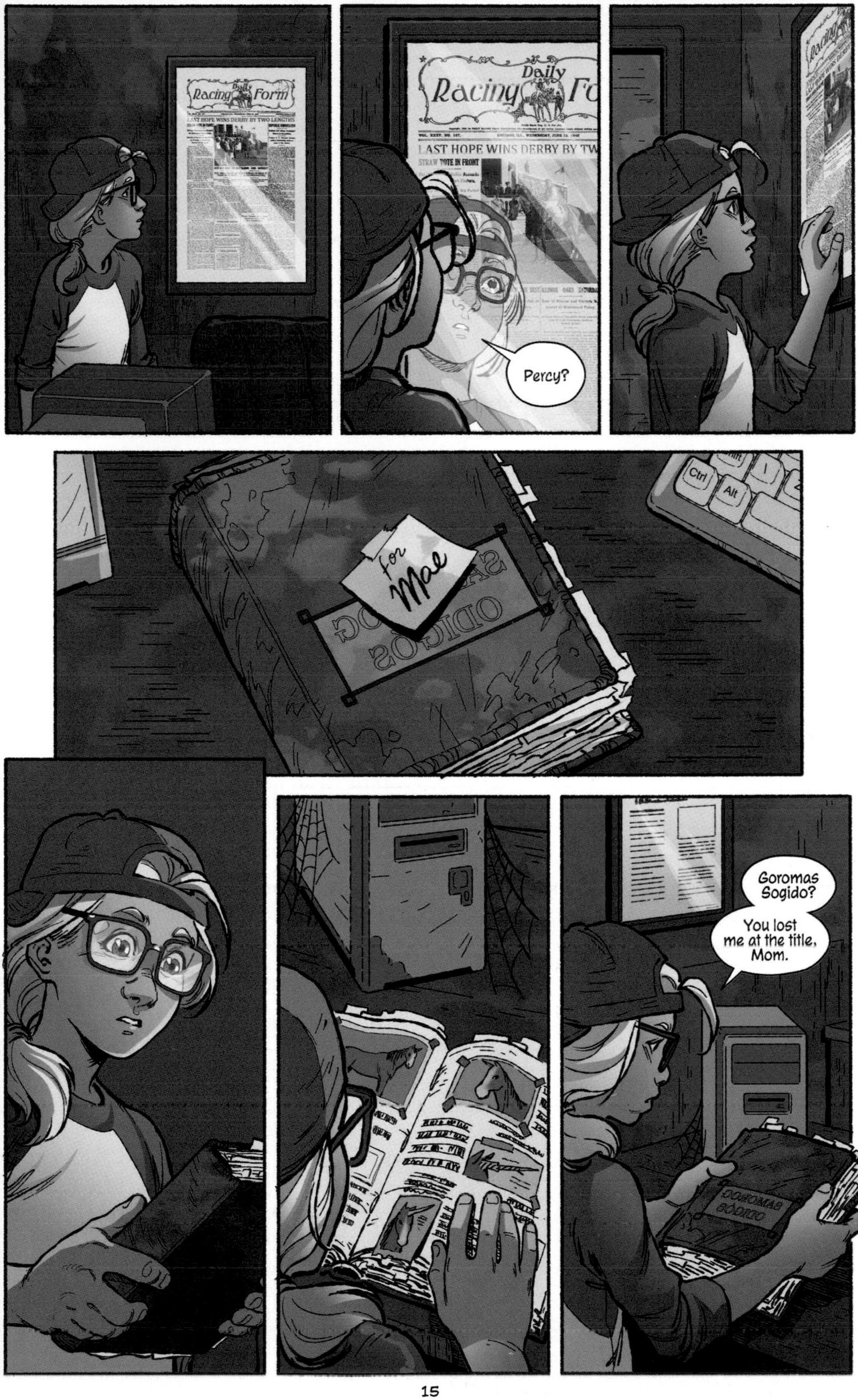
Daily Racing Form
LAST HOPE WINS DERBY BY TWO LENGTHS
STRAW VOTE IN FRONT
Percy?
Ctrl
Alt
for Mae
Goromas Sogido?
You lost me at the title, Mom.

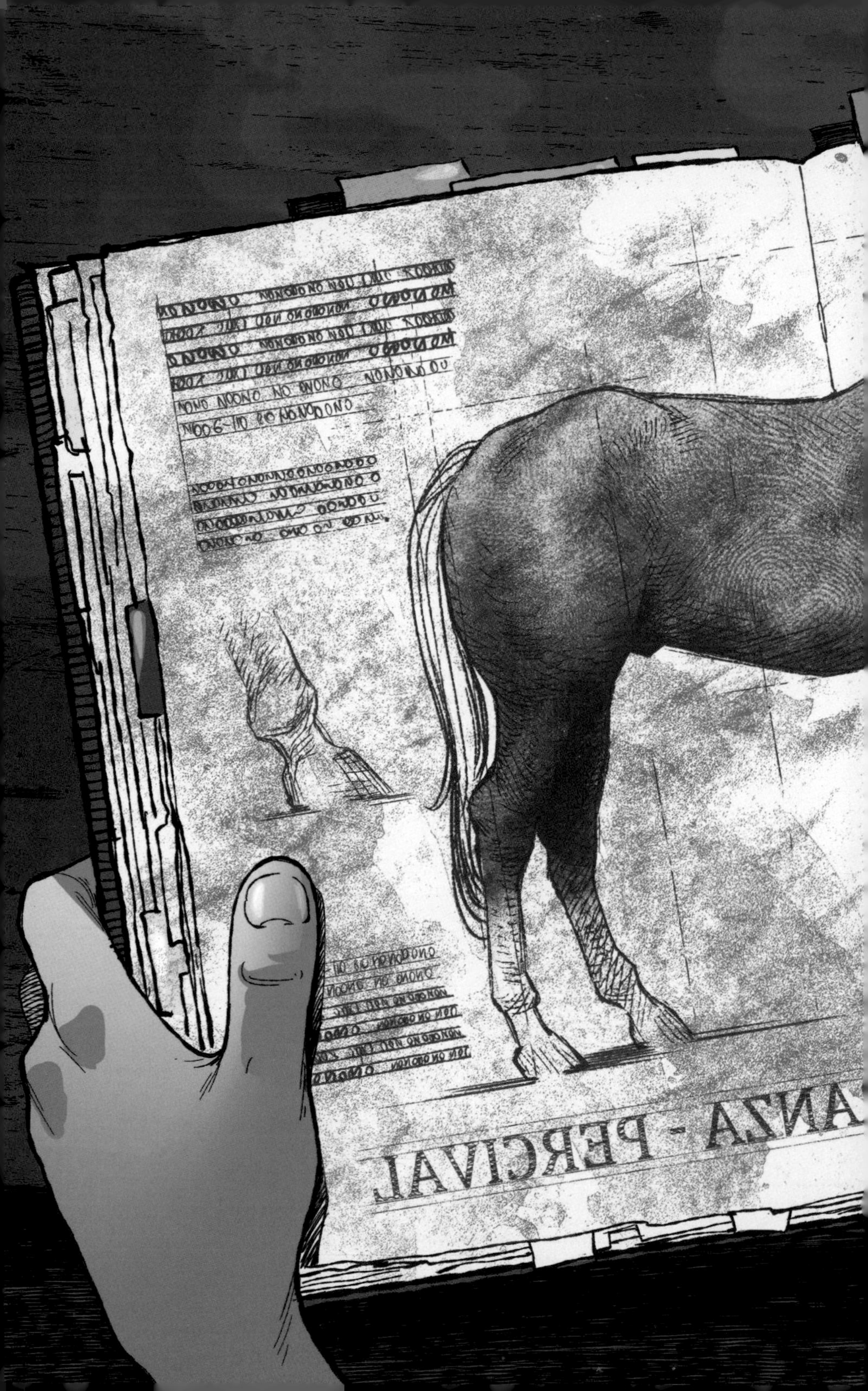
ANZA - PERCIVAL

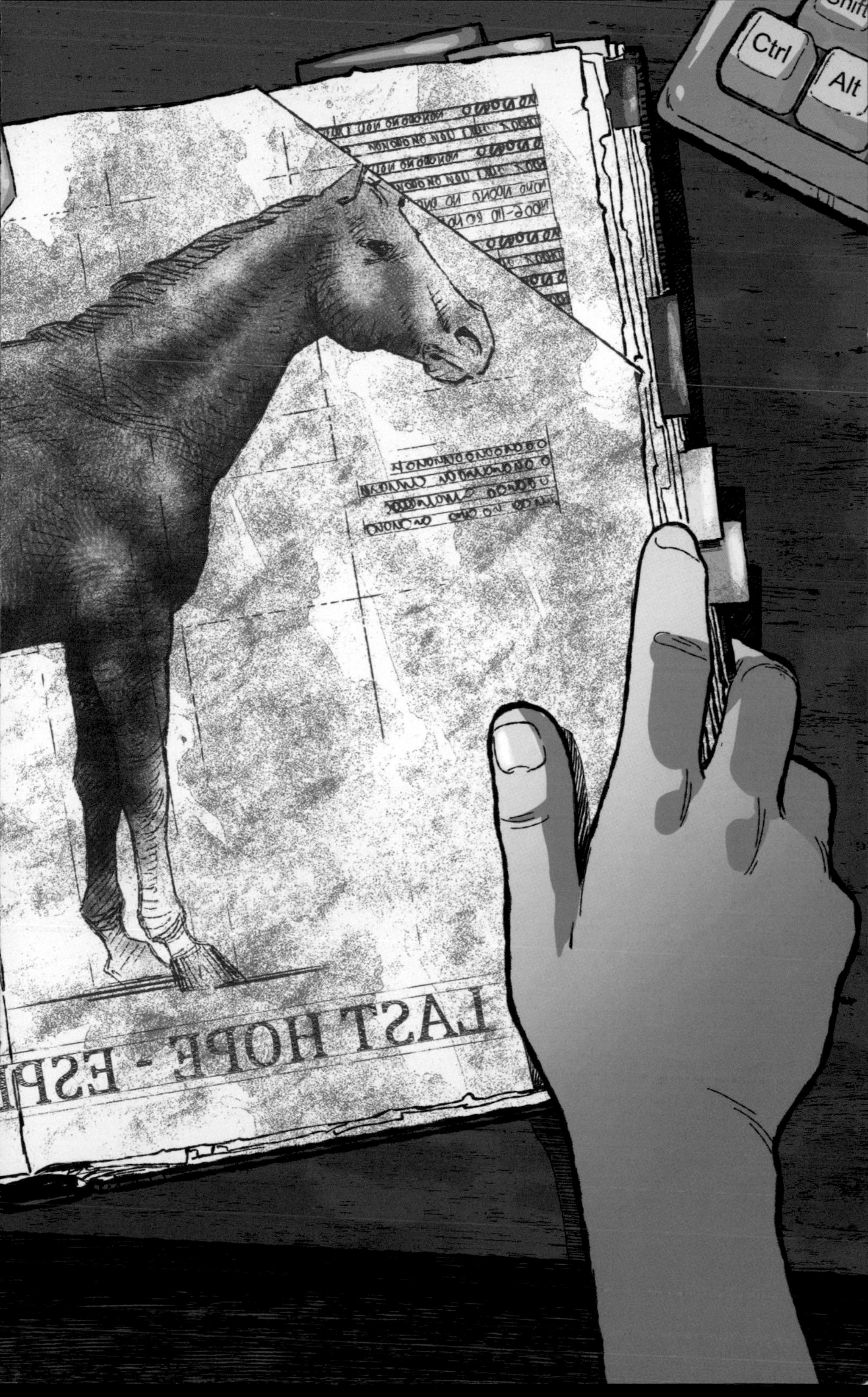
LAST HOPE
Ctrl
Alt

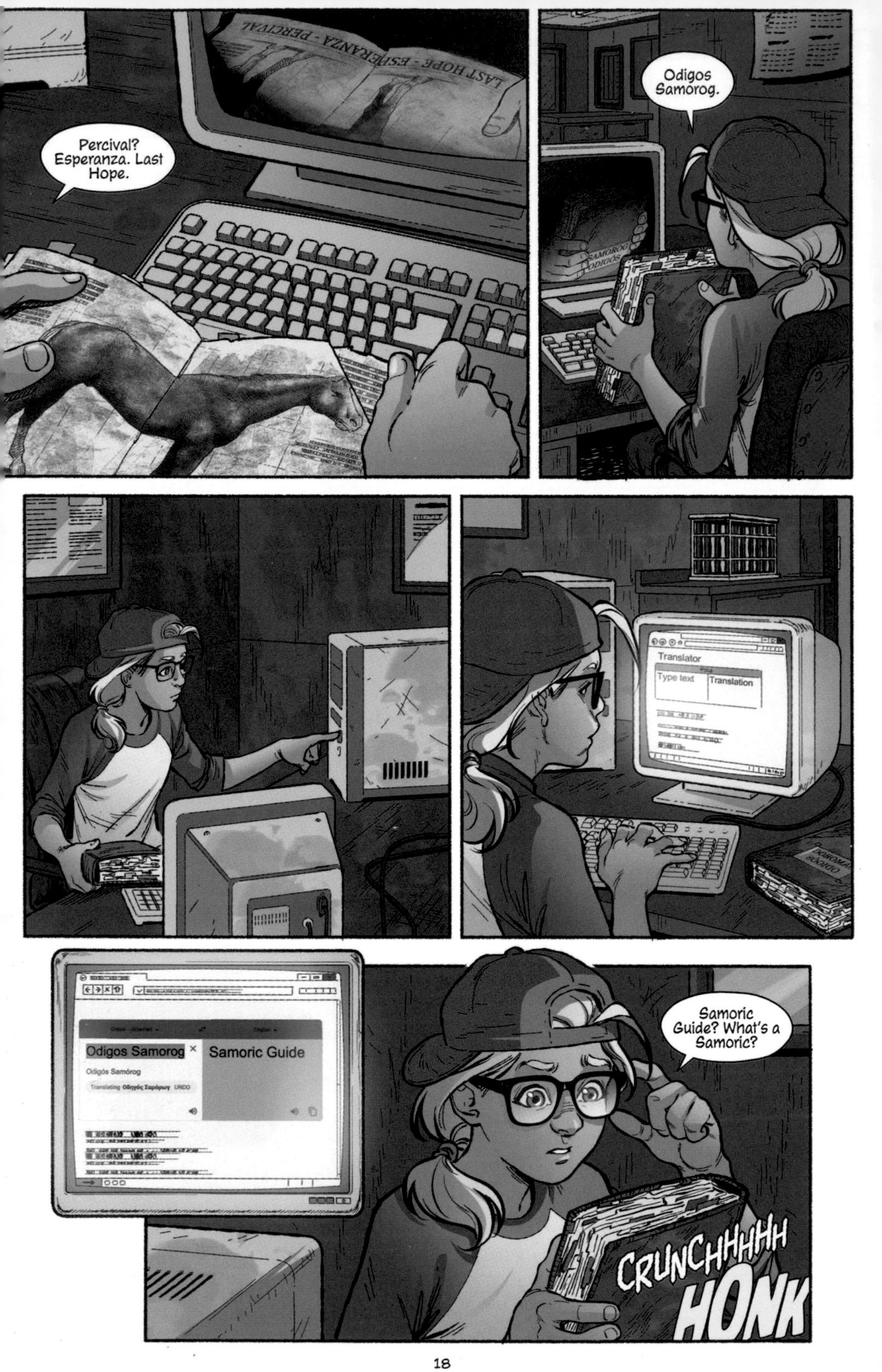
LAST HOPE - ESPERANZA - PERCIVAL
Percival? Esperanza. Last Hope.
Odigos Samorog.
SAMOROG ODIGOS
Translator
Type text
Translation
Odigos Samorog
Samoric Guide
Odigós Samórog
Samoric Guide? What's a Samoric?
CRUNCHHHHH
HONK

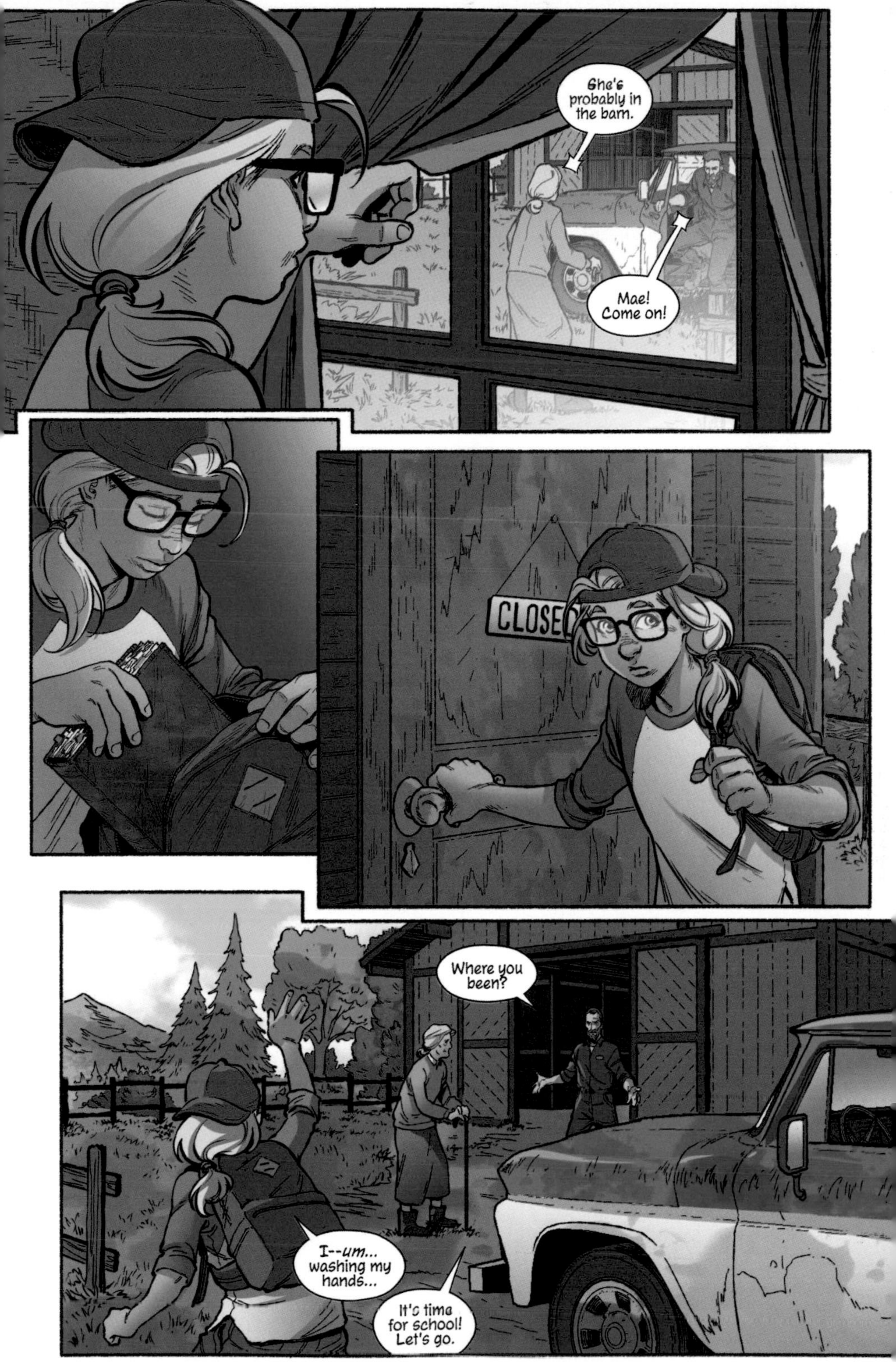
She's probably in the barn.
Mae! Come on!
CLOSED
Where you been?
I--*um*... washing my hands...
It's time for school! Let's go.

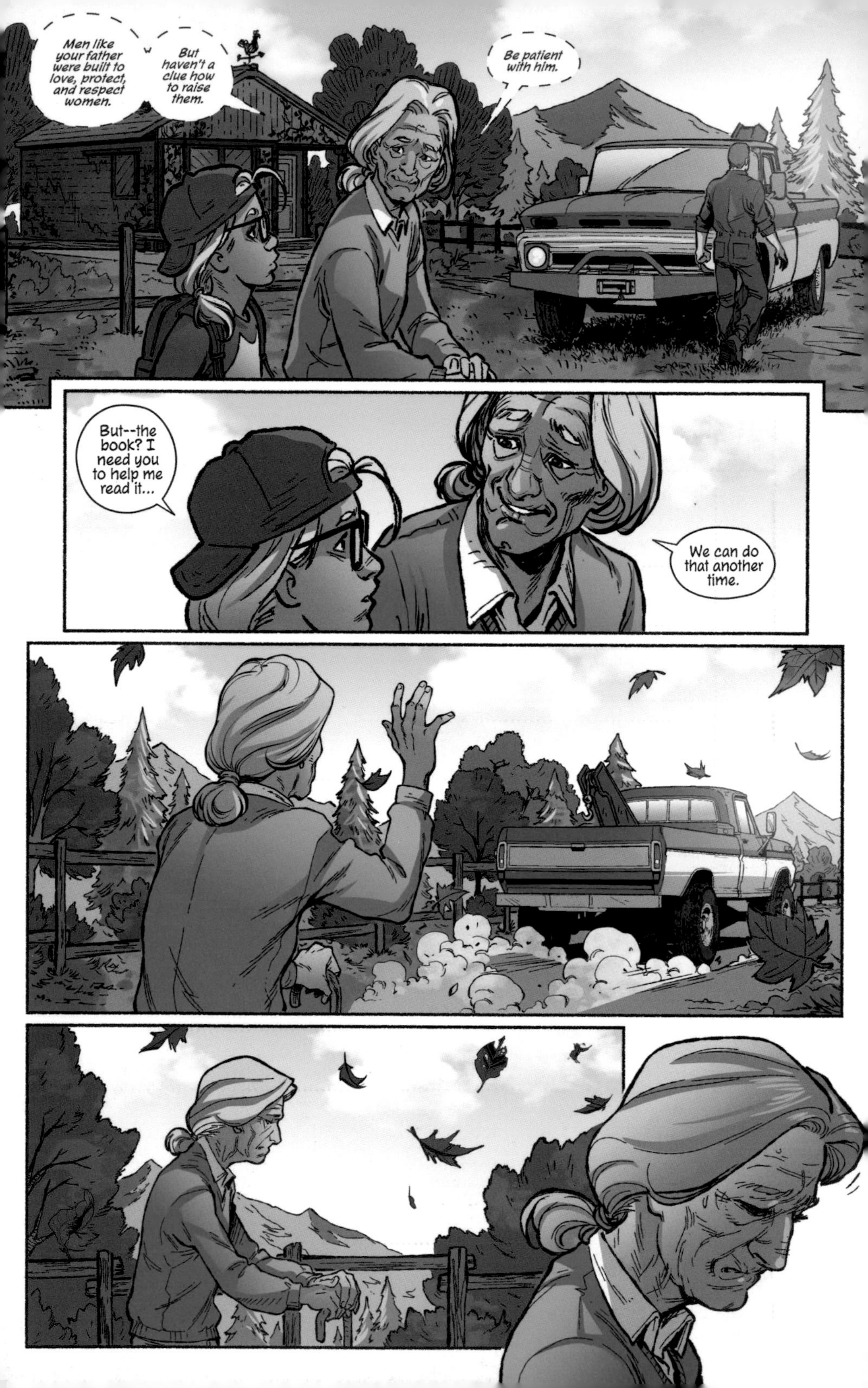

Men like your father were built to love, protect, and respect women.
But haven't a clue how to raise them.
Be patient with him.
But--the book? I need you to help me read it...
We can do that another time.

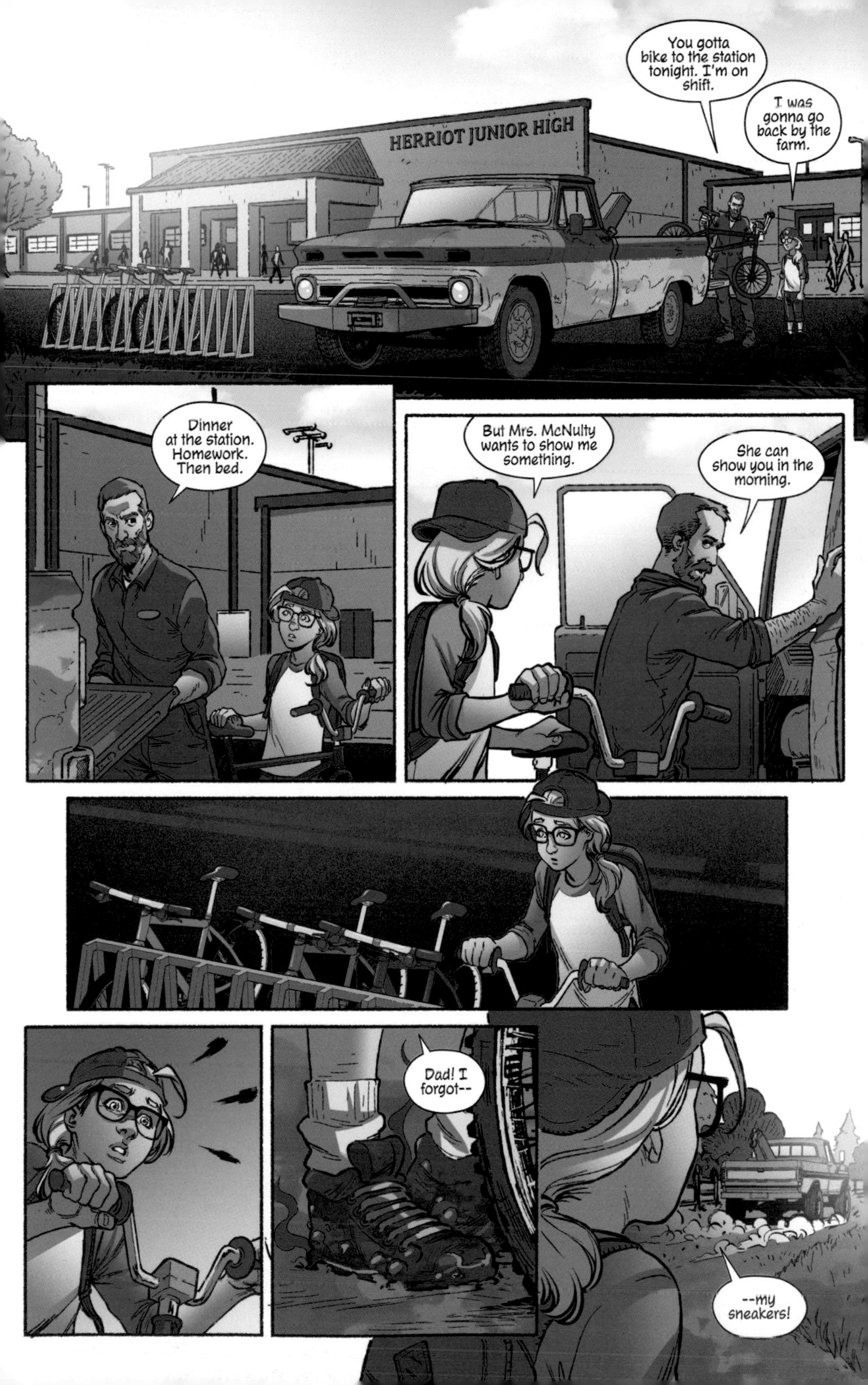
HERRIOT JUNIOR HIGH
You gotta bike to the station tonight. I'm on shift.
I was gonna go back by the farm.
Dinner at the station. Homework. Then bed.
But Mrs. McNulty wants to show me something.
She can show you in the morning.
Dad! I forgot--
--my sneakers!

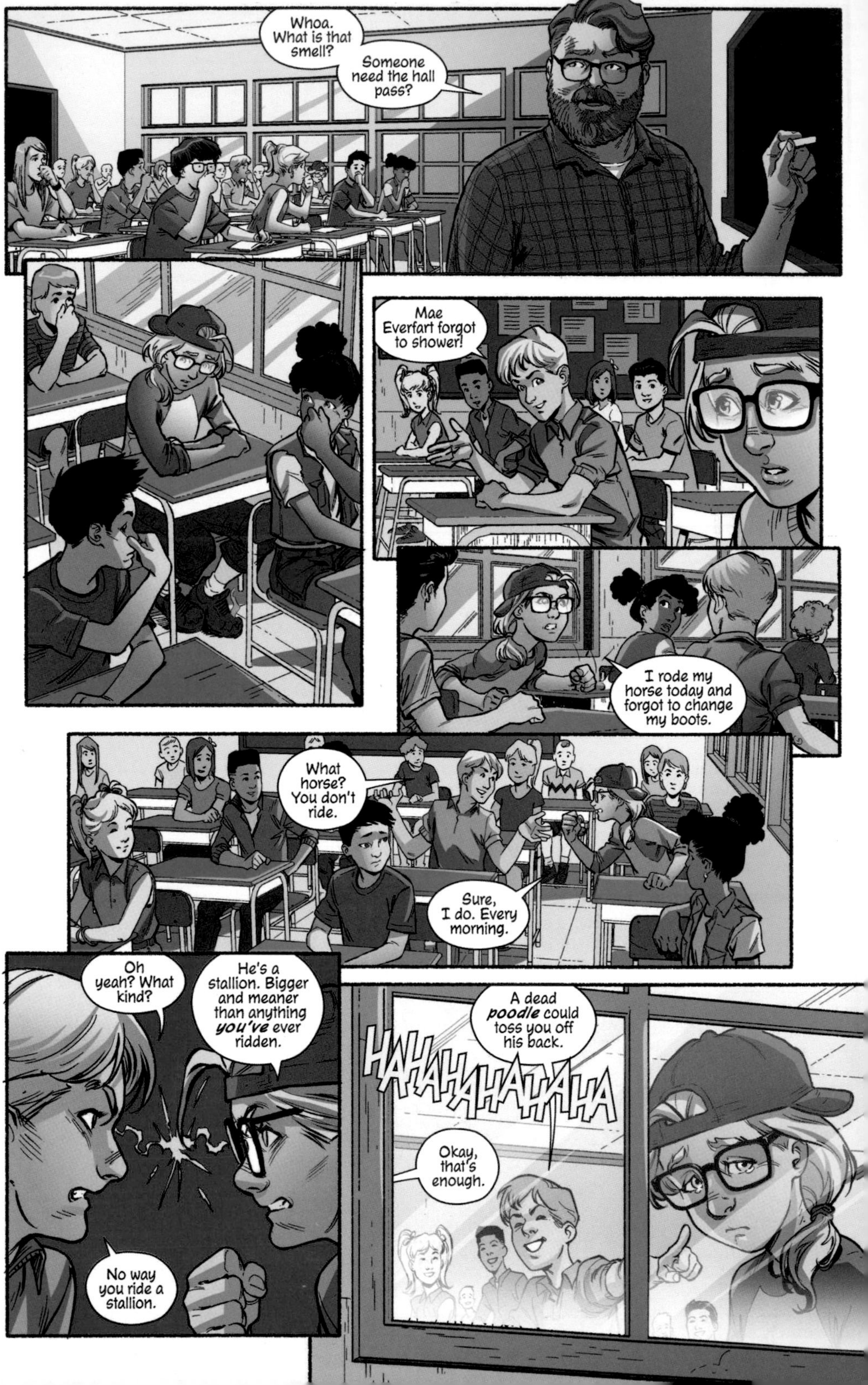

Whoa. What is that smell?
Someone need the hall pass?
Mae Everfart forgot to shower!
I rode my horse today and forgot to change my boots.
What horse? You don't ride.
Sure, I do. Every morning.
Oh yeah? What kind?
He's a stallion. Bigger and meaner than anything *you've* ever ridden.
No way you ride a stallion.
A dead *poodle* could toss you off his back.
HAHAHAHAHAHAHA
Okay, that's enough.

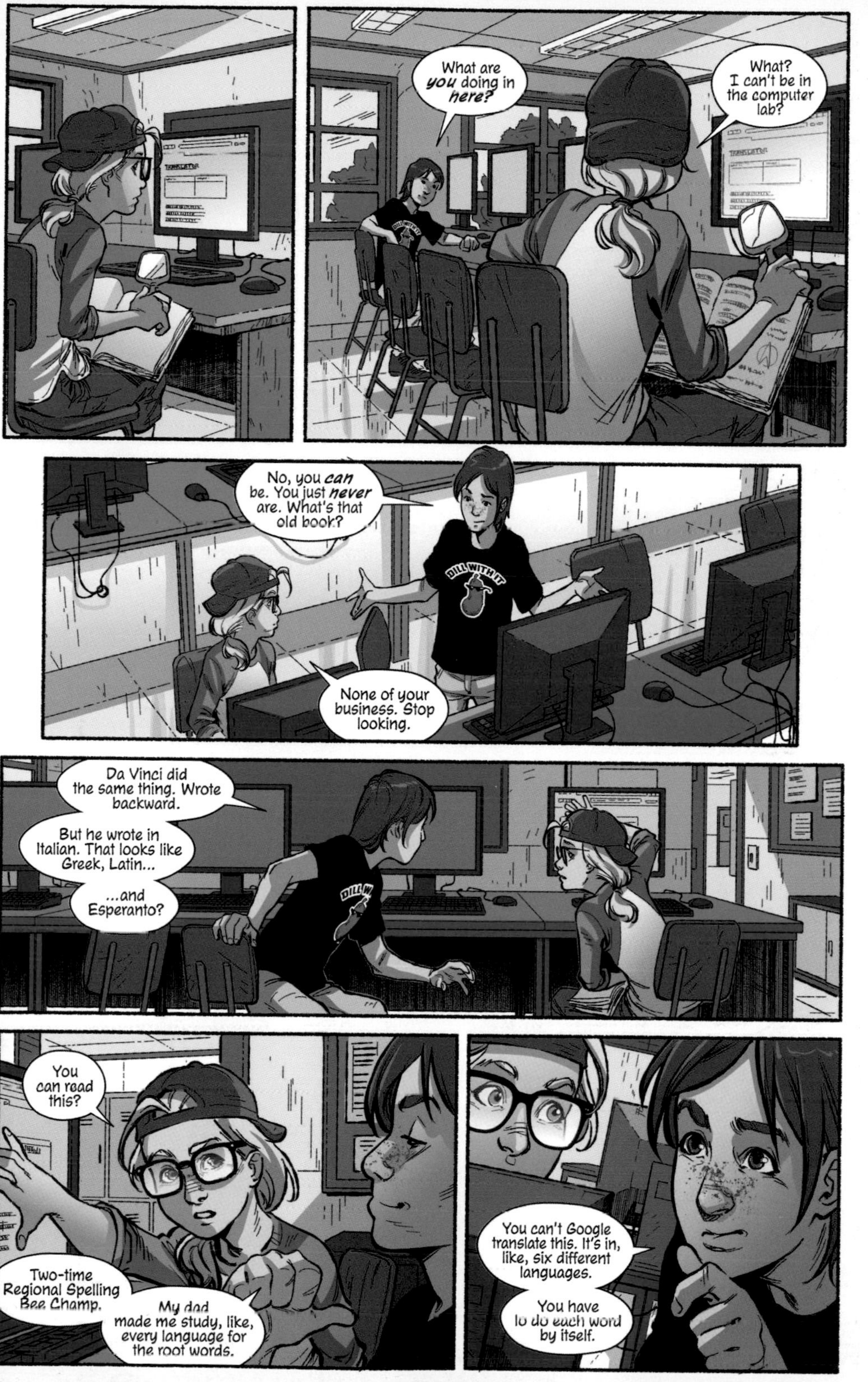
What are you doing in here?
What? I can't be in the computer lab?
No, you can be. You just never are. What's that old book?
None of your business. Stop looking.
Da Vinci did the same thing. Wrote backward.
But he wrote in Italian. That looks like Greek, Latin...
...and Esperanto?
You can read this?
Two-time Regional Spelling Bee Champ.
My dad made me study, like, every language for the root words.
You can't Google translate this. It's in, like, six different languages.
You have to do each word by itself.

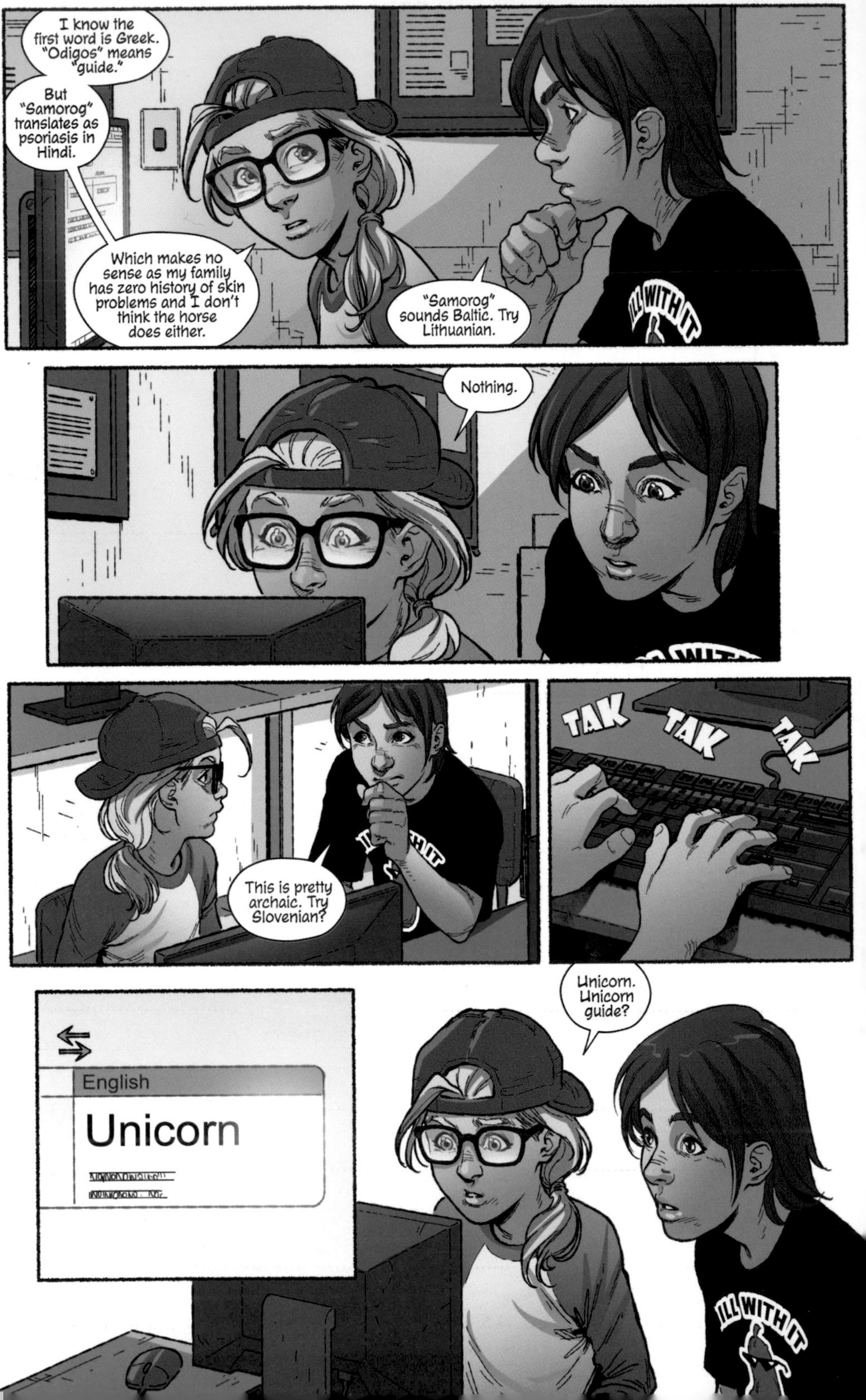
I know the first word is Greek. "Odigos" means "guide."
But "Samorog" translates as psoriasis in Hindi.
Which makes no sense as my family has zero history of skin problems and I don't think the horse does either.
"Samorog" sounds Baltic. Try Lithuanian.
Nothing.
This is pretty archaic. Try Slovenian?
TAK
TAK
TAK
English
Unicorn
Unicorn. Unicorn guide?
ILL WITH IT

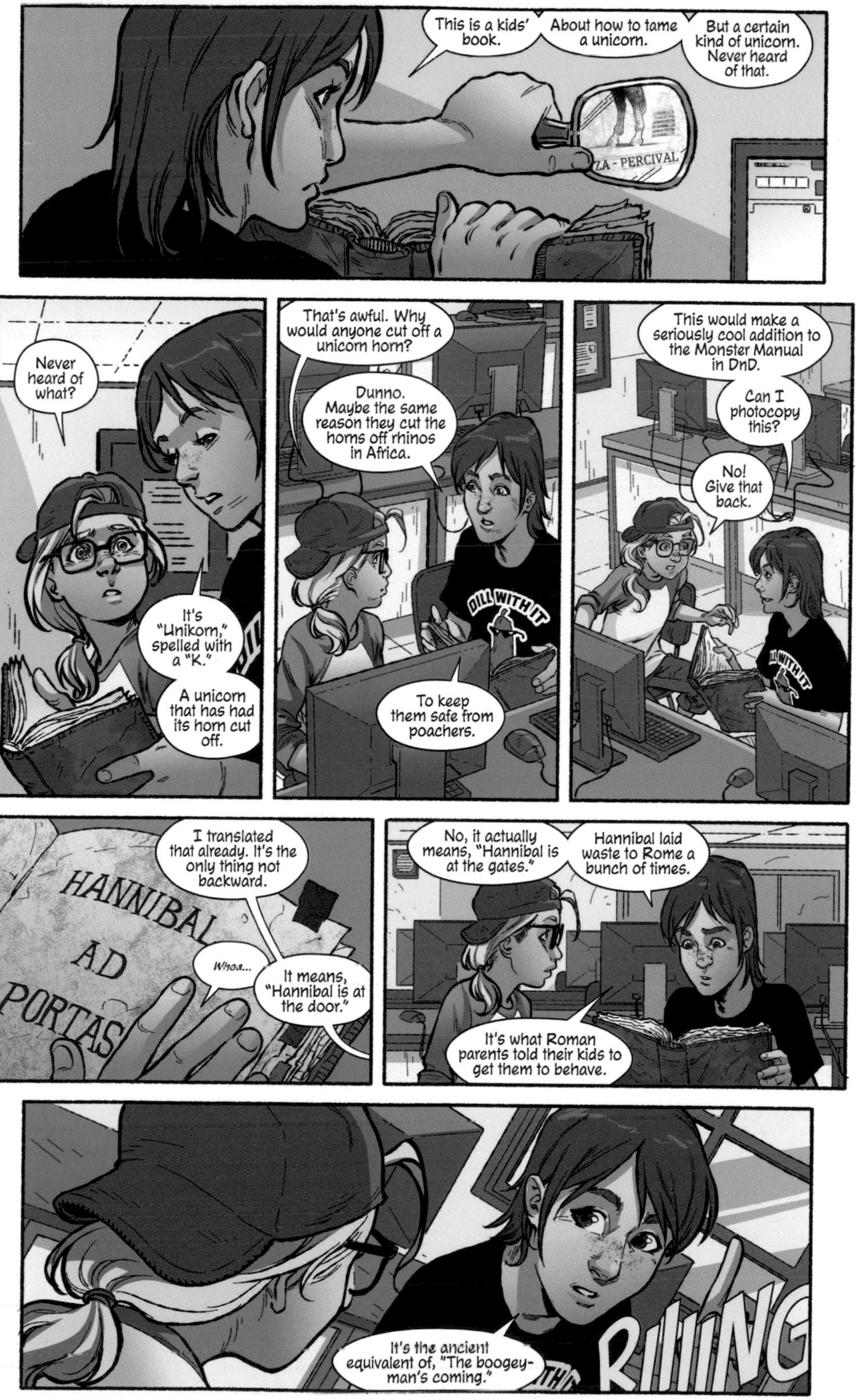
This is a kids' book.
About how to tame a unicorn.
But a certain kind of unicorn. Never heard of that.
ZA - PERCIVAL
Never heard of what?
It's "Unikorn," spelled with a "K."
A unicorn that has had its horn cut off.
That's awful. Why would anyone cut off a unicorn horn?
Dunno. Maybe the same reason they cut the horns off rhinos in Africa.
DILL WITH IT
To keep them safe from poachers.
This would make a seriously cool addition to the Monster Manual in DnD.
Can I photocopy this?
No! Give that back.
HANNIBAL AD PORTAS
I translated that already. It's the only thing not backward.
Whoa...
It means, "Hannibal is at the door."
No, it actually means, "Hannibal is at the gates."
Hannibal laid waste to Rome a bunch of times.
It's what Roman parents told their kids to get them to behave.
It's the ancient equivalent of, "The boogeyman's coming."
RIIIING

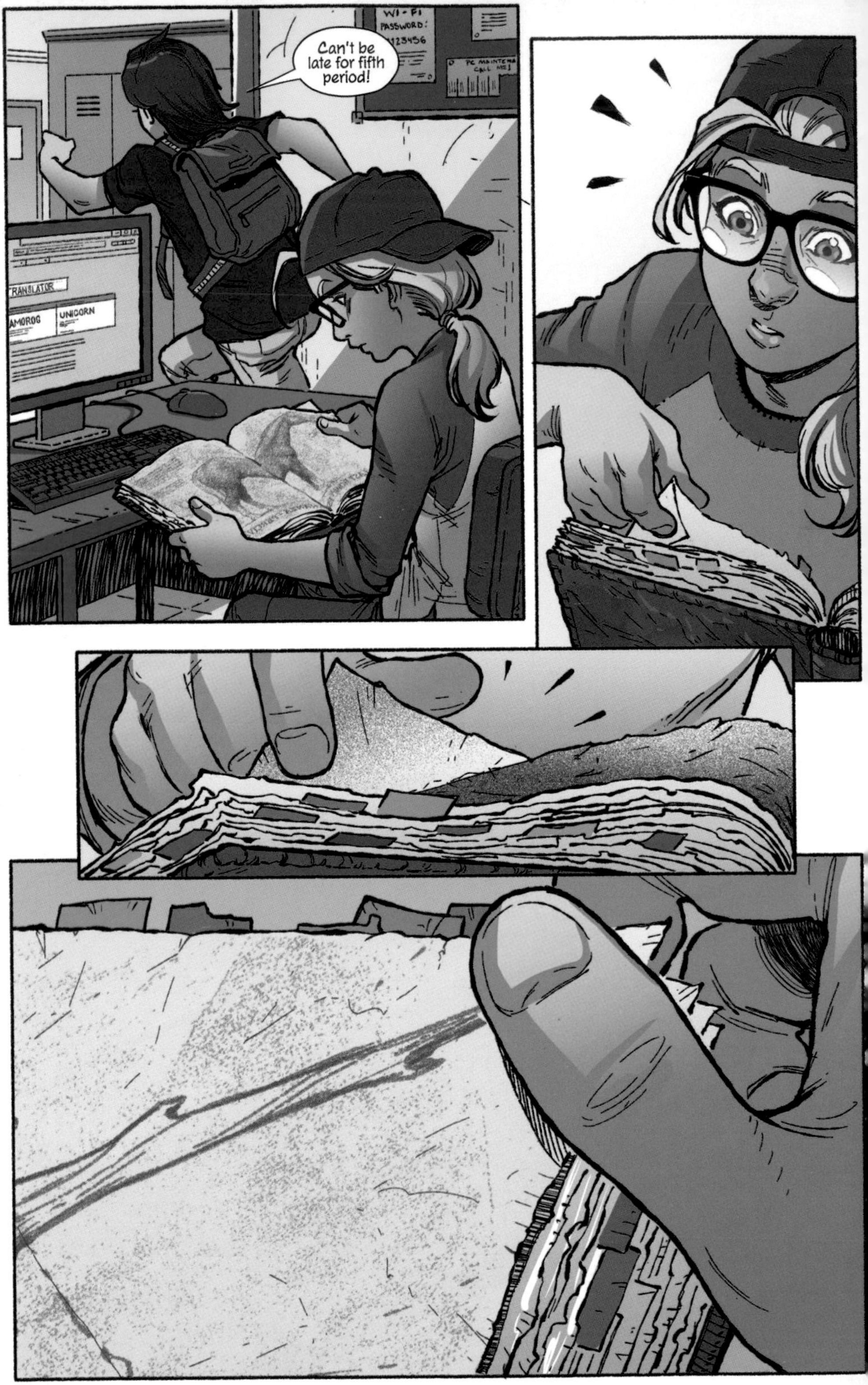
WI-FI
PASSWORD:
123456
Can't be late for fifth period!
TRANSLATOR
UNICORN

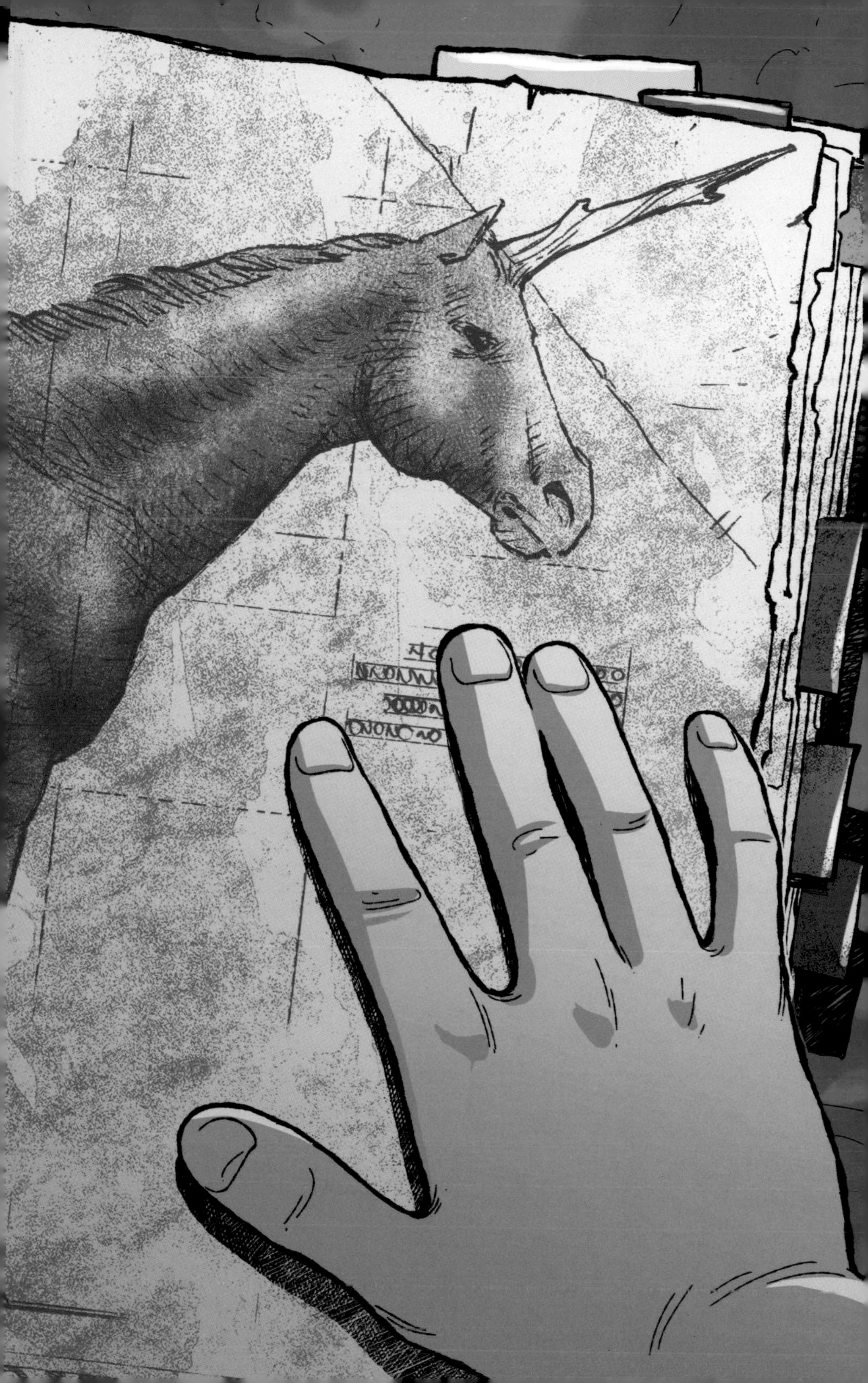

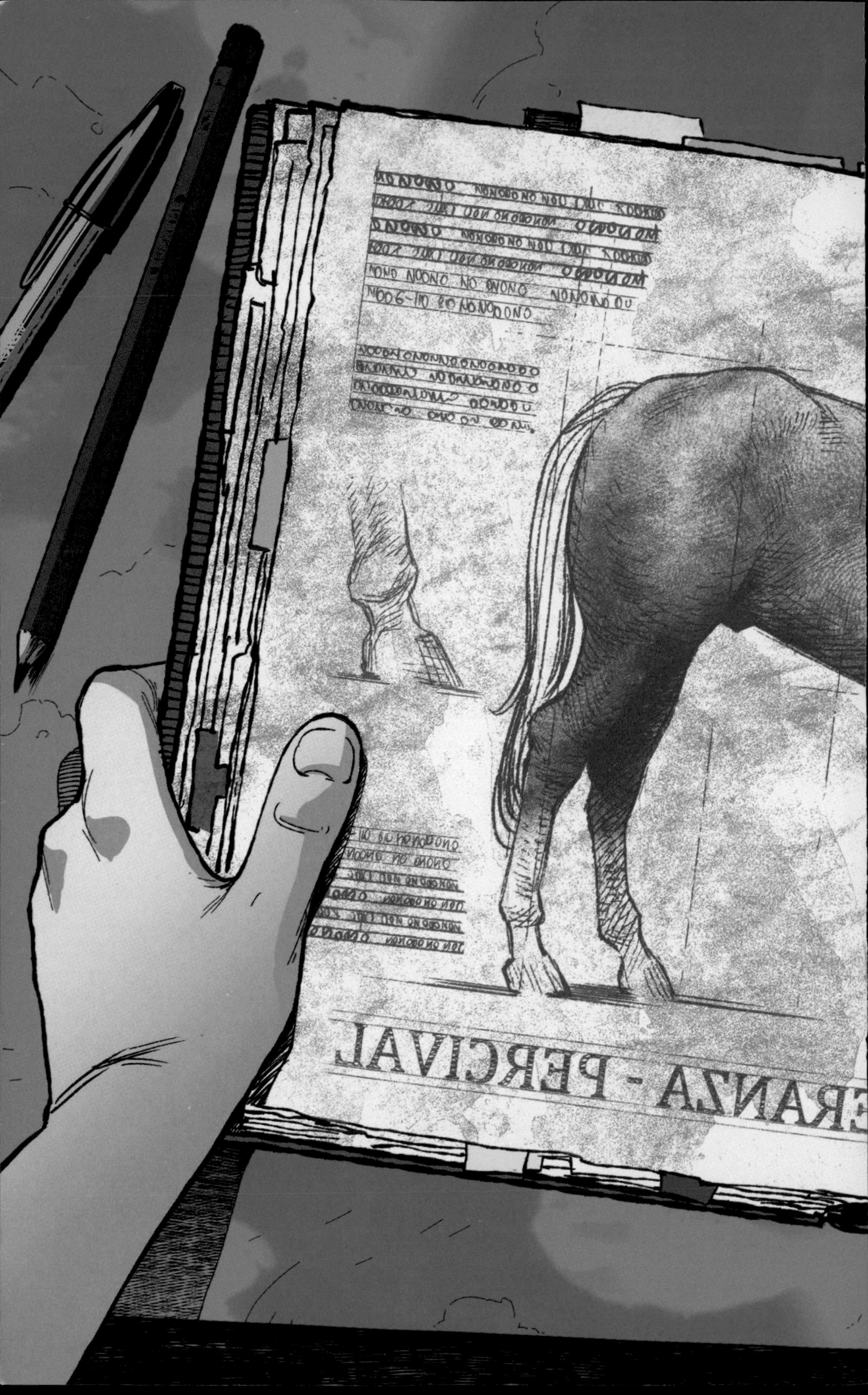
PERCIVAL

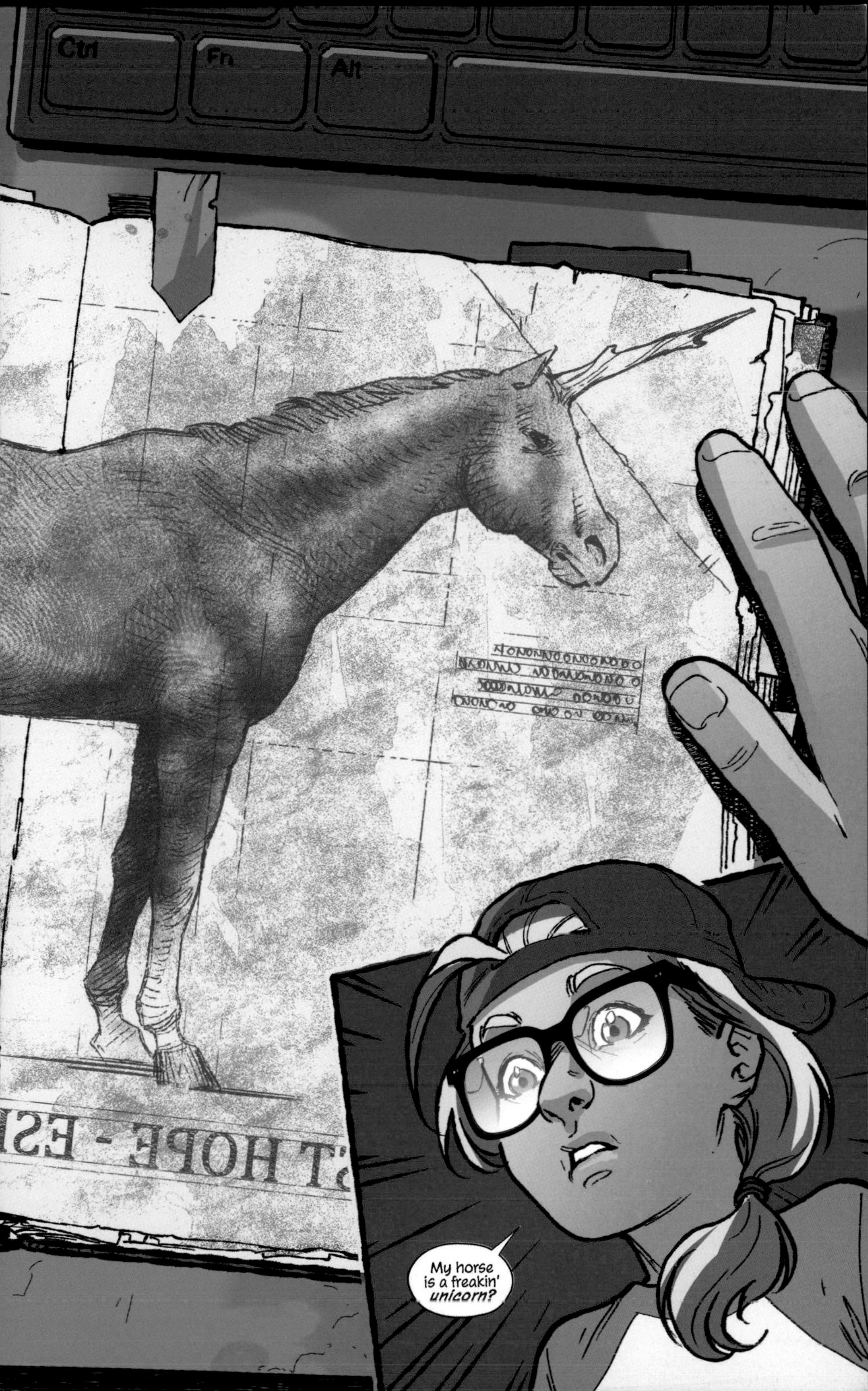
Ctrl
Fn
Alt
My horse is a freakin' *unicorn?*

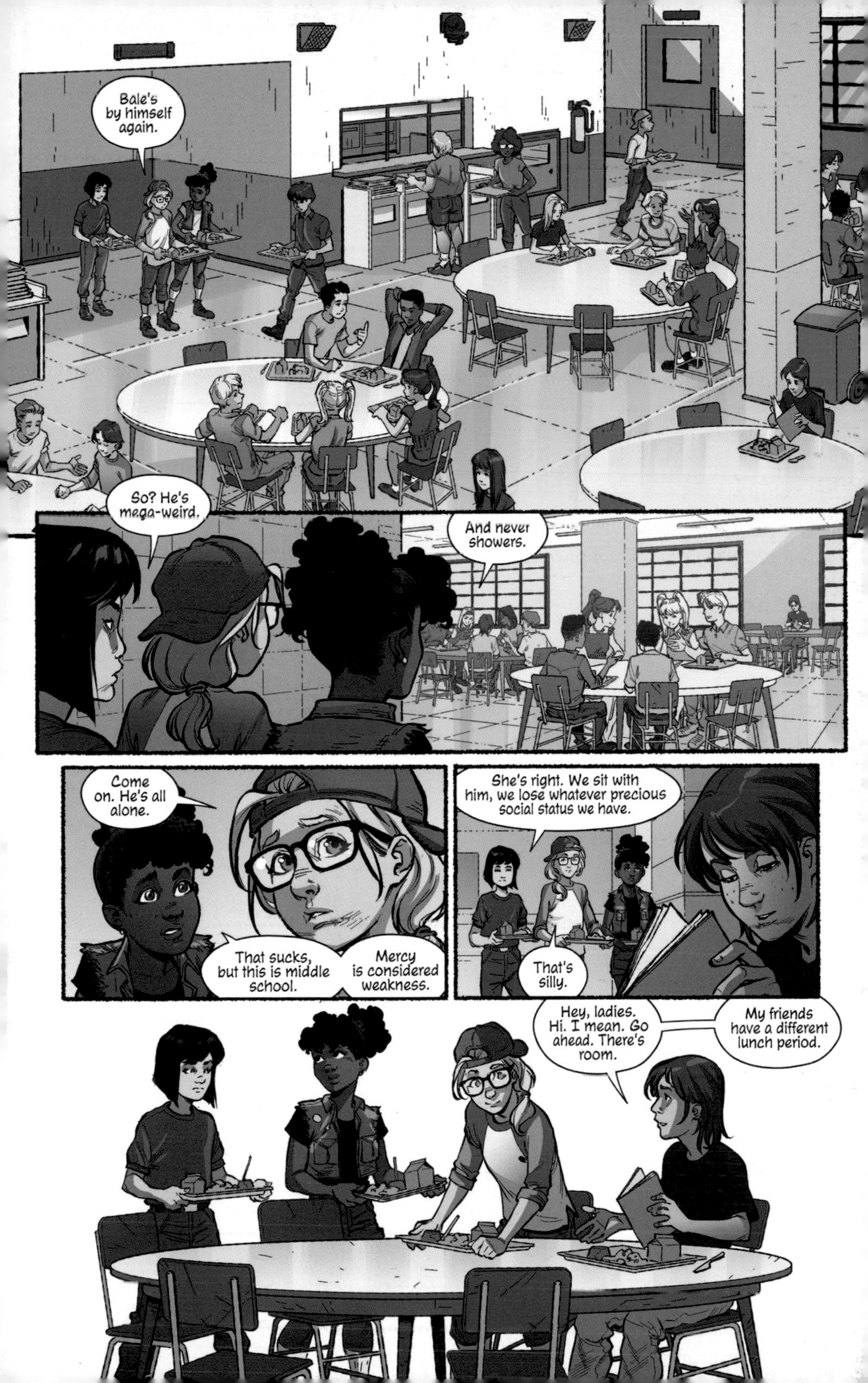

Bale's by himself again.
So? He's mega-weird.
And never showers.
Come on. He's all alone.
That sucks, but this is middle school.
Mercy is considered weakness.
She's right. We sit with him, we lose whatever precious social status we have.
That's silly.
Hey, ladies. Hi. I mean. Go ahead. There's room.
My friends have a different lunch period.

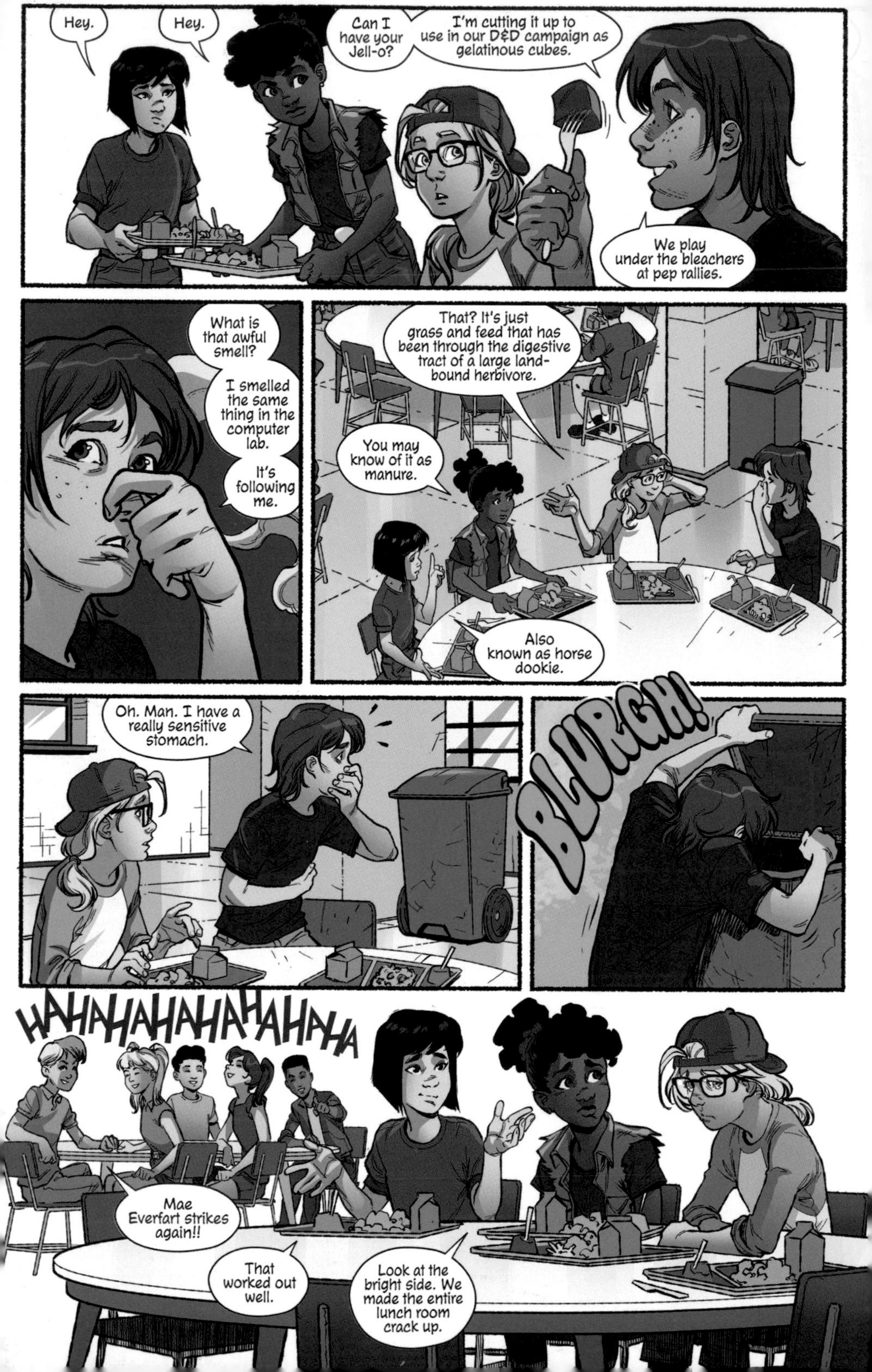
Hey.
Hey.
Can I have your Jell-o?
I'm cutting it up to use in our D&D campaign as gelatinous cubes.
We play under the bleachers at pep rallies.
What is that awful smell?
I smelled the same thing in the computer lab.
It's following me.
That? It's just grass and feed that has been through the digestive tract of a large land-bound herbivore.
You may know of it as manure.
Also known as horse dookie.
Oh. Man. I have a really sensitive stomach.
BLURGH!
HAHAHAHAHAHAHAHPHA
Mae Everfart strikes again!!
That worked out well.
Look at the bright side. We made the entire lunch room crack up.

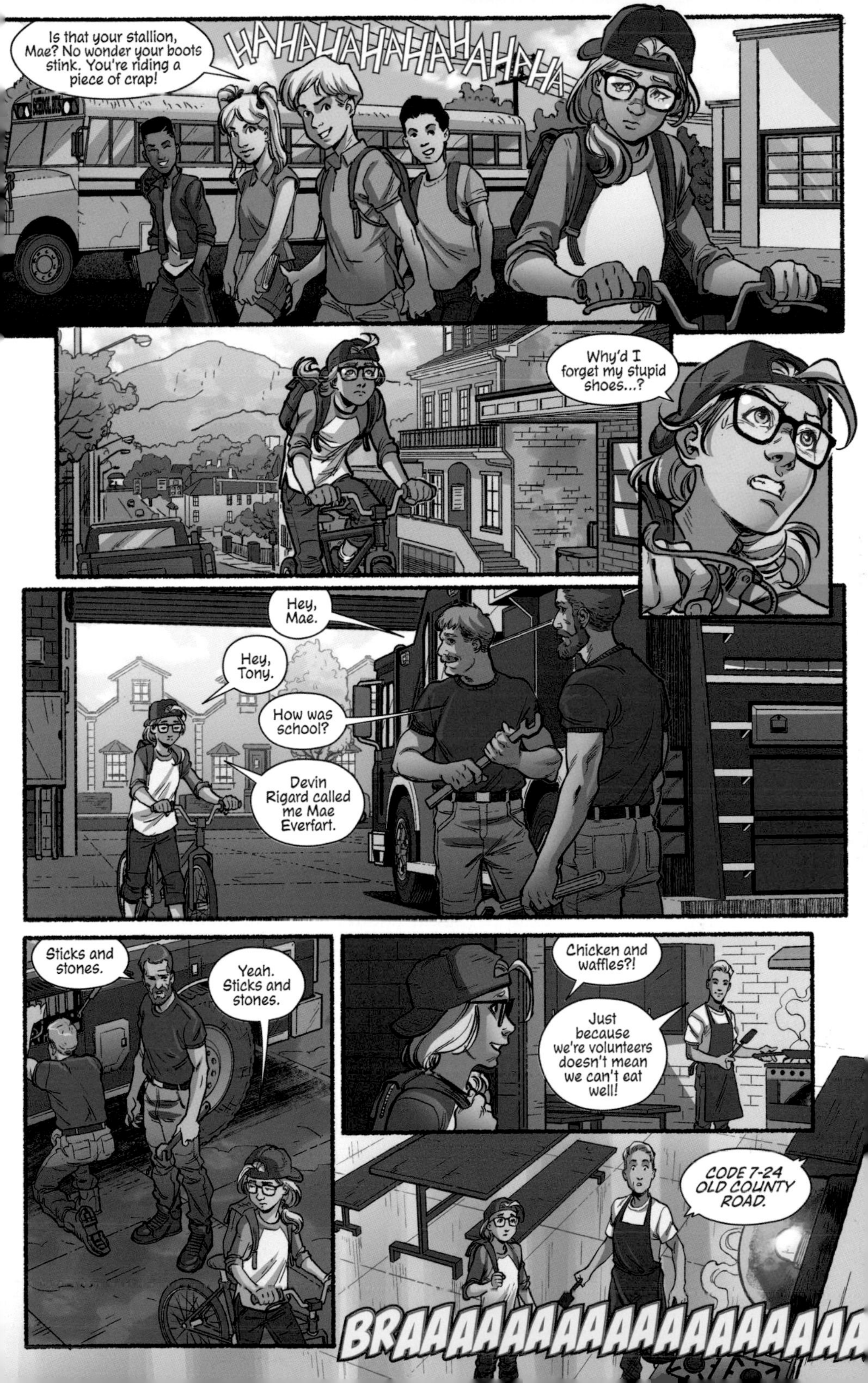
Is that your stallion, Mae? No wonder your boots stink. You're riding a piece of crap!
HAHAHAHAHAHAHAHAHA
Why'd I forget my stupid shoes...?
Hey, Mae.
Hey, Tony.
How was school?
Devin Rigard called me Mae Everfart.
Sticks and stones.
Yeah. Sticks and stones.
Chicken and waffles?!
Just because we're volunteers doesn't mean we can't eat well!
CODE 7-24 OLD COUNTY ROAD.
BRAAAAAAAAAAAAAAAA

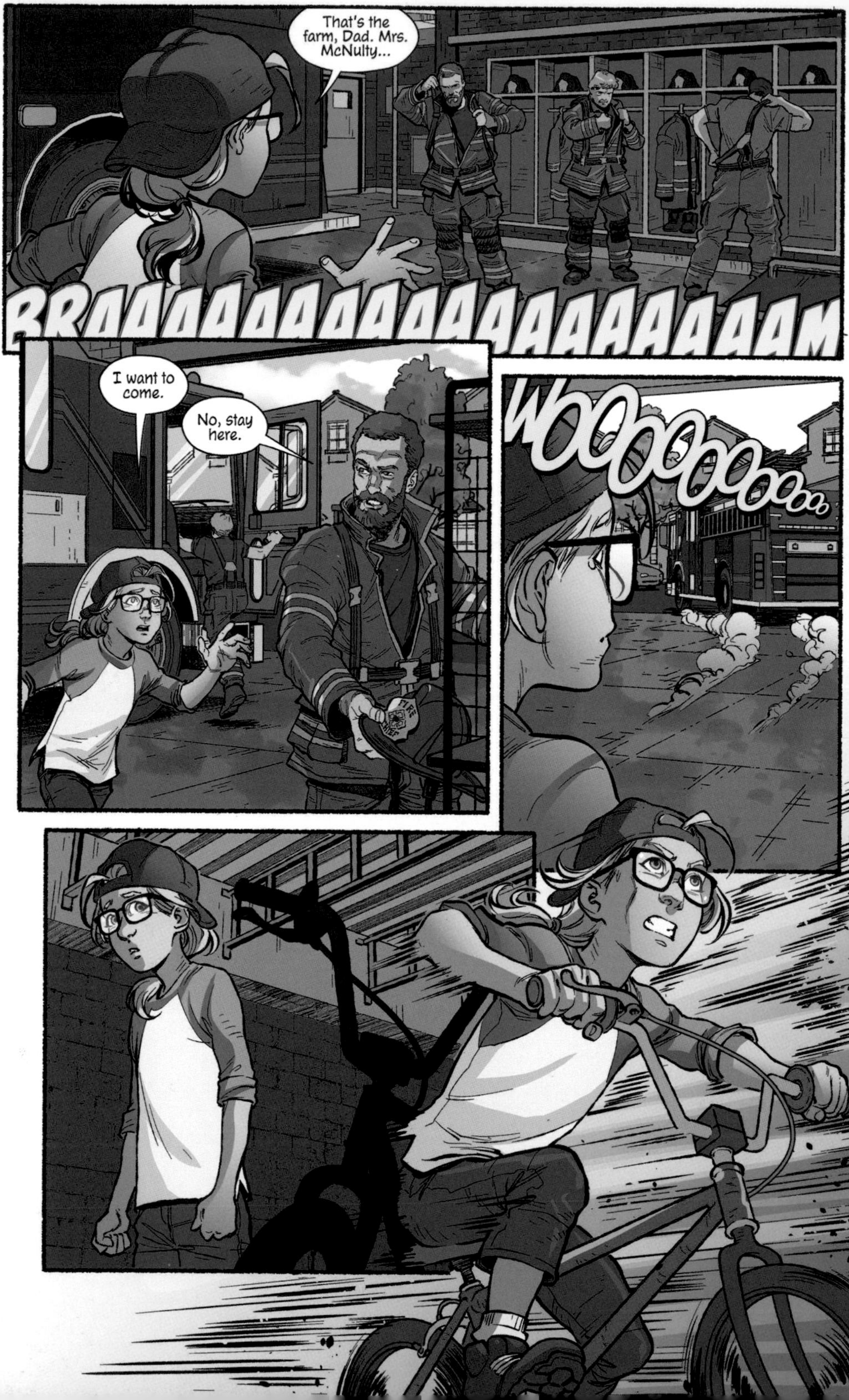
That's the farm, Dad. Mrs. McNulty...
BRAAAAAAAAAAAAAAAAAAM
I want to come.
No, stay here.
FIRE CHIEF
WOOOOOOOooo

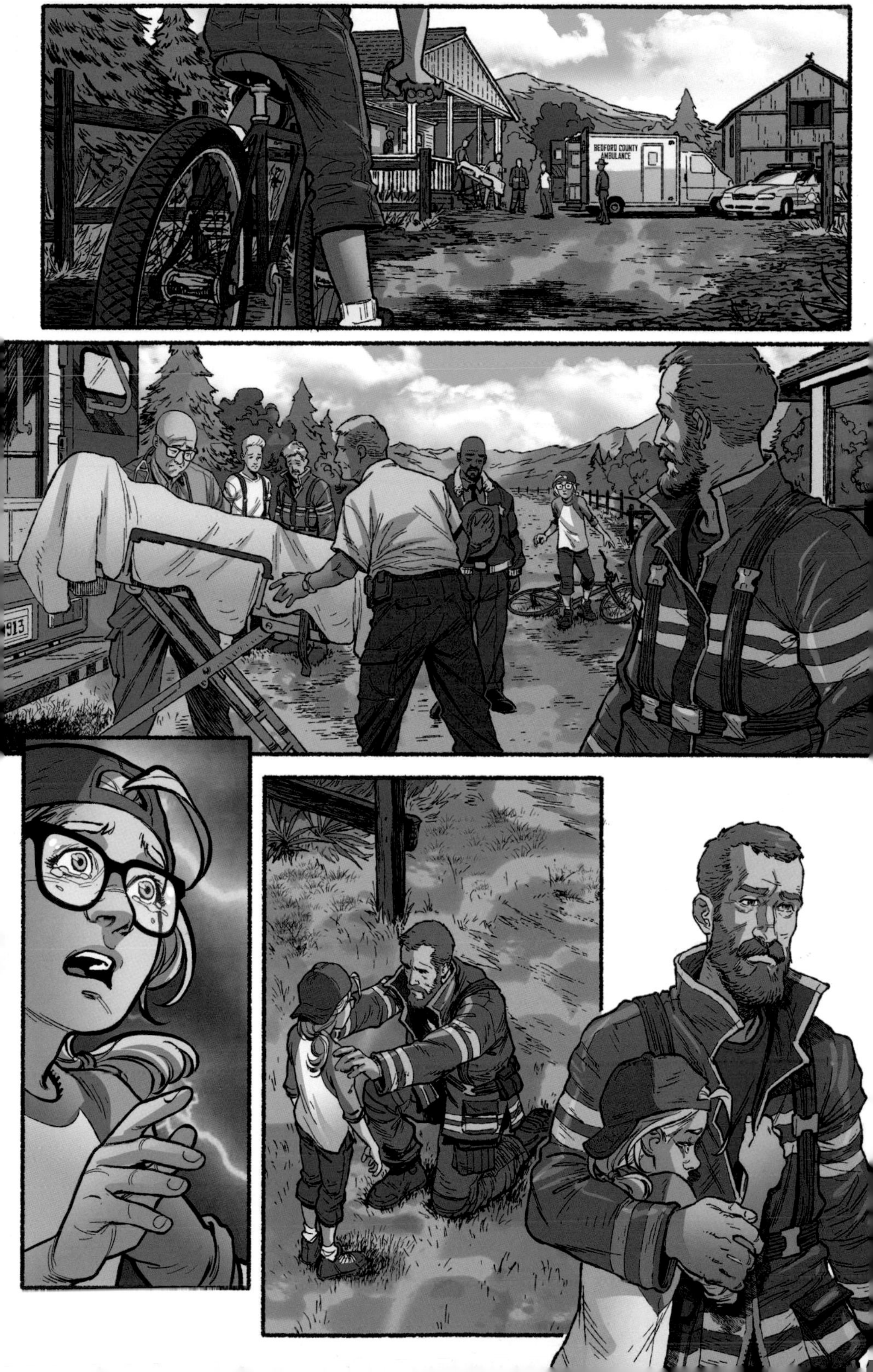
BEDFORD COUNTY
AMBULANCE

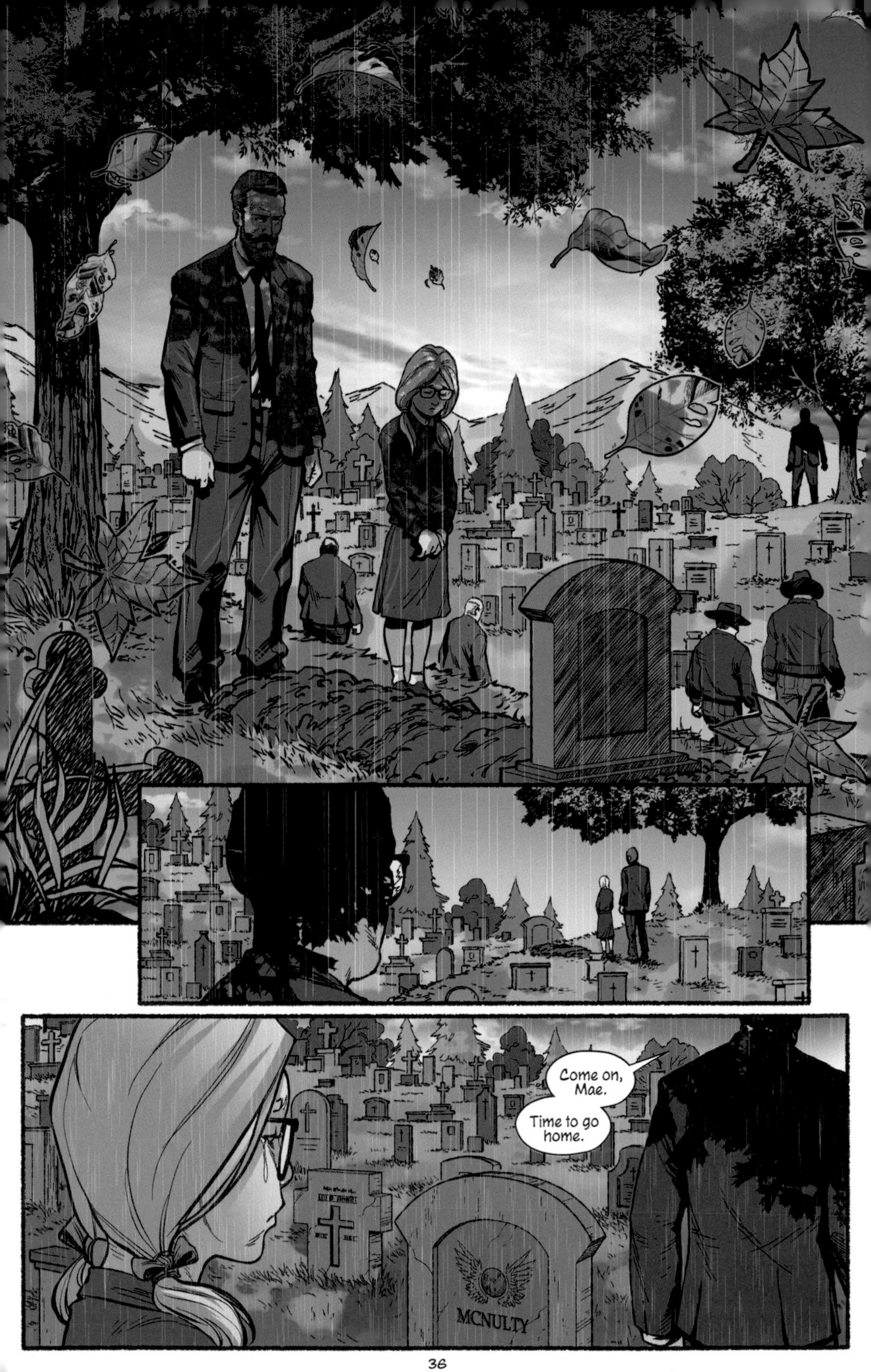
Come on, Mae.
Time to go home.
MCNULTY

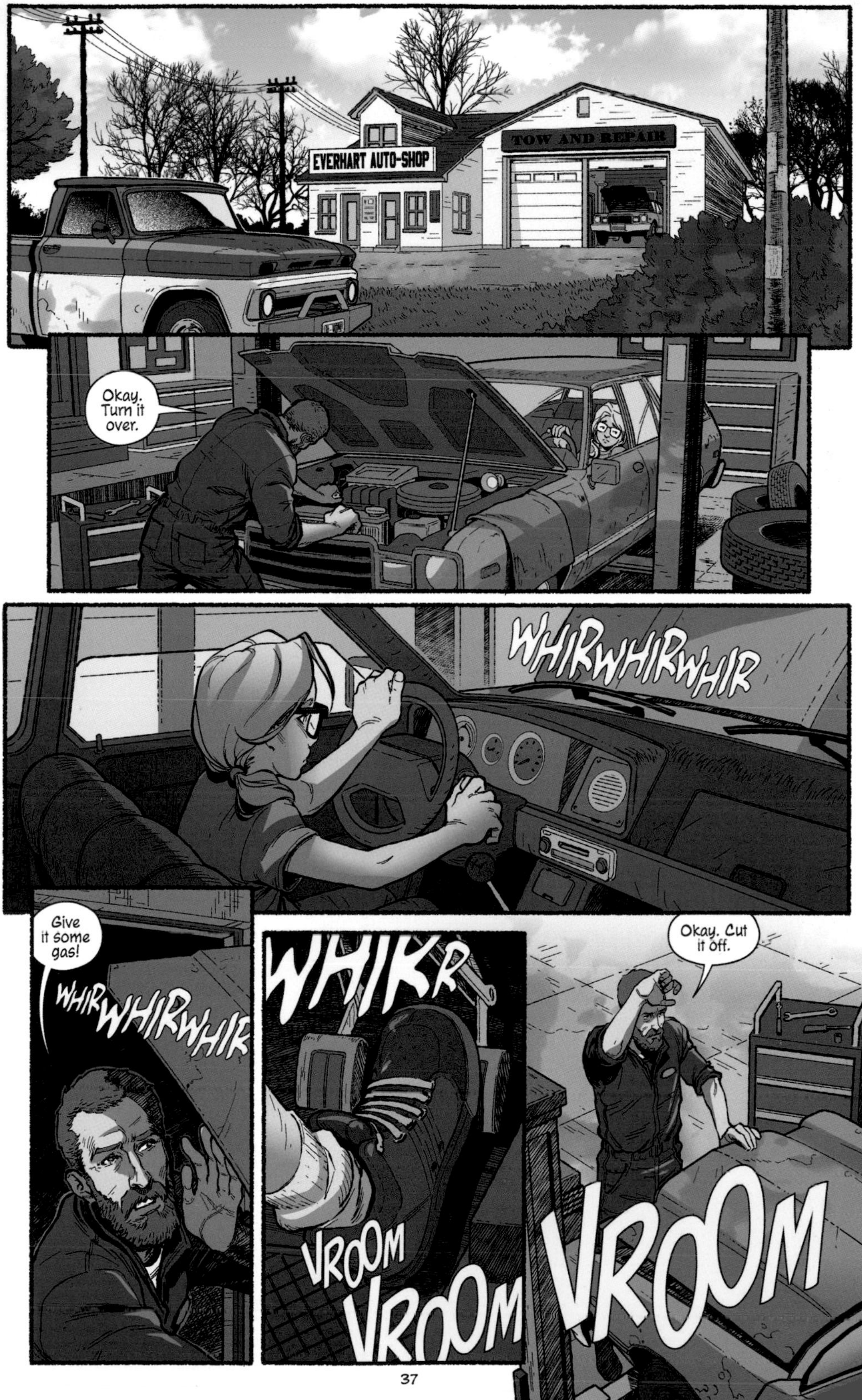
EVERHART AUTO-SHOP
TOW AND REPAIR
Okay. Turn it over.
WHIRWHIRWHIR
Give it some gas!
WHIRWHIRWHIR
WHIRR
VROOM
VROOM
Okay. Cut it off.
VROOM

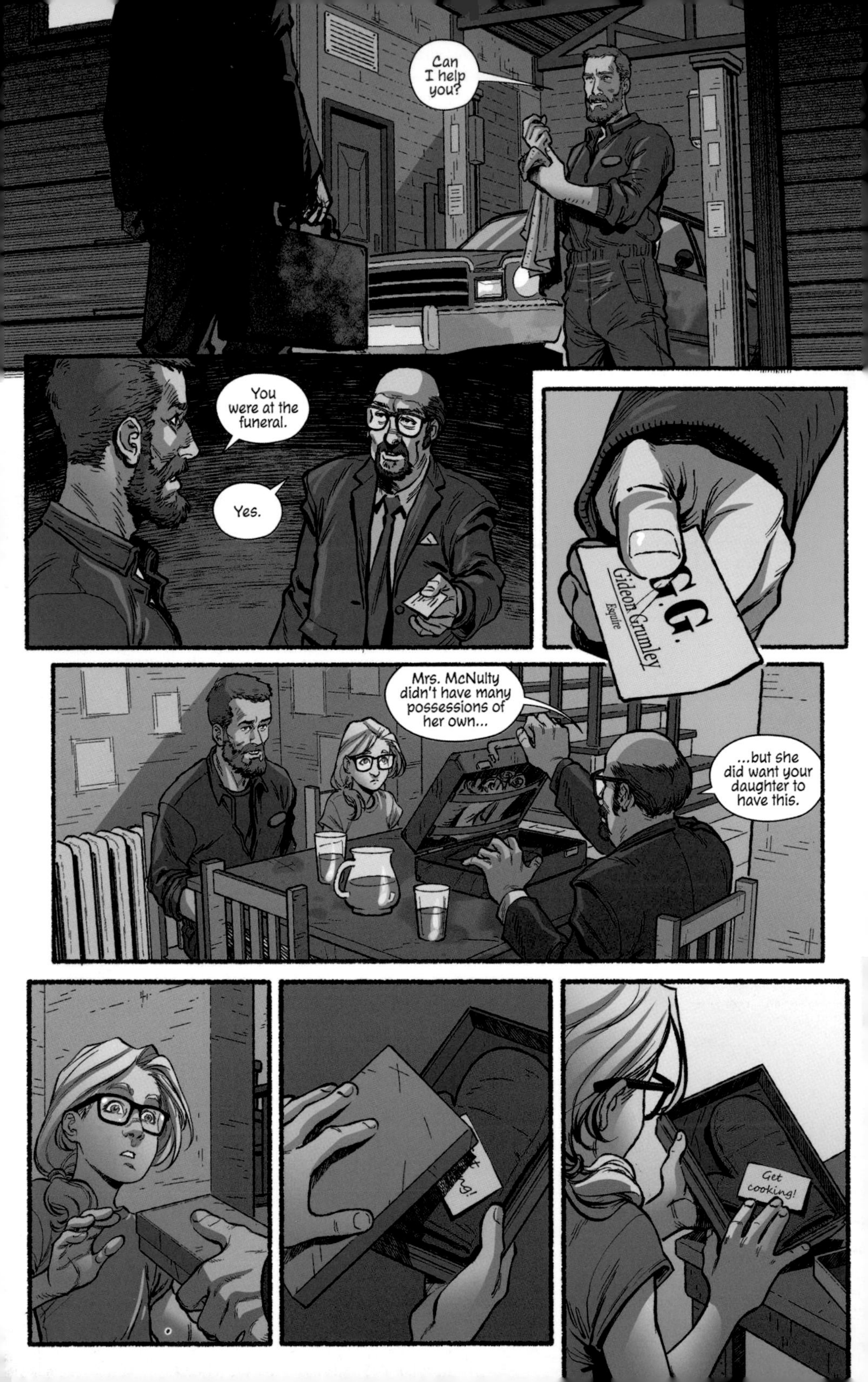
Can I help you?
You were at the funeral.
Yes.
G.G.
Gideon Grumley
Esquire
Mrs. McNulty didn't have many possessions of her own...
...but she did want your daughter to have this.
Get cooking!

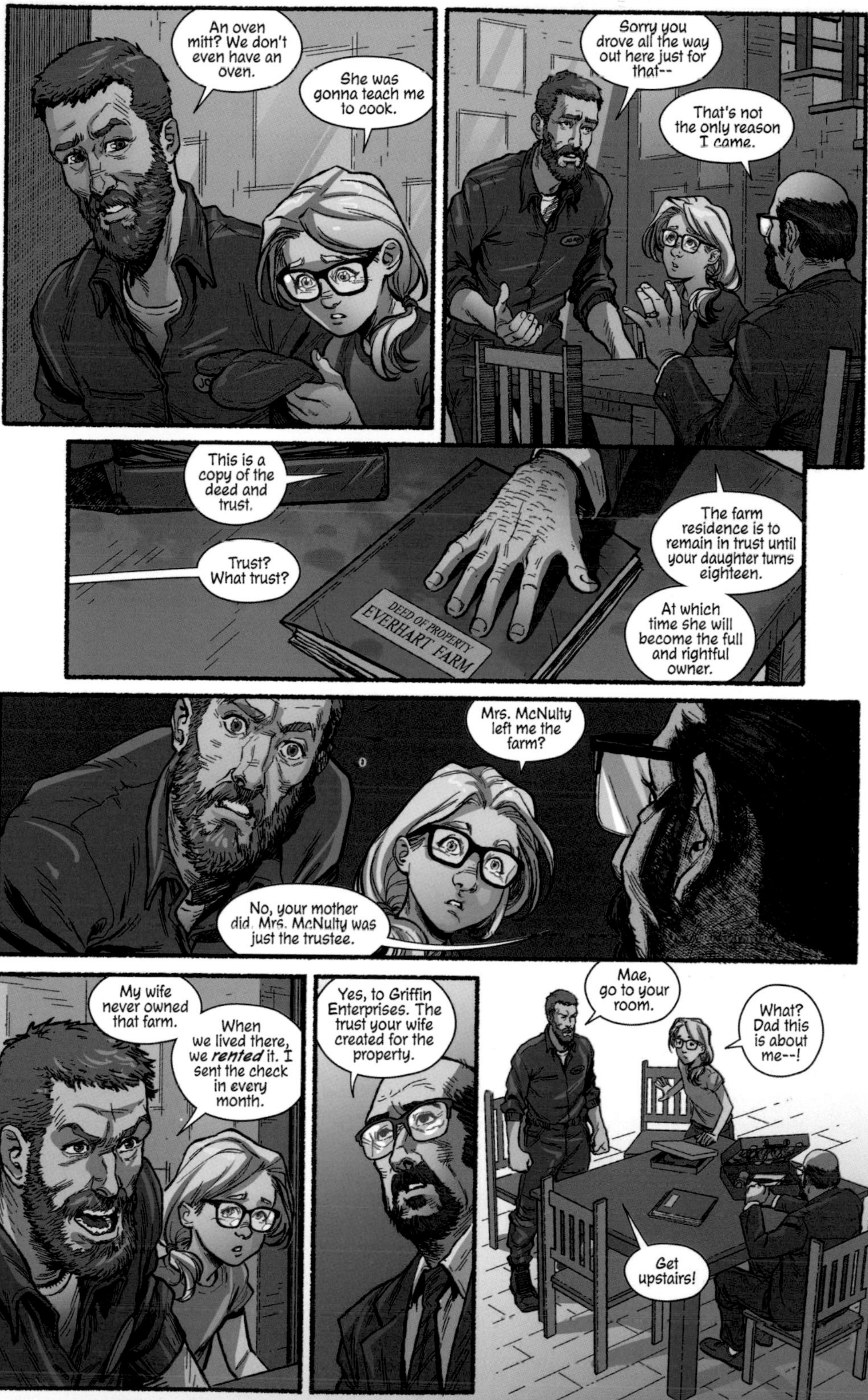

An oven mitt? We don't even have an oven.
She was gonna teach me to cook.
Sorry you drove all the way out here just for that--
That's not the only reason I came.
This is a copy of the deed and trust.
Trust? What trust?
DEED OF PROPERTY
EVERHART FARM
The farm residence is to remain in trust until your daughter turns eighteen.
At which time she will become the full and rightful owner.
Mrs. McNulty left me the farm?
No, your mother did. Mrs. McNulty was just the trustee.
My wife never owned that farm.
When we lived there, we *rented* it. I sent the check in every month.
Yes, to Griffin Enterprises. The trust your wife created for the property.
Mae, go to your room.
What? Dad this is about me--!
Get upstairs!

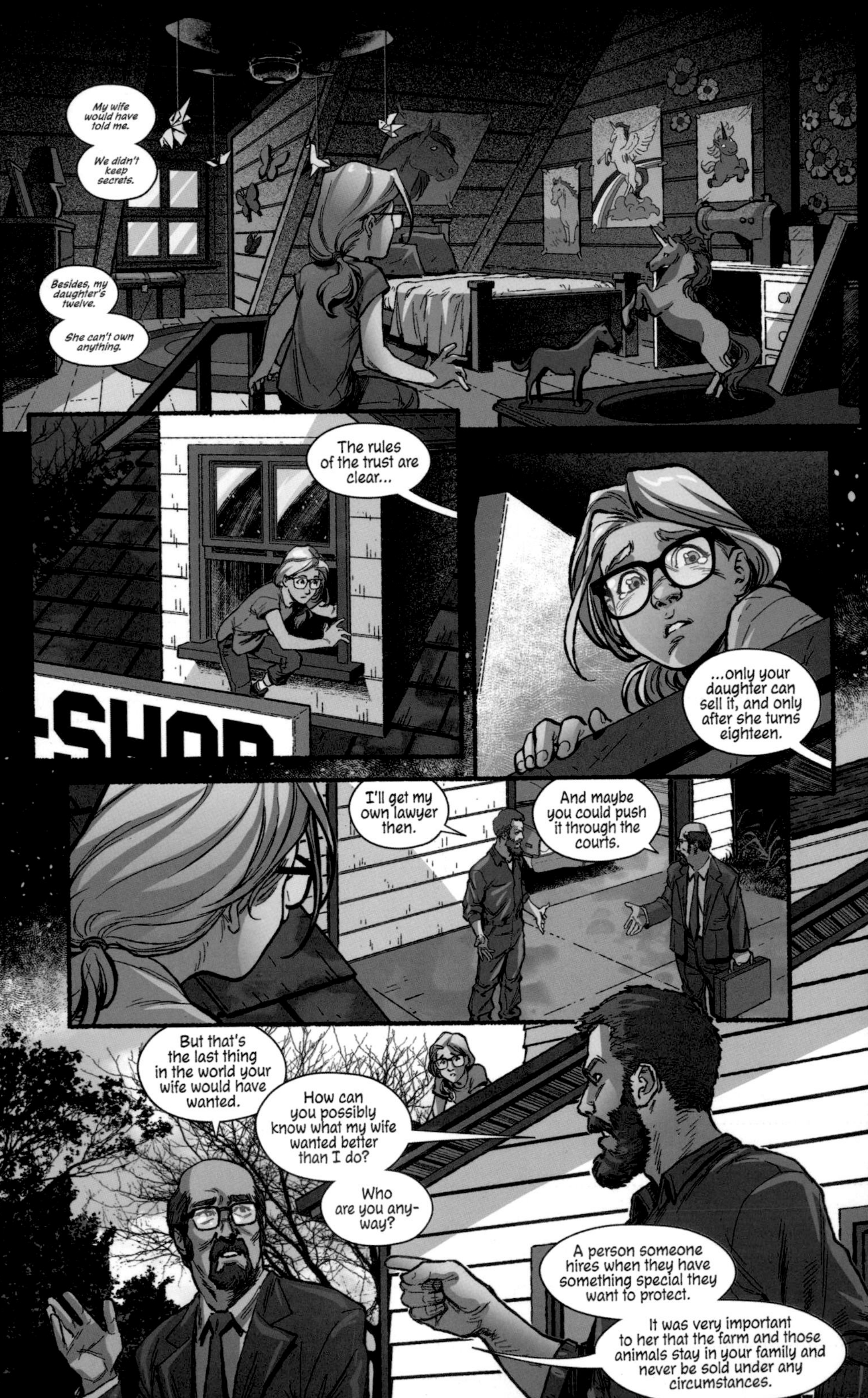

My wife would have told me.
We didn't keep secrets.
Besides, my daughter's twelve.
She can't own anything.
The rules of the trust are clear...
SHOP
...only your daughter can sell it, and only after she turns eighteen.
I'll get my own lawyer then.
And maybe you could push it through the courts.
But that's the last thing in the world your wife would have wanted.
How can you possibly know what my wife wanted better than I do?
Who are you any-way?
A person someone hires when they have something special they want to protect.
It was very important to her that the farm and those animals stay in your family and never be sold under any circumstances.

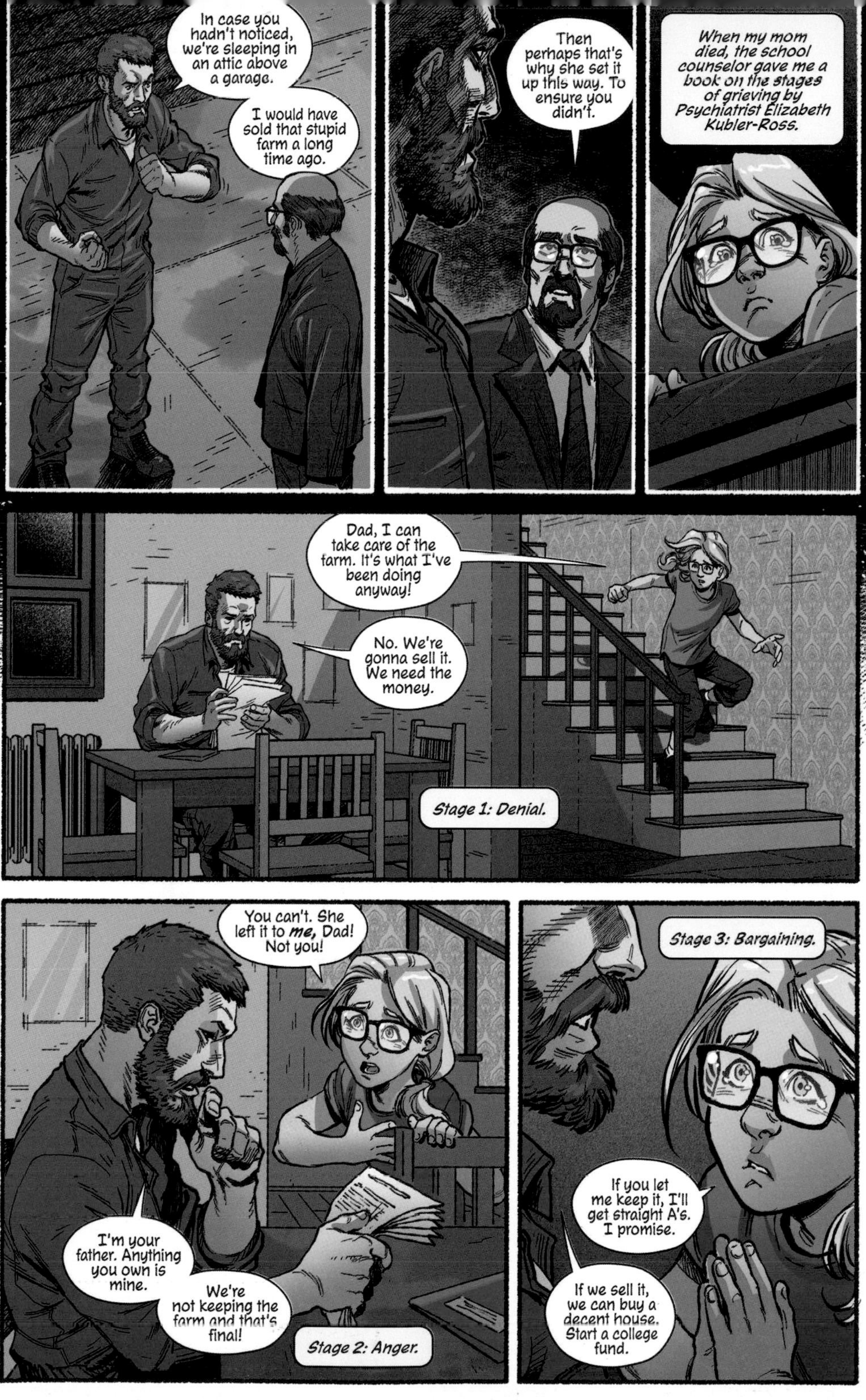
In case you hadn't noticed, we're sleeping in an attic above a garage.
I would have sold that stupid farm a long time ago.
Then perhaps that's why she set it up this way. To ensure you didn't.
When my mom died, the school counselor gave me a book on the stages of grieving by Psychiatrist Elizabeth Kubler-Ross.
Dad, I can take care of the farm. It's what I've been doing anyway!
No. We're gonna sell it. We need the money.
Stage 1: Denial.
You can't. She left it to me, Dad! Not you!
I'm your father. Anything you own is mine.
We're not keeping the farm and that's final!
Stage 2: Anger.
Stage 3: Bargaining.
If you let me keep it, I'll get straight A's. I promise.
If we sell it, we can buy a decent house. Start a college fund.

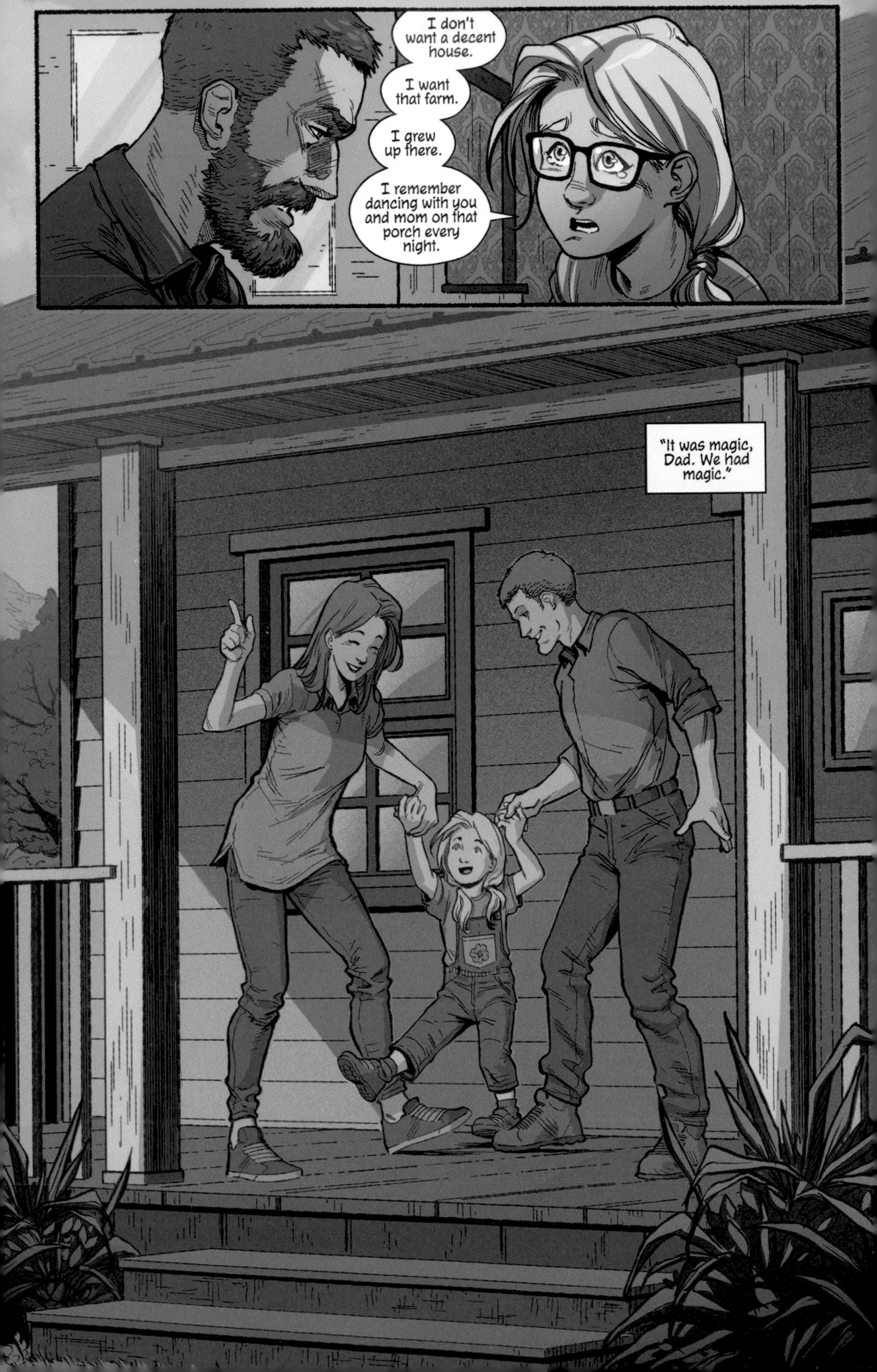
I don't want a decent house.
I want that farm.
I grew up there.
I remember dancing with you and mom on that porch every night.
"It was magic, Dad. We had magic."

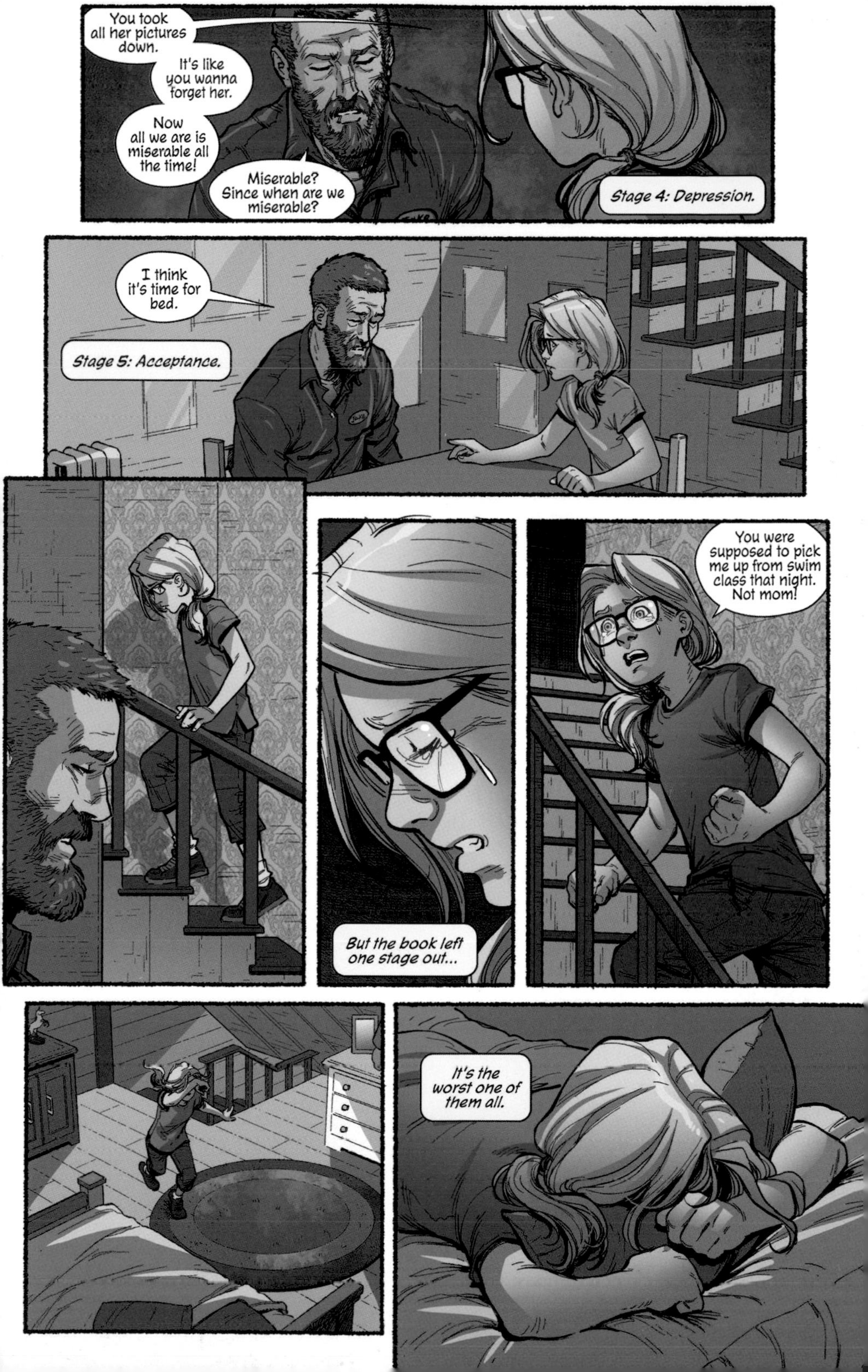
You took all her pictures down.
It's like you wanna forget her.
Now all we are is miserable all the time!
Miserable? Since when are we miserable?
Stage 4: Depression.
I think it's time for bed.
Stage 5: Acceptance.
But the book left one stage out...
You were supposed to pick me up from swim class that night. Not mom!
It's the worst one of them all.

BLAME

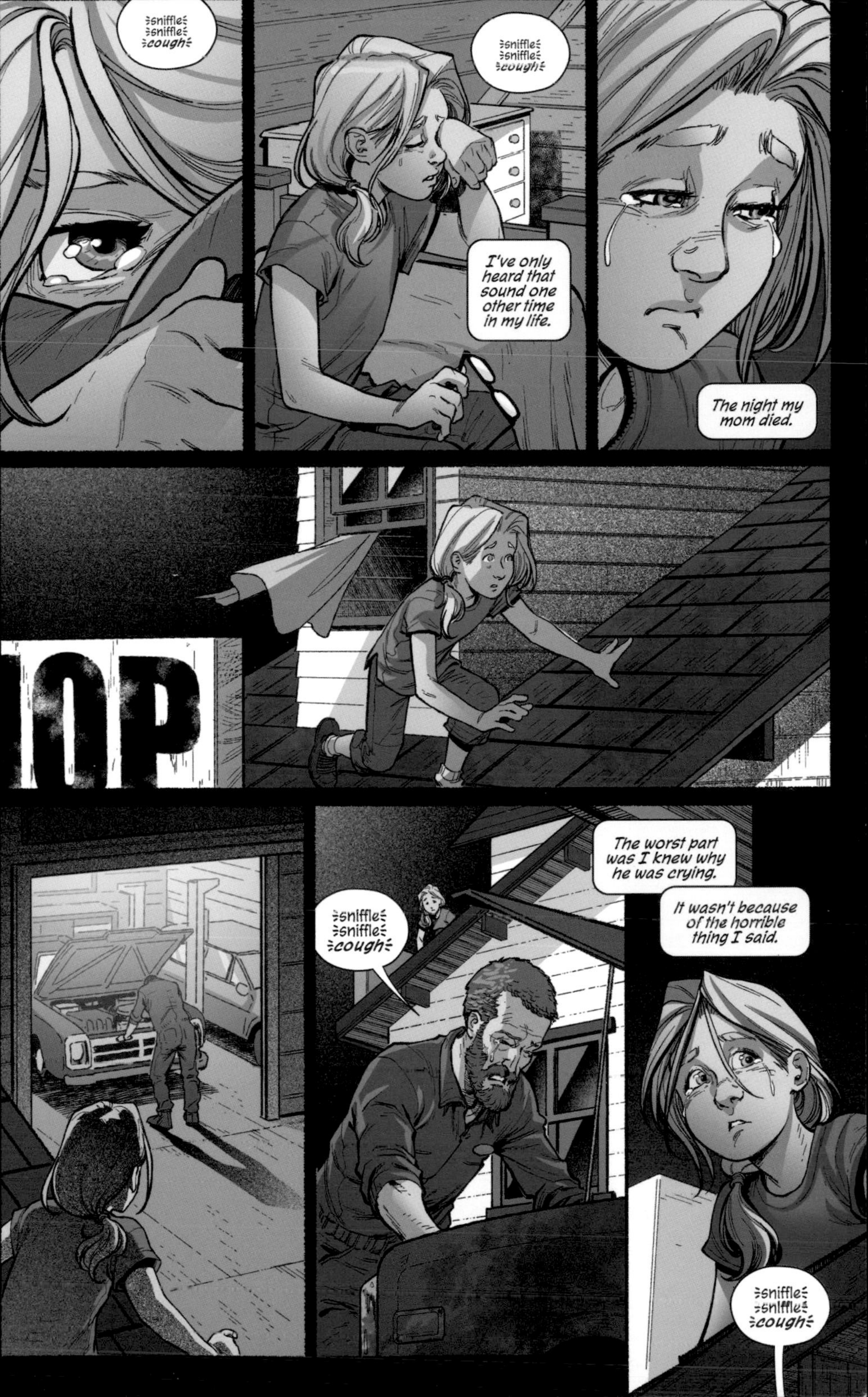
sniffle sniffle cough
sniffle sniffle cough
I've only heard that sound one other time in my life.
The night my mom died.
The worst part was I knew why he was crying.
sniffle sniffle cough
It wasn't because of the horrible thing I said.
sniffle sniffle cough

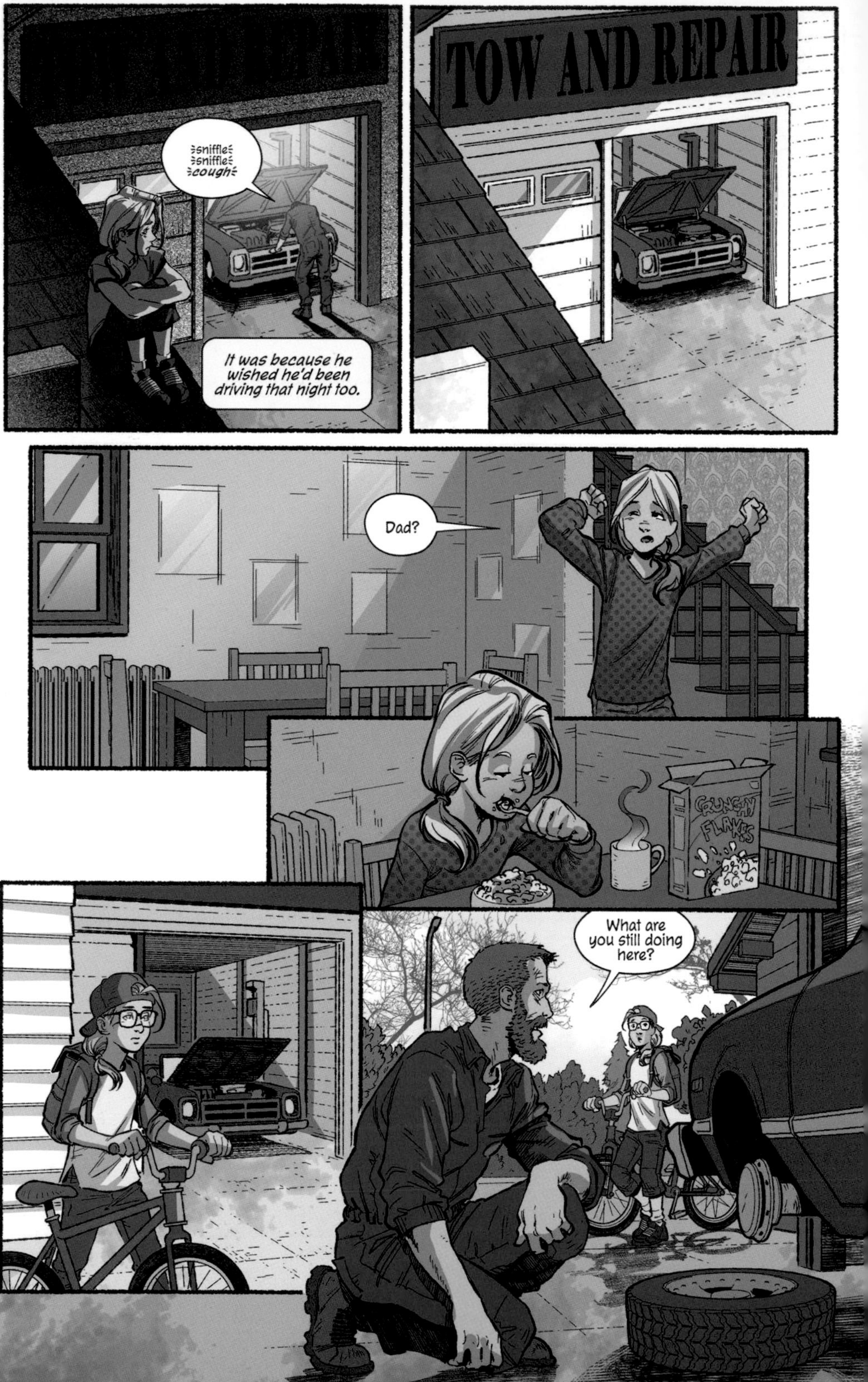

sniffle sniffle cough
It was because he wished he'd been driving that night too.
TOW AND REPAIR
Dad?
CRUNCHY FLAKES
What are you still doing here?

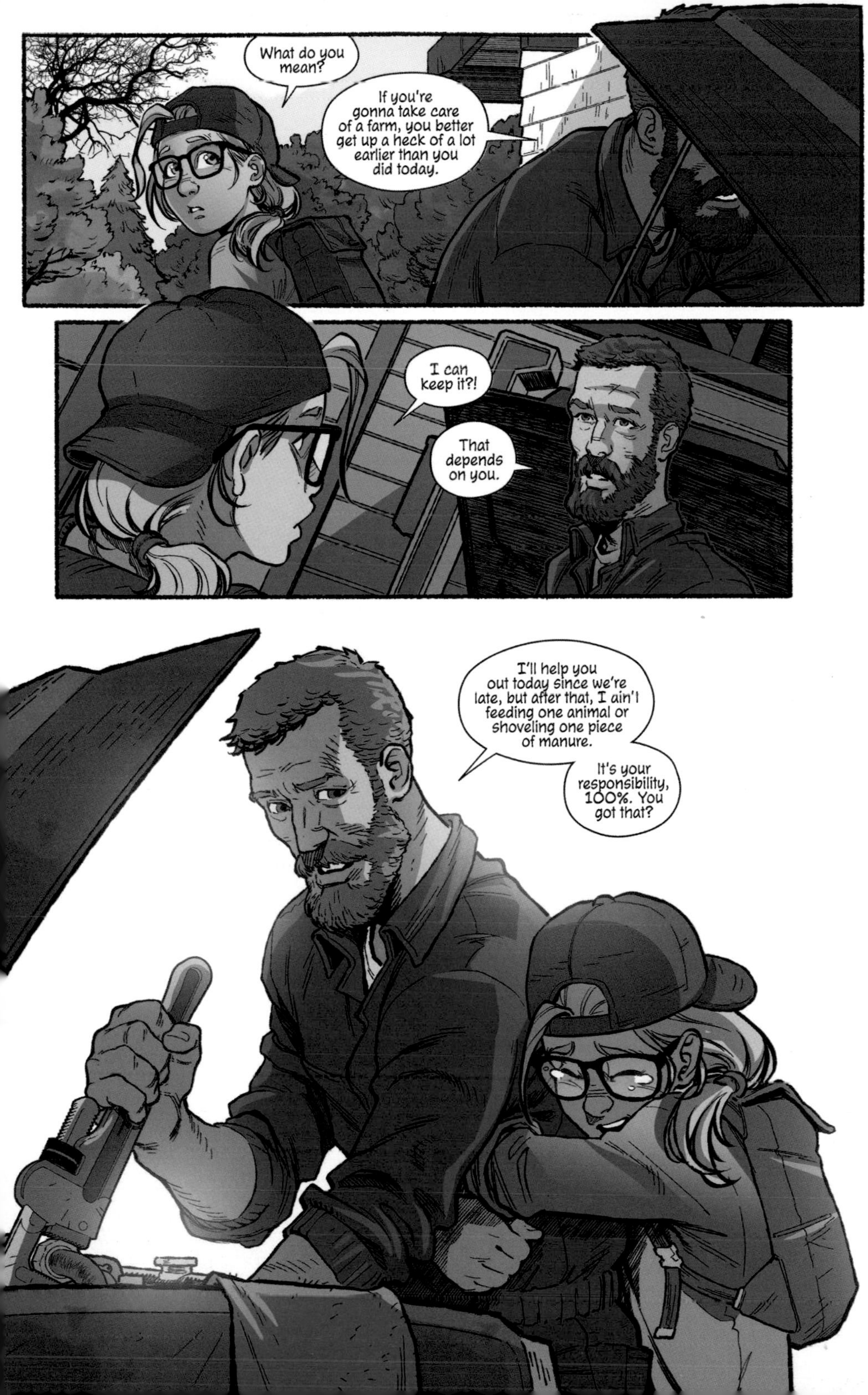
What do you mean?
If you're gonna take care of a farm, you better get up a heck of a lot earlier than you did today.
I can keep it?!
That depends on you.
I'll help you out today since we're late, but after that, I ain't feeding one animal or shoveling one piece of manure.
It's your responsibility, 100%. You got that?

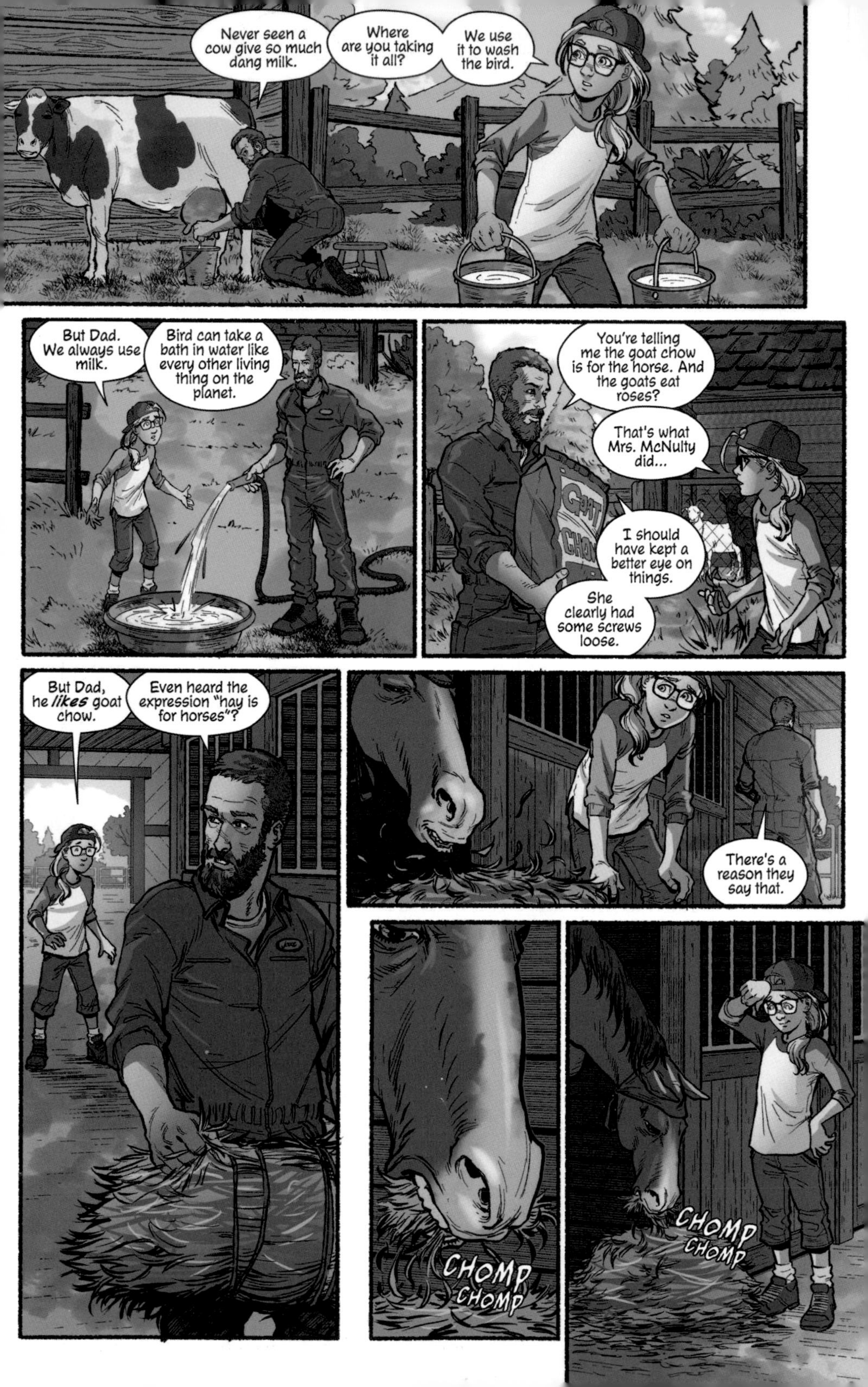

Never seen a cow give so much dang milk.
Where are you taking it all?
We use it to wash the bird.
But Dad. We always use milk.
Bird can take a bath in water like every other living thing on the planet.
You're telling me the goat chow is for the horse. And the goats eat roses?
That's what Mrs. McNulty did...
GOAT CHOW
I should have kept a better eye on things.
She clearly had some screws loose.
But Dad, he *likes* goat chow.
Even heard the expression "hay is for horses"?
There's a reason they say that.
CHOMP CHOMP
CHOMP CHOMP

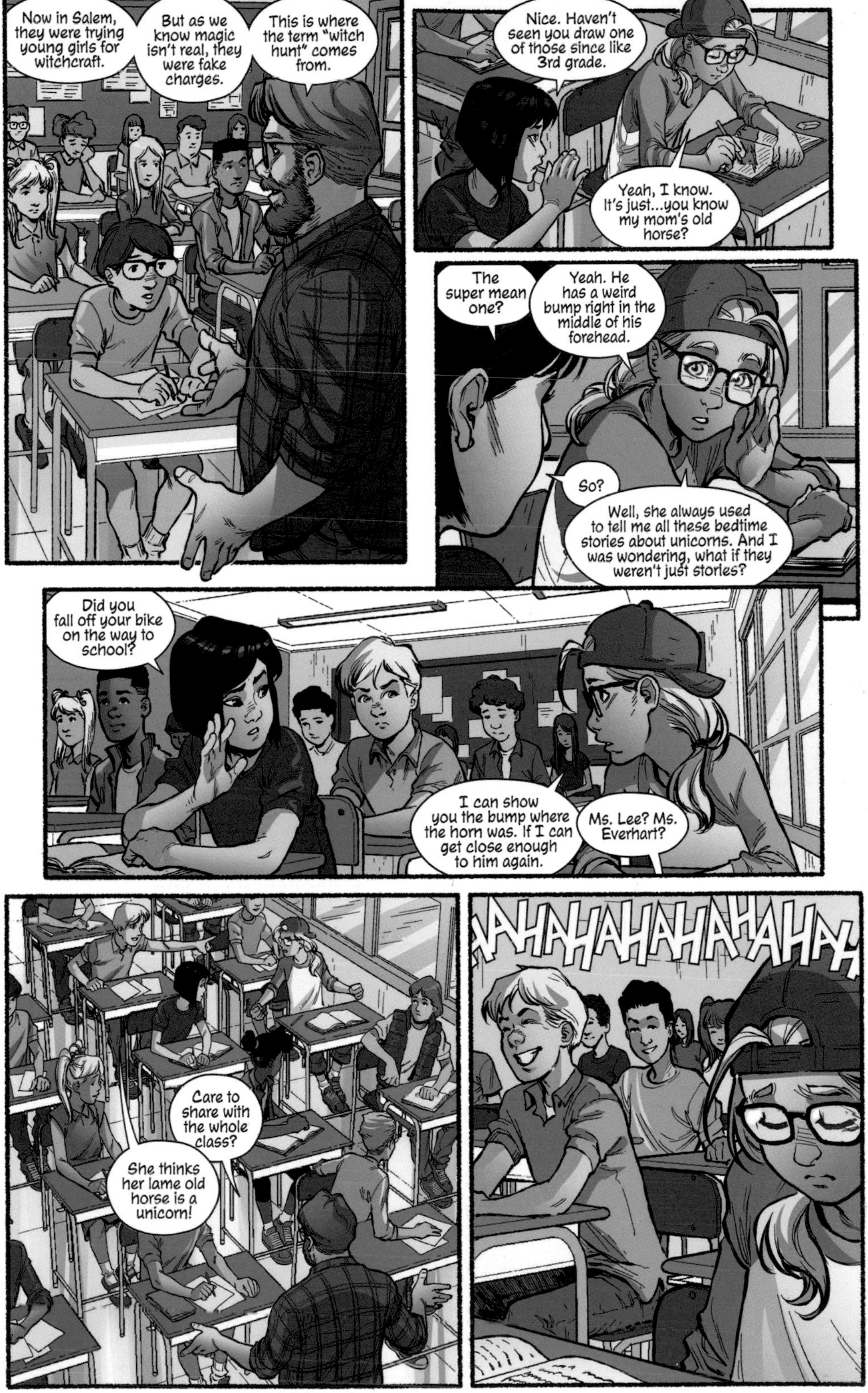
Now in Salem, they were trying young girls for witchcraft.
But as we know magic isn't real, they were fake charges.
This is where the term "witch hunt" comes from.
Nice. Haven't seen you draw one of those since like 3rd grade.
Yeah, I know. It's just...you know my mom's old horse?
The super mean one?
Yeah. He has a weird bump right in the middle of his forehead.
So?
Well, she always used to tell me all these bedtime stories about unicorns. And I was wondering, what if they weren't just stories?
Did you fall off your bike on the way to school?
I can show you the bump where the horn was. If I can get close enough to him again.
Ms. Lee? Ms. Everhart?
Care to share with the whole class?
She thinks her lame old horse is a unicorn!
HAHAHAHAHAHAHAHAHA

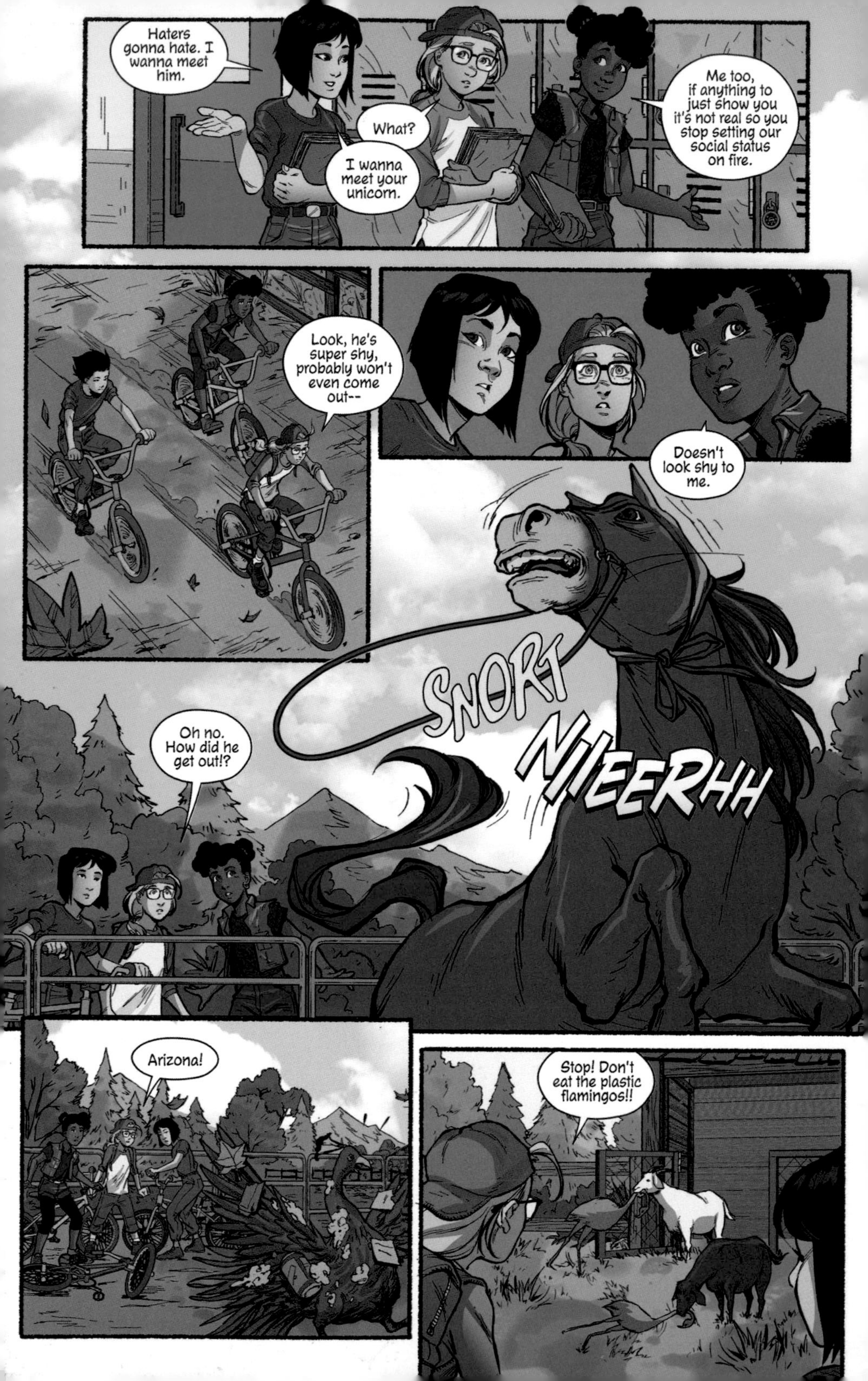
Haters gonna hate. I wanna meet him.
What?
I wanna meet your unicorn.
Me too, if anything to just show you it's not real so you stop setting our social status on fire.
Look, he's super shy, probably won't even come out--
Doesn't look shy to me.
SNORT
NIIEERHH
Oh no. How did he get out!?
Arizona!
Stop! Don't eat the plastic flamingos!!

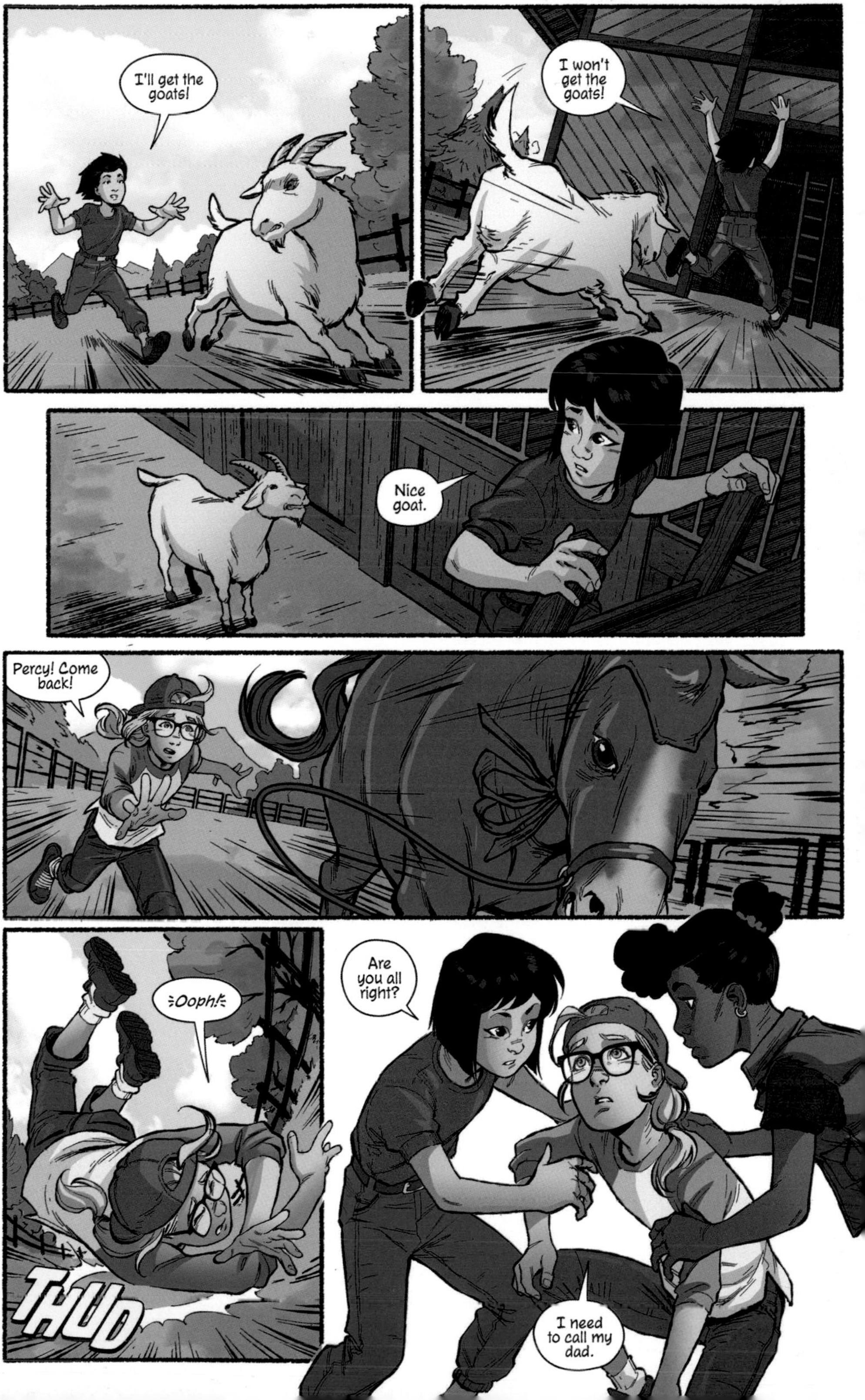
I'll get the goats!
I won't get the goats!
Nice goat.
Percy! Come back!
Ooph!
THUD
Are you all right?
I need to call my dad.

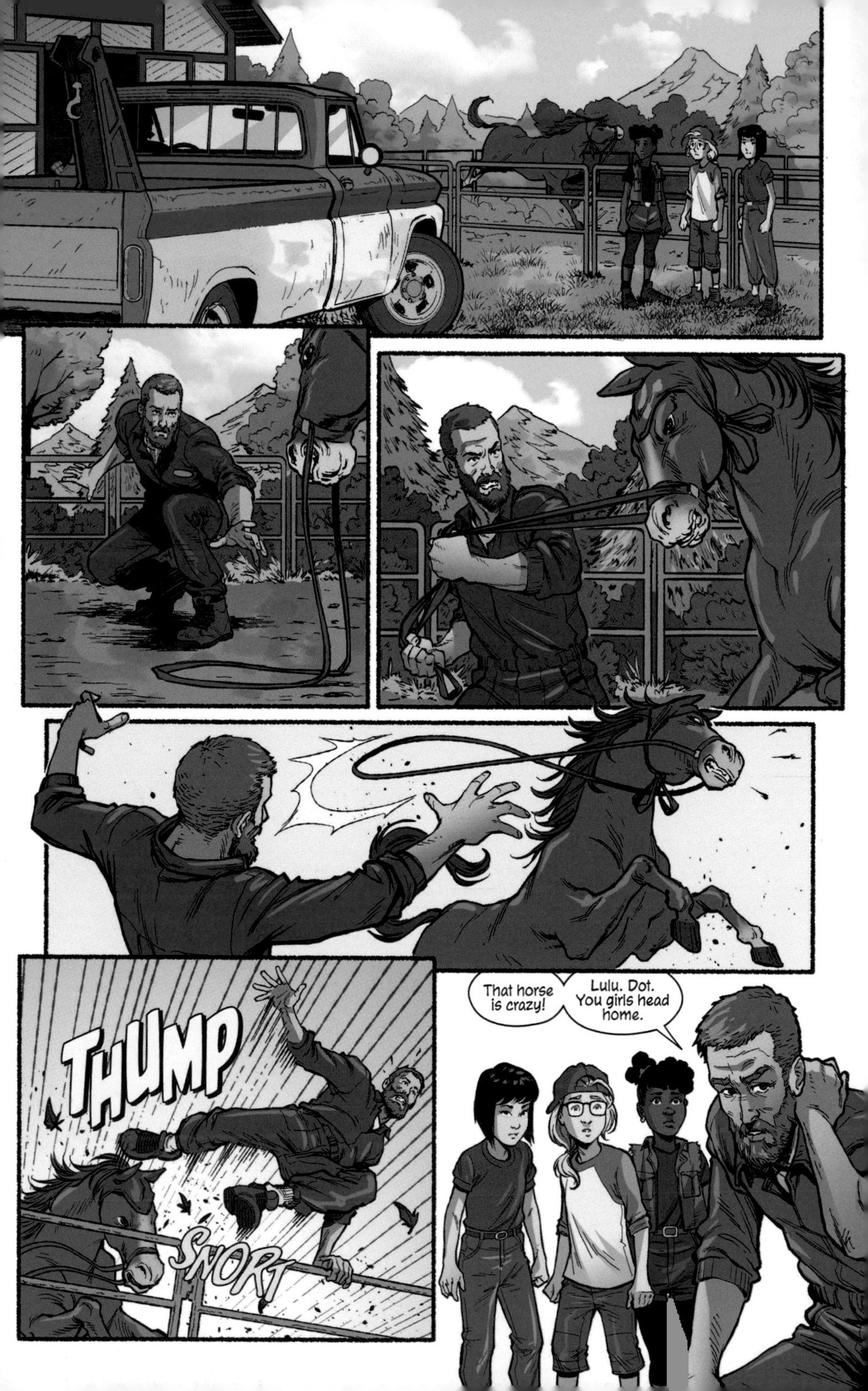
THUMP
SNORT
That horse is crazy!
Lulu. Dot. You girls head home.

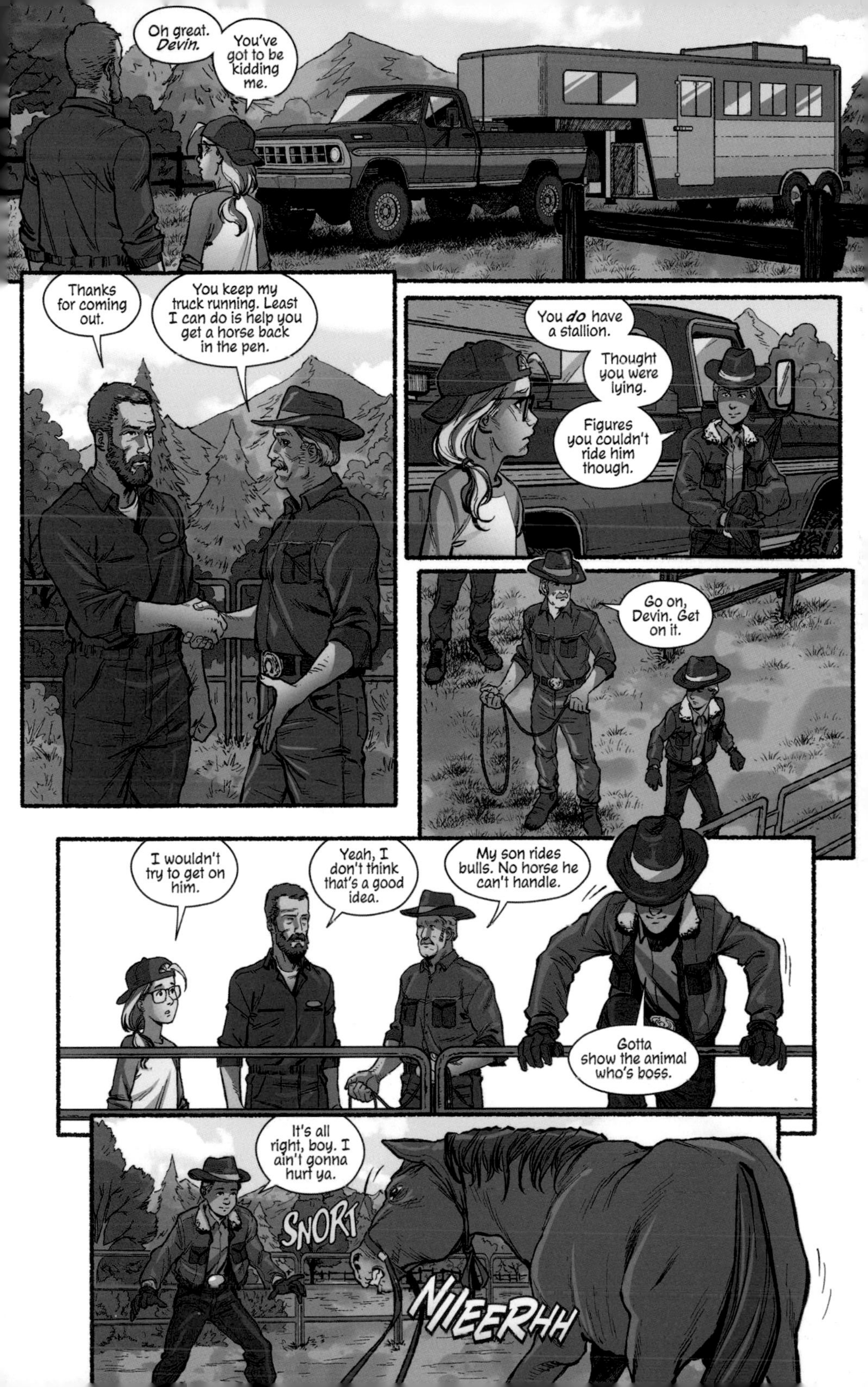
Oh great. *Devin.*
You've got to be kidding me.
Thanks for coming out.
You keep my truck running. Least I can do is help you get a horse back in the pen.
You *do* have a stallion.
Thought you were lying.
Figures you couldn't ride him though.
Go on, Devin. Get on it.
I wouldn't try to get on him.
Yeah, I don't think that's a good idea.
My son rides bulls. No horse he can't handle.
Gotta show the animal who's boss.
It's all right, boy. I ain't gonna hurt ya.
SNORT
NIIEERHH

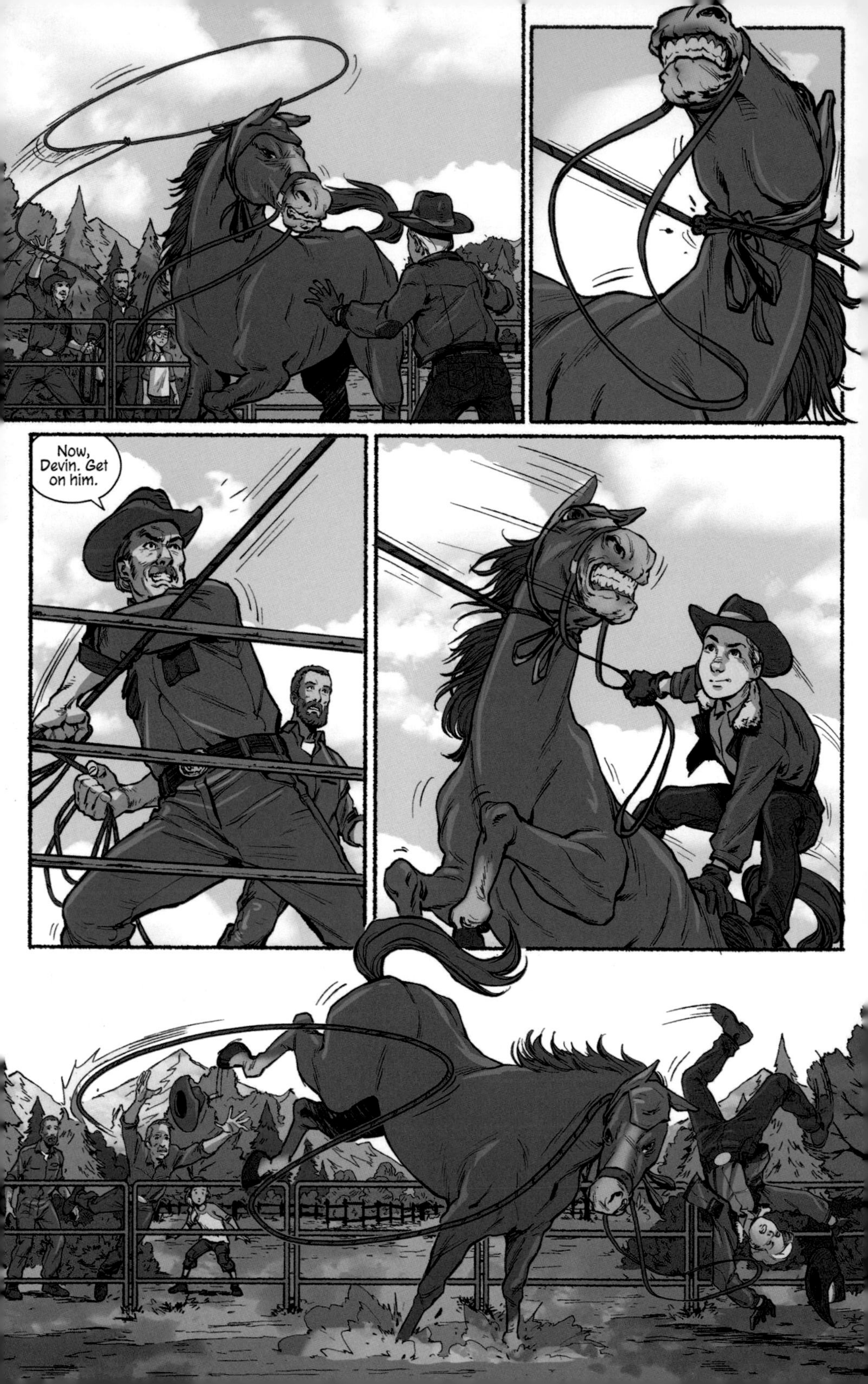
Now, Devin. Get on him.

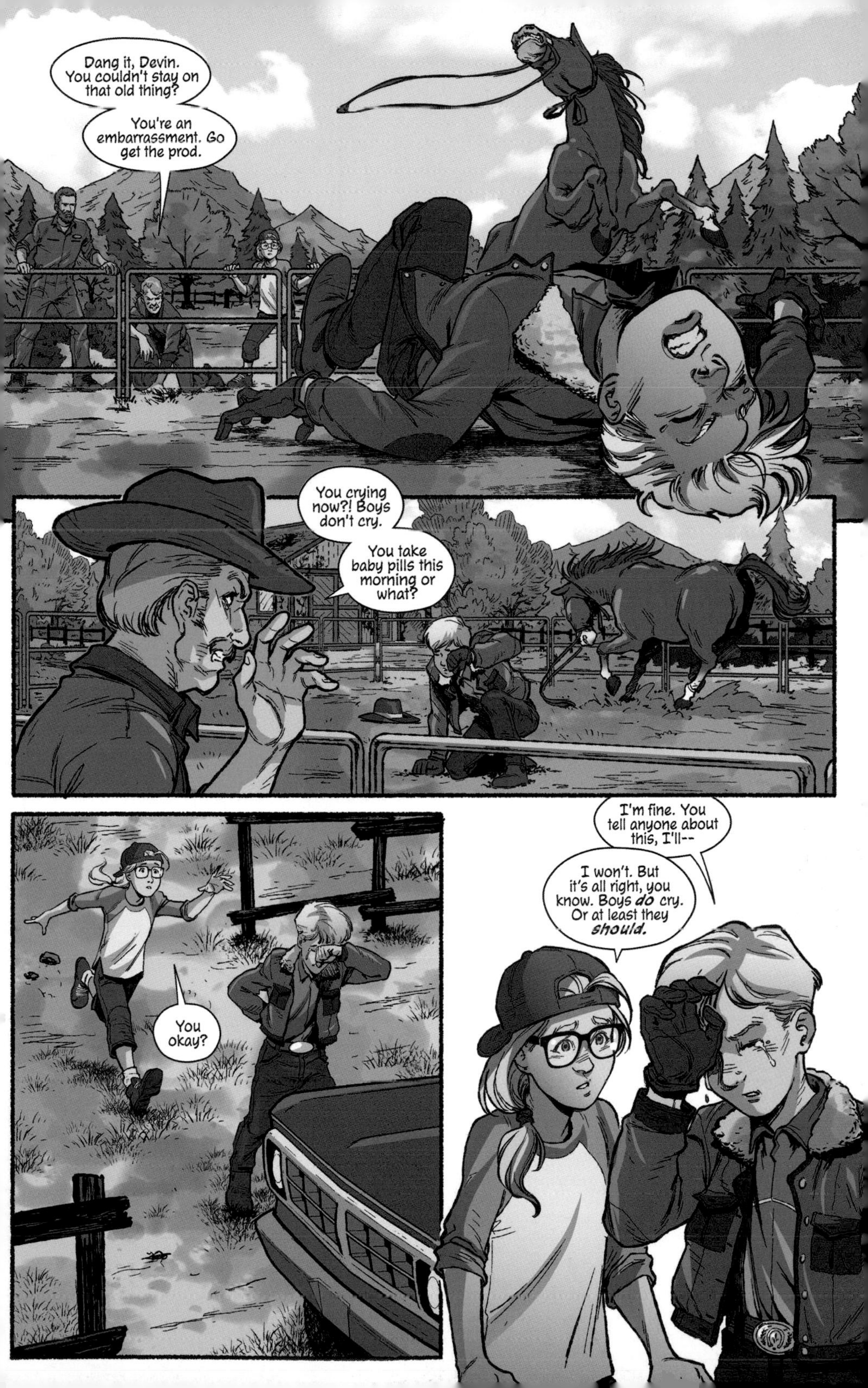
Dang it, Devin. You couldn't stay on that old thing?
You're an embarrassment. Go get the prod.
You crying now?! Boys don't cry.
You take baby pills this morning or what?
You okay?
I'm fine. You tell anyone about this, I'll--
I won't. But it's all right, you know. Boys *do* cry. Or at least they ***should.***

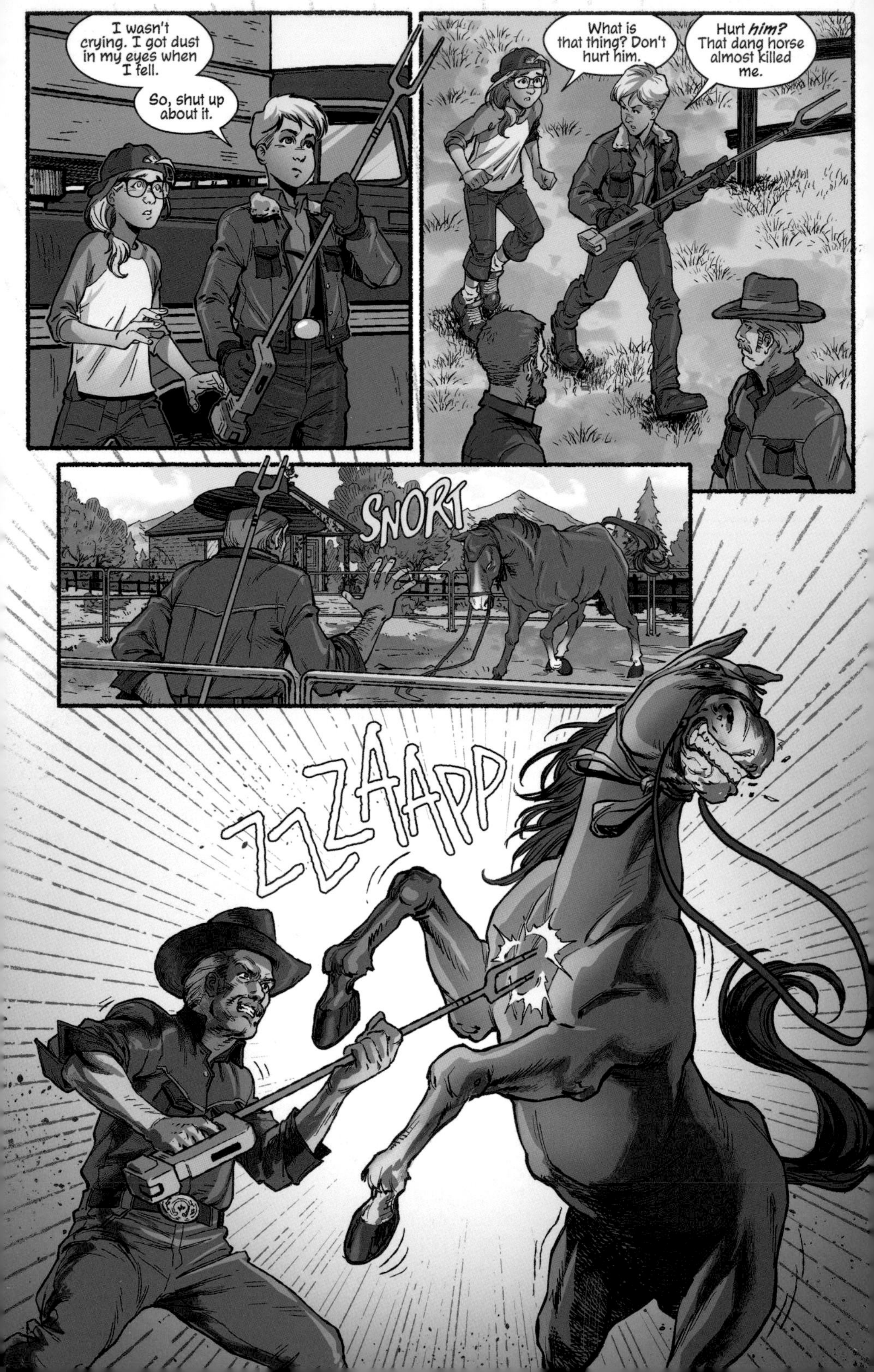
I wasn't crying. I got dust in my eyes when I fell.
So, shut up about it.
What is that thing? Don't hurt him.
Hurt *him?* That dang horse almost killed me.
SNORT
ZZZAAPP

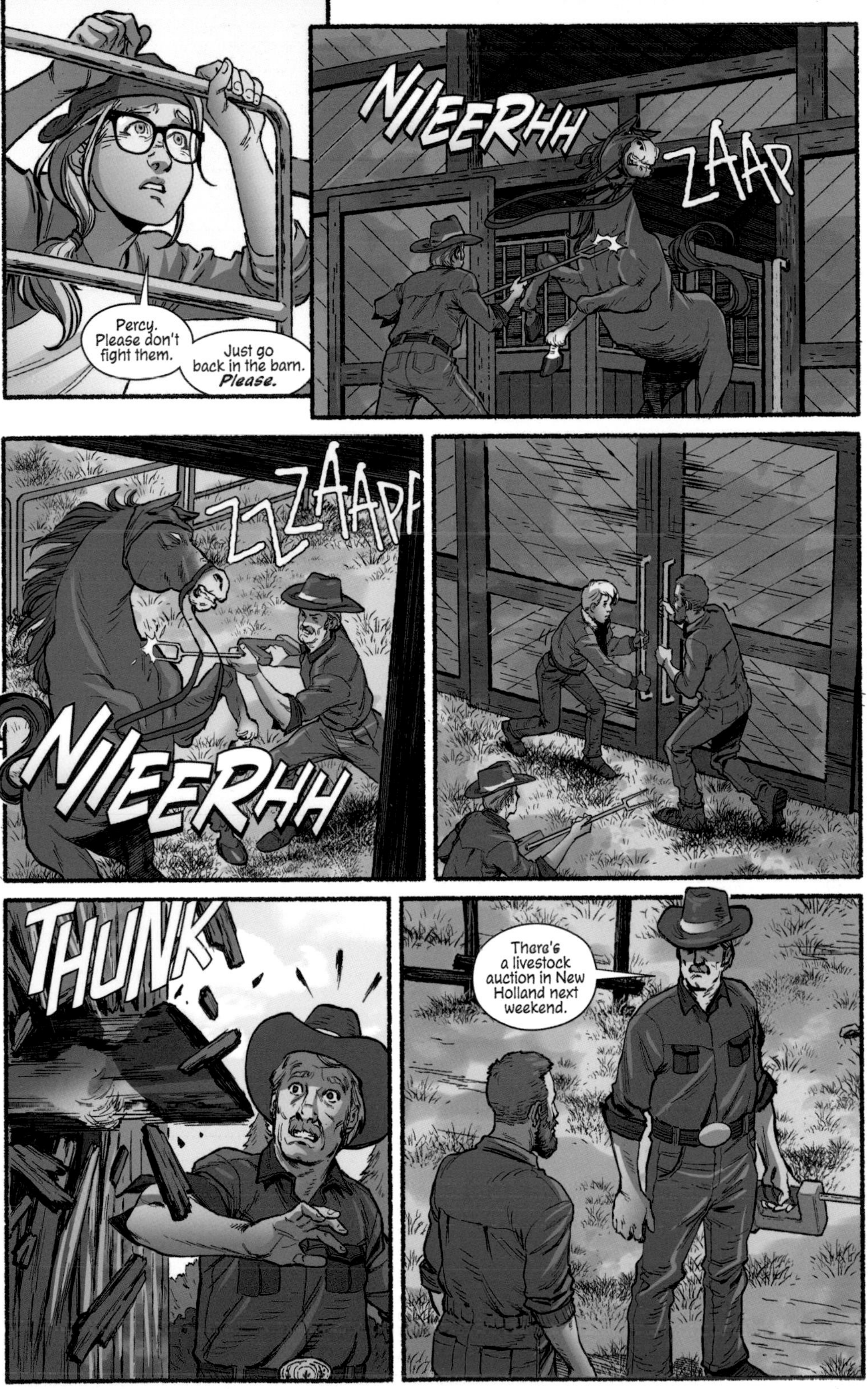
Percy. Please don't fight them.
Just go back in the barn. *Please.*
NIIEERHH
ZAAP
ZZZAAPP
NIIEERHH
THUNK
There's a livestock auction in New Holland next weekend.

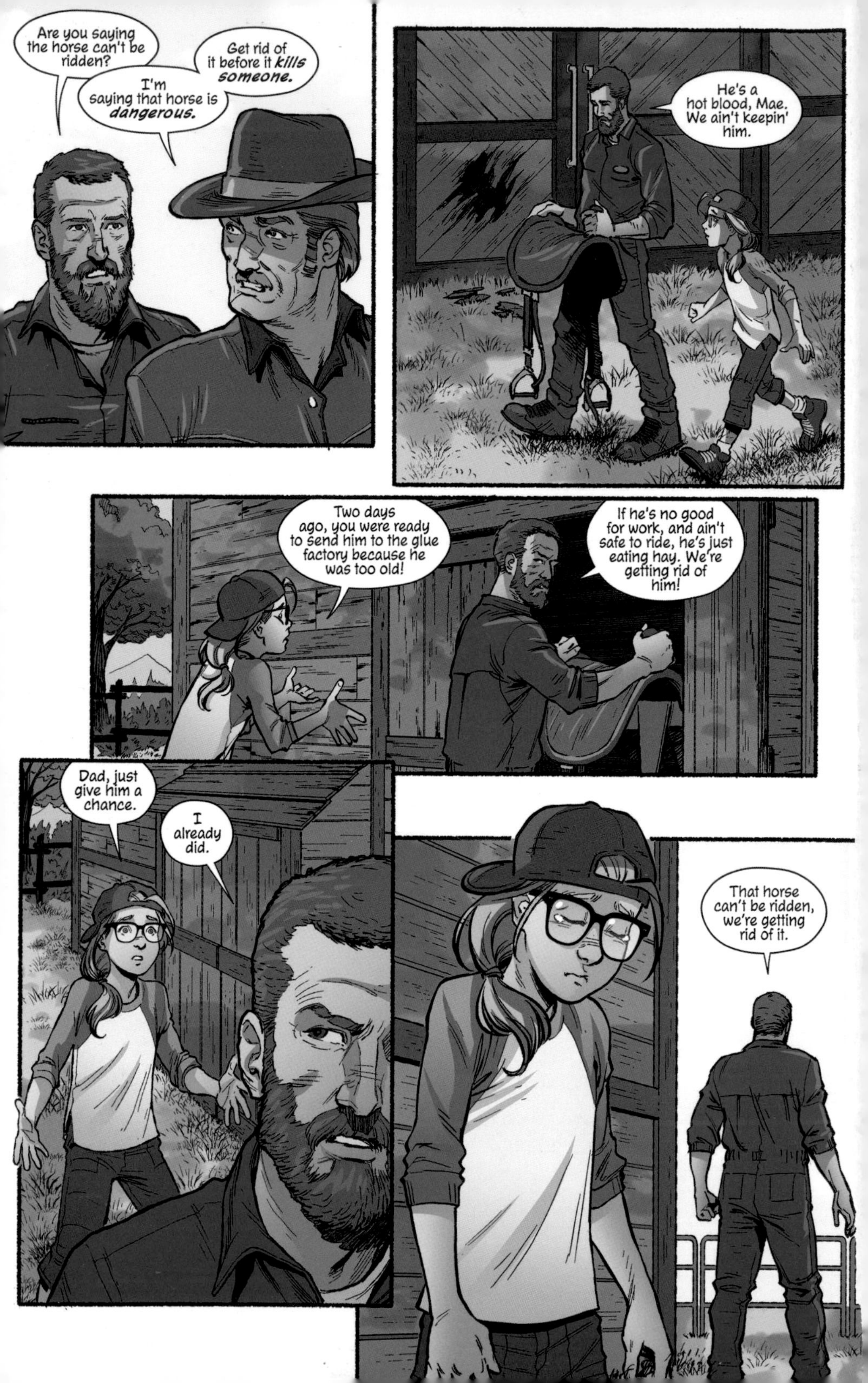
Are you saying the horse can't be ridden?
I'm saying that horse is *dangerous.*
Get rid of it before it *kills someone.*
He's a hot blood, Mae. We ain't keepin' him.
Two days ago, you were ready to send him to the glue factory because he was too old!
If he's no good for work, and ain't safe to ride, he's just eating hay. We're getting rid of him!
Dad, just give him a chance.
I already did.
That horse can't be ridden, we're getting rid of it.

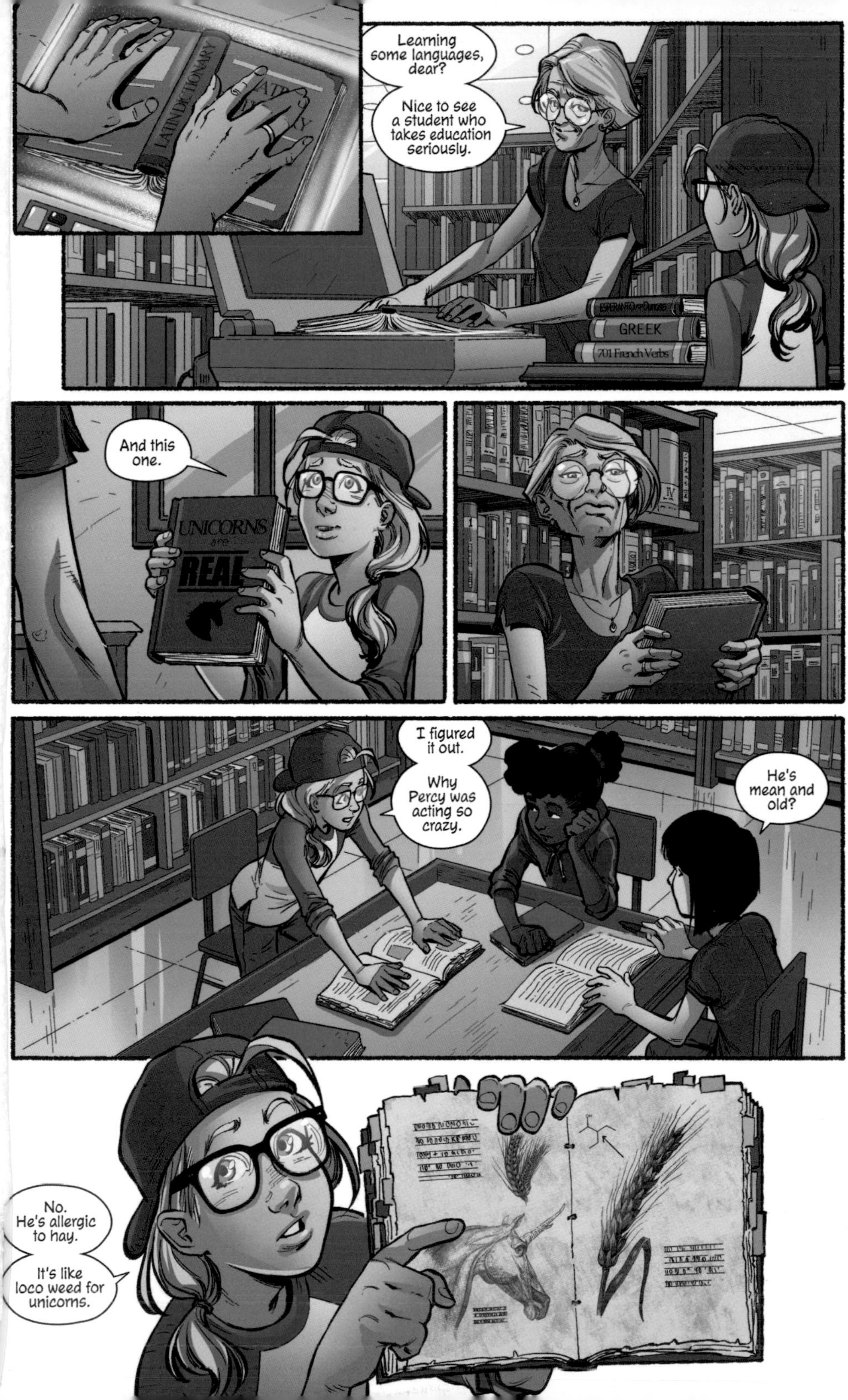
LATIN DICTIONARY
Learning some languages, dear?
Nice to see a student who takes education seriously.
ESPERANTO and Duncan
GREEK
701 French Verbs
And this one.
UNICORNS are REAL
I figured it out.
Why Percy was acting so crazy.
He's mean and old?
No. He's allergic to hay.
It's like loco weed for unicorns.

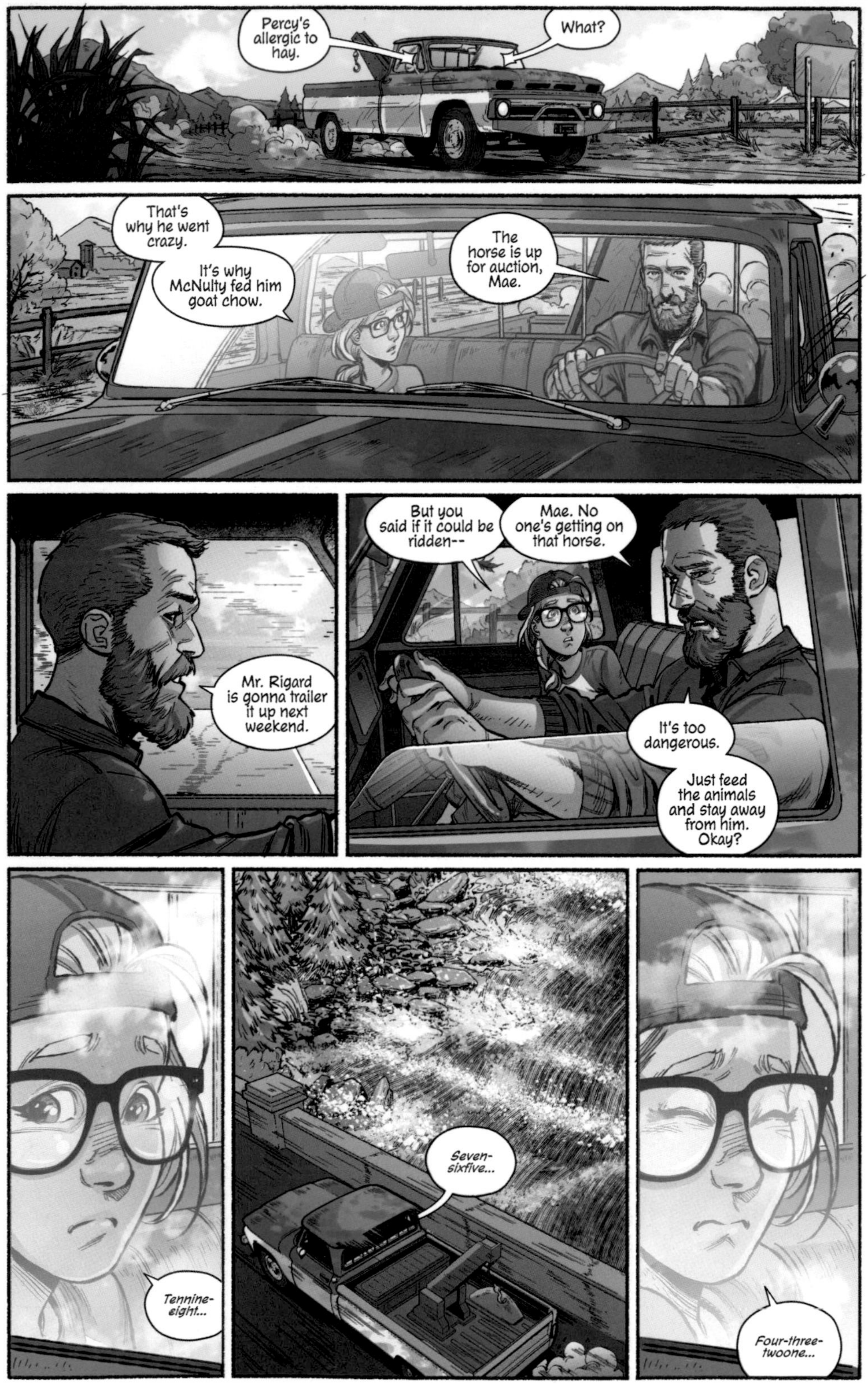
Percy's allergic to hay.
What?
That's why he went crazy.
It's why McNulty fed him goat chow.
The horse is up for auction, Mae.
Mr. Rigard is gonna trailer it up next weekend.
But you said if it could be ridden--
Mae. No one's getting on that horse.
It's too dangerous.
Just feed the animals and stay away from him. Okay?
Tennine-eight...
Seven-sixfive...
Four-three-twoone...

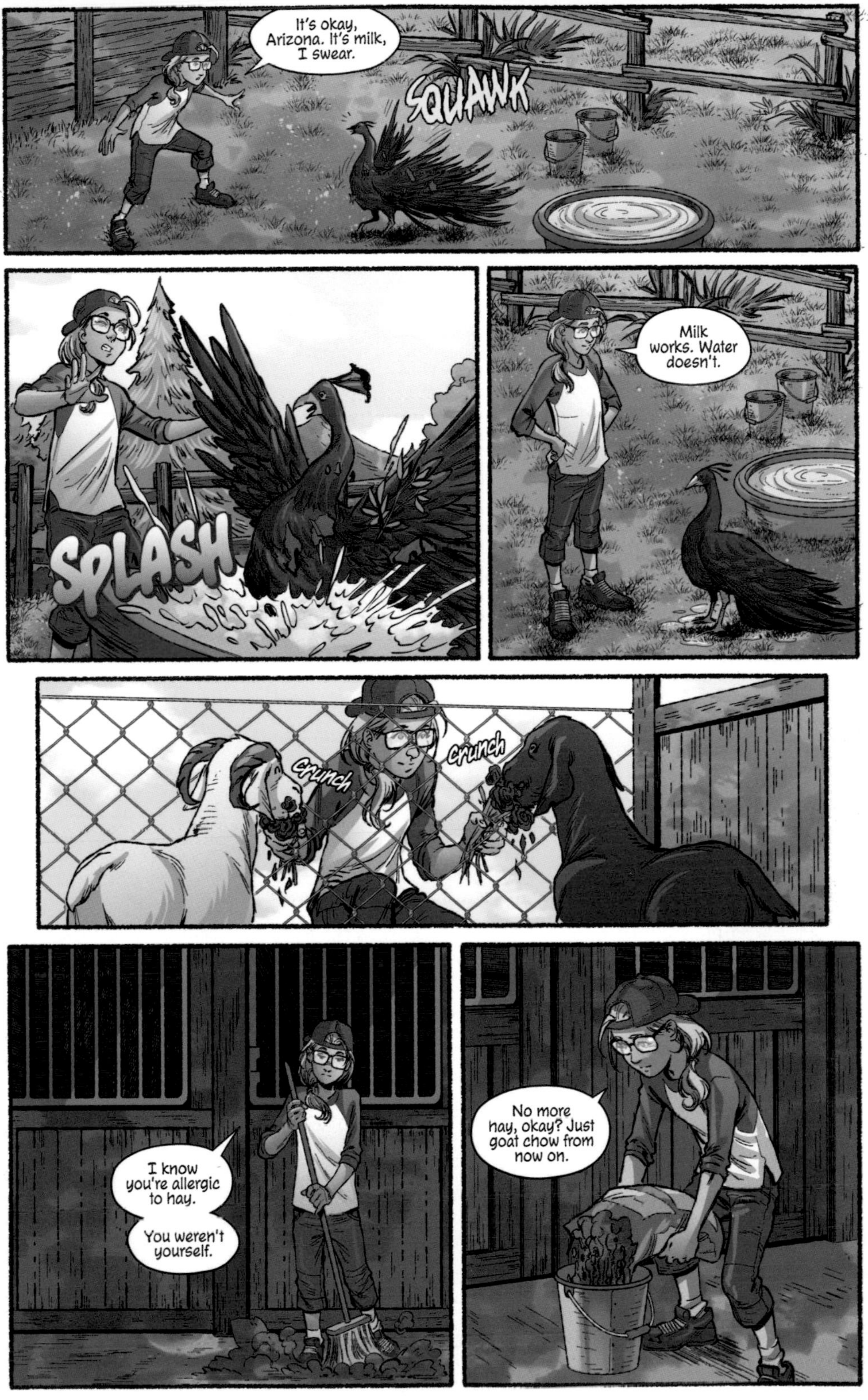
It's okay, Arizona. It's milk, I swear.
SQUAWK
SPLASH
Milk works. Water doesn't.
crunch
crunch
I know you're allergic to hay.
You weren't yourself.
No more hay, okay? Just goat chow from now on.

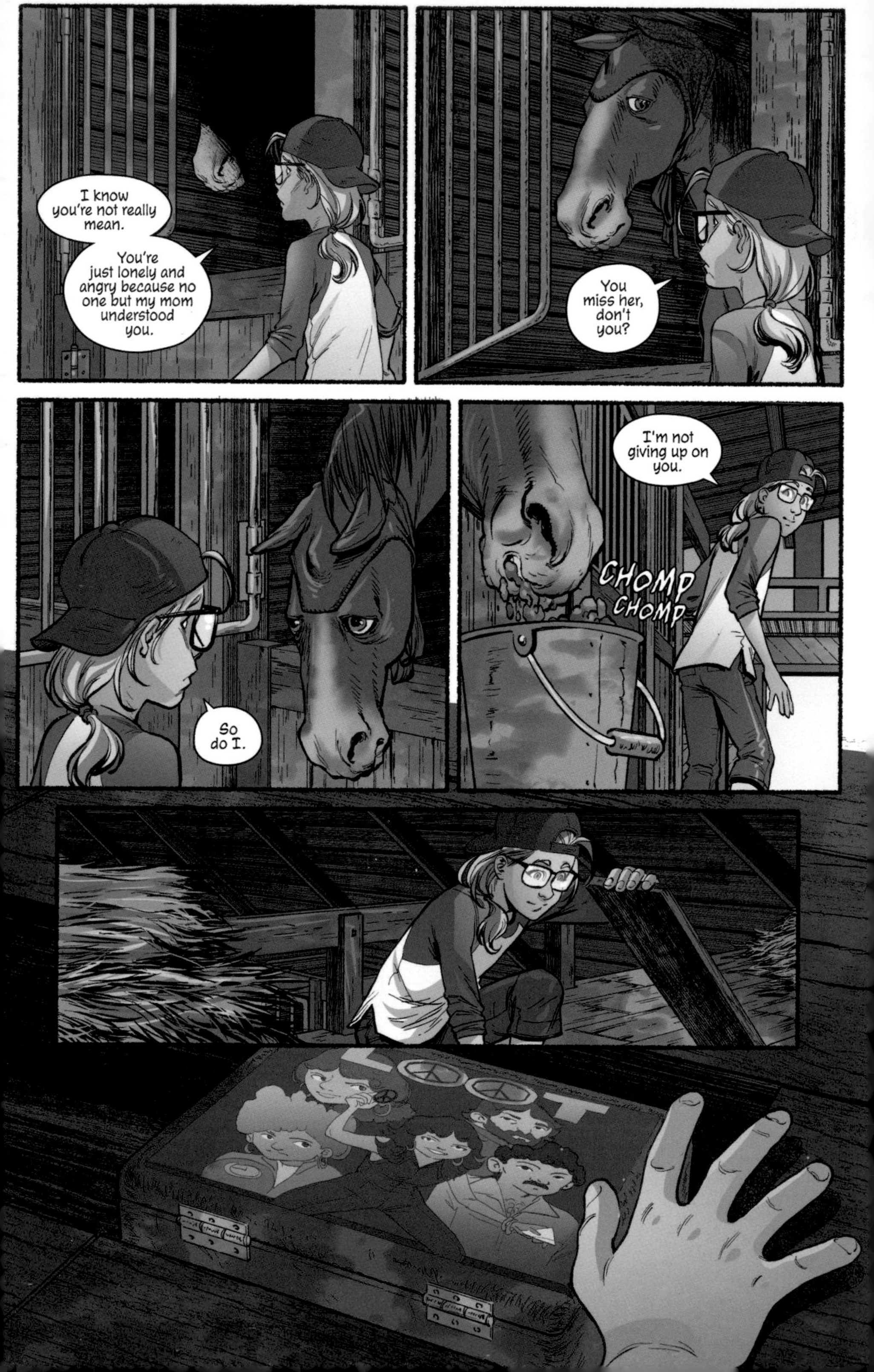
I know you're not really mean.
You're just lonely and angry because no one but my mom understood you.
You miss her, don't you?
So do I.
I'm not giving up on you.
CHOMP CHOMP

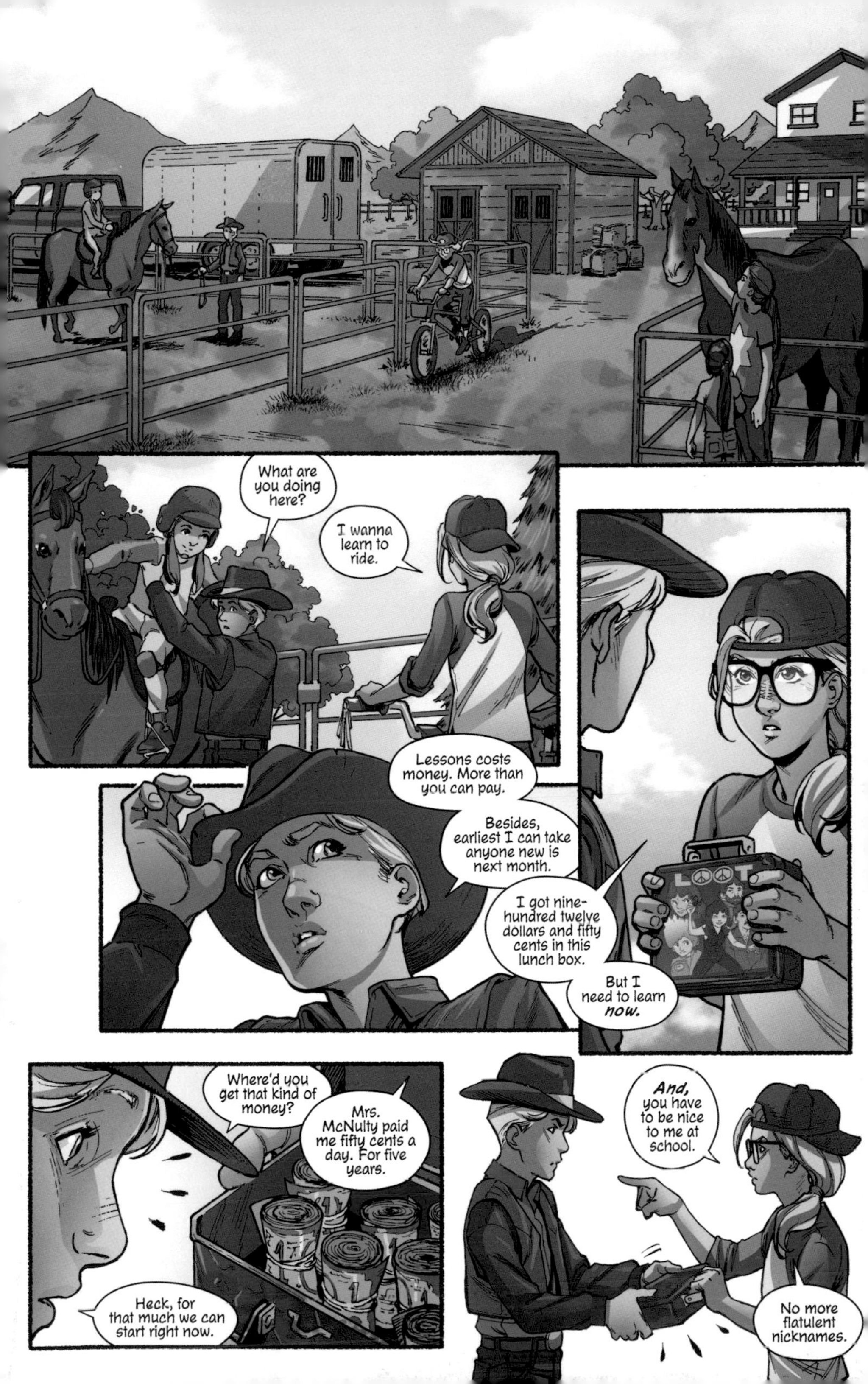
What are you doing here?
I wanna learn to ride.
Lessons costs money. More than you can pay.
Besides, earliest I can take anyone new is next month.
I got nine-hundred twelve dollars and fifty cents in this lunch box.
But I need to learn *now.*
Where'd you get that kind of money?
Mrs. McNulty paid me fifty cents a day. For five years.
Heck, for that much we can start right now.
And, you have to be nice to me at school.
No more flatulent nicknames.

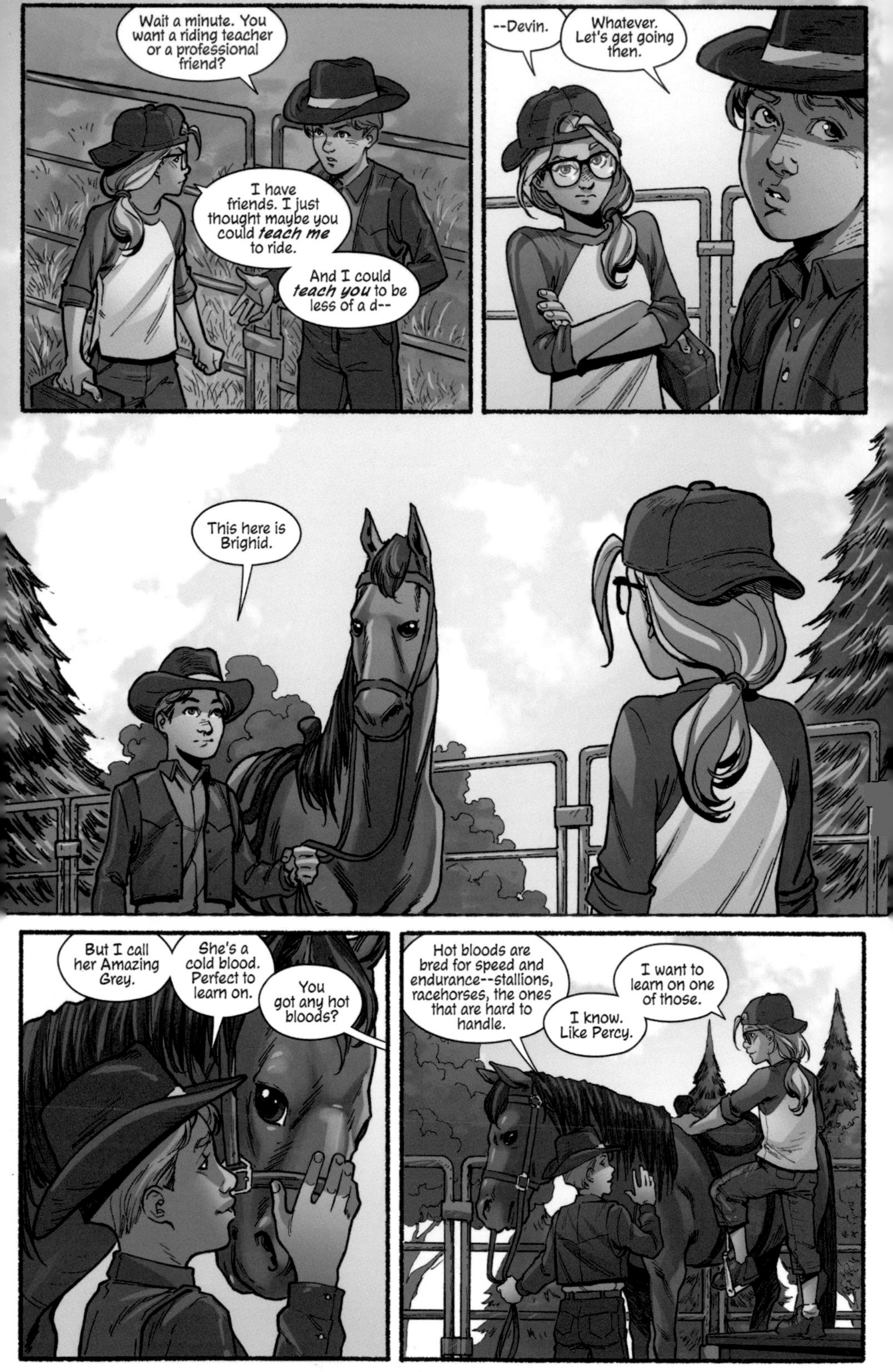
Wait a minute. You want a riding teacher or a professional friend?
I have friends. I just thought maybe you could *teach me* to ride.
And I could *teach you* to be less of a d--
--Devin.
Whatever. Let's get going then.
This here is Brighid.
But I call her Amazing Grey.
She's a cold blood. Perfect to learn on.
You got any hot bloods?
Hot bloods are bred for speed and endurance--stallions, racehorses, the ones that are hard to handle.
I want to learn on one of those.
I know. Like Percy.

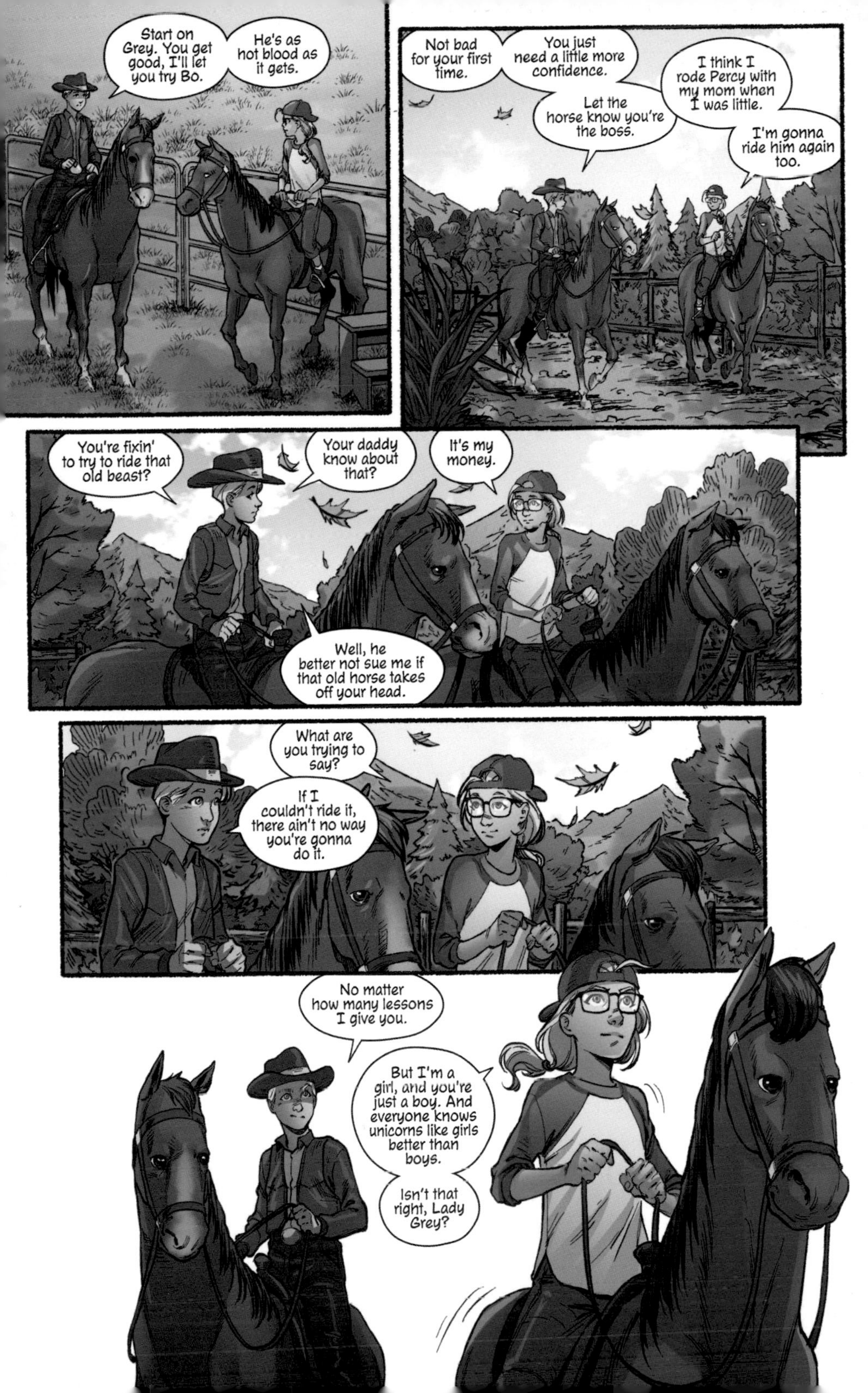
Start on Grey. You get good, I'll let you try Bo.
He's as hot blood as it gets.
Not bad for your first time.
You just need a little more confidence.
Let the horse know you're the boss.
I think I rode Percy with my mom when I was little.
I'm gonna ride him again too.
You're fixin' to try to ride that old beast?
Your daddy know about that?
It's my money.
Well, he better not sue me if that old horse takes off your head.
What are you trying to say?
If I couldn't ride it, there ain't no way you're gonna do it.
No matter how many lessons I give you.
But I'm a girl, and you're just a boy. And everyone knows unicorns like girls better than boys.
Isn't that right, Lady Grey?

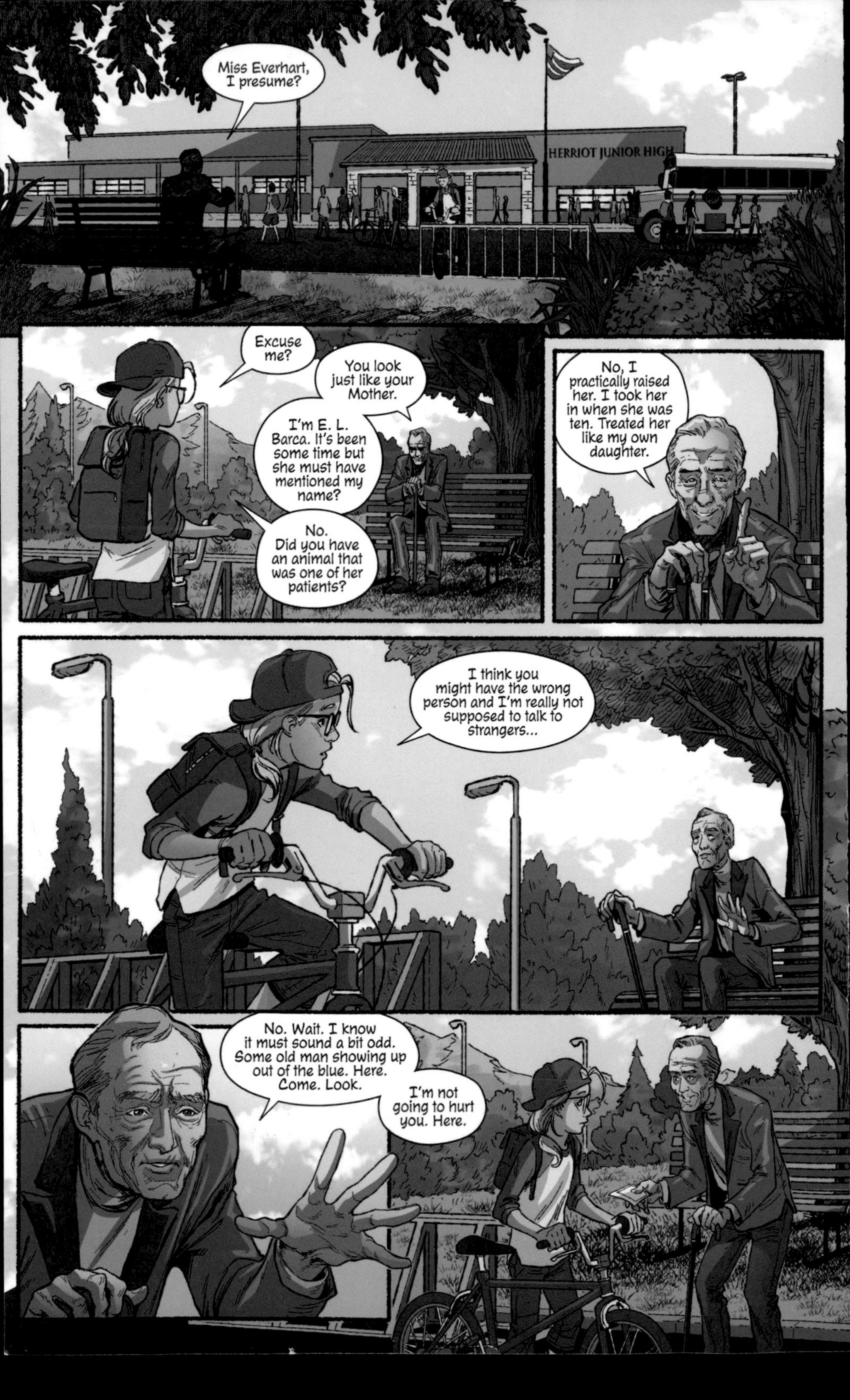
Miss Everhart, I presume?
HERRIOT JUNIOR HIGH
Excuse me?
You look just like your Mother.
I'm E. L. Barca. It's been some time but she must have mentioned my name?
No. Did you have an animal that was one of her patients?
No, I practically raised her. I took her in when she was ten. Treated her like my own daughter.
I think you might have the wrong person and I'm really not supposed to talk to strangers...
No. Wait. I know it must sound a bit odd. Some old man showing up out of the blue. Here. Come. Look.
I'm not going to hurt you. Here.

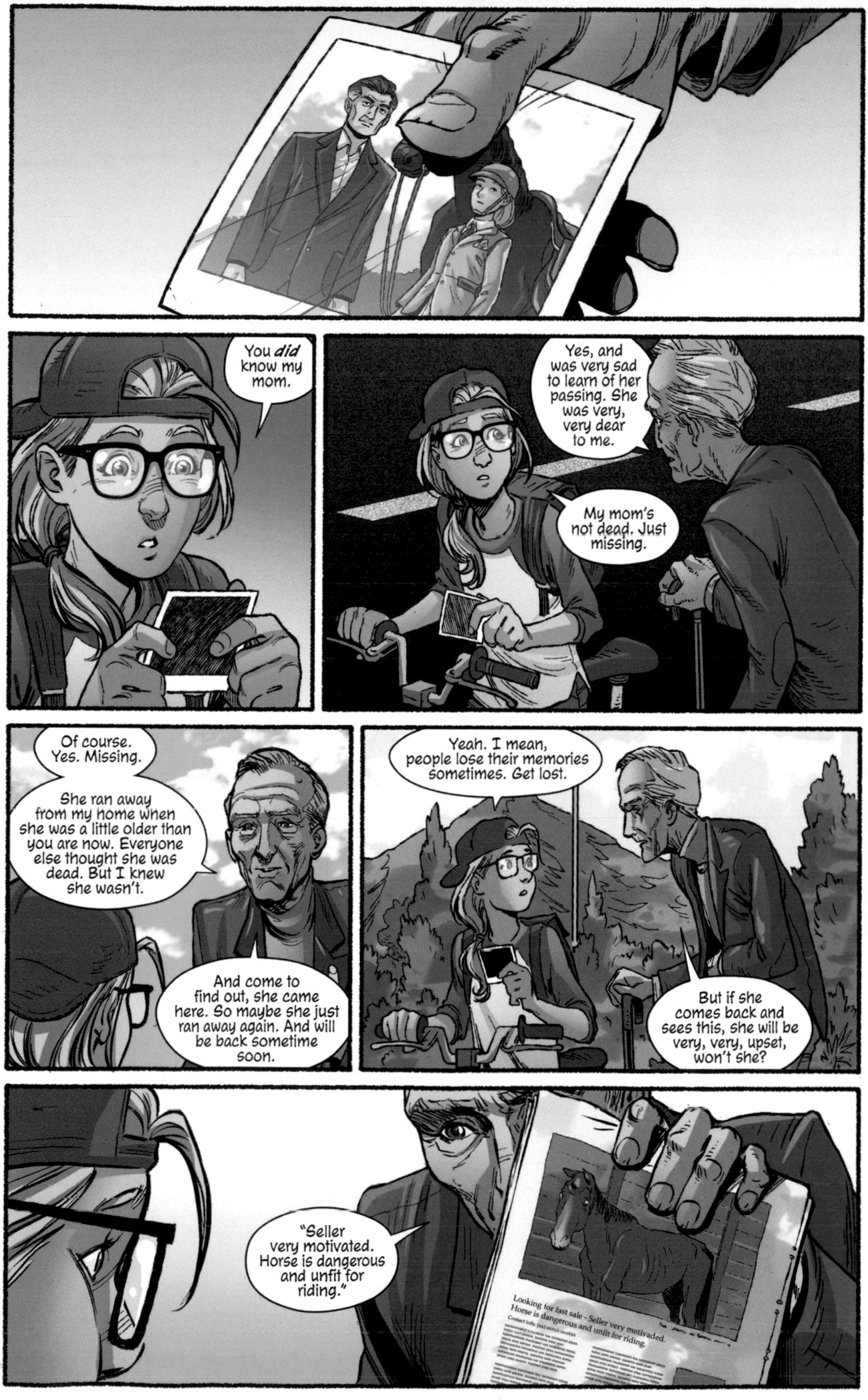
You *did* know my mom.
Yes, and was very sad to learn of her passing. She was very, very dear to me.
My mom's not dead. Just missing.
Of course. Yes. Missing.
She ran away from my home when she was a little older than you are now. Everyone else thought she was dead. But I knew she wasn't.
And come to find out, she came here. So maybe she just ran away again. And will be back sometime soon.
Yeah. I mean, people lose their memories sometimes. Get lost.
But if she comes back and sees this, she will be very, very, upset, won't she?
"Seller very motivated. Horse is dangerous and unfit for riding."
Looking for fast sale - Seller very motivated.
Horse is dangerous and unfit for riding.

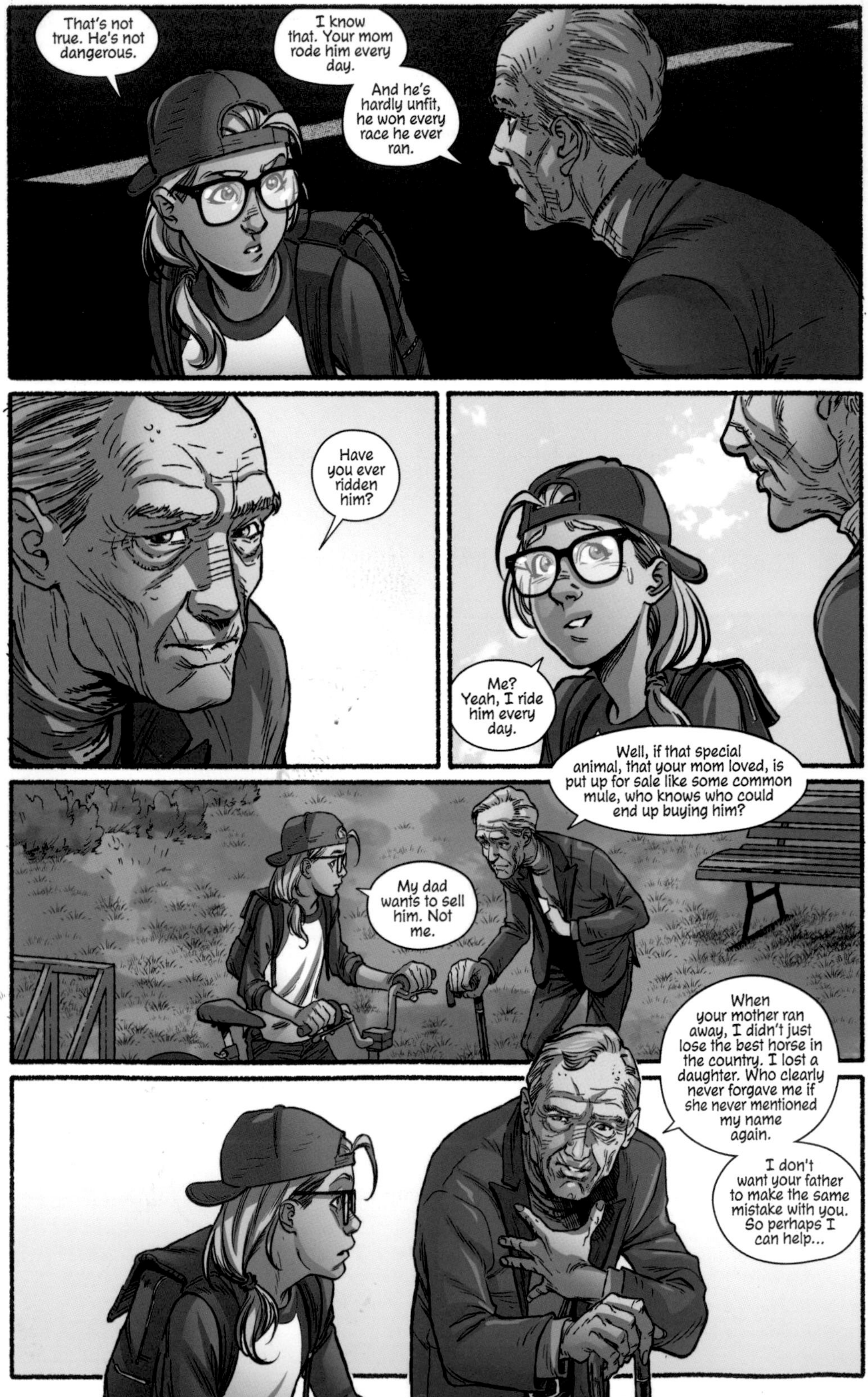
That's not true. He's not dangerous.
I know that. Your mom rode him every day.
And he's hardly unfit, he won every race he ever ran.
Have you ever ridden him?
Me? Yeah, I ride him every day.
Well, if that special animal, that your mom loved, is put up for sale like some common mule, who knows who could end up buying him?
My dad wants to sell him. Not me.
When your mother ran away, I didn't just lose the best horse in the country. I lost a daughter. Who clearly never forgave me if she never mentioned my name again.
I don't want your father to make the same mistake with you. So perhaps I can help...

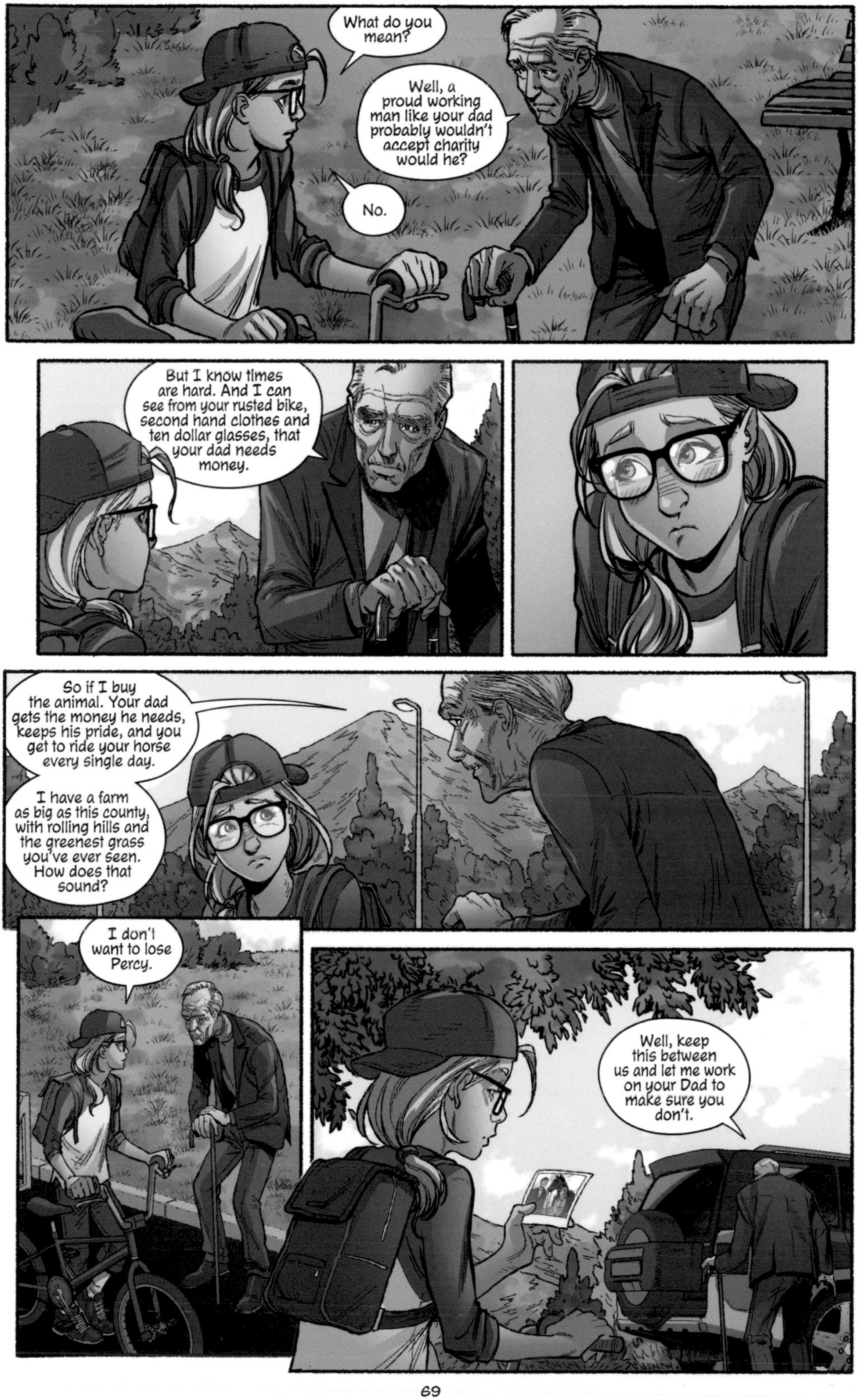
What do you mean?
Well, a proud working man like your dad probably wouldn't accept charity would he?
No.
But I know times are hard. And I can see from your rusted bike, second hand clothes and ten dollar glasses, that your dad needs money.
So if I buy the animal. Your dad gets the money he needs, keeps his pride, and you get to ride your horse every single day.
I have a farm as big as this county, with rolling hills and the greenest grass you've ever seen. How does that sound?
I don't want to lose Percy.
Well, keep this between us and let me work on your Dad to make sure you don't.

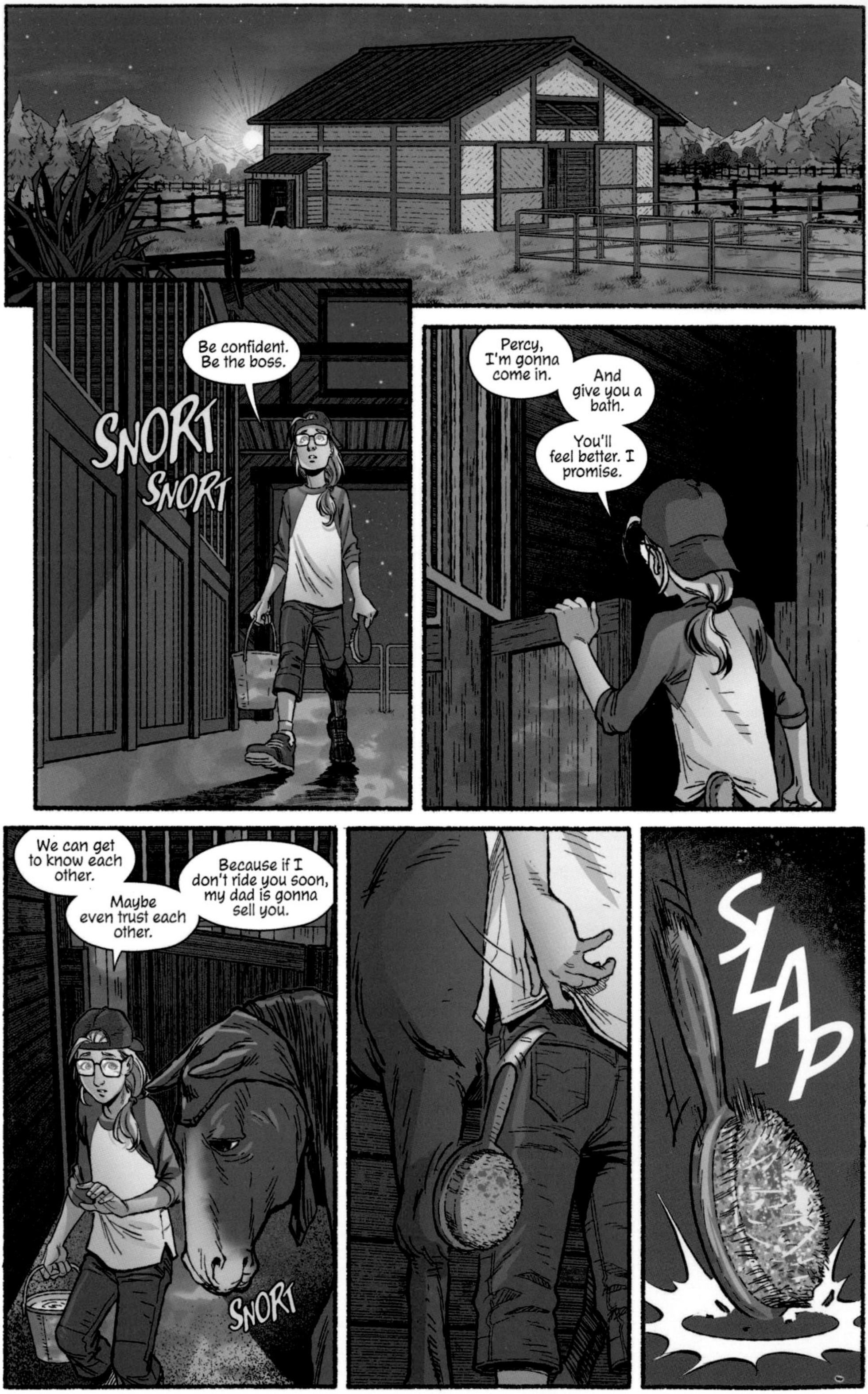
Be confident. Be the boss.
SNORT
SNORT
Percy, I'm gonna come in.
And give you a bath.
You'll feel better. I promise.
We can get to know each other.
Maybe even trust each other.
Because if I don't ride you soon, my dad is gonna sell you.
SNORT
SLAP

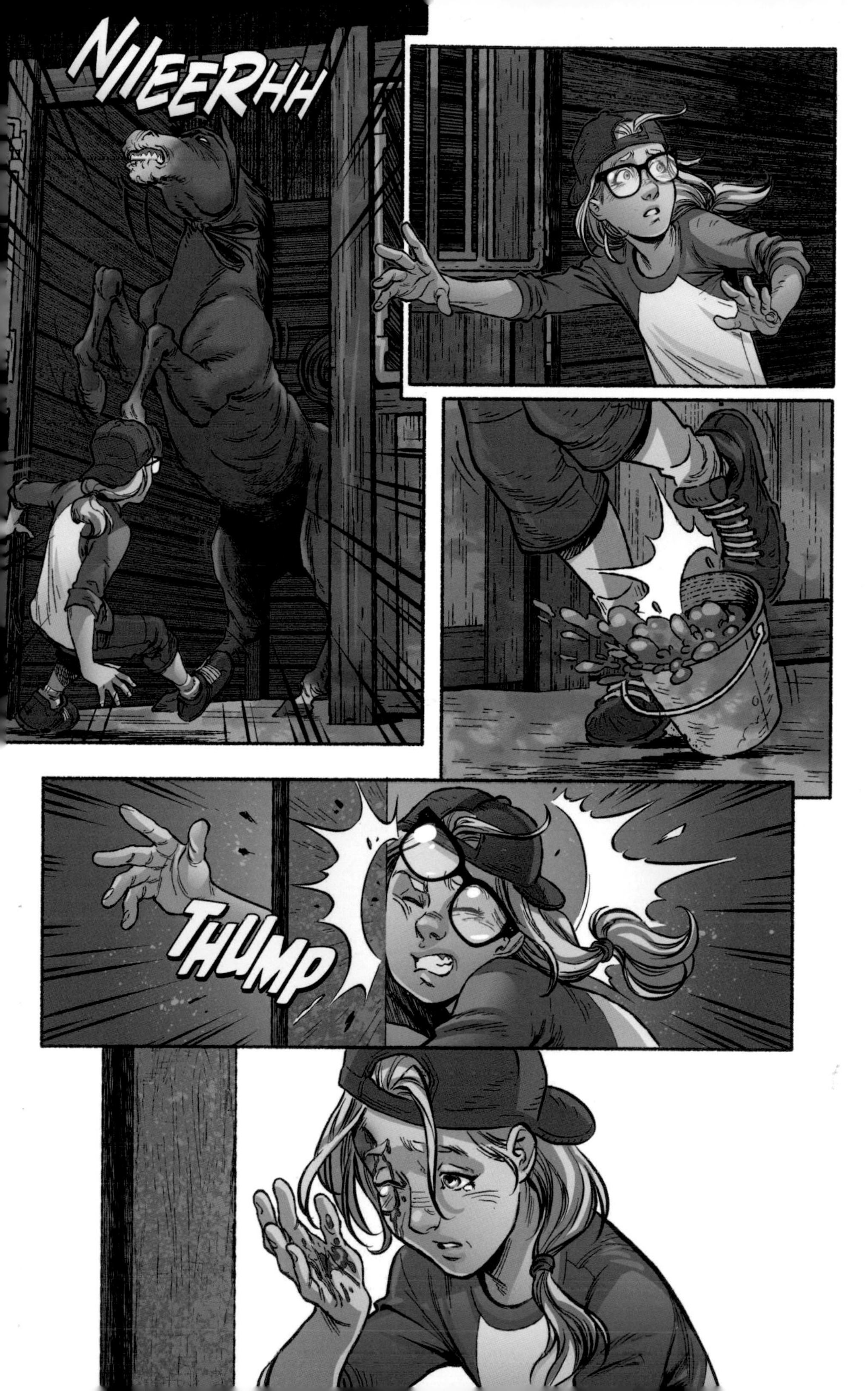
NIIEERHH
THUMP

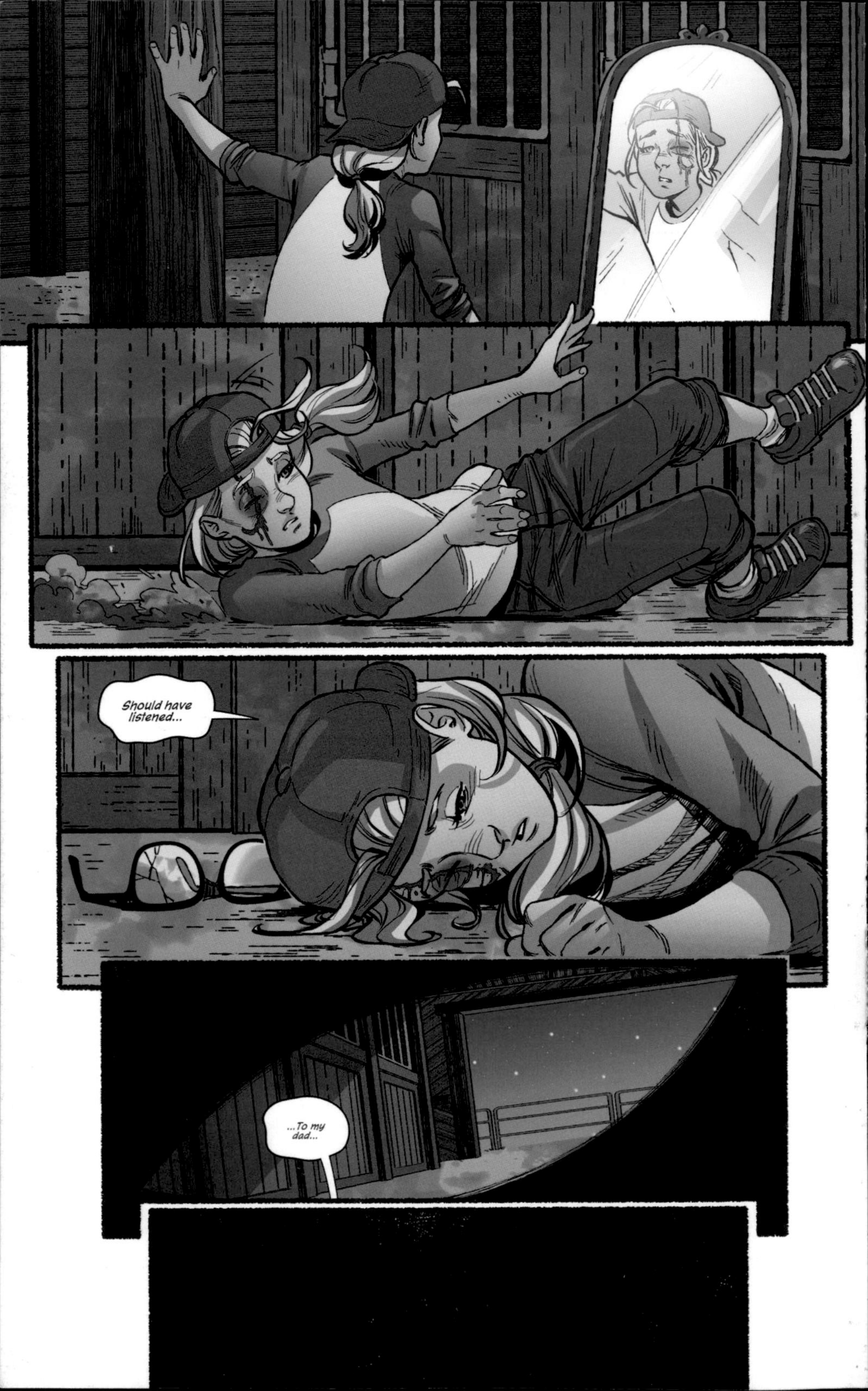
Should have listened...
...To my dad...

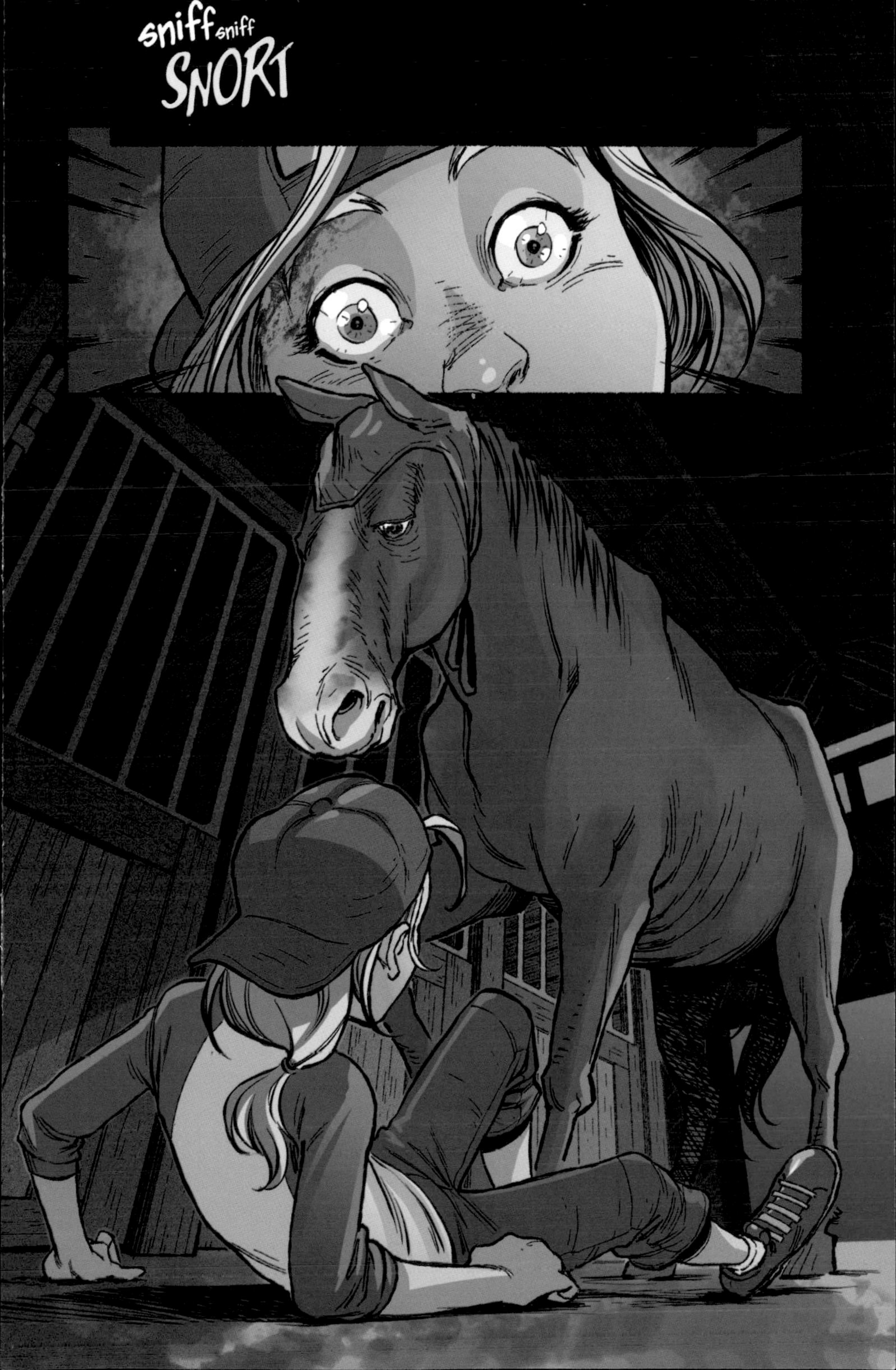
sniff sniff
SNORT

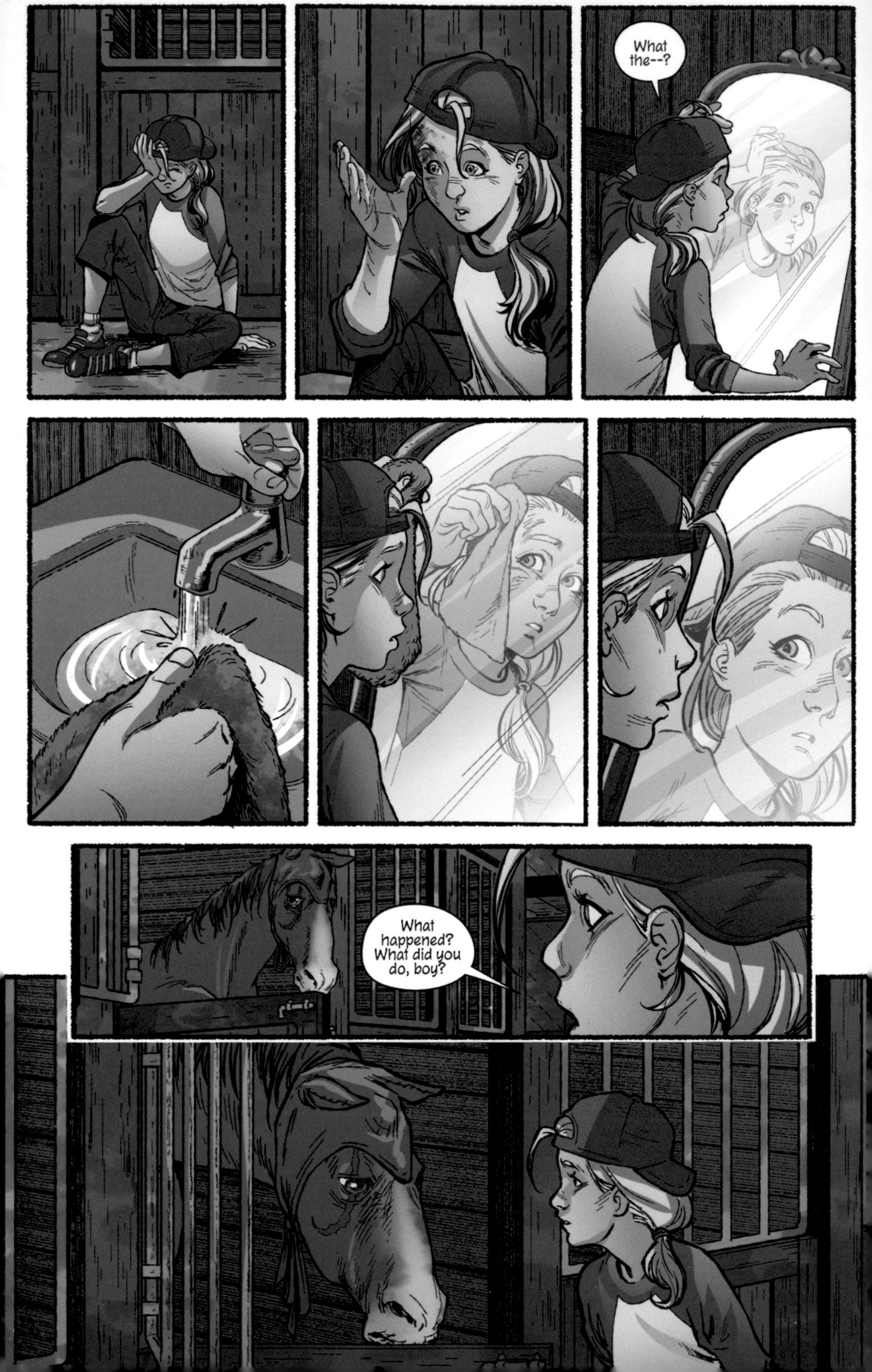
What the--?
What happened? What did you do, boy?

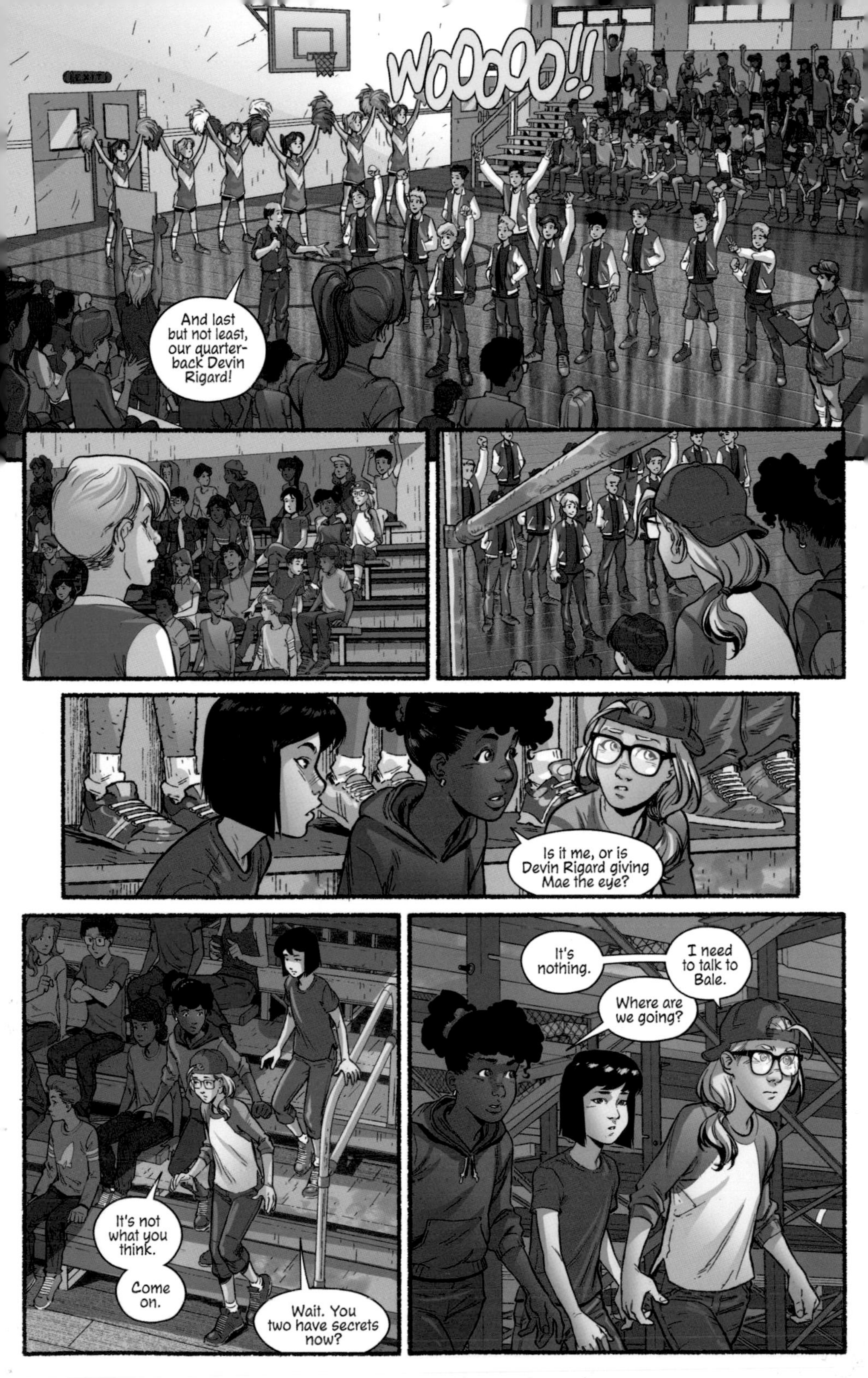
EXIT
WOOOOO!!
And last but not least, our quarter-back Devin Rigard!
Is it me, or is Devin Rigard giving Mae the eye?
It's not what you think.
Come on.
Wait. You two have secrets now?
It's nothing.
I need to talk to Bale.
Where are we going?

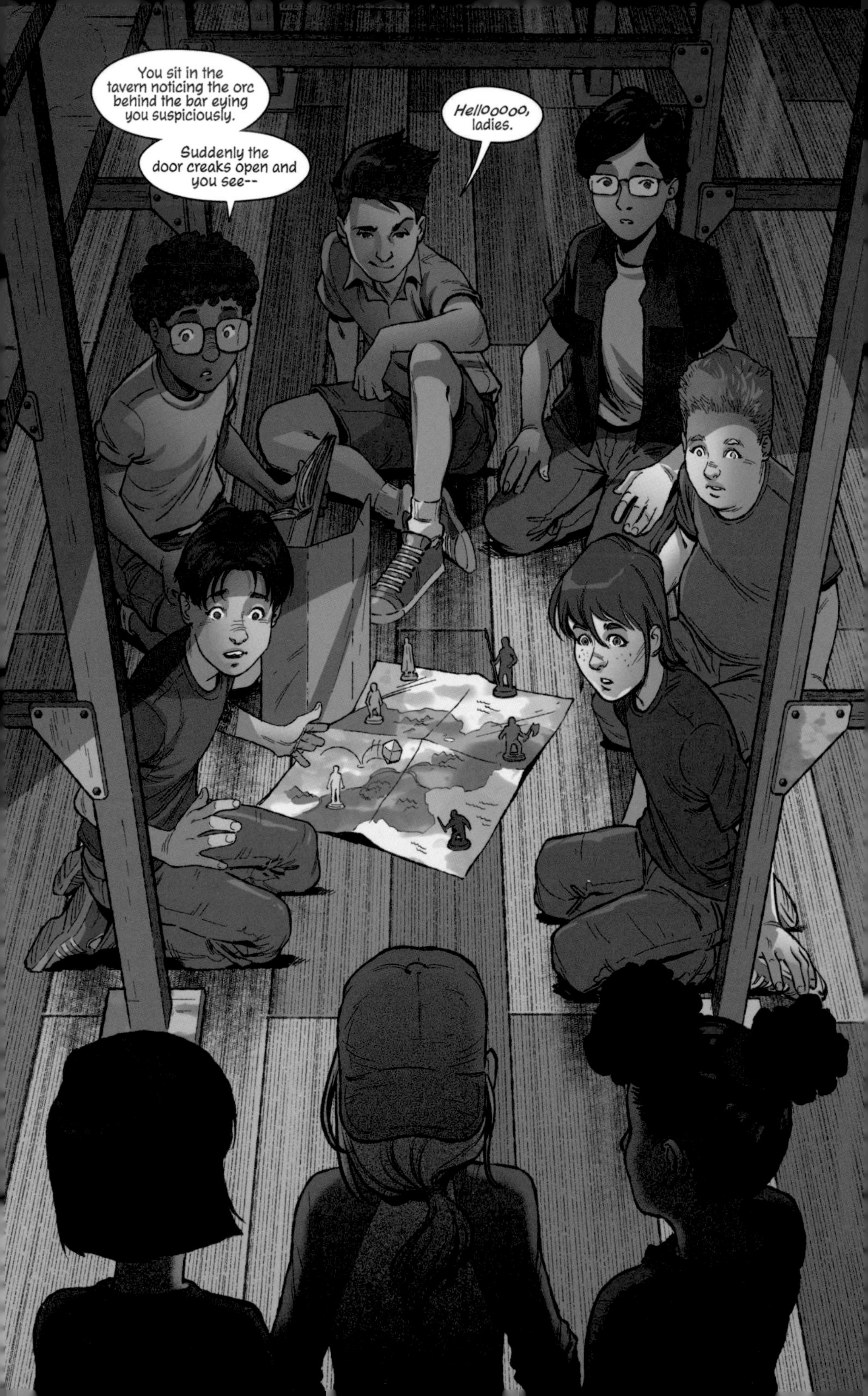
You sit in the tavern noticing the orc behind the bar eying you suspiciously.
Suddenly the door creaks open and you see--
Hellooooo, ladies.

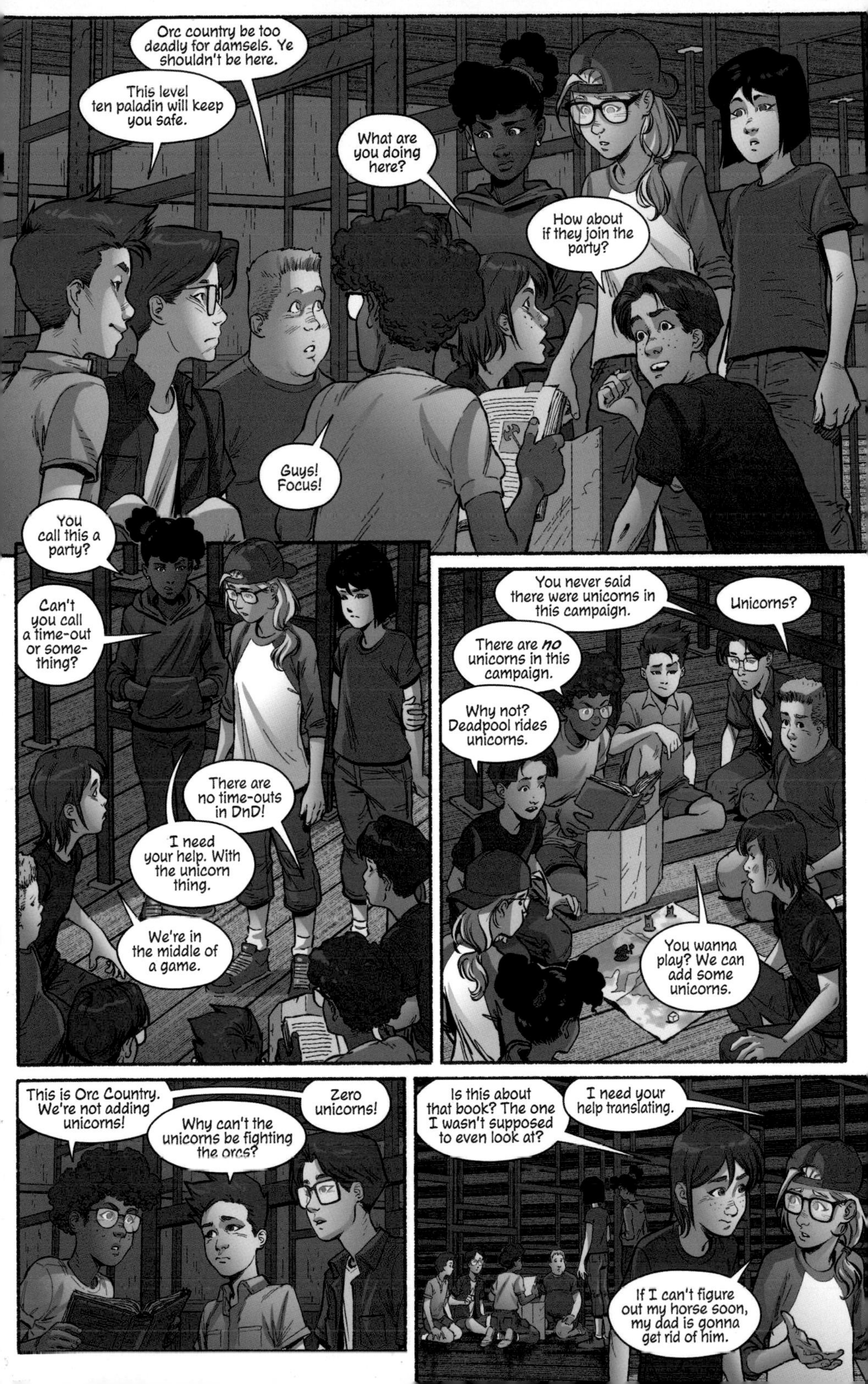
This level ten paladin will keep you safe.
Orc country be too deadly for damsels. Ye shouldn't be here.
What are you doing here?
How about if they join the party?
Guys! Focus!
You call this a party?
Can't you call a time-out or some-thing?
There are no time-outs in DnD!
I need your help. With the unicorn thing.
We're in the middle of a game.
You never said there were unicorns in this campaign.
Unicorns?
There are *no* unicorns in this campaign.
Why not? Deadpool rides unicorns.
You wanna play? We can add some unicorns.
This is Orc Country. We're not adding unicorns!
Zero unicorns!
Why can't the unicorns be fighting the orcs?
Is this about that book? The one I wasn't supposed to even look at?
I need your help translating.
If I can't figure out my horse soon, my dad is gonna get rid of him.

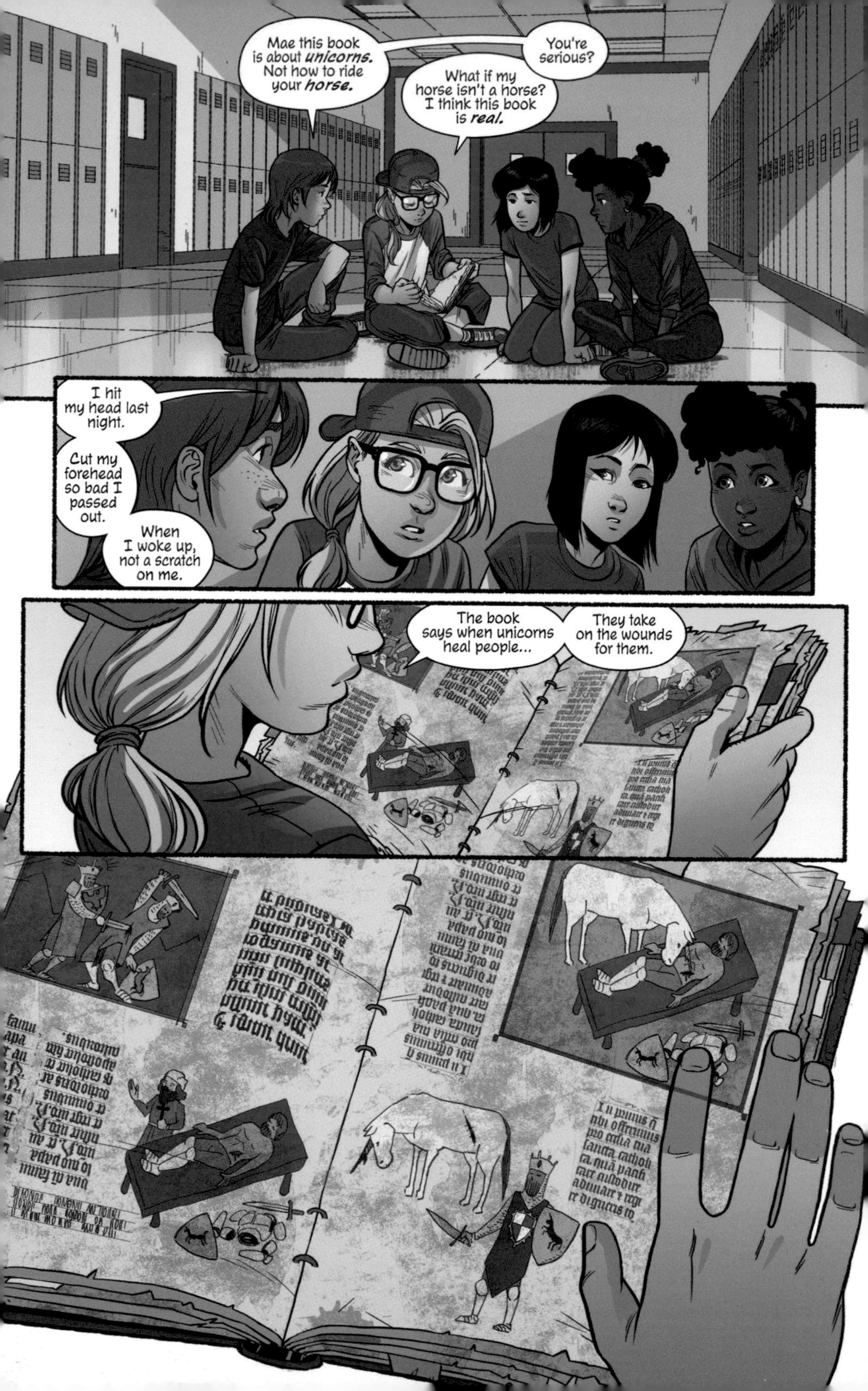

Mae this book is about *unicorns.* Not how to ride your *horse.*
You're serious?
What if my horse isn't a horse? I think this book is *real.*
I hit my head last night.
Cut my forehead so bad I passed out.
When I woke up, not a scratch on me.
The book says when unicorns heal people...
They take on the wounds for them.

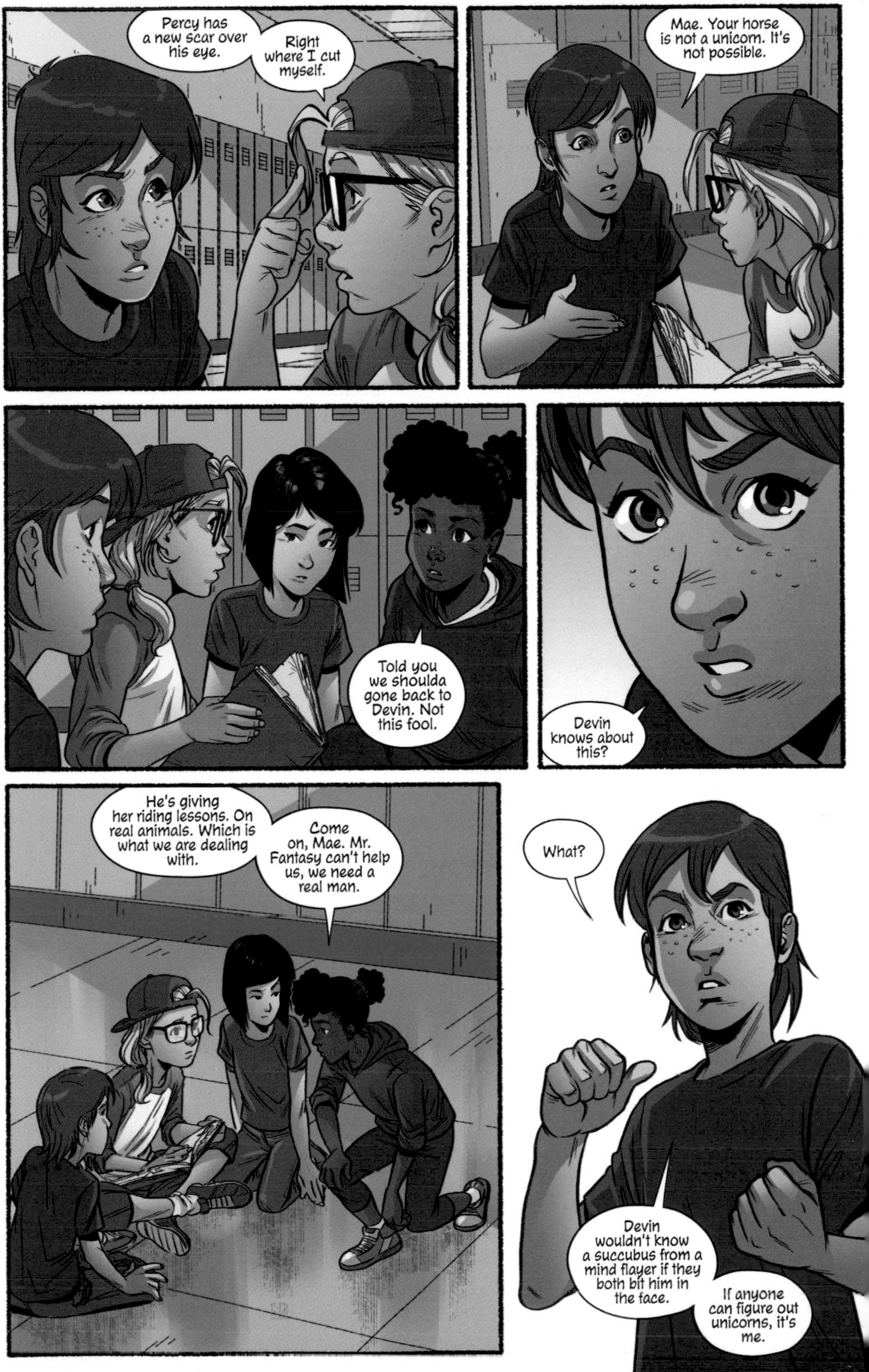
Percy has a new scar over his eye.
Right where I cut myself.
Mae. Your horse is not a unicorn. It's not possible.
Told you we shoulda gone back to Devin. Not this fool.
Devin knows about this?
He's giving her riding lessons. On real animals. Which is what we are dealing with.
Come on, Mae. Mr. Fantasy can't help us, we need a real man.
What?
Devin wouldn't know a succubus from a mind flayer if they both bit him in the face.
If anyone can figure out unicorns, it's me.

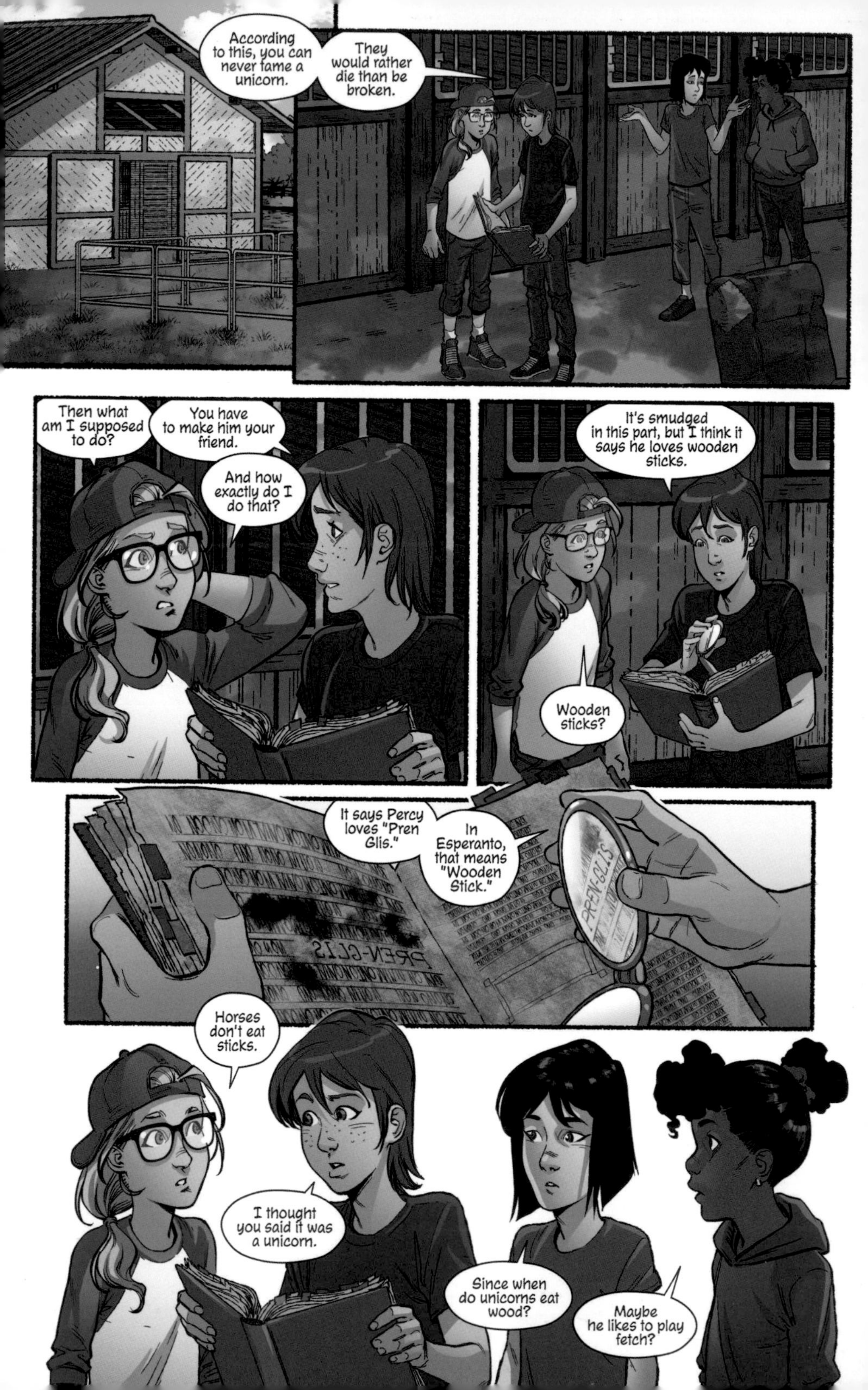
According to this, you can never tame a unicorn.
They would rather die than be broken.
Then what am I supposed to do?
You have to make him your friend.
And how exactly do I do that?
It's smudged in this part, but I think it says he loves wooden sticks.
Wooden sticks?
It says Percy loves "Pren Glis."
In Esperanto, that means "Wooden Stick."
PREN-GLIS
Horses don't eat sticks.
I thought you said it was a unicorn.
Since when do unicorns eat wood?
Maybe he likes to play fetch?

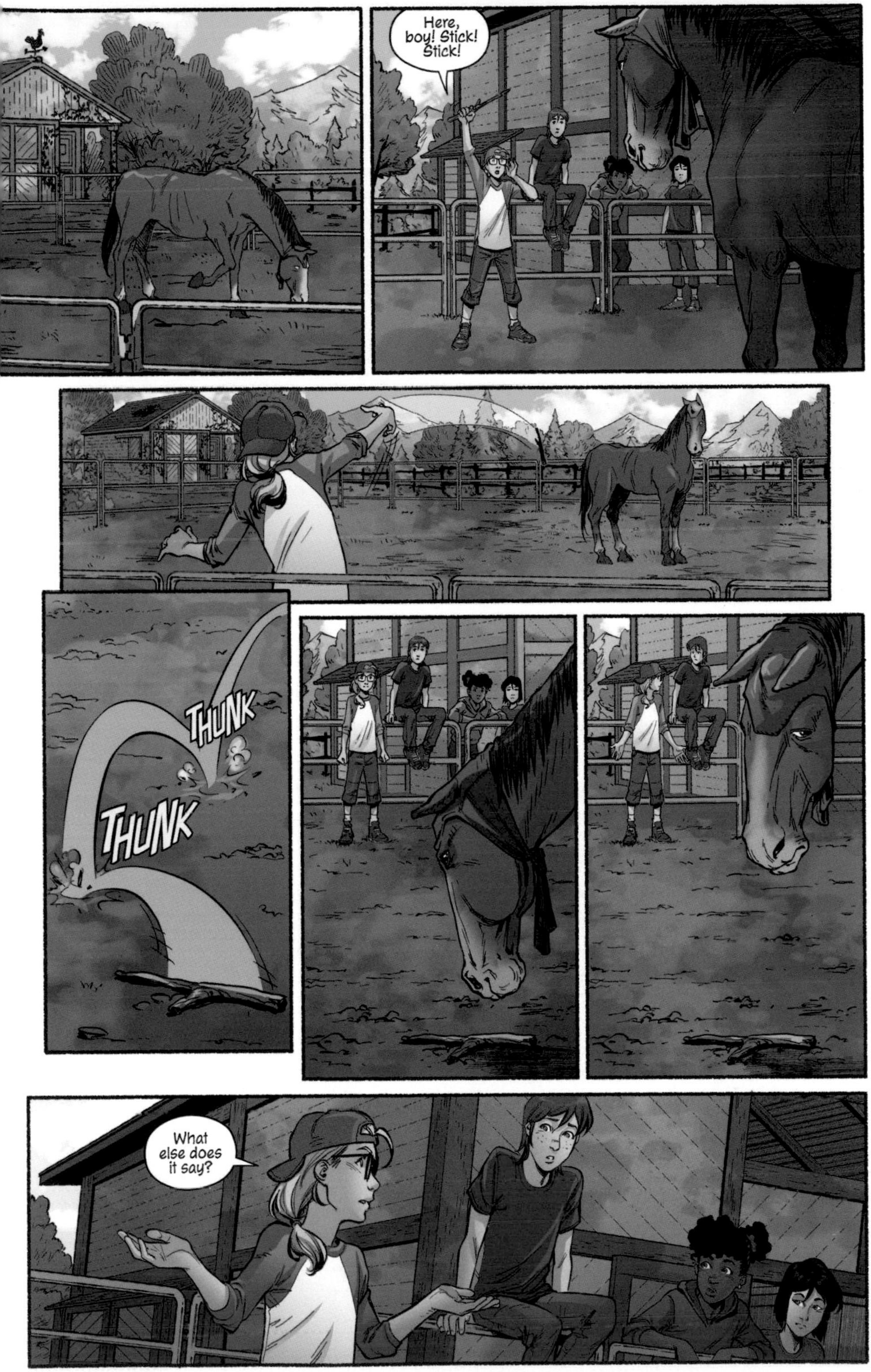
Here, boy! Stick! Stick!
THUNK
THUNK
What else does it say?

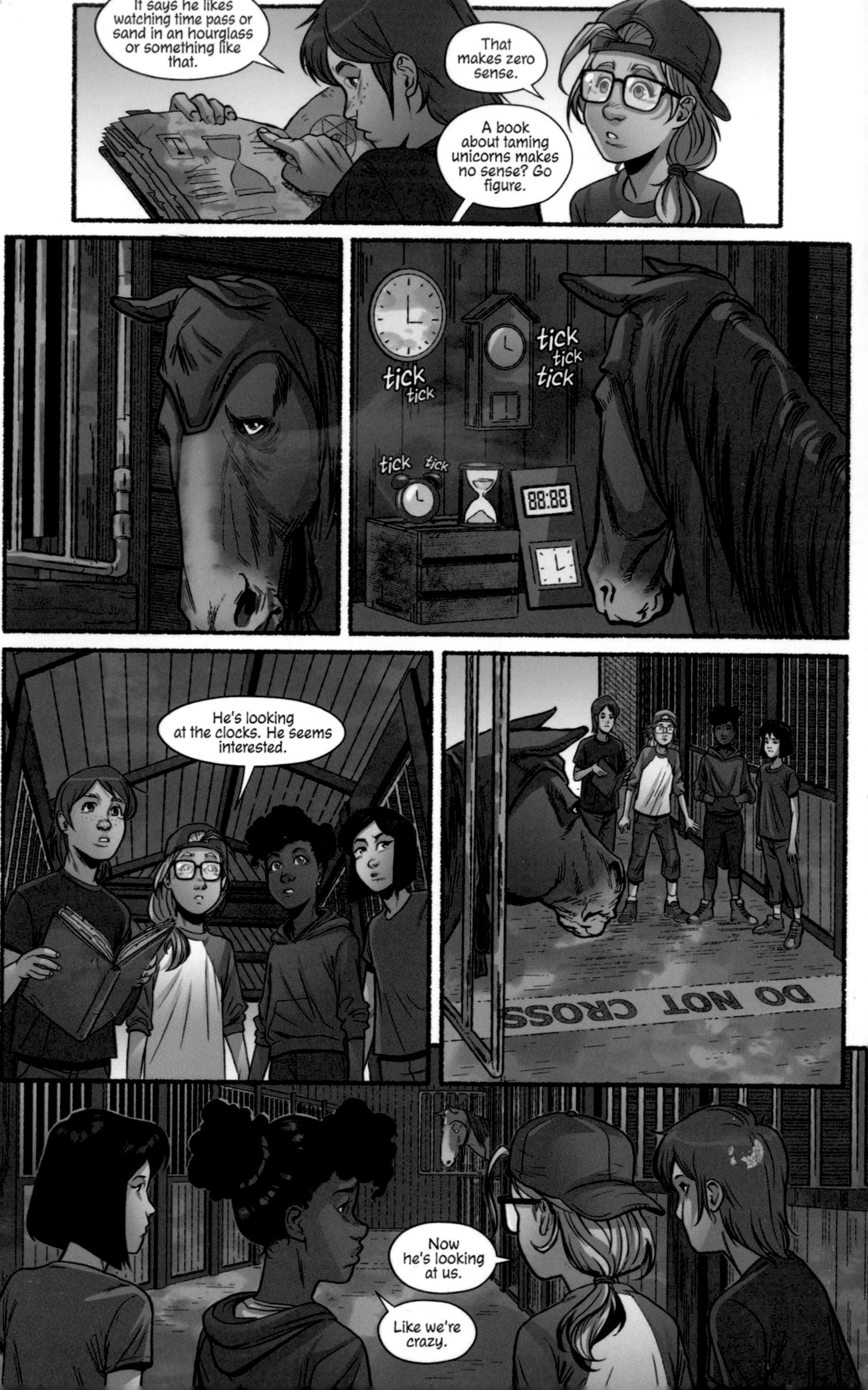
It says he likes watching time pass or sand in an hourglass or something like that.
That makes zero sense.
A book about taming unicorns makes no sense? Go figure.
tick tick
tick tick tick
tick tick
88:88
He's looking at the clocks. He seems interested.
DO NOT CROSS
Now he's looking at us.
Like we're crazy.

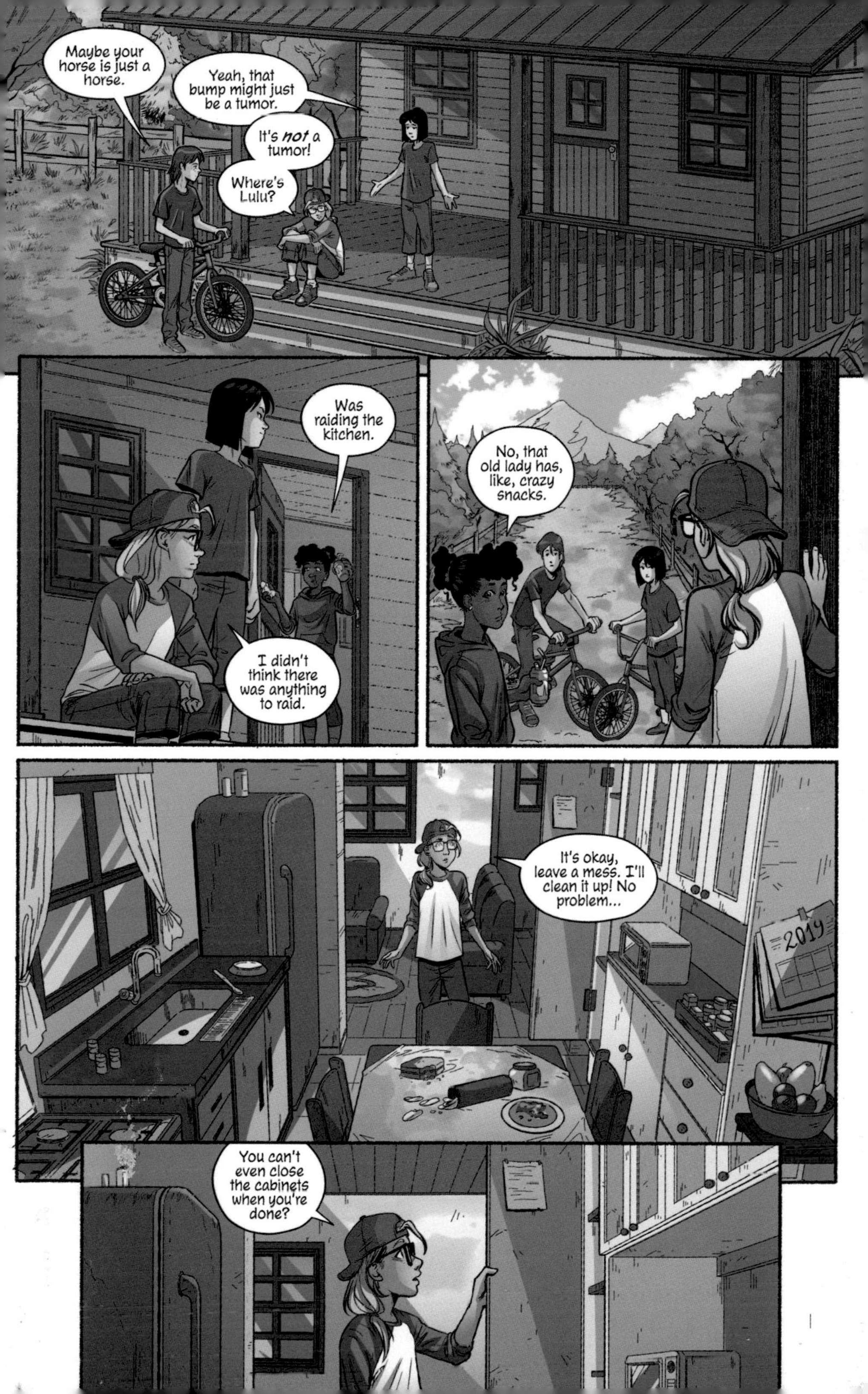
Maybe your horse is just a horse.
Yeah, that bump might just be a tumor.
It's *not* a tumor!
Where's Lulu?
Was raiding the kitchen.
I didn't think there was anything to raid.
No, that old lady has, like, crazy snacks.
It's okay, leave a mess. I'll clean it up! No problem...
2019
You can't even close the cabinets when you're done?

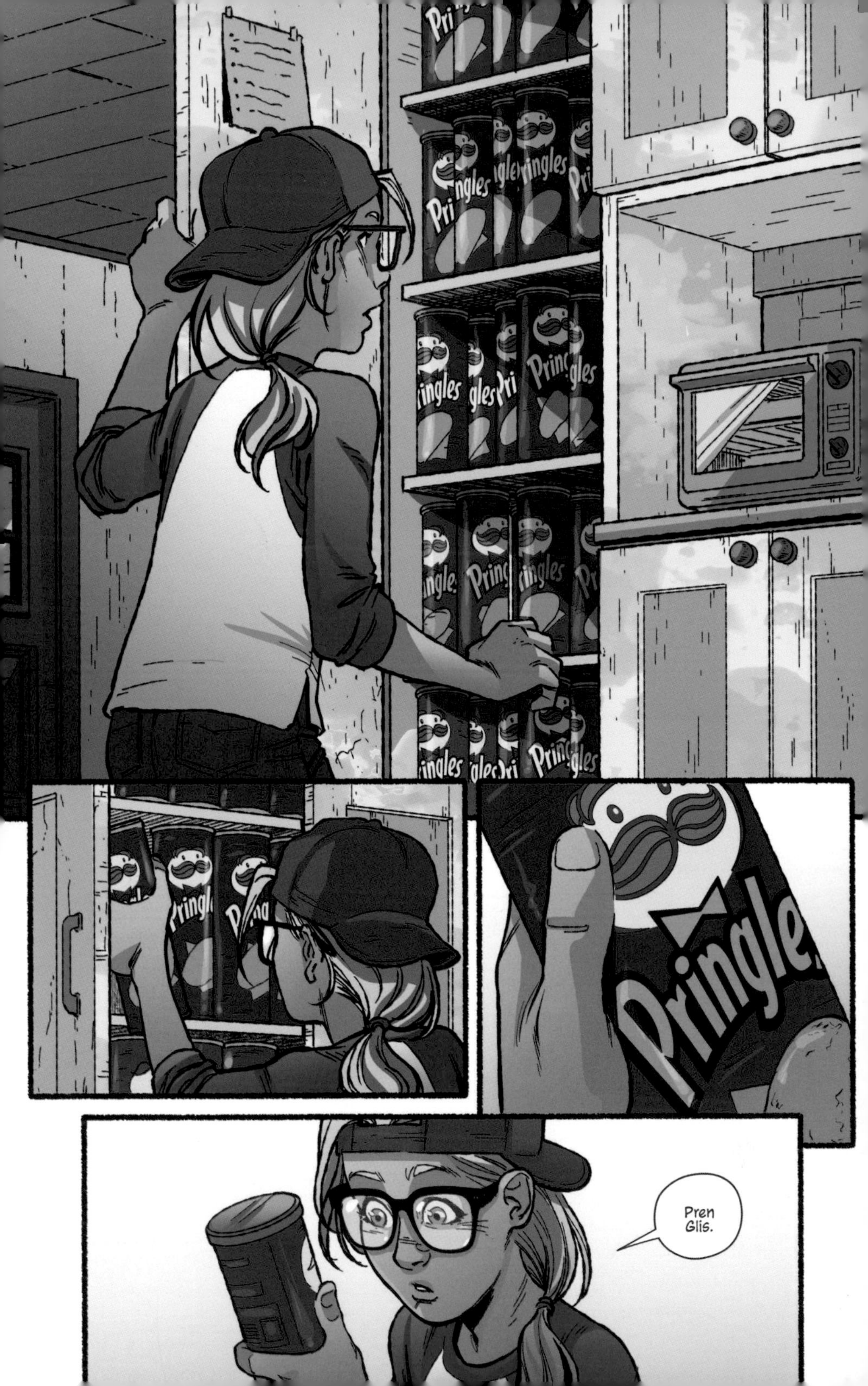
Pren
Glis.

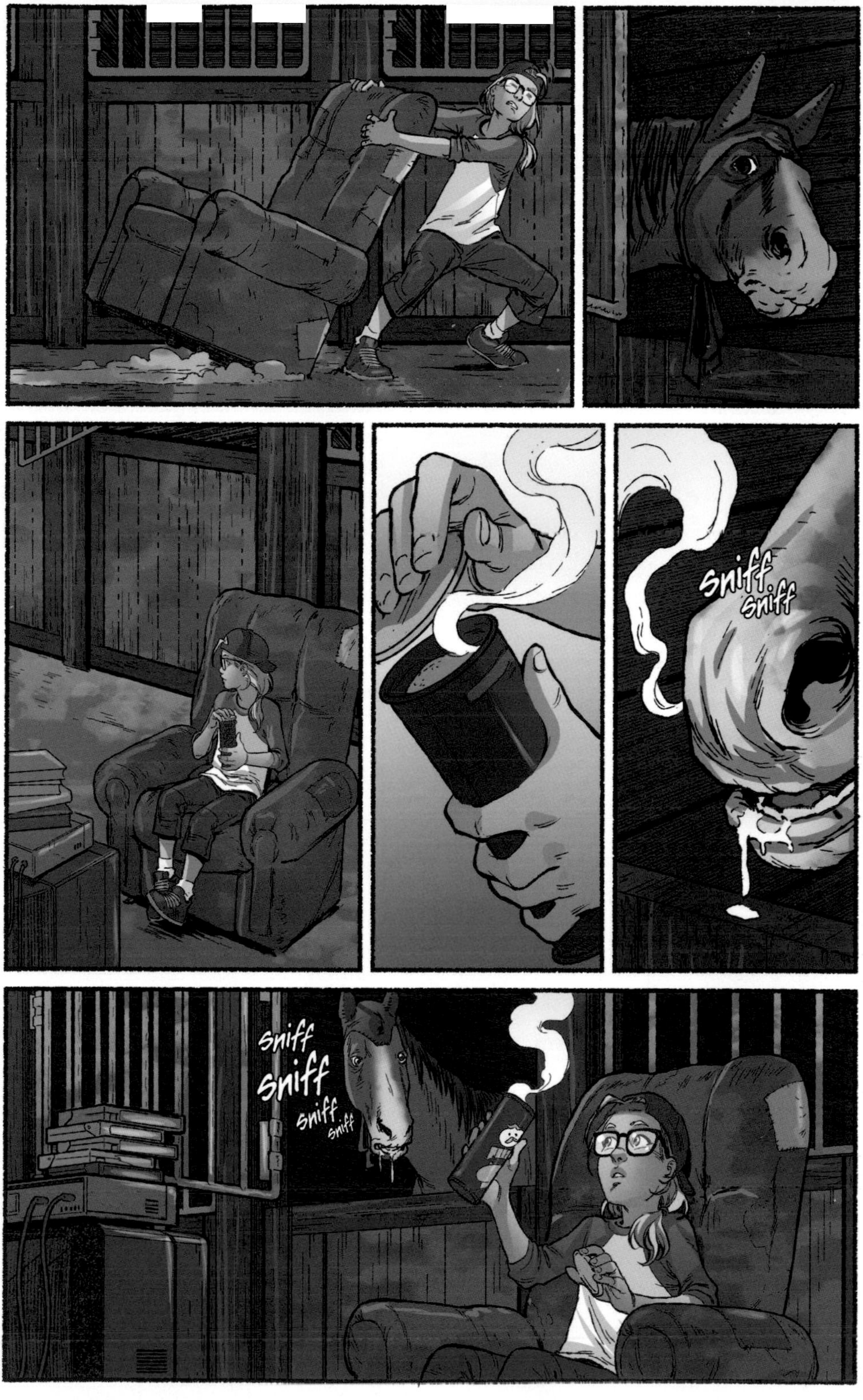
sniff
sniff
sniff
sniff
sniff
sniff

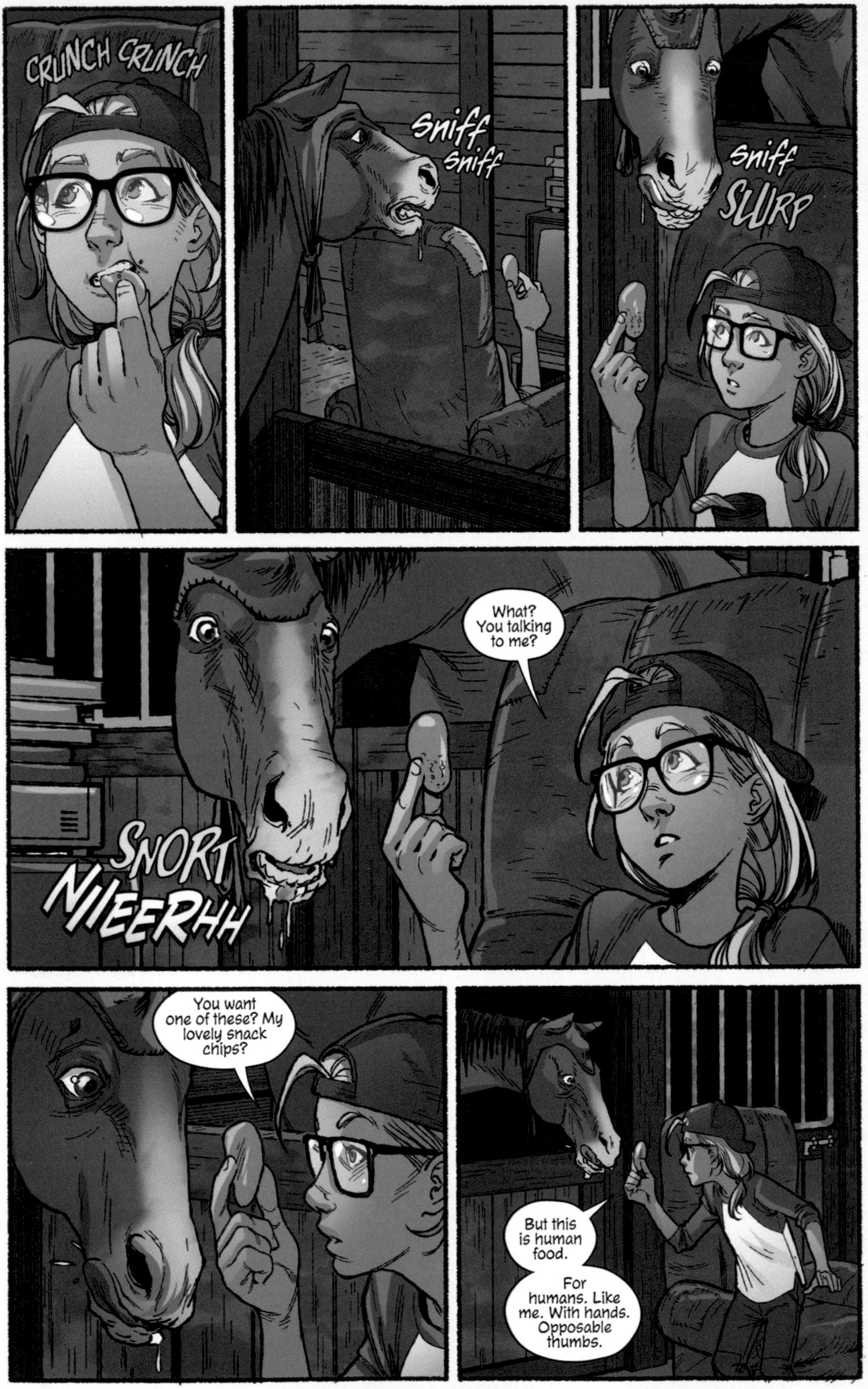
CRUNCH CRUNCH
Sniff sniff
Sniff SLURP
What? You talking to me?
SNORT NIIEERHH
You want one of these? My lovely snack chips?
But this is human food.
For humans. Like me. With hands. Opposable thumbs.

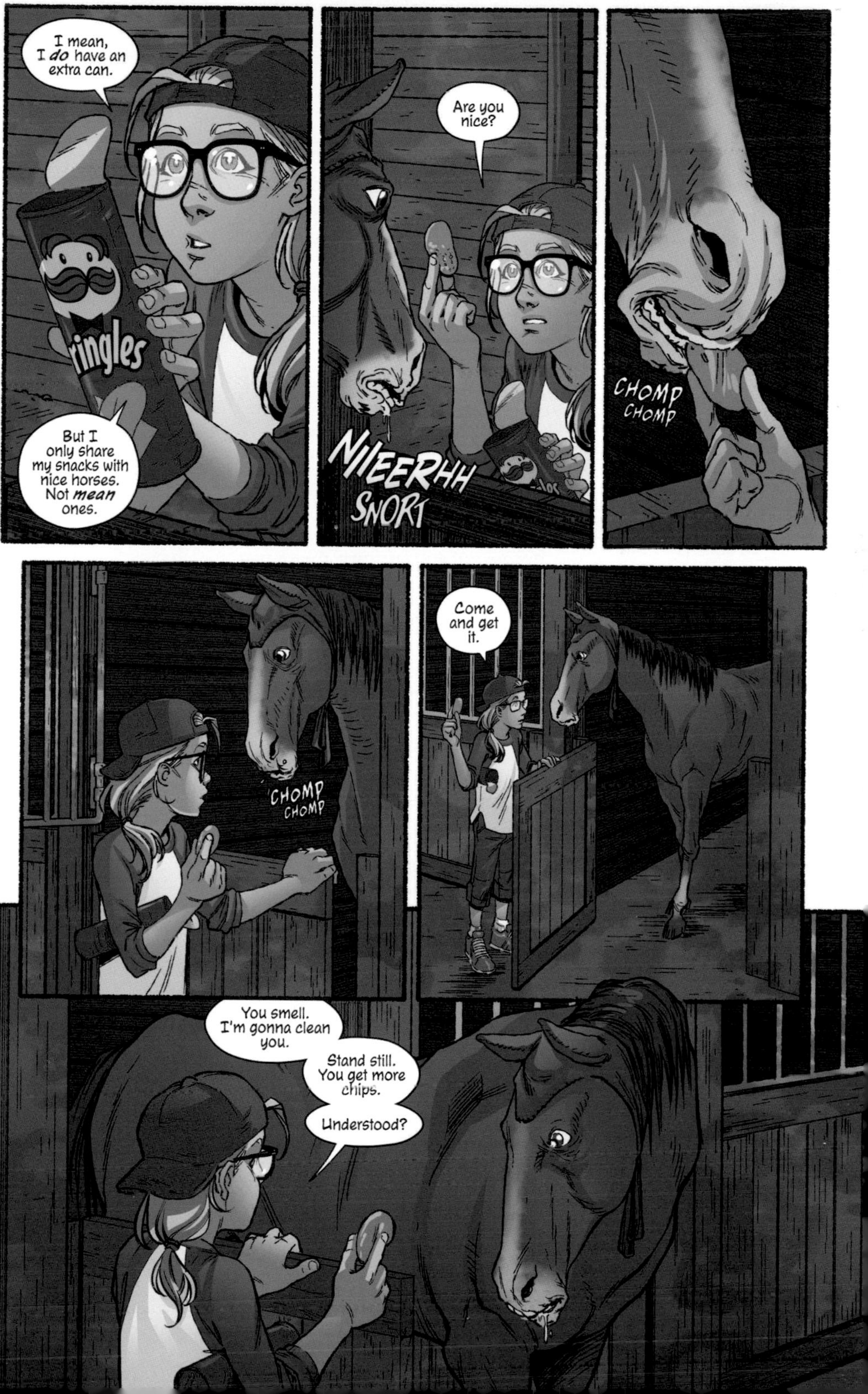
I mean, I *do* have an extra can.
Pringles
But I only share my snacks with nice horses. Not *mean* ones.
Are you nice?
NIIEERHH
SNORT
CHOMP CHOMP
CHOMP CHOMP
Come and get it.
You smell. I'm gonna clean you.
Stand still. You get more chips.
Understood?

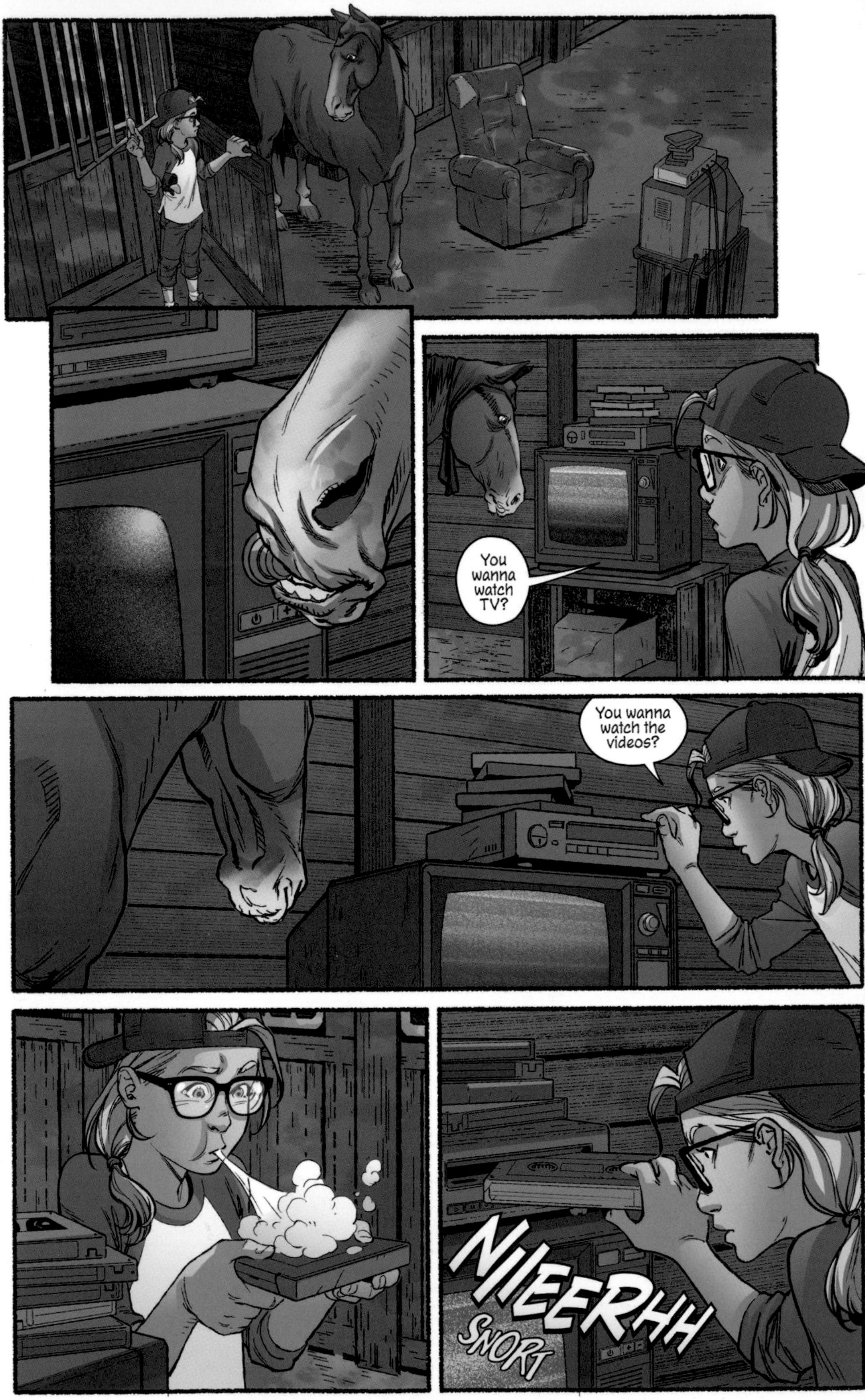
You wanna watch TV?
You wanna watch the videos?
NIIEERHH
SNORT

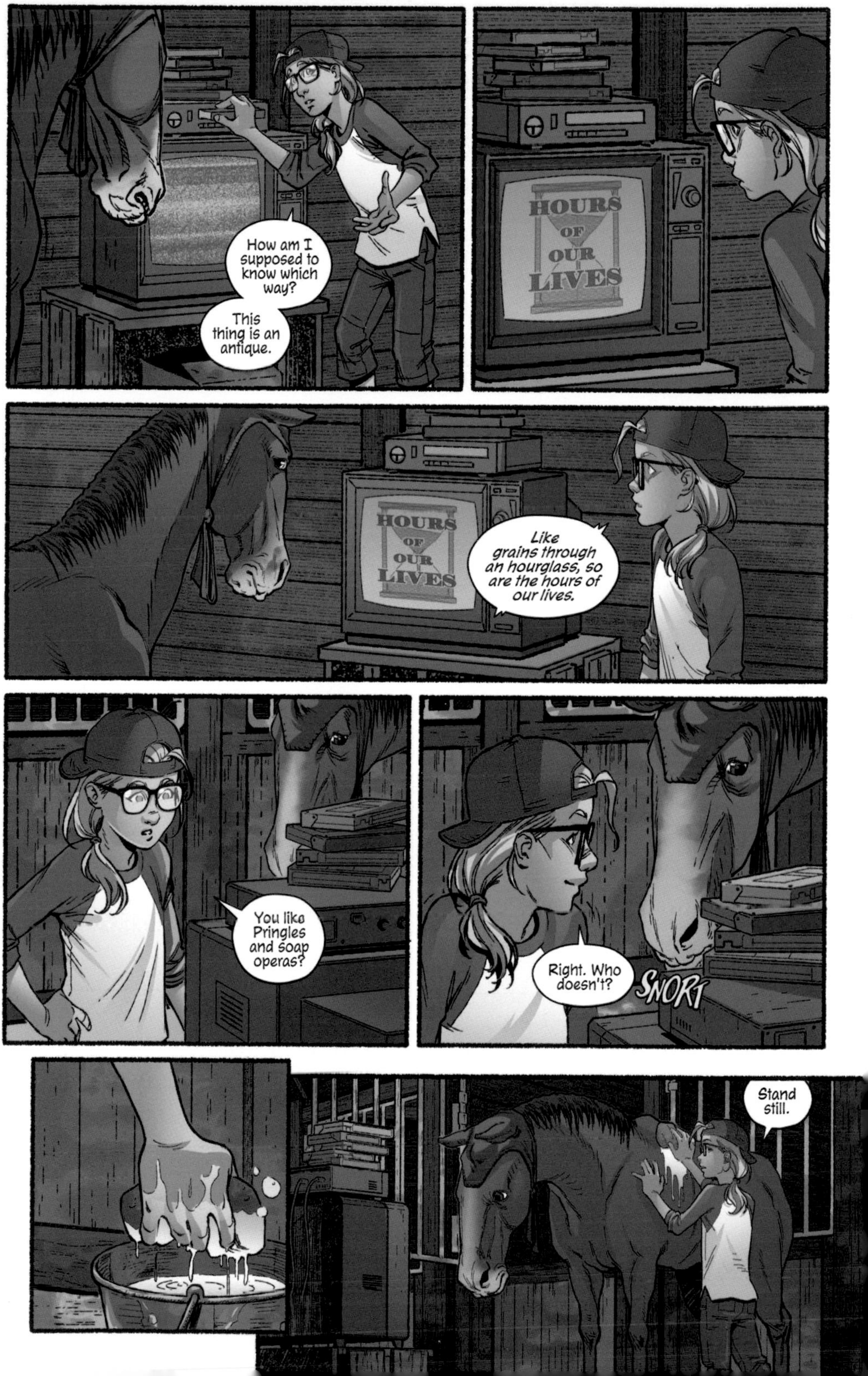
How am I supposed to know which way?
This thing is an antique.
HOURS OF OUR LIVES
HOURS OF OUR LIVES
Like grains through an hourglass, so are the hours of our lives.
You like Pringles and soap operas?
Right. Who doesn't?
SNORT
Stand still.

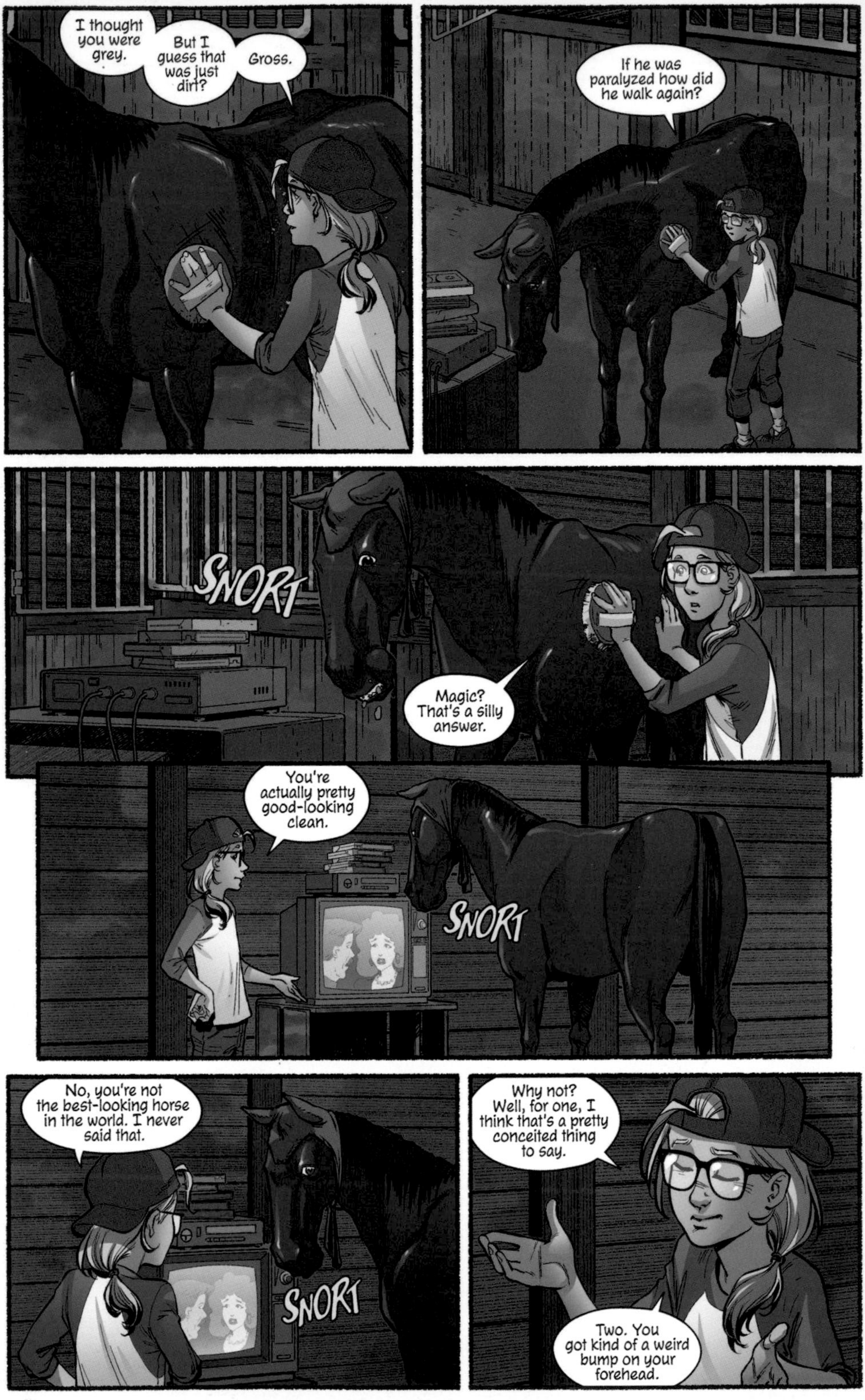

I thought you were grey.
But I guess that was just dirt?
Gross.
If he was paralyzed how did he walk again?
SNORT
Magic? That's a silly answer.
You're actually pretty good-looking clean.
SNORT
No, you're not the best-looking horse in the world. I never said that.
SNORT
Why not? Well, for one, I think that's a pretty conceited thing to say.
Two. You got kind of a weird bump on your forehead.

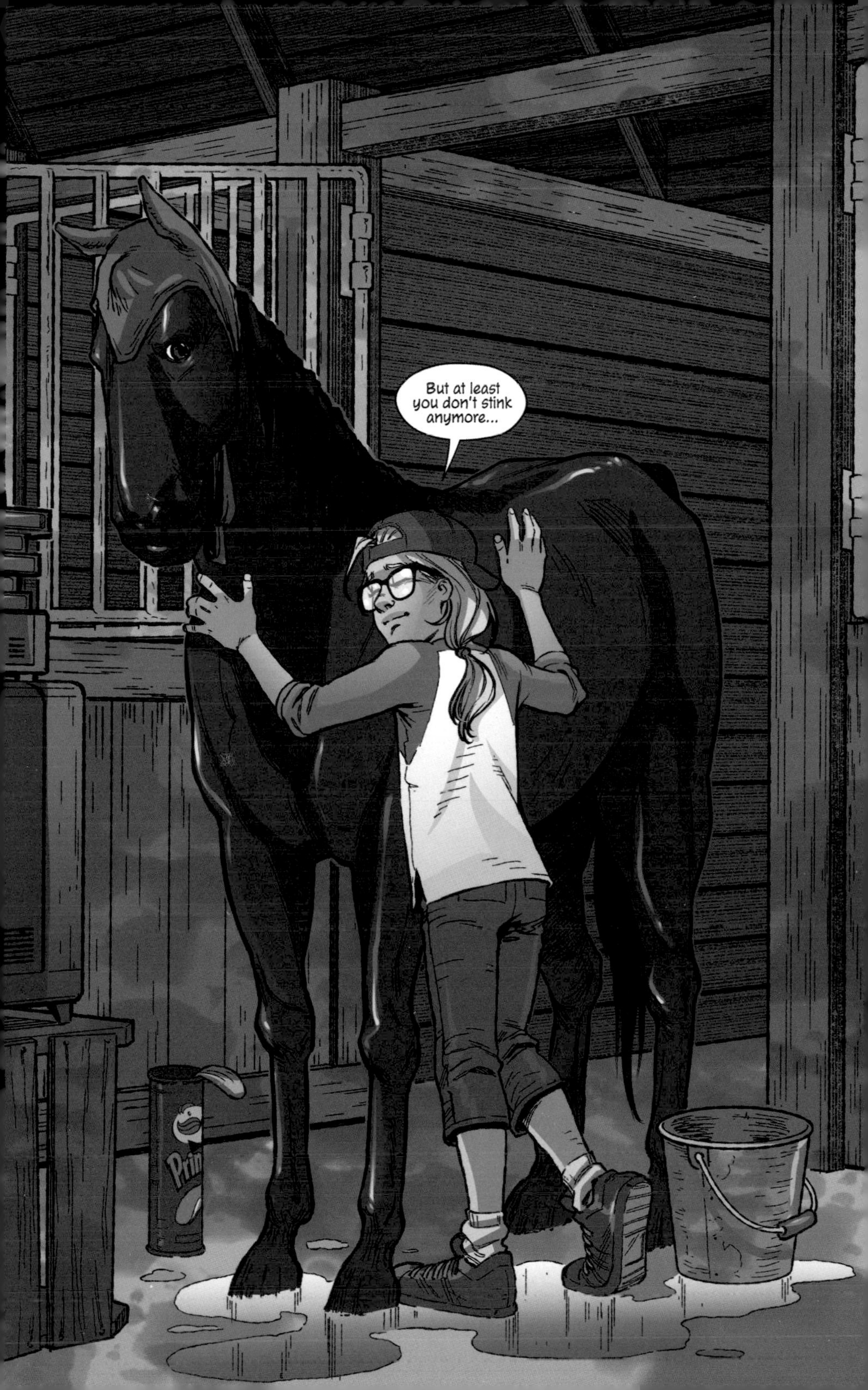
But at least you don't stink anymore...

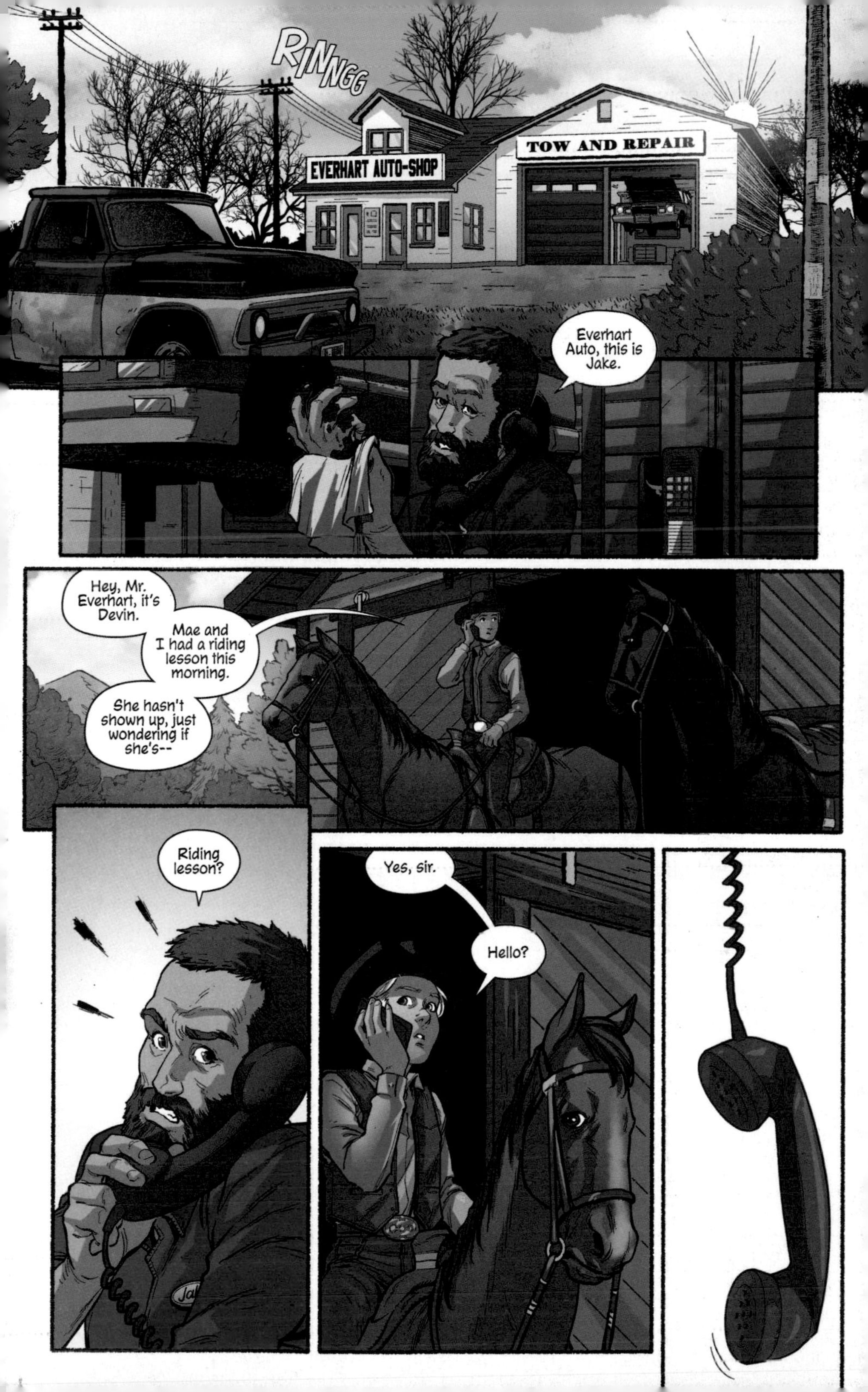
RINNGG
EVERHART AUTO-SHOP
TOW AND REPAIR
Everhart Auto, this is Jake.
Hey, Mr. Everhart, it's Devin.
Mae and I had a riding lesson this morning.
She hasn't shown up, just wondering if she's--
Riding lesson?
Yes, sir.
Hello?

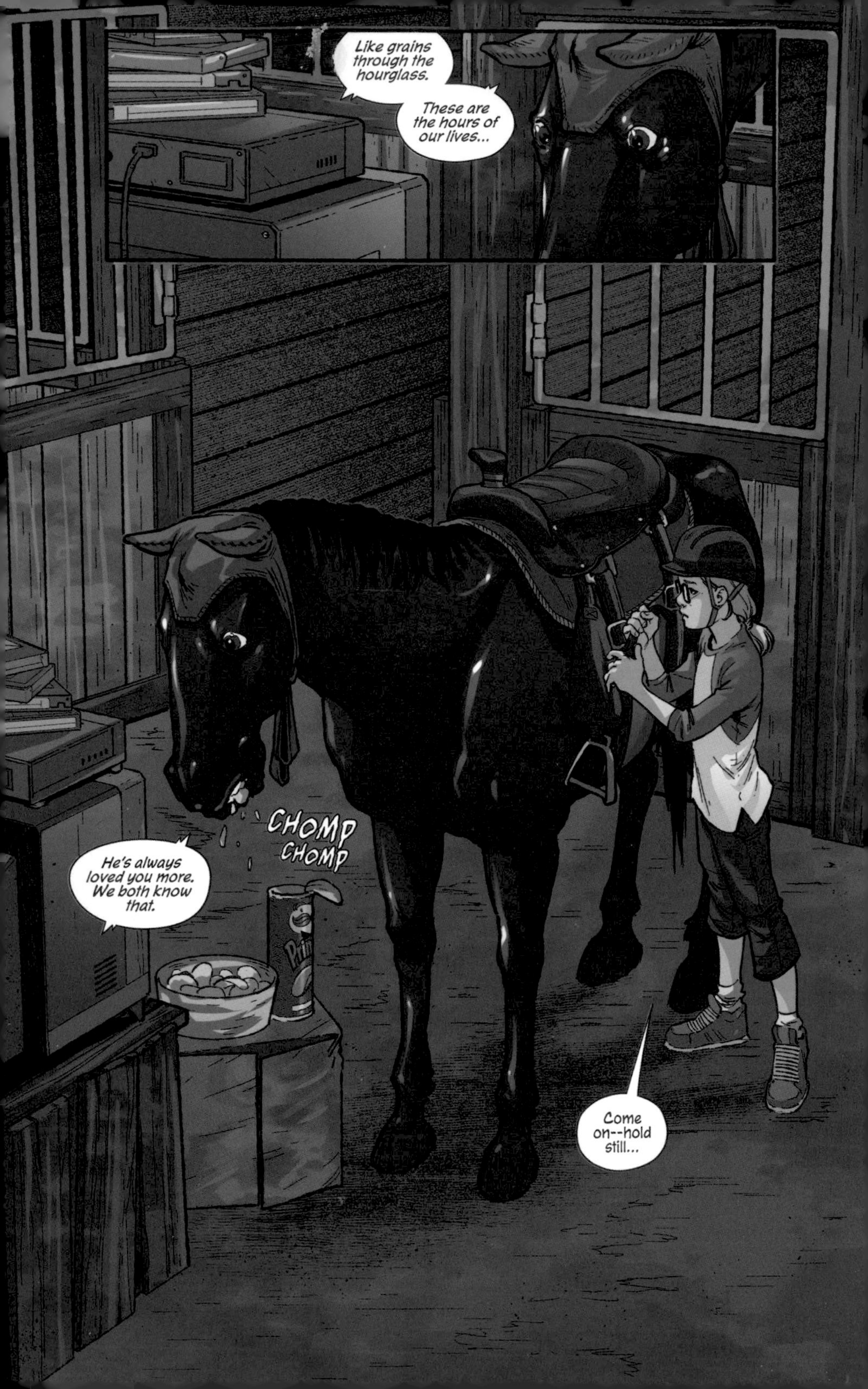

Like grains through the hourglass.
These are the hours of our lives...
CHOMP CHOMP
He's always loved you more. We both know that.
Come on--hold still...

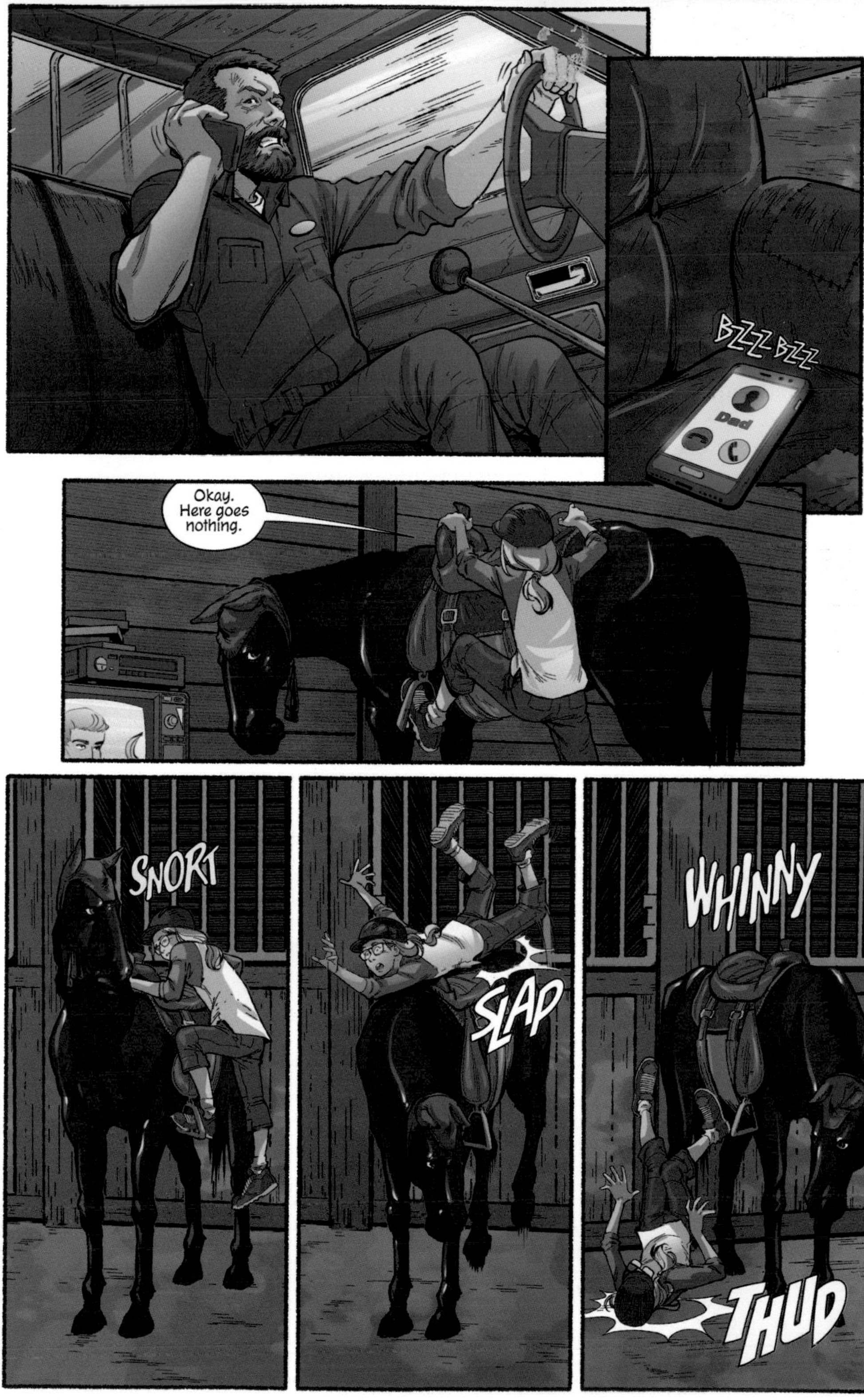
BZZZ BZZZ
Dad
Okay. Here goes nothing.
SNORT
SLAP
WHINNY
THUD

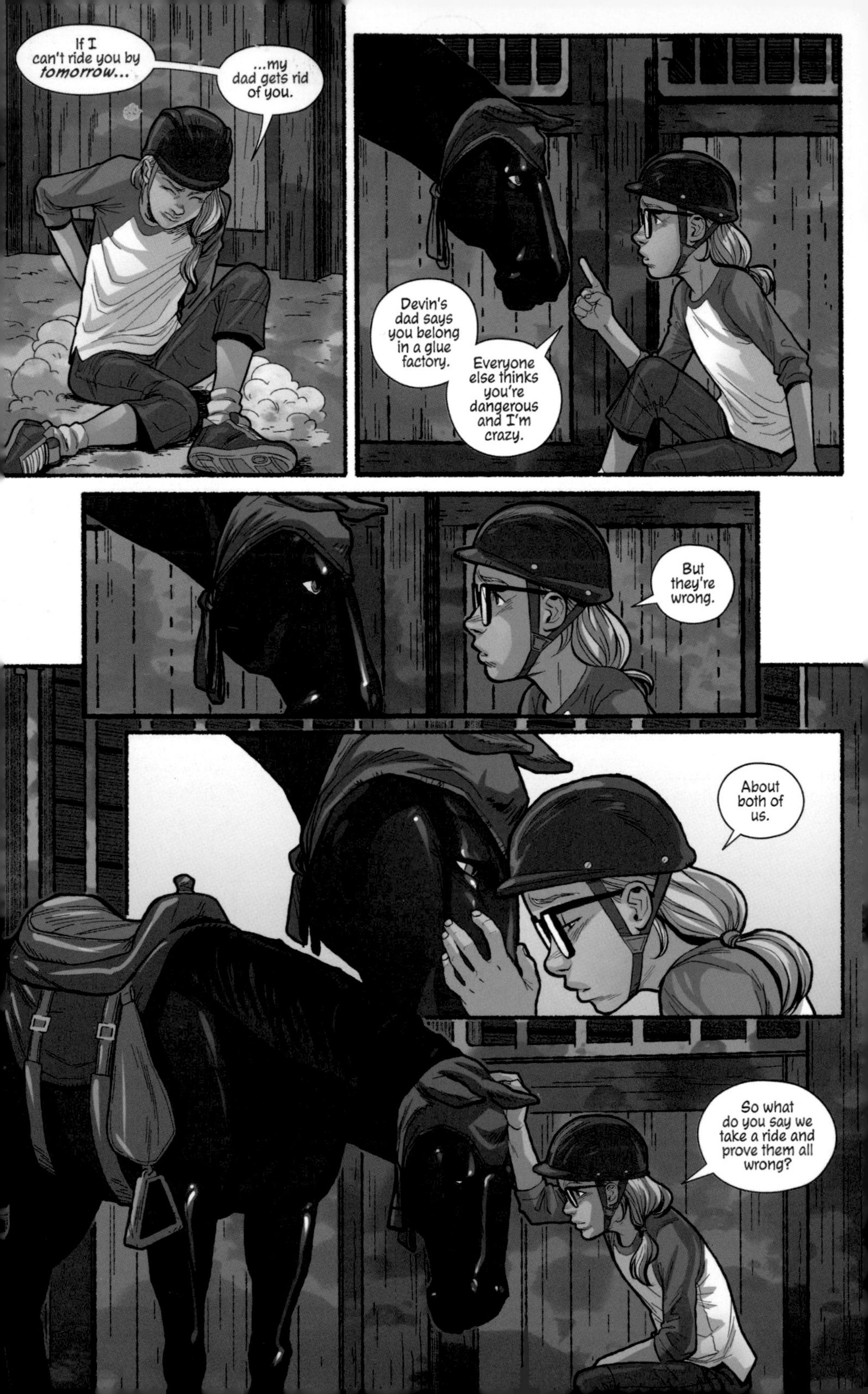
If I can't ride you by *tomorrow...*
...my dad gets rid of you.
Devin's dad says you belong in a glue factory.
Everyone else thinks you're dangerous and I'm crazy.
But they're wrong.
About both of us.
So what do you say we take a ride and prove them all wrong?

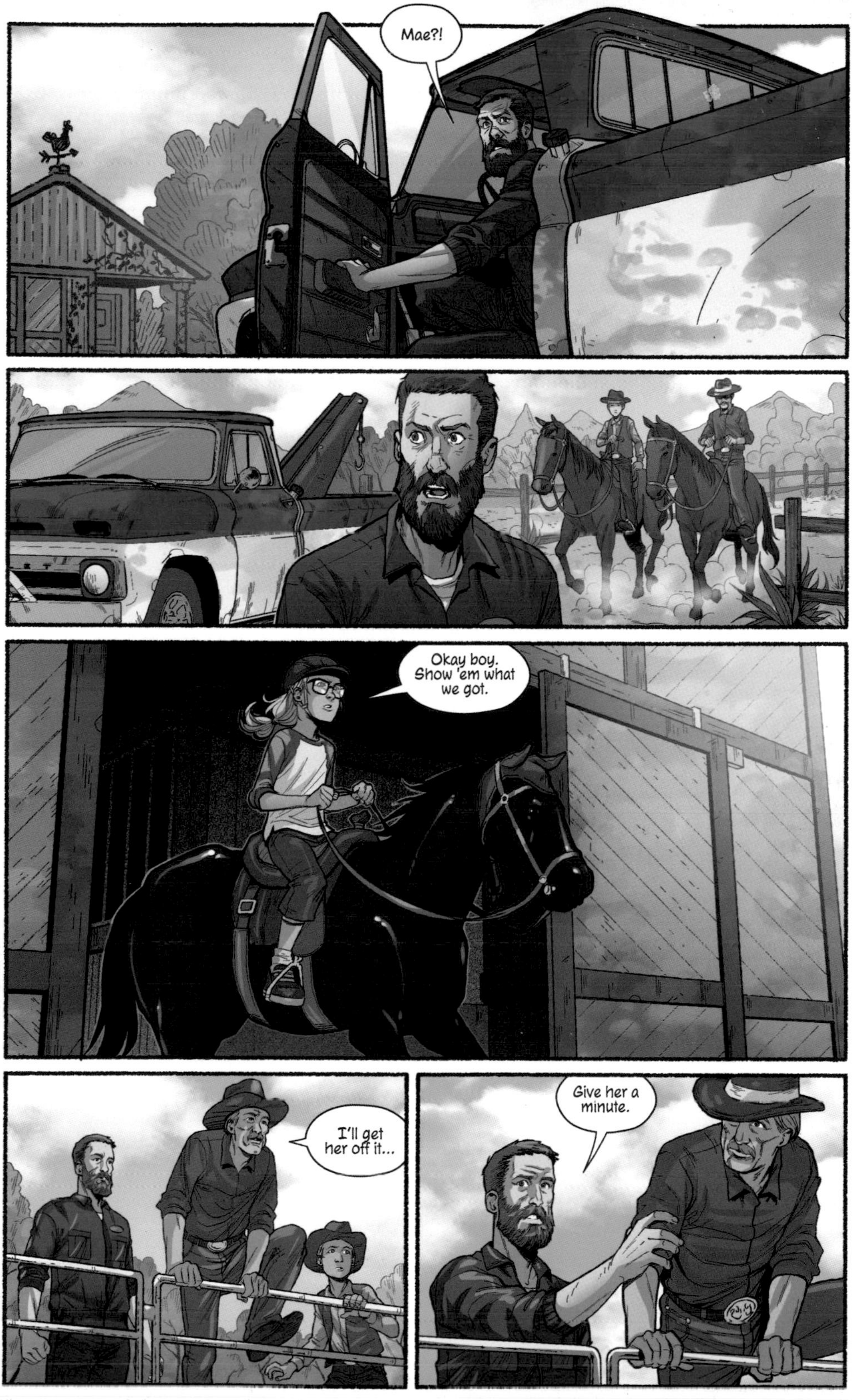
Mae?!
Okay boy. Show 'em what we got.
I'll get her off it...
Give her a minute.

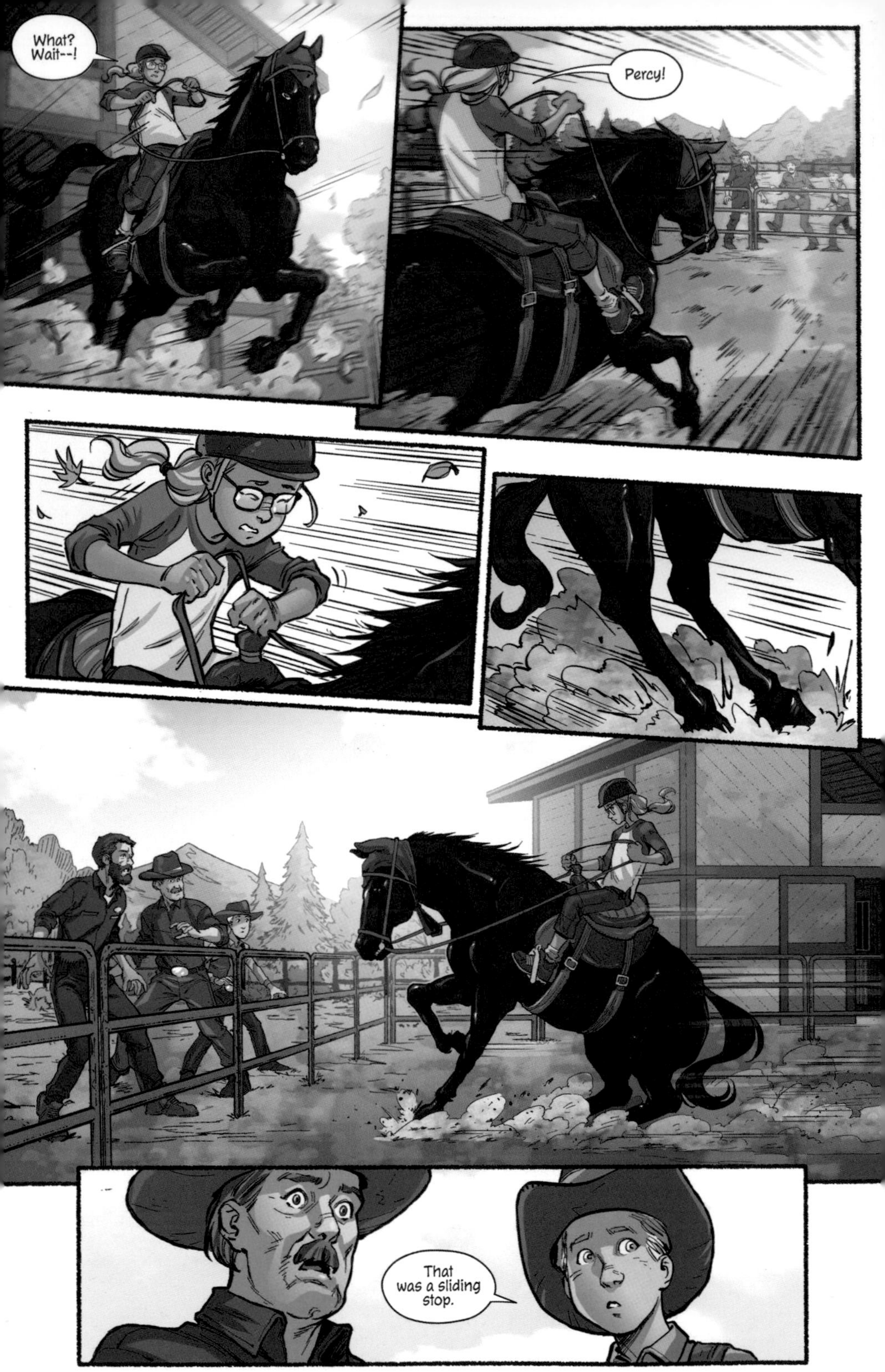
What? Wait--!
Percy!
That was a sliding stop.

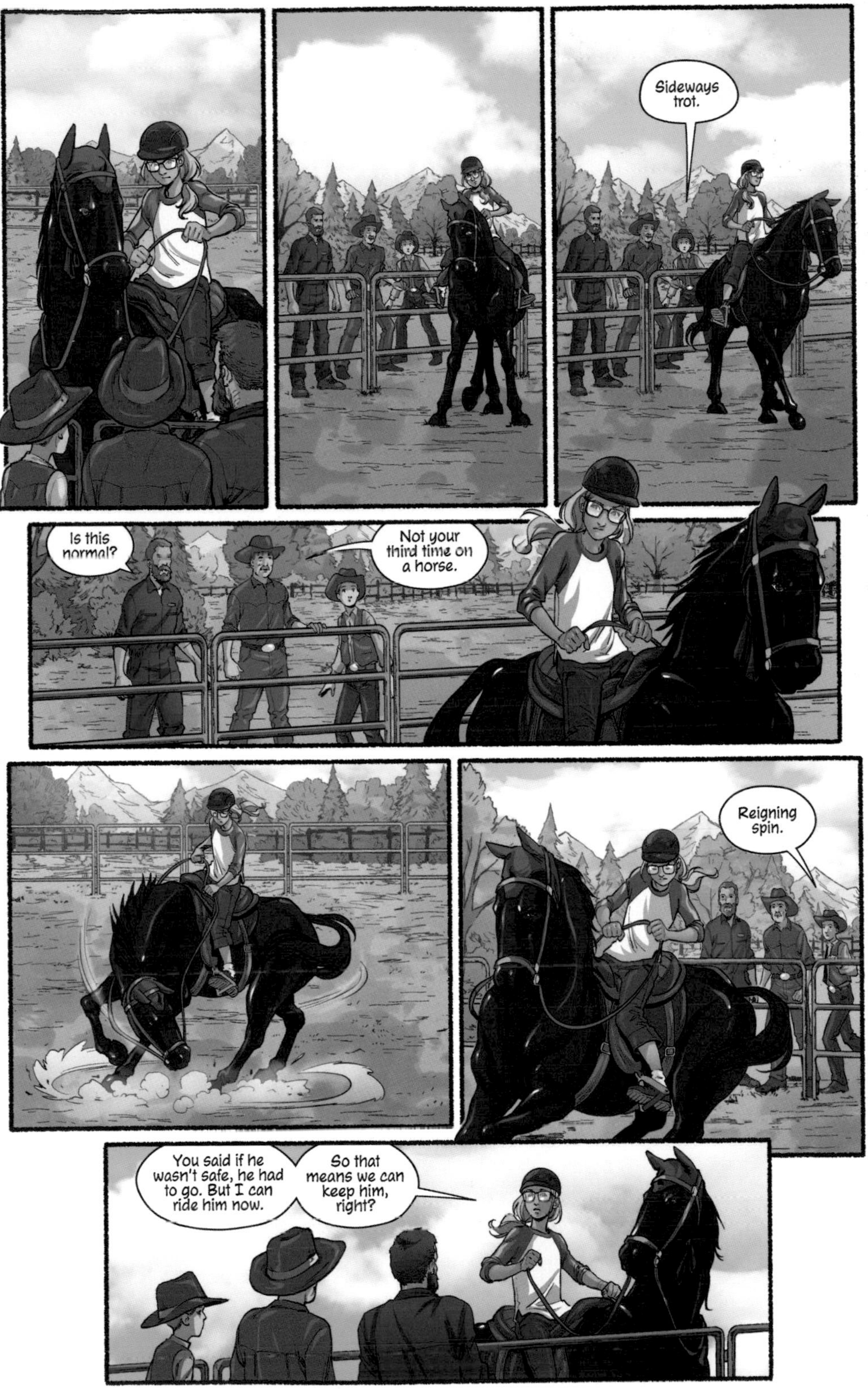

Sideways trot.
Is this normal?
Not your third time on a horse.
Reigning spin.
You said if he wasn't safe, he had to go. But I can ride him now.
So that means we can keep him, right?

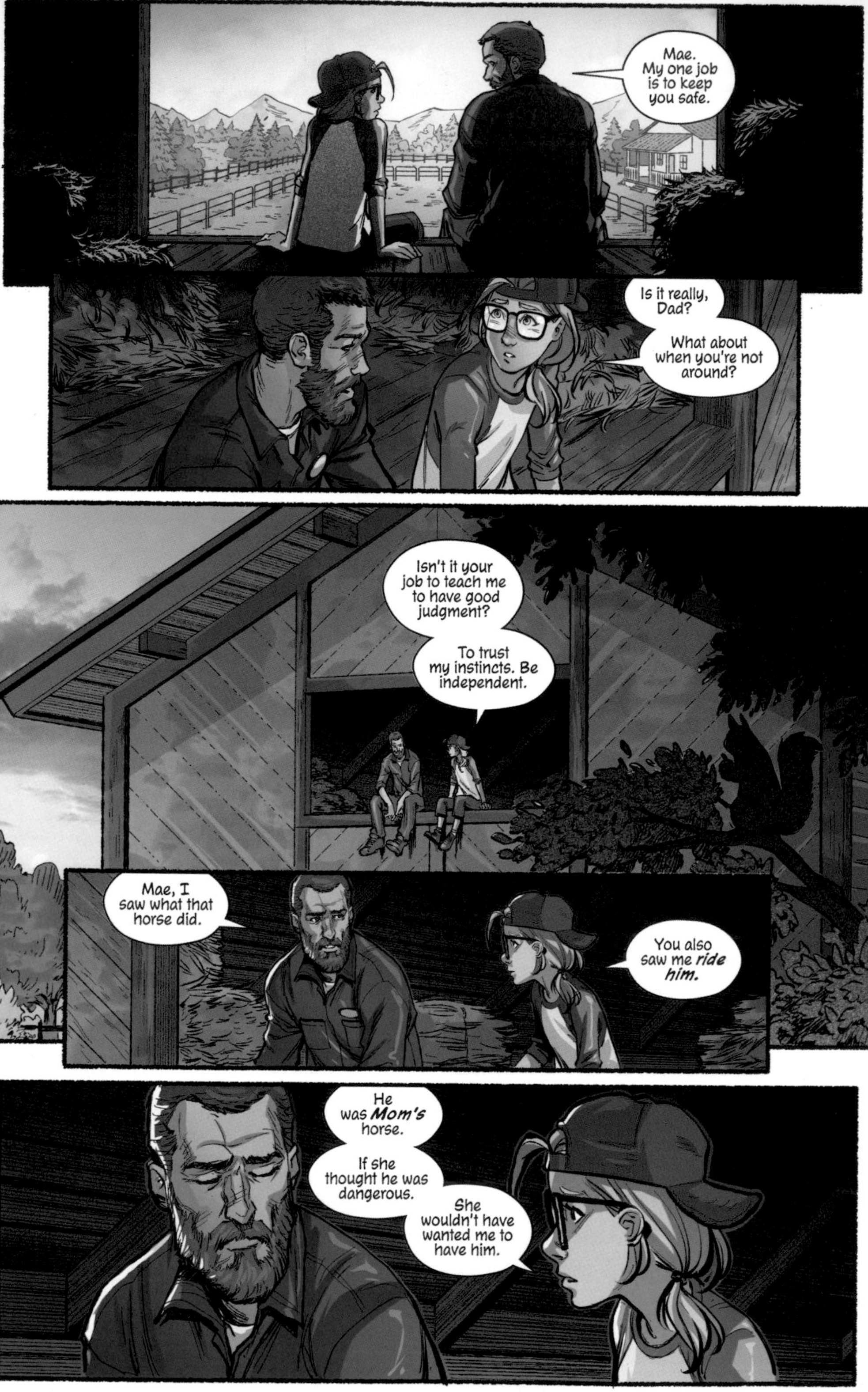
Mae. My one job is to keep you safe.
Is it really, Dad?
What about when you're not around?
Isn't it your job to teach me to have good judgment?
To trust my instincts. Be independent.
Mae, I saw what that horse did.
You also saw me *ride him.*
He was **Mom's** horse.
If she thought he was dangerous.
She wouldn't have wanted me to have him.

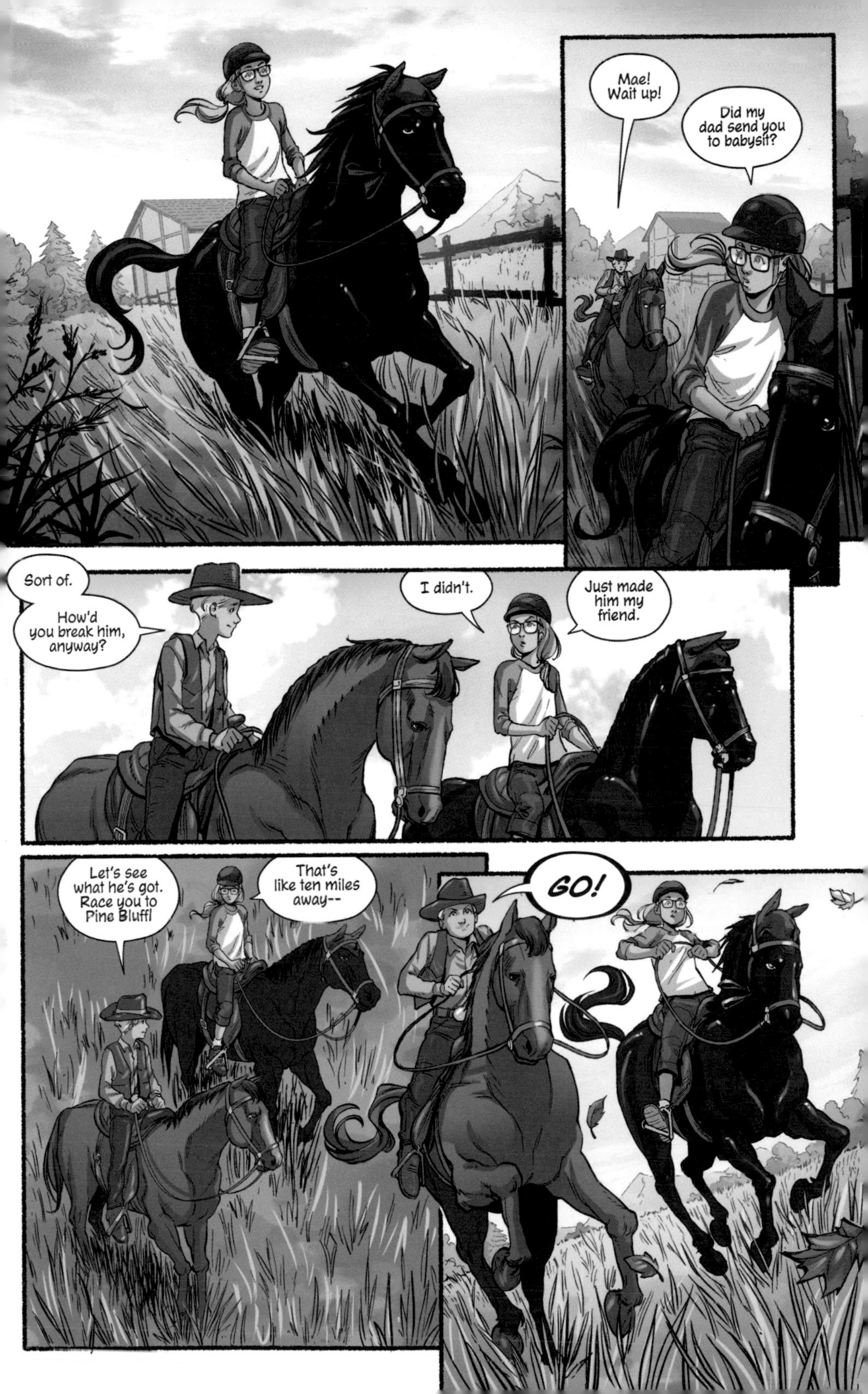
Mae! Wait up!
Did my dad send you to babysit?
Sort of.
How'd you break him, anyway?
I didn't.
Just made him my friend.
Let's see what he's got. Race you to Pine Bluff!
That's like ten miles away--
GO!

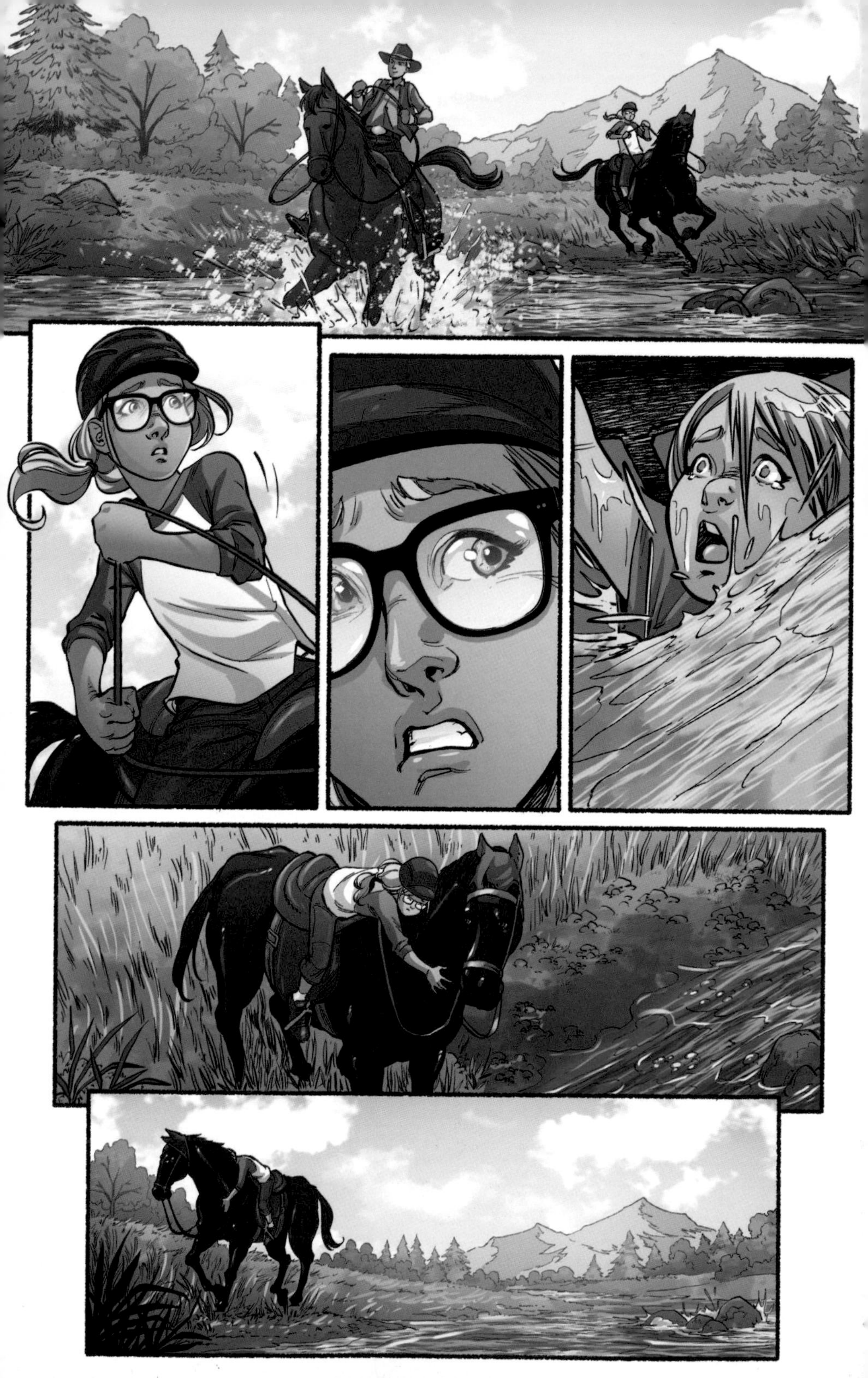

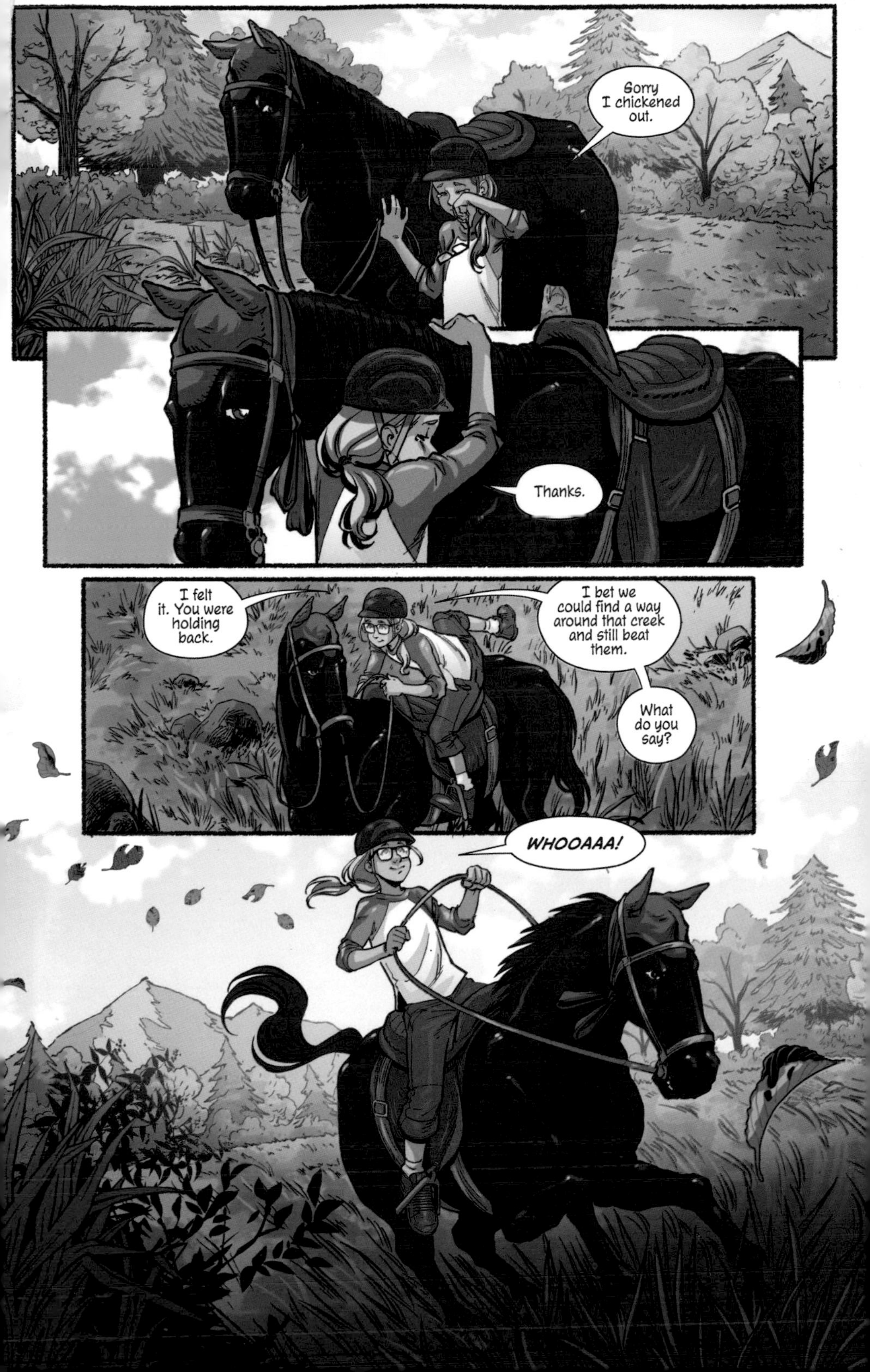
Sorry I chickened out.
Thanks.
I felt it. You were holding back.
I bet we could find a way around that creek and still beat them.
What do you say?
WHOOAAA!

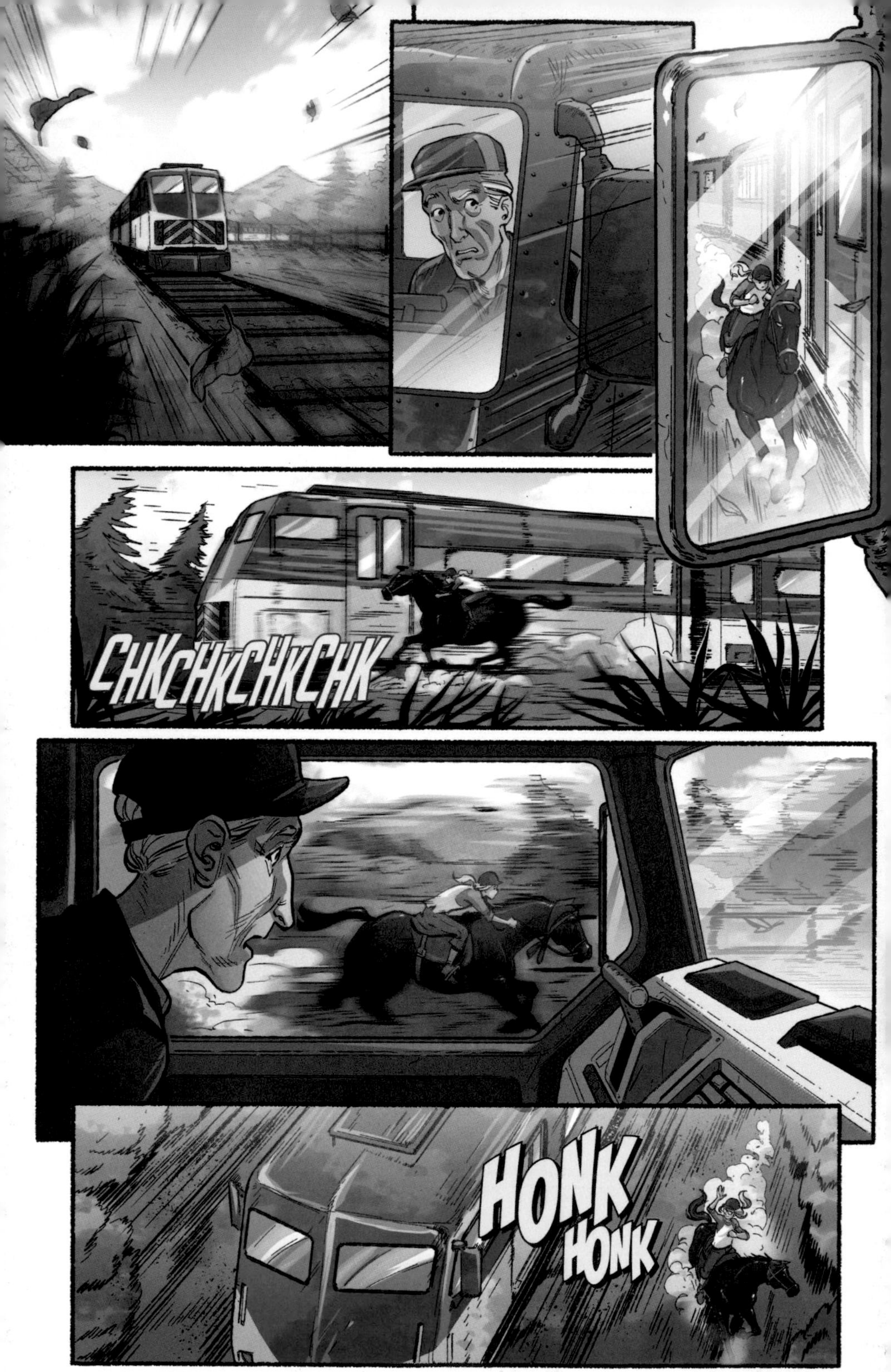
CHKCHKCHKCHK
HONK
HONK

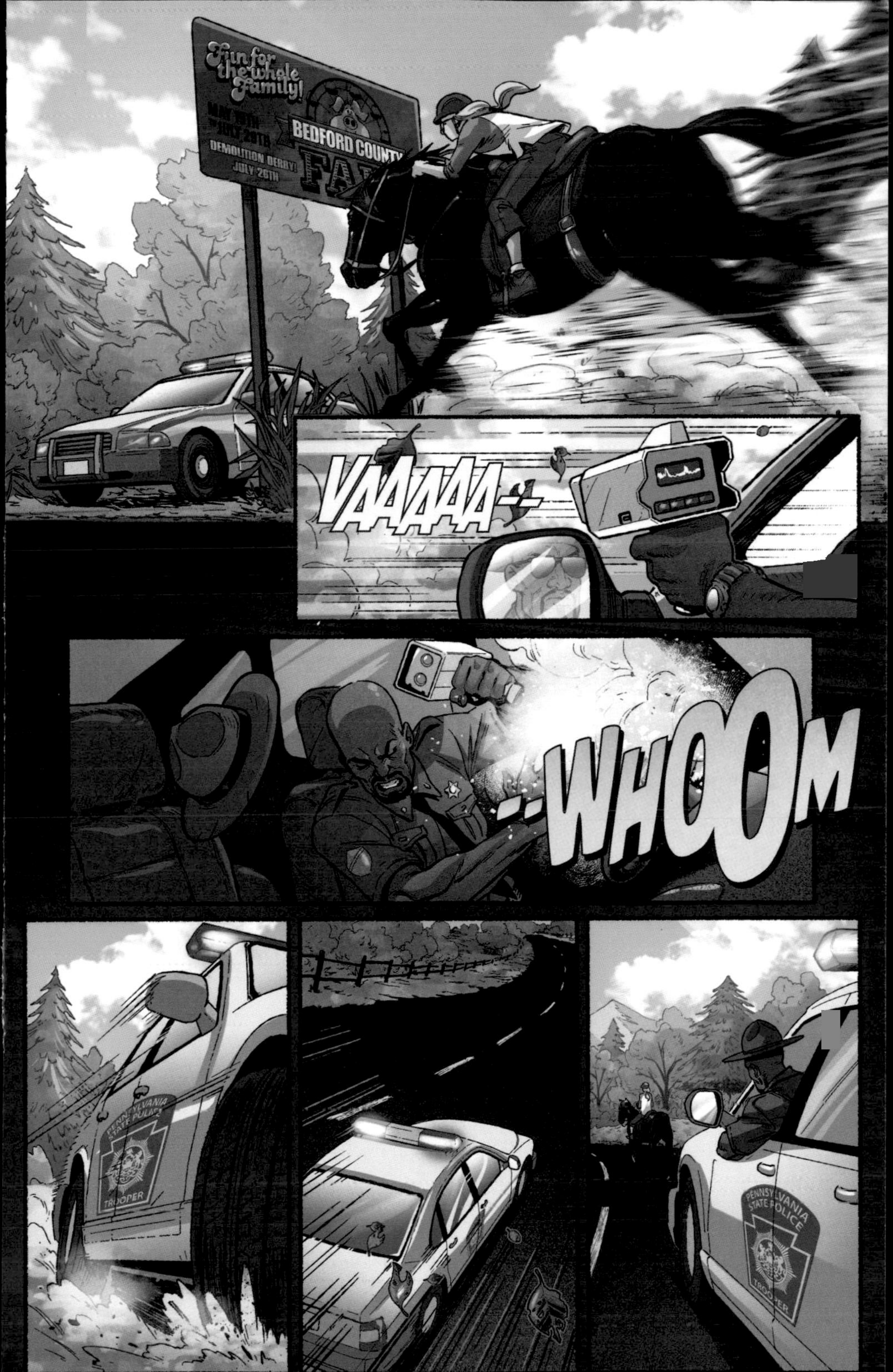
Fun for the whole Family!
BEDFORD COUNTY
DEMOLITION DERBY!
JULY 26TH
VAAAAA--
--WHOOM
PENNSYLVANIA STATE POLICE
TROOPER
PENNSYLVANIA STATE POLICE
TROOPER

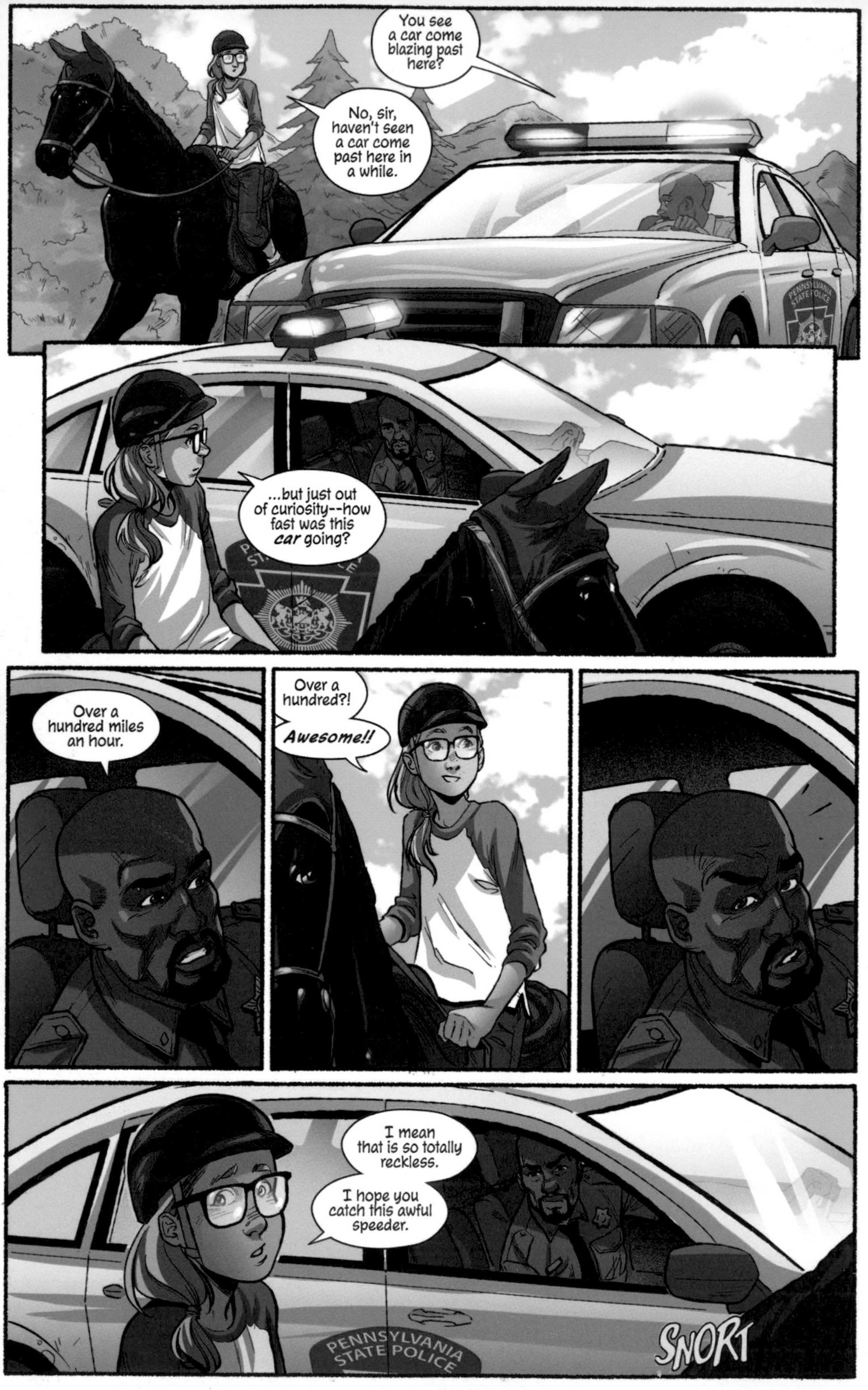
You see a car come blazing past here?
No, sir, haven't seen a car come past here in a while.
...but just out of curiosity--how fast was this *car* going?
Over a hundred miles an hour.
Over a hundred?!
Awesome!!
I mean that is so totally reckless.
I hope you catch this awful speeder.
PENNSYLVANIA STATE POLICE
SNORT

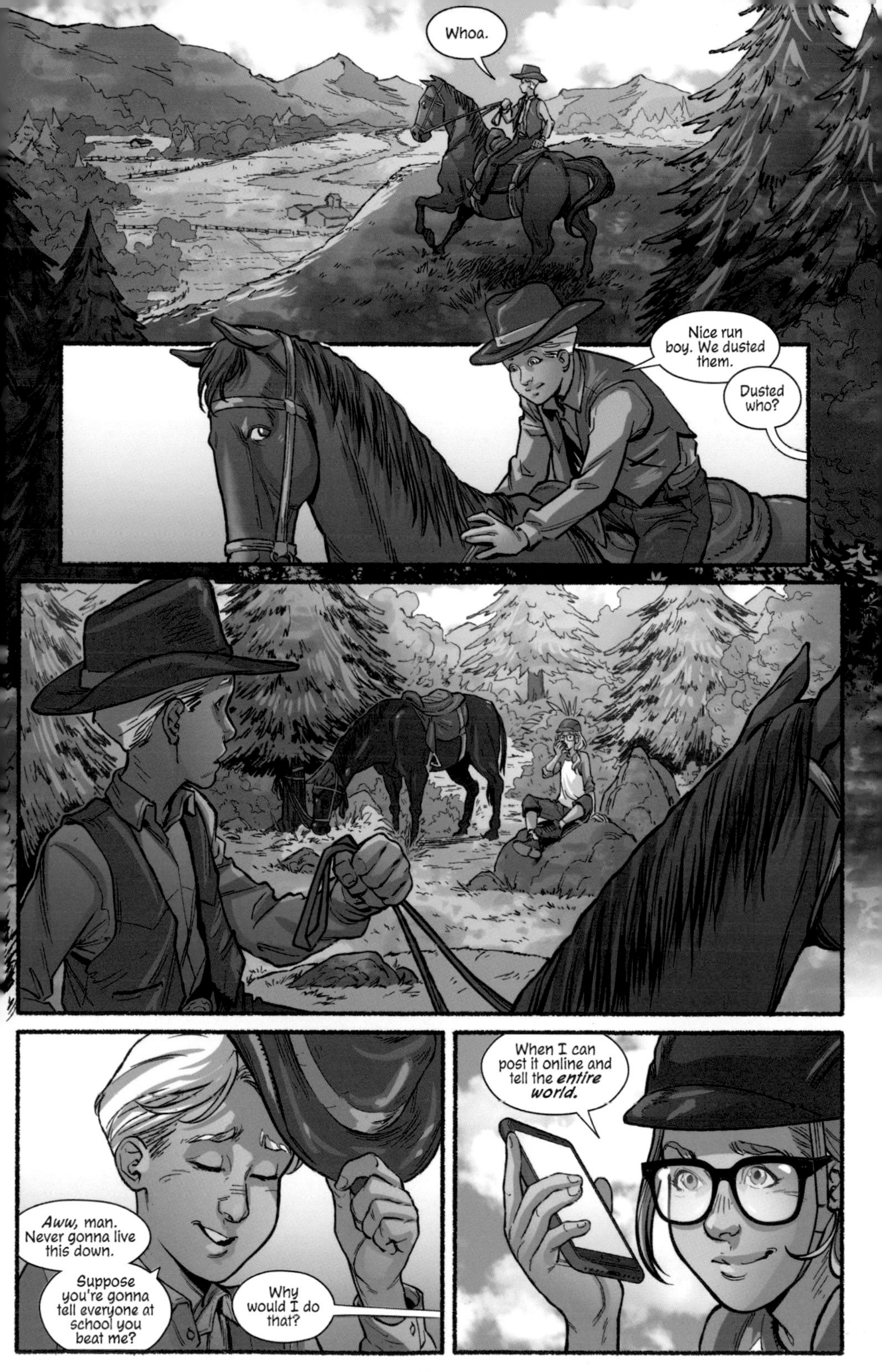
Whoa.
Nice run boy. We dusted them.
Dusted who?
Aww, man. Never gonna live this down.
Suppose you're gonna tell everyone at school you beat me?
Why would I do that?
When I can post it online and tell the *entire world.*

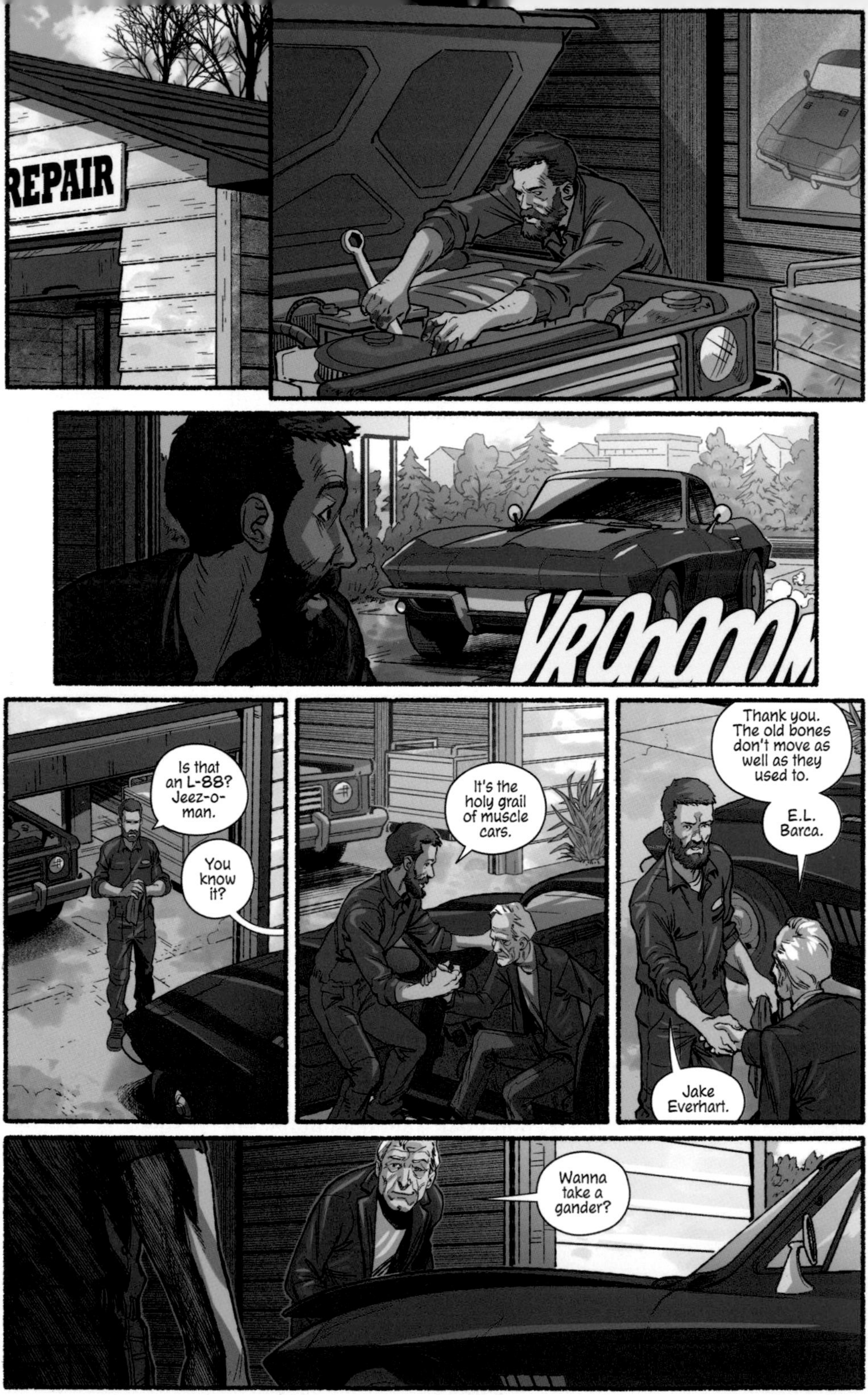
REPAIR
VROOOOOM
Is that an L-88? Jeez-o-man.
You know it?
It's the holy grail of muscle cars.
Thank you. The old bones don't move as well as they used to.
E.L. Barca.
Jake Everhart.
Wanna take a gander?

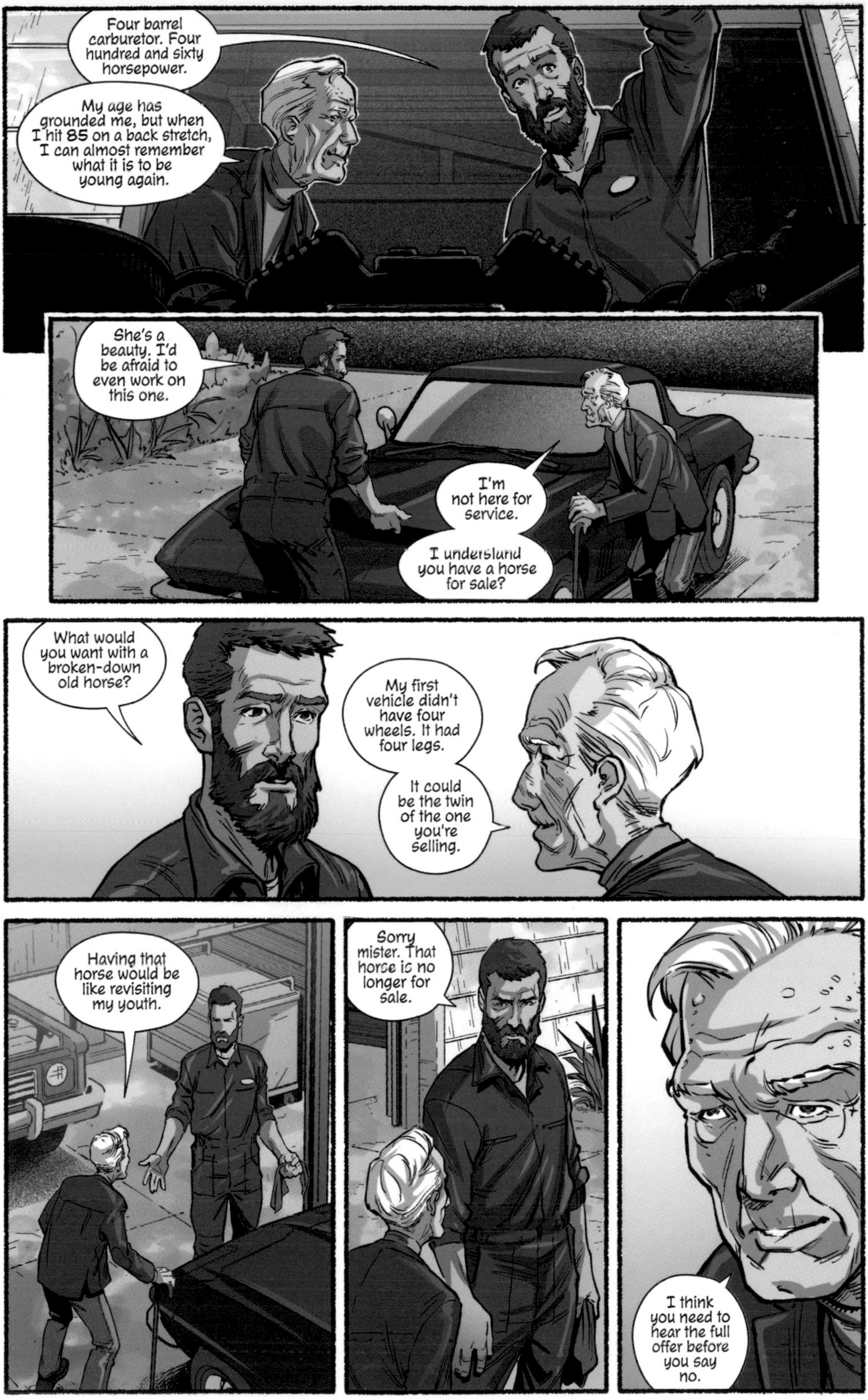
Four barrel carburetor. Four hundred and sixty horsepower.
My age has grounded me, but when I hit 85 on a back stretch, I can almost remember what it is to be young again.
She's a beauty. I'd be afraid to even work on this one.
I'm not here for service.
I understand you have a horse for sale?
What would you want with a broken-down old horse?
My first vehicle didn't have four wheels. It had four legs.
It could be the twin of the one you're selling.
Having that horse would be like revisiting my youth.
Sorry mister. That horse is no longer for sale.
I think you need to hear the full offer before you say no.

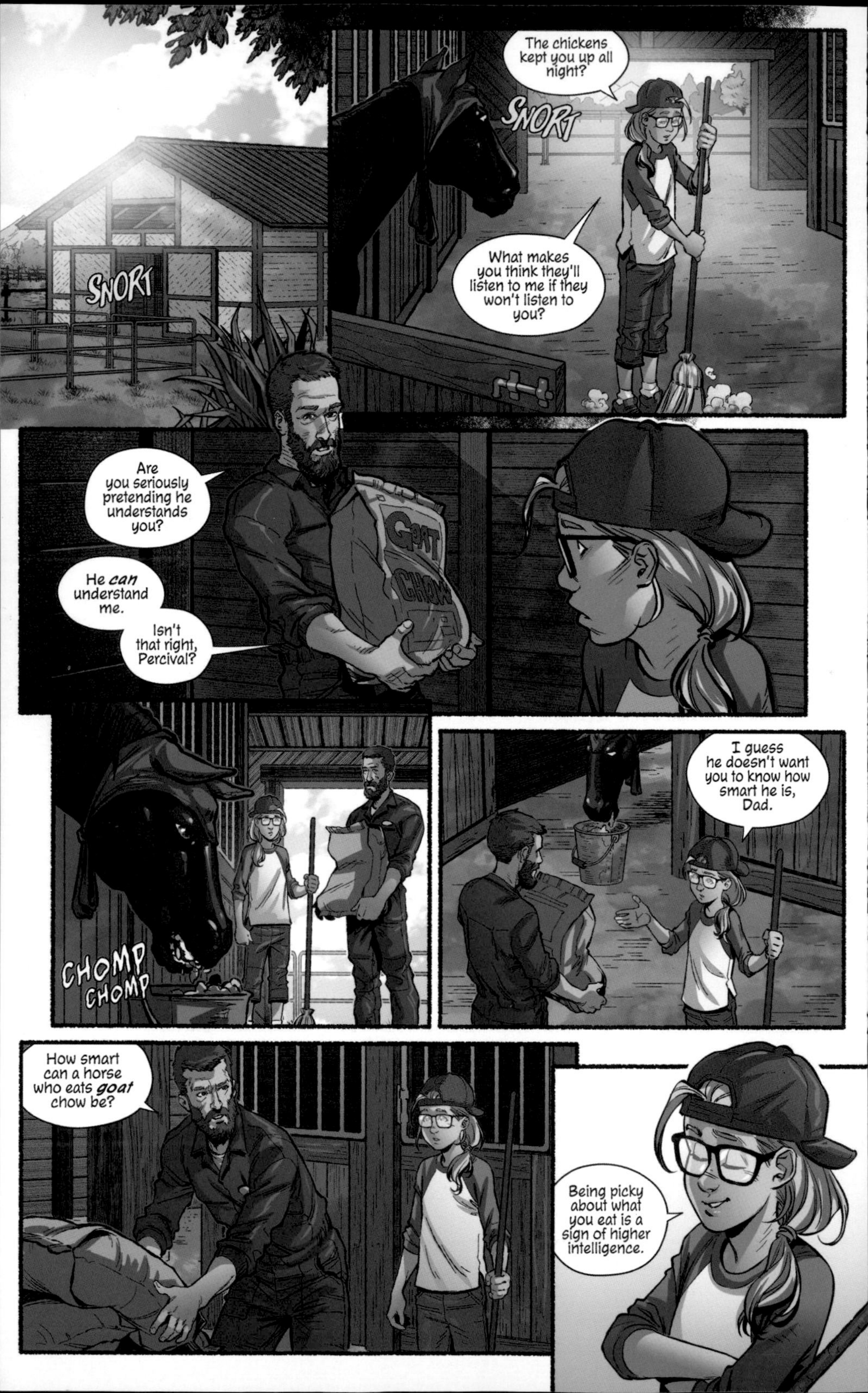
SNORT
SNORT
The chickens kept you up all night?
What makes you think they'll listen to me if they won't listen to you?
Are you seriously pretending he understands you?
GOAT CHOW
He *can* understand me.
Isn't that right, Percival?
CHOMP CHOMP
I guess he doesn't want you to know how smart he is, Dad.
How smart can a horse who eats *goat* chow be?
Being picky about what you eat is a sign of higher intelligence.

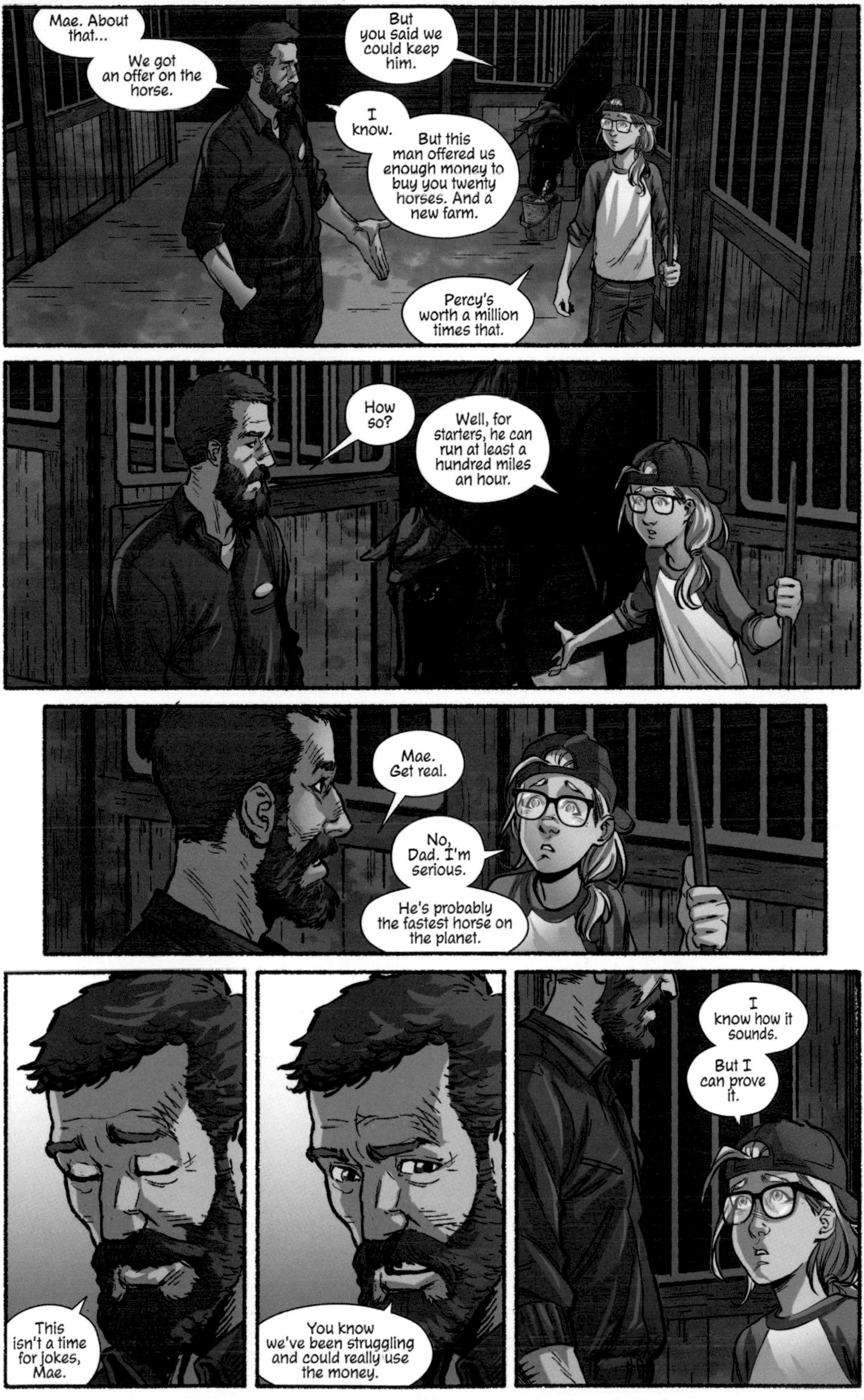
Mae. About that...
We got an offer on the horse.
But you said we could keep him.
I know.
But this man offered us enough money to buy you twenty horses. And a new farm.
Percy's worth a million times that.
How so?
Well, for starters, he can run at least a hundred miles an hour.
Mae. Get real.
No, Dad. I'm serious.
He's probably the fastest horse on the planet.
This isn't a time for jokes, Mae.
You know we've been struggling and could really use the money.
I know how it sounds.
But I can prove it.

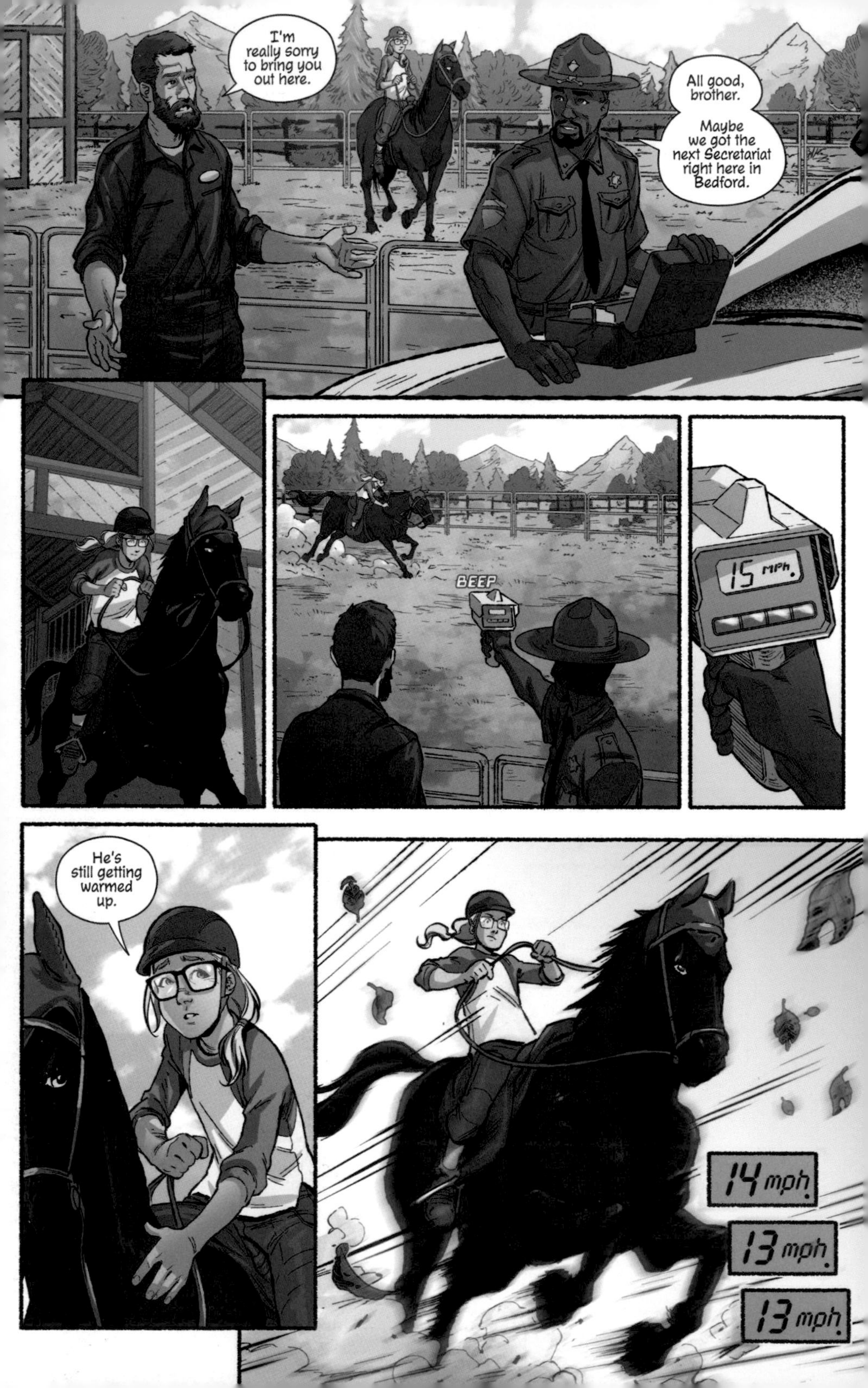
I'm really sorry to bring you out here.
All good, brother.
Maybe we got the next Secretariat right here in Bedford.
BEEP
15 mph.
He's still getting warmed up.
14 mph.
13 mph.
13 mph.

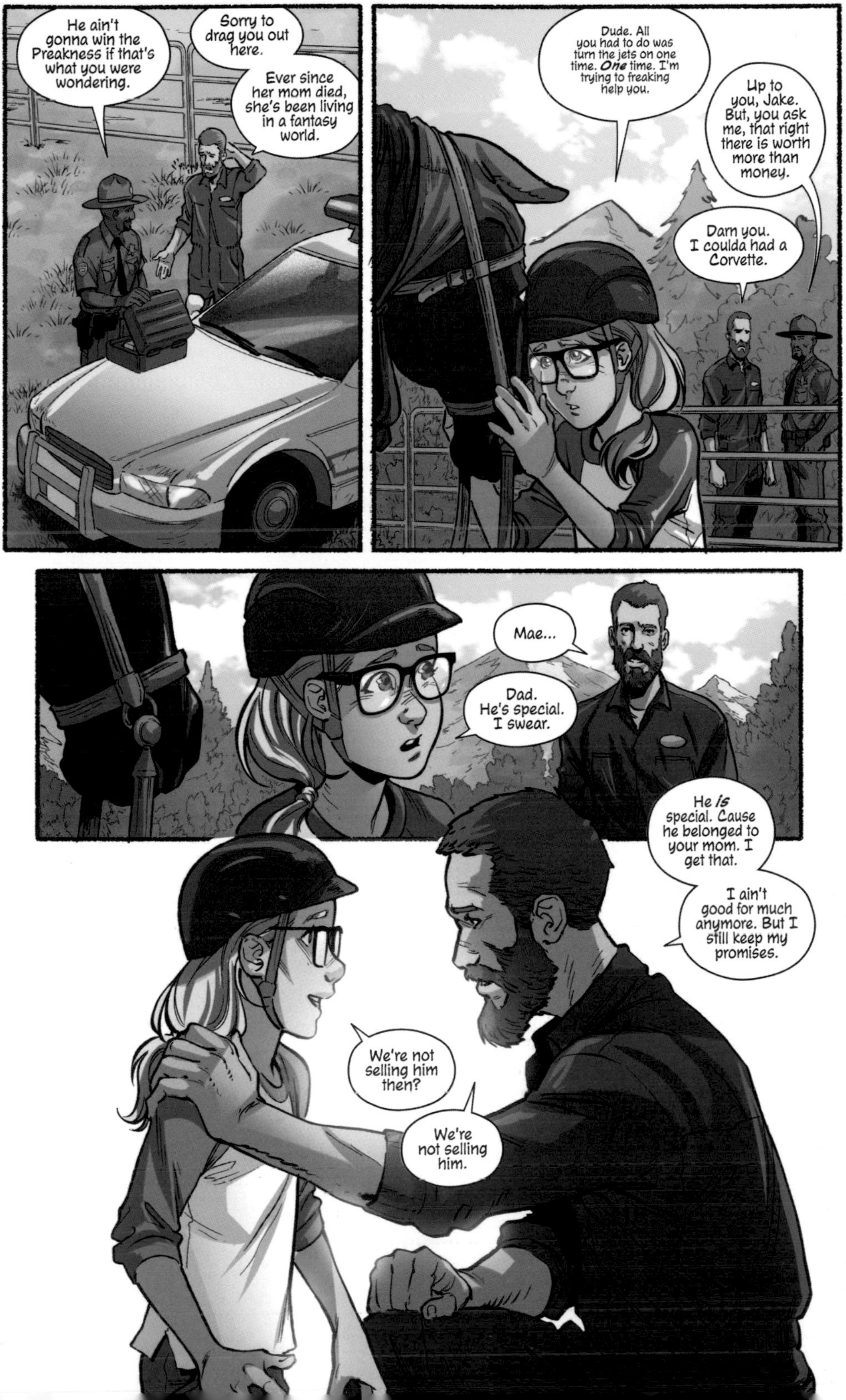
He ain't gonna win the Preakness if that's what you were wondering.
Sorry to drag you out here.
Ever since her mom died, she's been living in a fantasy world.
Dude. All you had to do was turn the jets on one time. *One* time. I'm trying to freaking help you.
Up to you, Jake. But, you ask me, that right there is worth more than money.
Darn you. I coulda had a Corvette.
Mae...
Dad. He's special. I swear.
He *is* special. Cause he belonged to your mom. I get that.
I ain't good for much anymore. But I still keep my promises.
We're not selling him then?
We're not selling him.

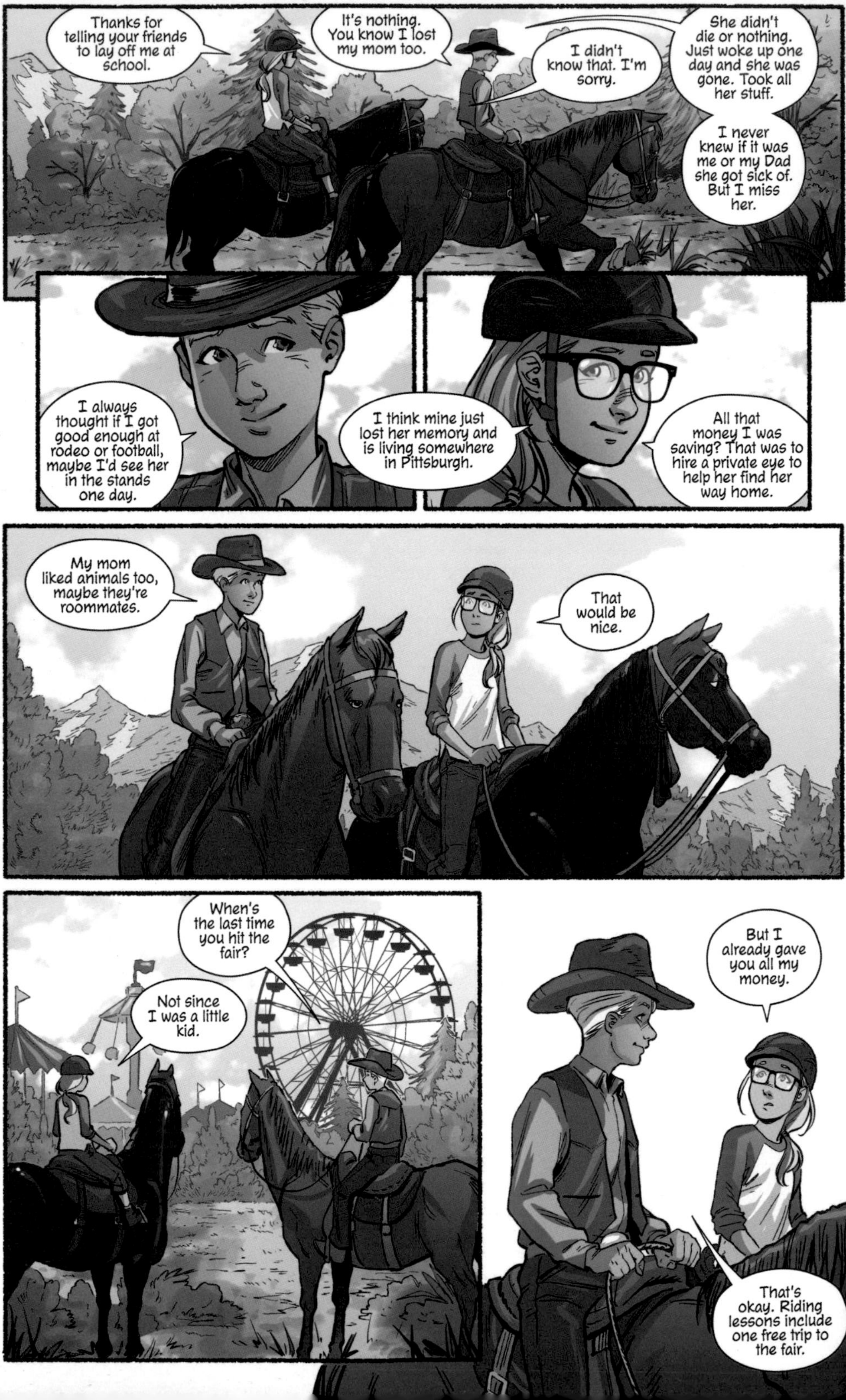
Thanks for telling your friends to lay off me at school.
It's nothing. You know I lost my mom too.
I didn't know that. I'm sorry.
She didn't die or nothing. Just woke up one day and she was gone. Took all her stuff.
I never knew if it was me or my Dad she got sick of. But I miss her.
I always thought if I got good enough at rodeo or football, maybe I'd see her in the stands one day.
I think mine just lost her memory and is living somewhere in Pittsburgh.
All that money I was saving? That was to hire a private eye to help her find her way home.
My mom liked animals too, maybe they're roommates.
That would be nice.
When's the last time you hit the fair?
Not since I was a little kid.
But I already gave you all my money.
That's okay. Riding lessons include one free trip to the fair.

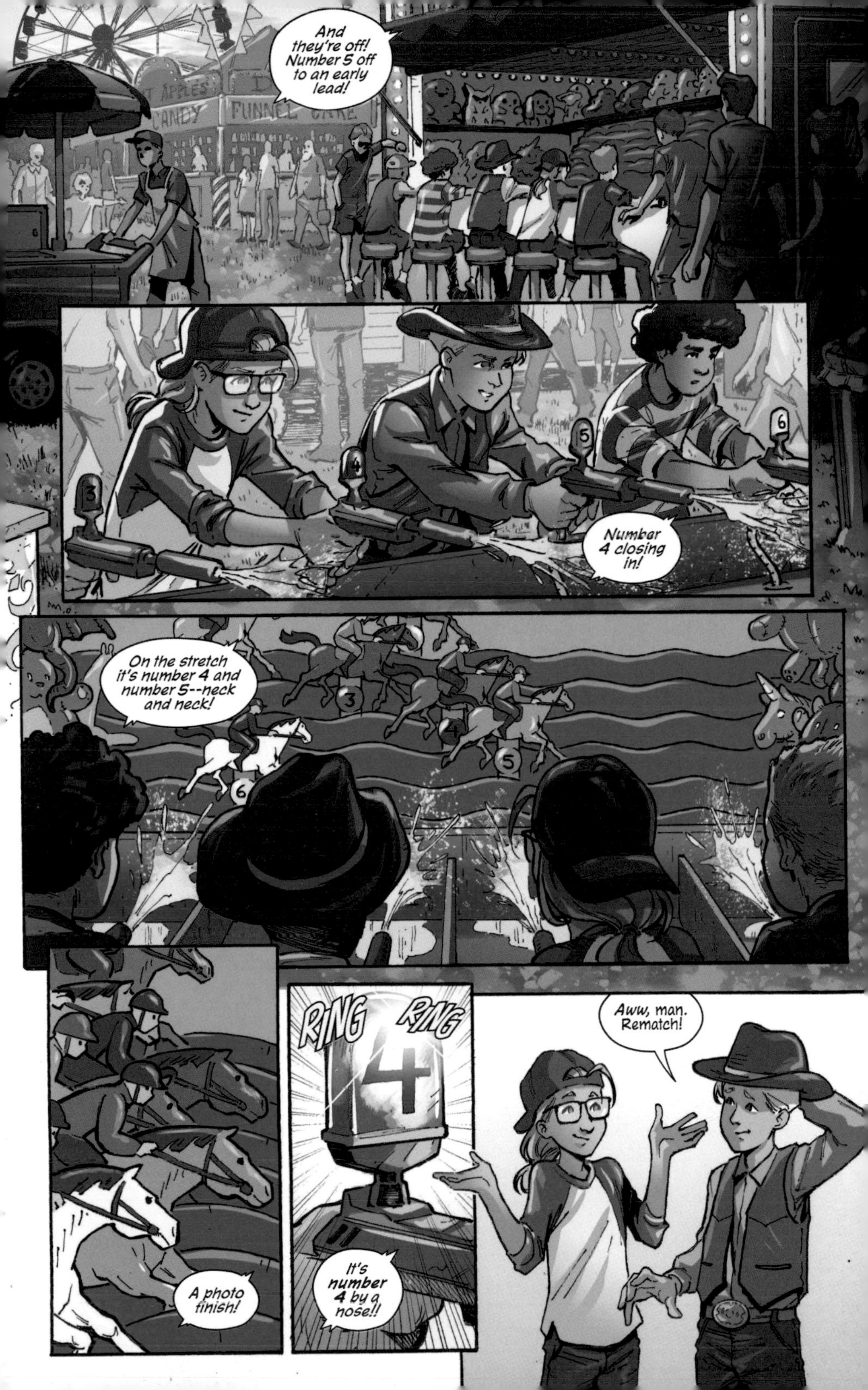
And they're off! Number 5 off to an early lead!
Number 4 closing in!
On the stretch it's number 4 and number 5--neck and neck!
A photo finish!
RING RING
It's number 4 by a nose!!
Aww, man. Rematch!

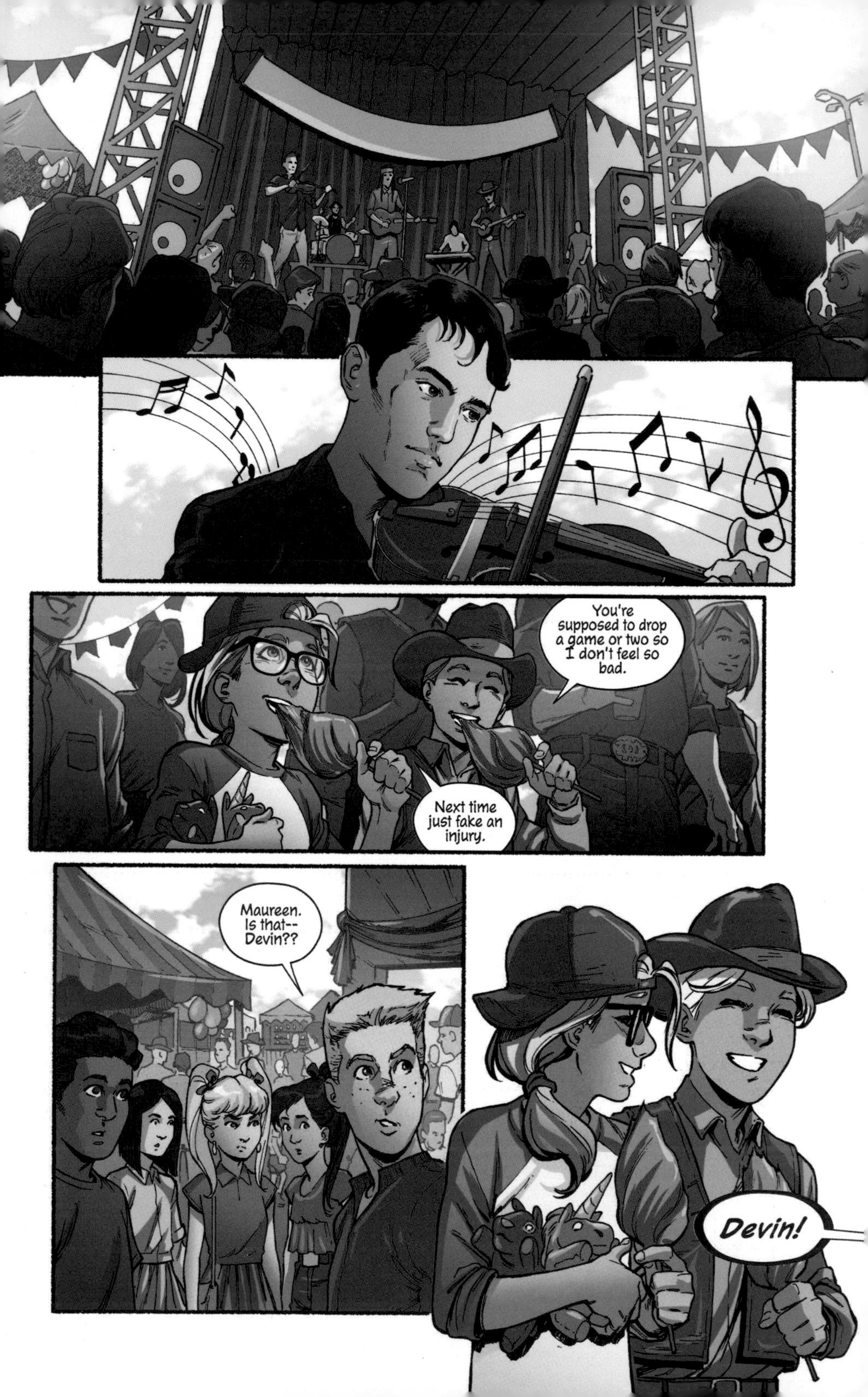

You're supposed to drop a game or two so I don't feel so bad.
Next time just fake an injury.
Maureen. Is that-- Devin??
Devin!

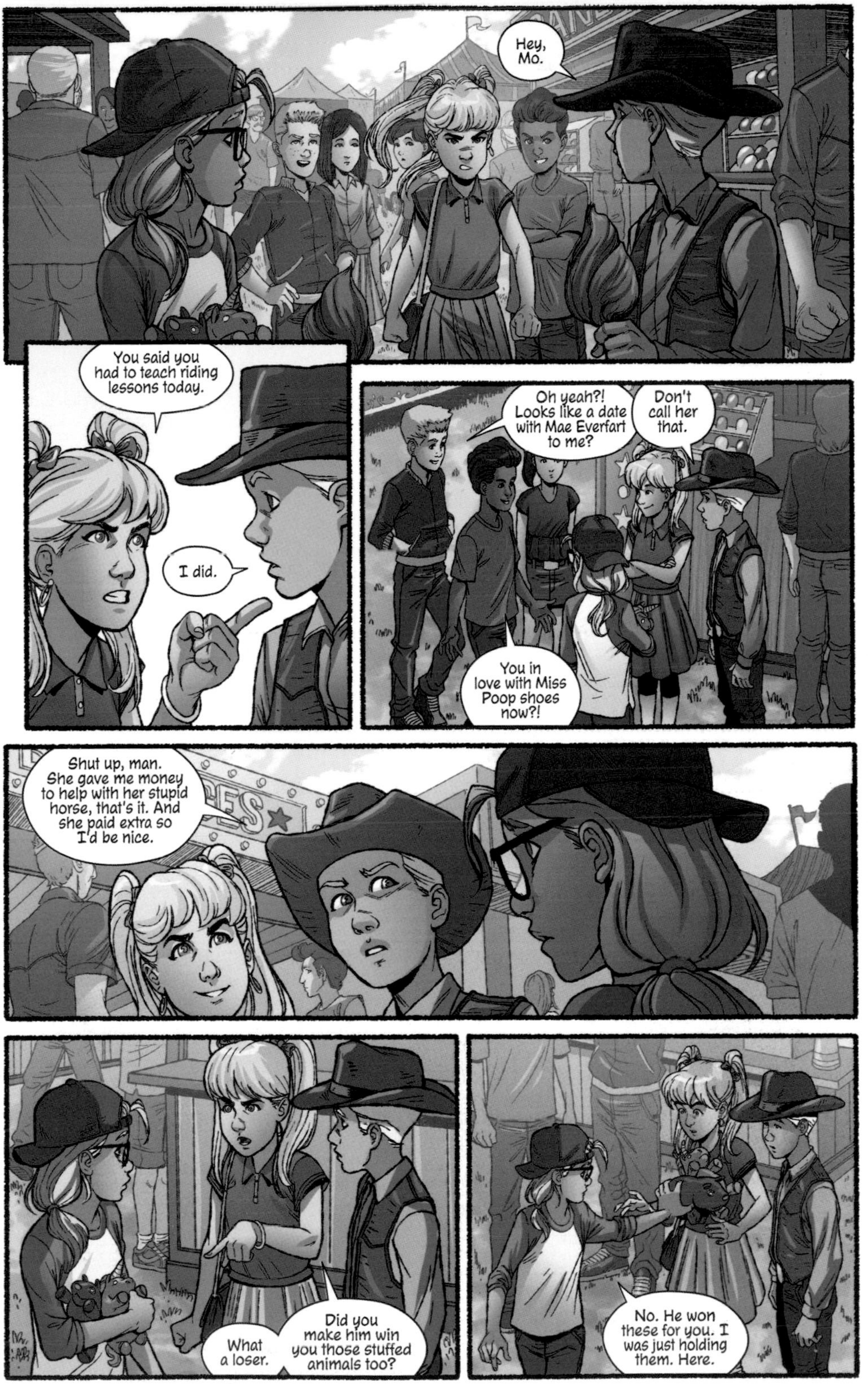
Hey, Mo.
You said you had to teach riding lessons today.
I did.
Oh yeah?! Looks like a date with Mae Everfart to me?
Don't call her that.
You in love with Miss Poop shoes now?!
Shut up, man. She gave me money to help with her stupid horse, that's it. And she paid extra so I'd be nice.
What a loser.
Did you make him win you those stuffed animals too?
No. He won these for you. I was just holding them. Here.

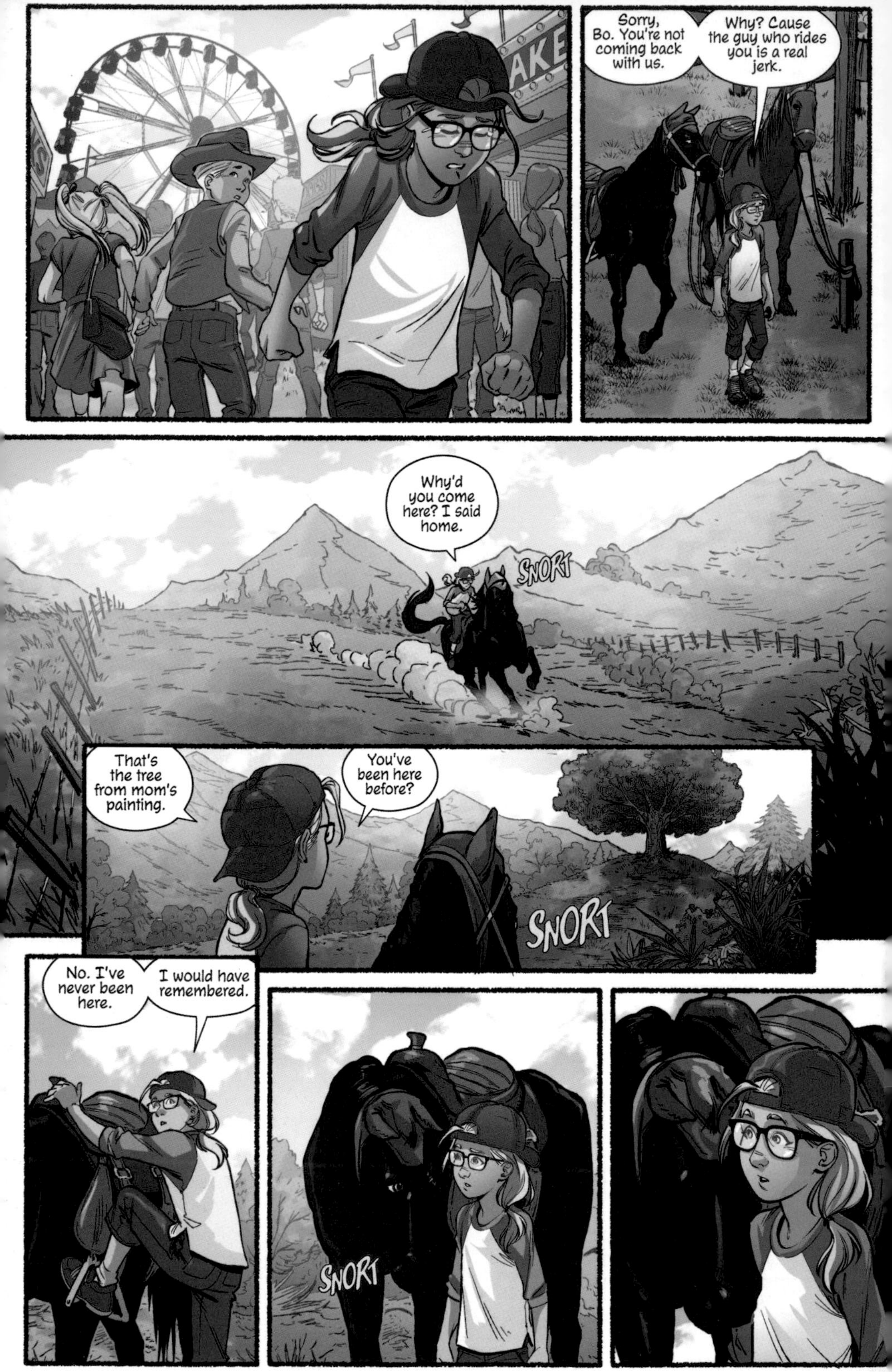
Sorry, Bo. You're not coming back with us.
Why? Cause the guy who rides you is a real jerk.
Why'd you come here? I said home.
SNORT
That's the tree from mom's painting.
You've been here before?
SNORT
No. I've never been here.
I would have remembered.
SNORT

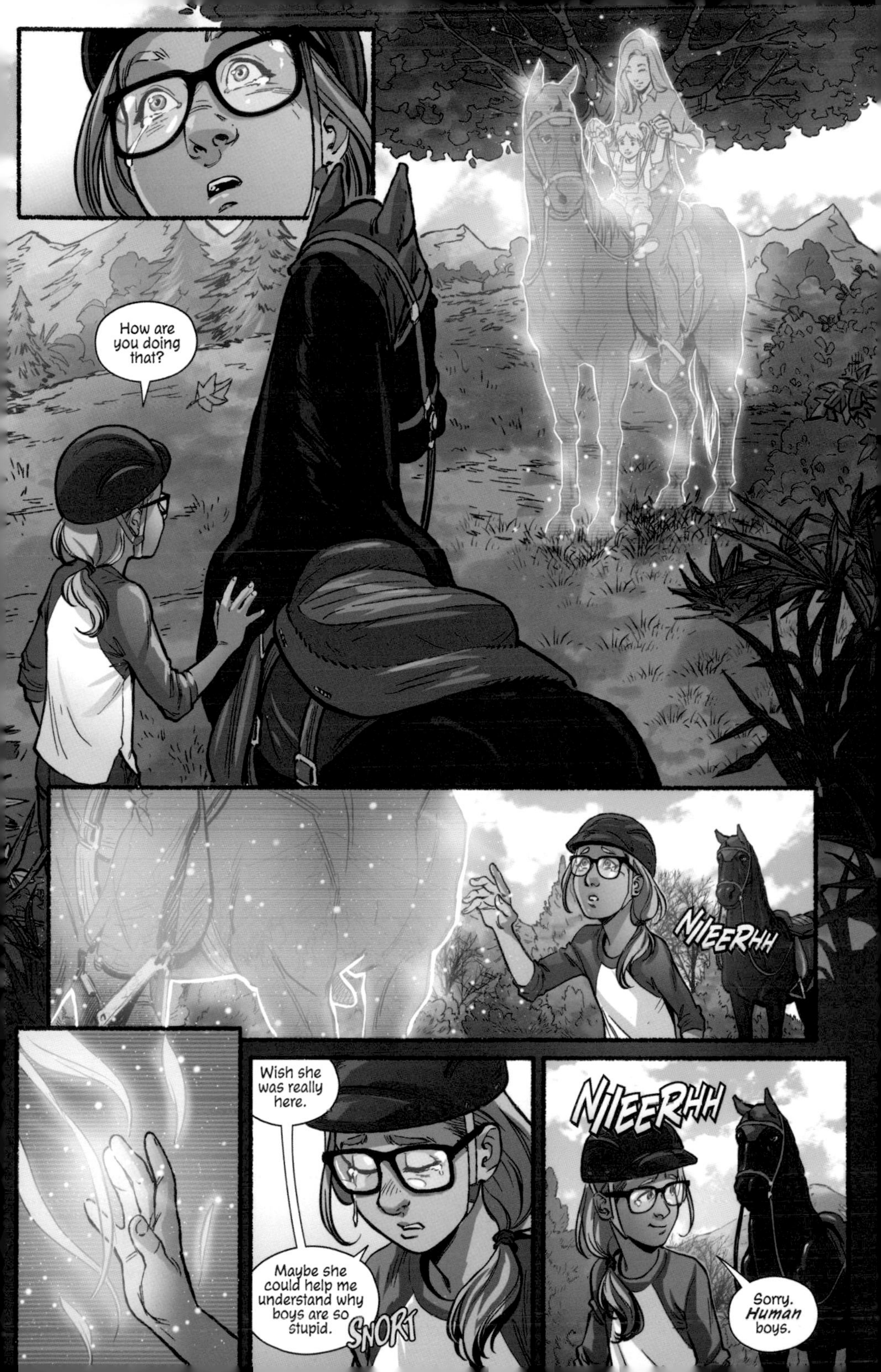
How are you doing that?
NIIEERHH
Wish she was really here.
Maybe she could help me understand why boys are so stupid.
SNORT
NIIEERHH
Sorry. *Human* boys.

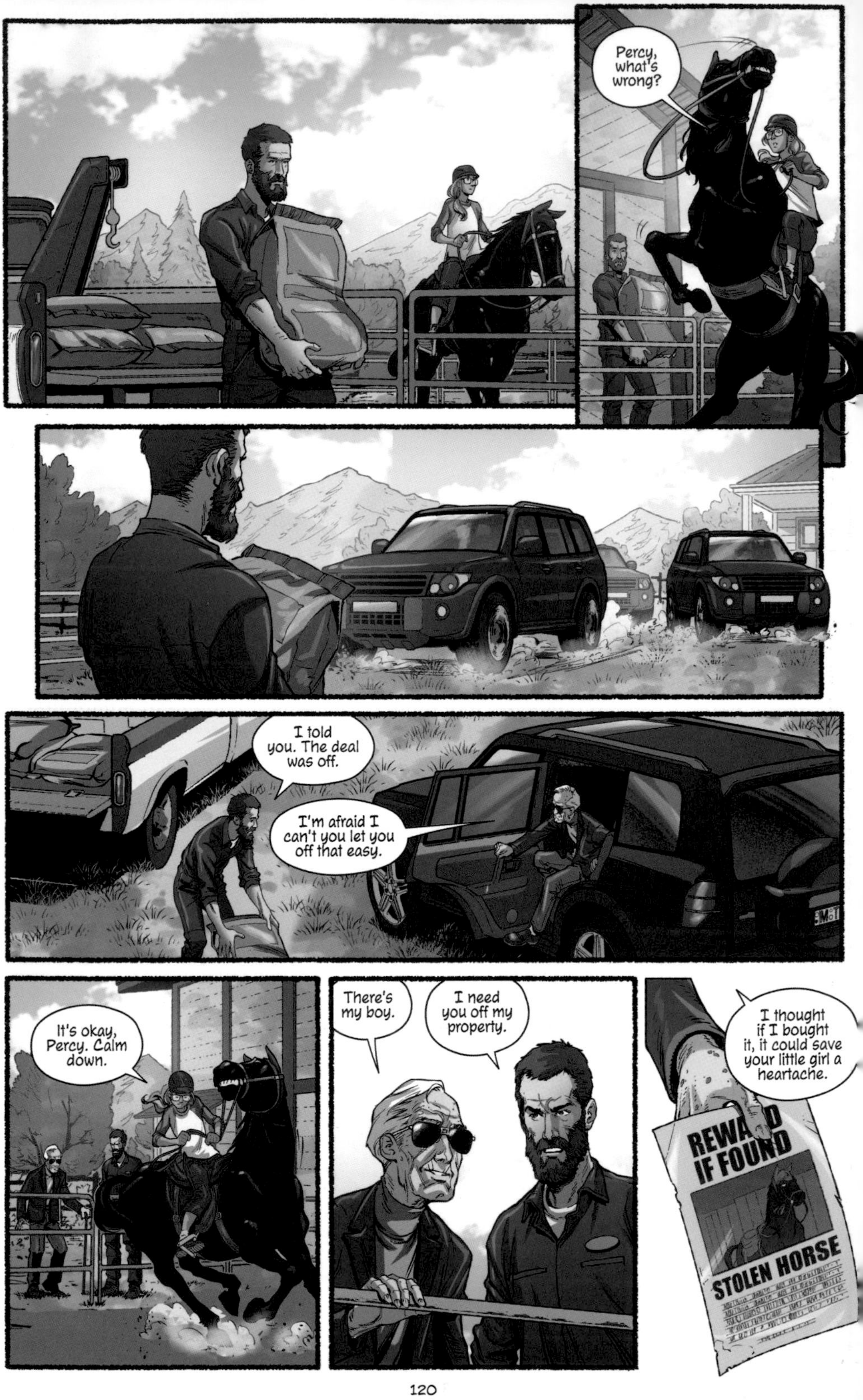
Percy, what's wrong?
I told you. The deal was off.
I'm afraid I can't you let you off that easy.
It's okay, Percy. Calm down.
There's my boy.
I need you off my property.
I thought if I bought it, it could save your little girl a heartache.
REWA D IF FOUND
STOLEN HORSE

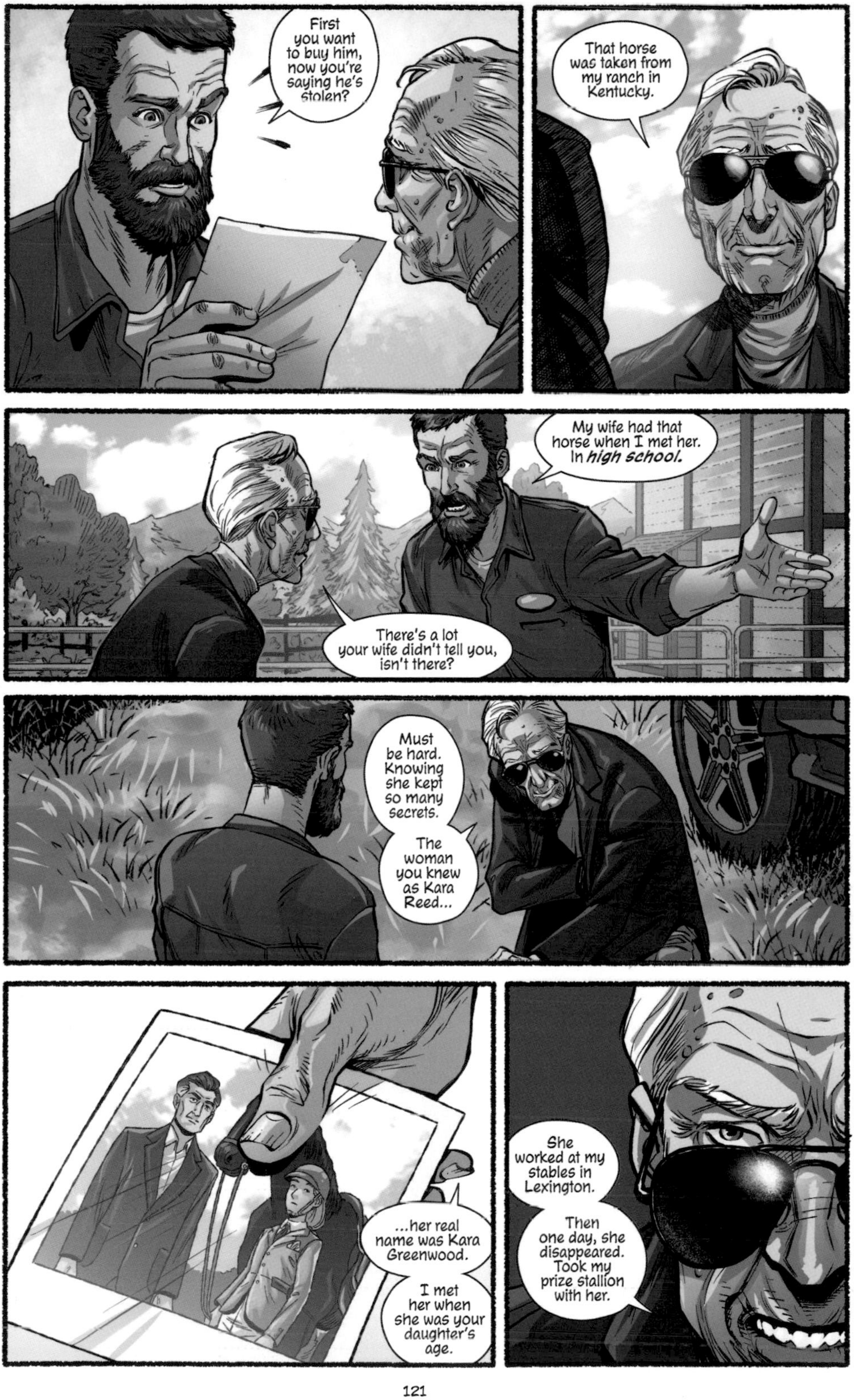
First you want to buy him, now you're saying he's stolen?
That horse was taken from my ranch in Kentucky.
My wife had that horse when I met her. In *high school.*
There's a lot your wife didn't tell you, isn't there?
Must be hard. Knowing she kept so many secrets.
The woman you knew as Kara Reed...
...her real name was Kara Greenwood.
I met her when she was your daughter's age.
She worked at my stables in Lexington.
Then one day, she disappeared. Took my prize stallion with her.

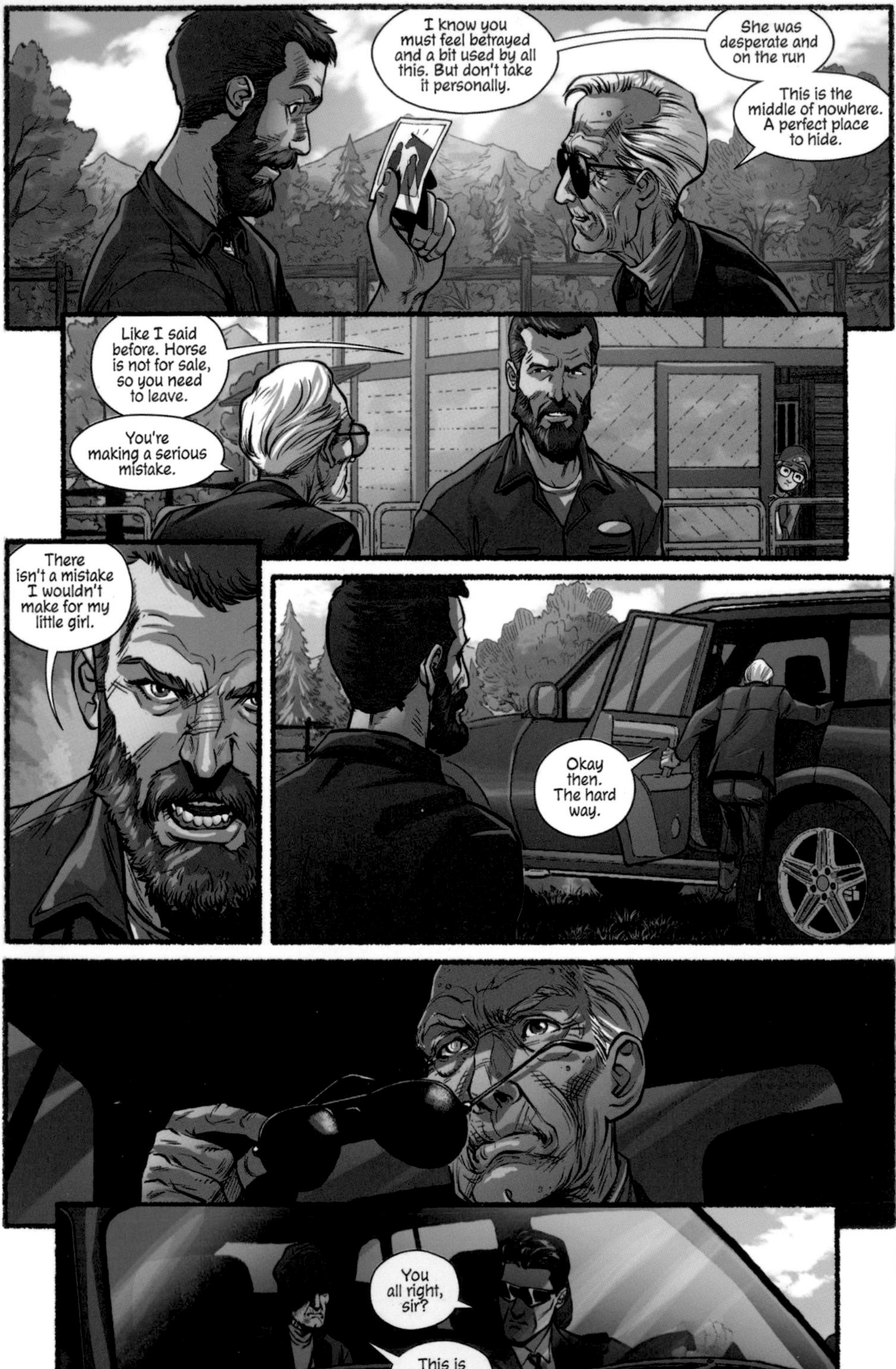
I know you must feel betrayed and a bit used by all this. But don't take it personally.
She was desperate and on the run
This is the middle of nowhere. A perfect place to hide.
Like I said before. Horse is not for sale, so you need to leave.
You're making a serious mistake.
There isn't a mistake I wouldn't make for my little girl.
Okay then. The hard way.
You all right, sir?
This is taking too long.

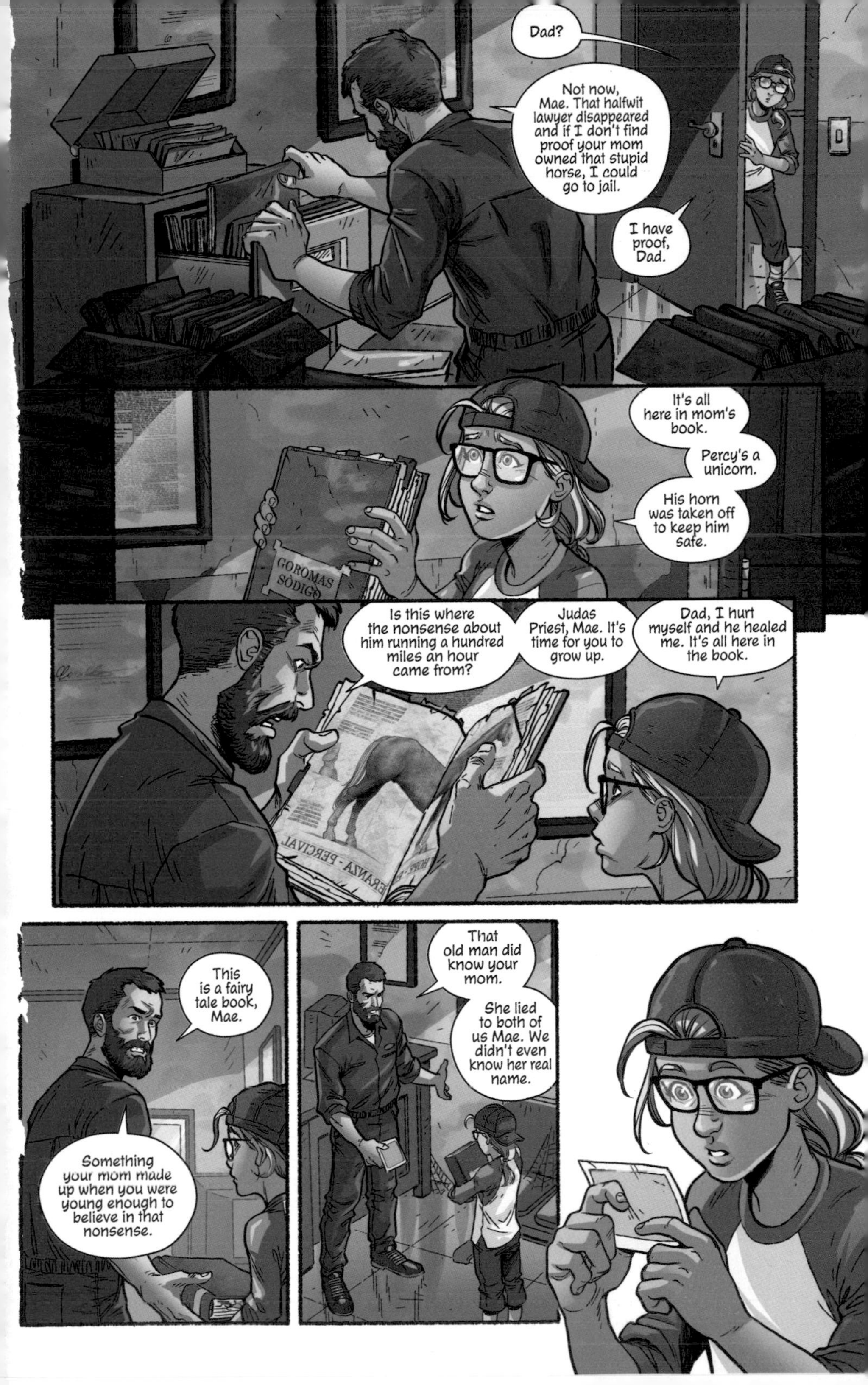

Dad?
Not now, Mae. That halfwit lawyer disappeared and if I don't find proof your mom owned that stupid horse, I could go to jail.
I have proof, Dad.
GOROMAS SÓDIGO
It's all here in mom's book.
Percy's a unicorn.
His horn was taken off to keep him safe.
Is this where the nonsense about him running a hundred miles an hour came from?
Judas Priest, Mae. It's time for you to grow up.
Dad, I hurt myself and he healed me. It's all here in the book.
ERANZA - PERCIVAL
This is a fairy tale book, Mae.
Something your mom made up when you were young enough to believe in that nonsense.
That old man did know your mom.
She lied to both of us Mae. We didn't even know her real name.

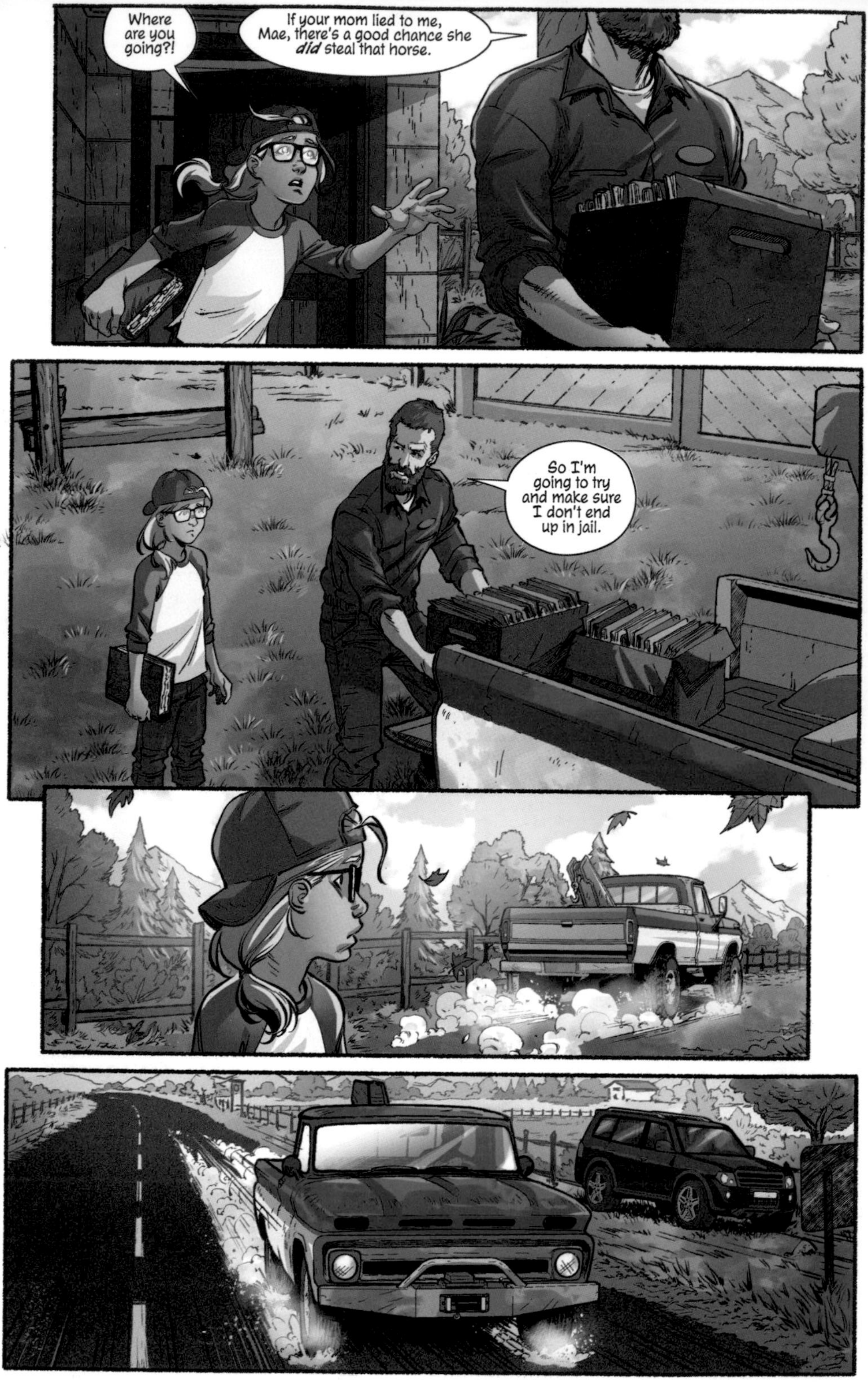
Where are you going?!
If your mom lied to me, Mae, there's a good chance she *did* steal that horse.
So I'm going to try and make sure I don't end up in jail.

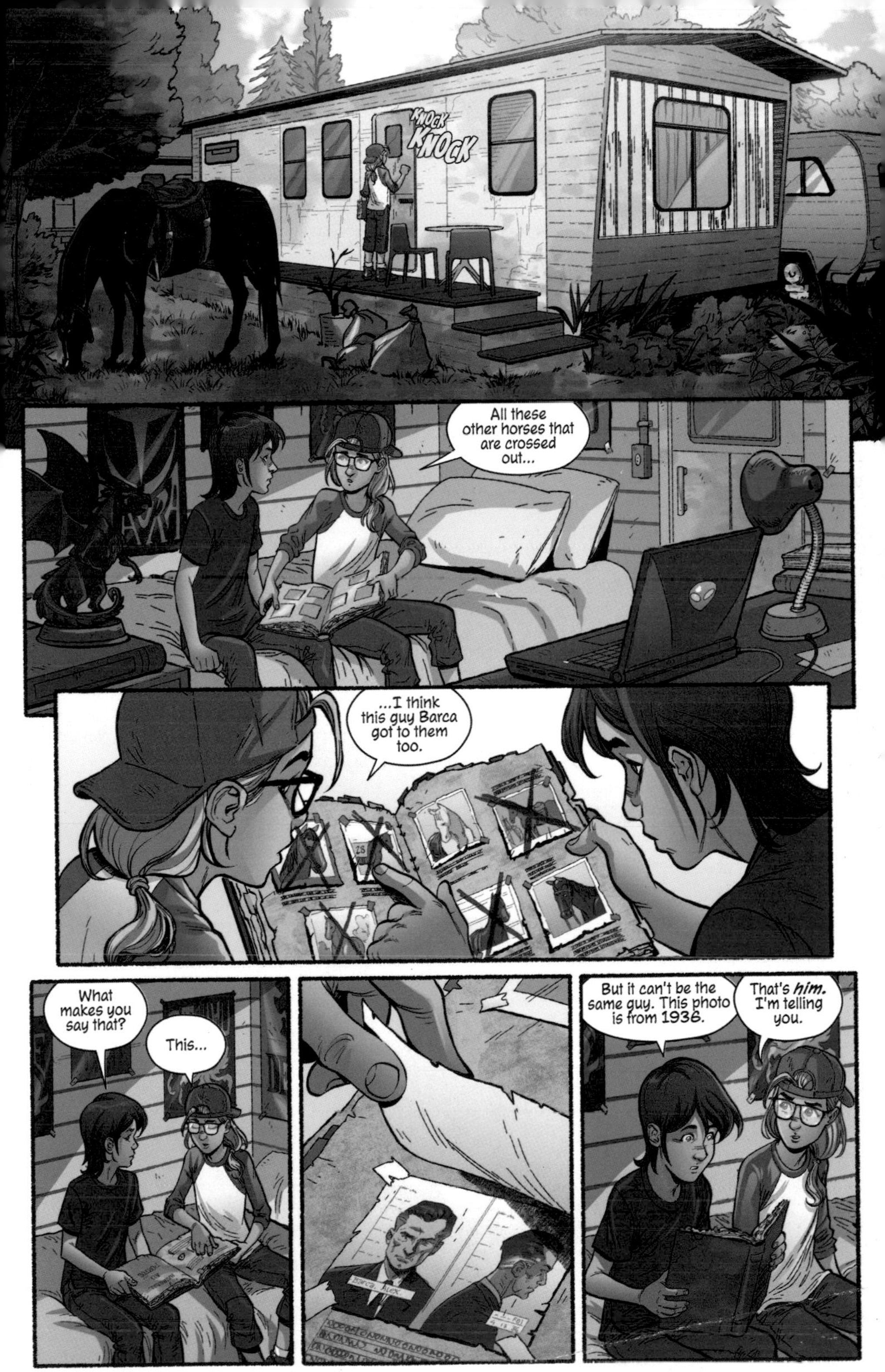
KNOCK KNOCK
All these other horses that are crossed out...
...I think this guy Barca got to them too.
What makes you say that?
This...
Barca, Alex
But it can't be the same guy. This photo is from 1936.
That's *him.* I'm telling you.

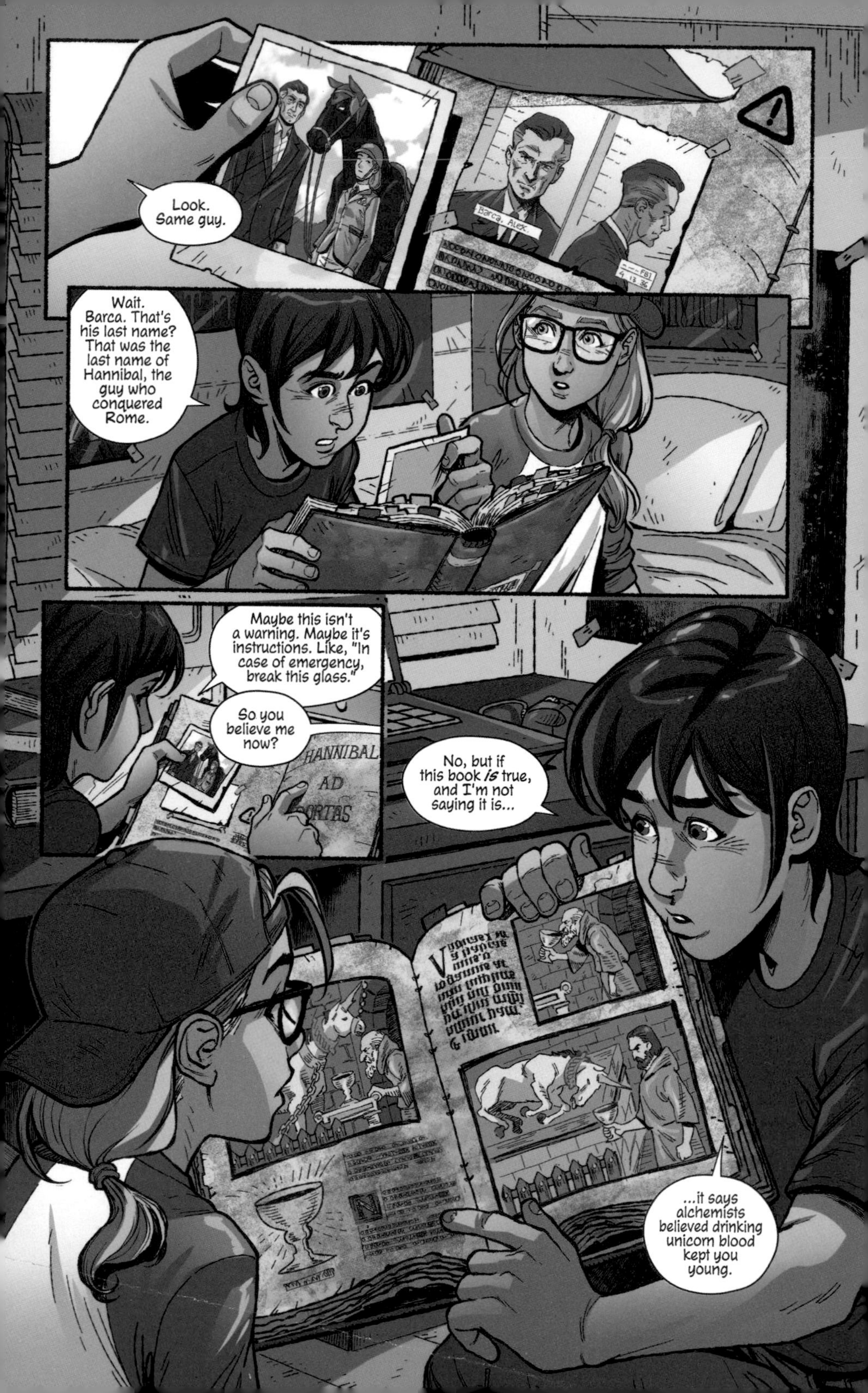
Look. Same guy.
Barca, Alex.
FBI 4 13 36
Wait. Barca. That's his last name? That was the last name of Hannibal, the guy who conquered Rome.
Maybe this isn't a warning. Maybe it's instructions. Like, "In case of emergency, break this glass."
So you believe me now?
HANNIBAL AD PORTAS
No, but if this book *is* true, and I'm not saying it is...
...it says alchemists believed drinking unicorn blood kept you young.

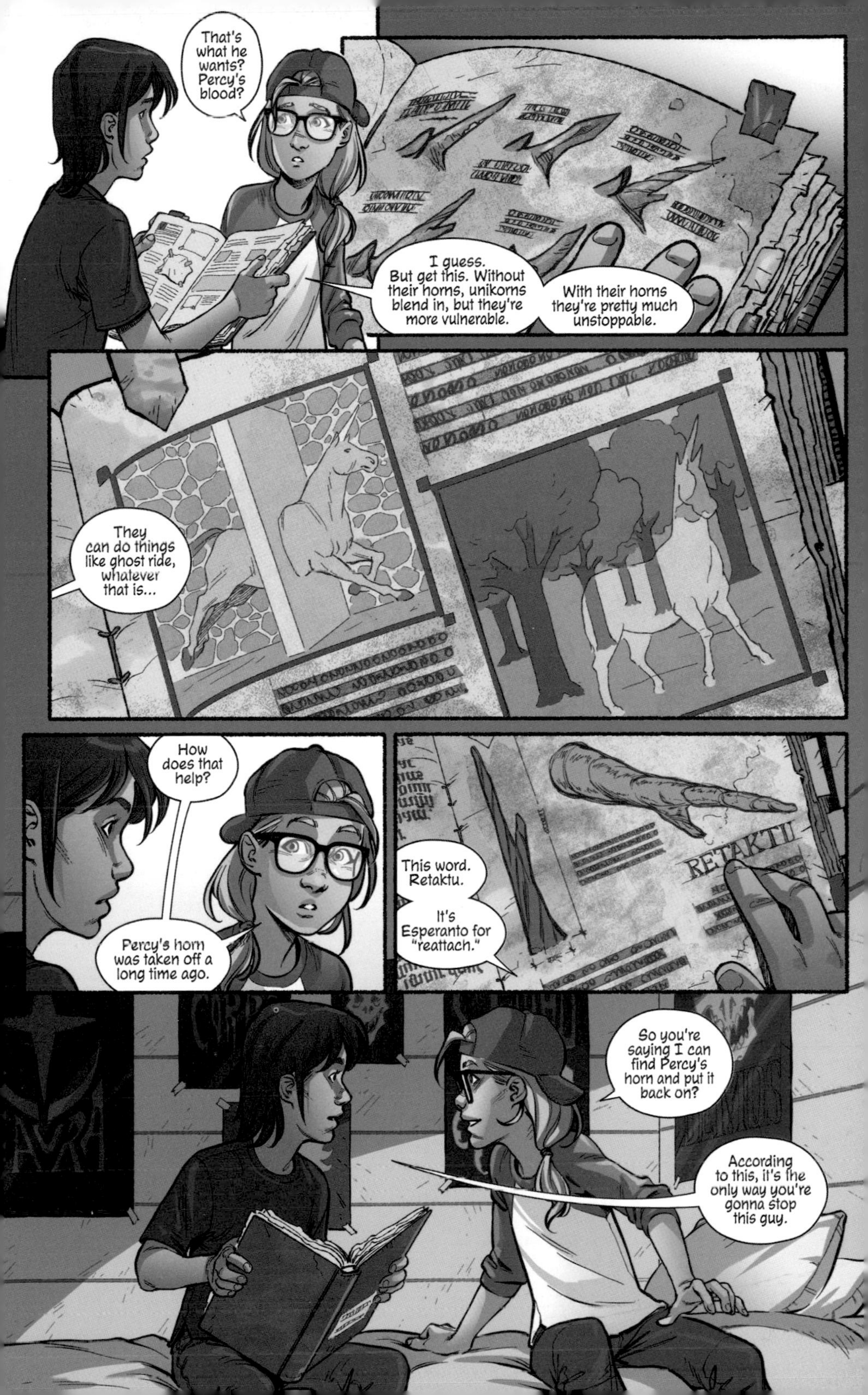
That's what he wants? Percy's blood?
I guess. But get this. Without their horns, unikorns blend in, but they're more vulnerable.
With their horns they're pretty much unstoppable.
They can do things like ghost ride, whatever that is...
How does that help?
Percy's horn was taken off a long time ago.
This word. Retaktu.
It's Esperanto for "reattach."
RETAKTU
So you're saying I can find Percy's horn and put it back on?
According to this, it's the only way you're gonna stop this guy.

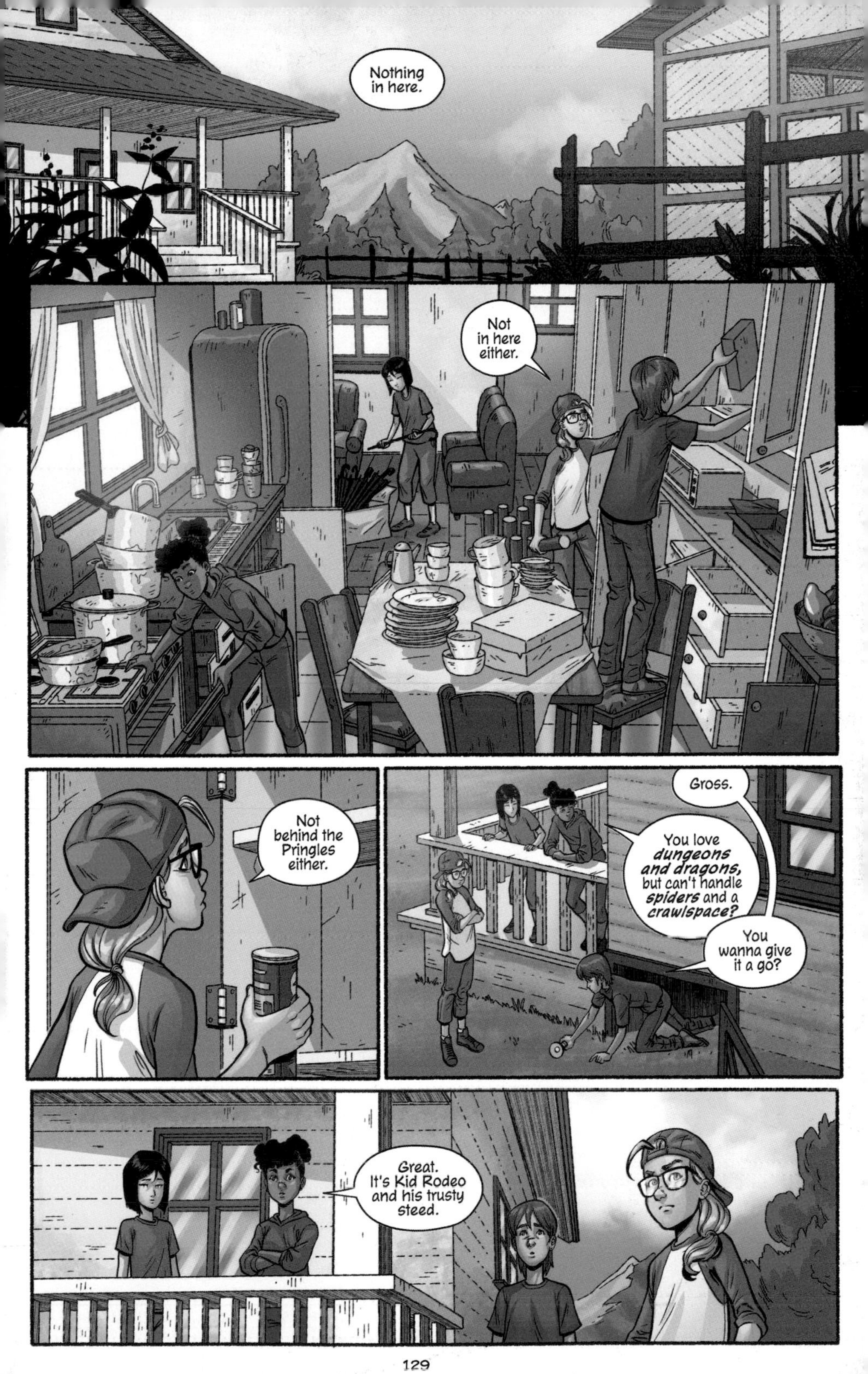
Nothing in here.
Not in here either.
Not behind the Pringles either.
Gross.
You love *dungeons and dragons,* but can't handle *spiders* and a *crawlspace?*
You wanna give it a go?
Great. It's Kid Rodeo and his trusty steed.

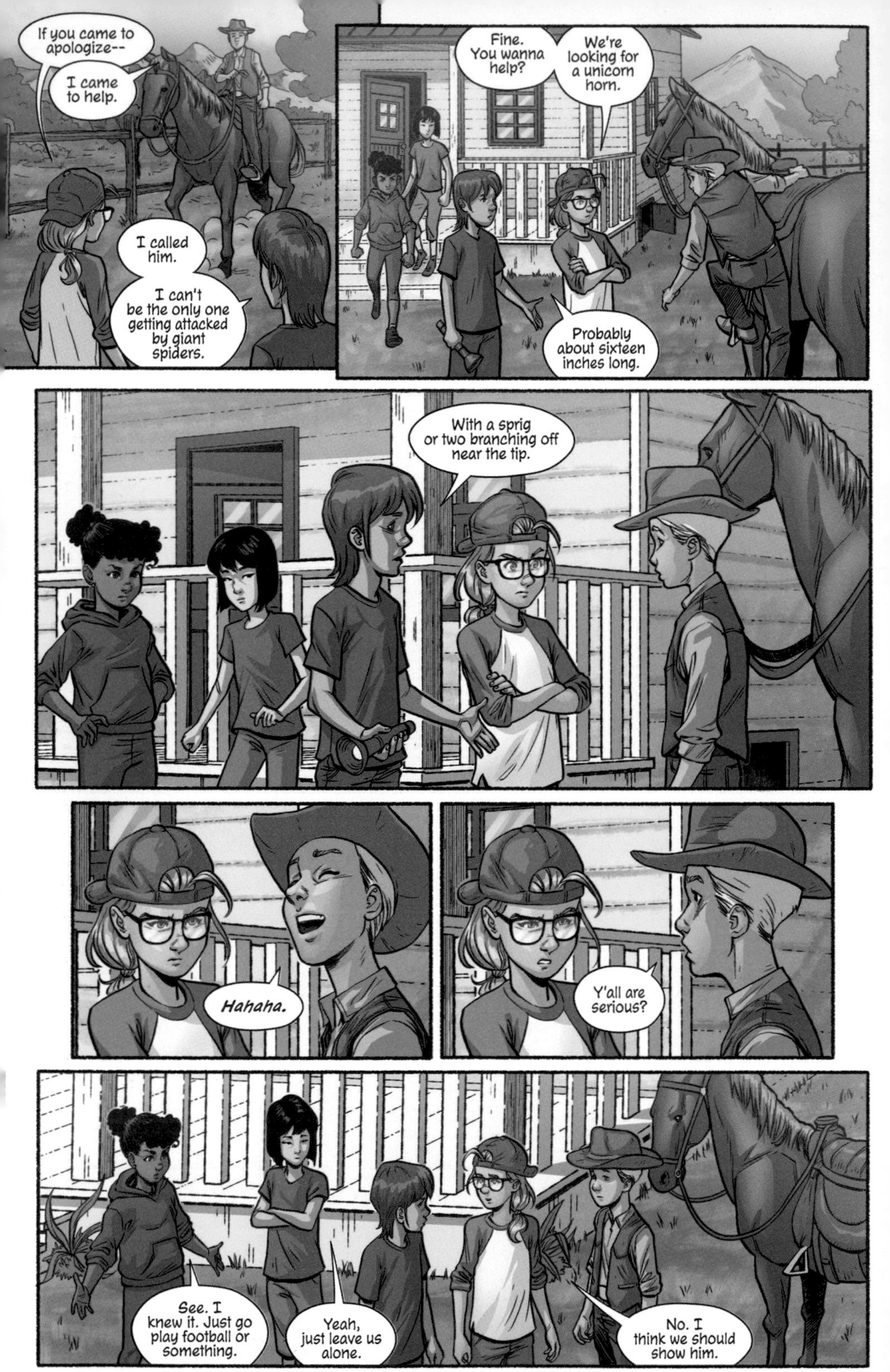
If you came to apologize--
I came to help.
I called him.
I can't be the only one getting attacked by giant spiders.
Fine. You wanna help?
We're looking for a unicorn horn.
Probably about sixteen inches long.
With a sprig or two branching off near the tip.
Hahaha.
Y'all are serious?
See. I knew it. Just go play football or something.
Yeah, just leave us alone.
No. I think we should show him.

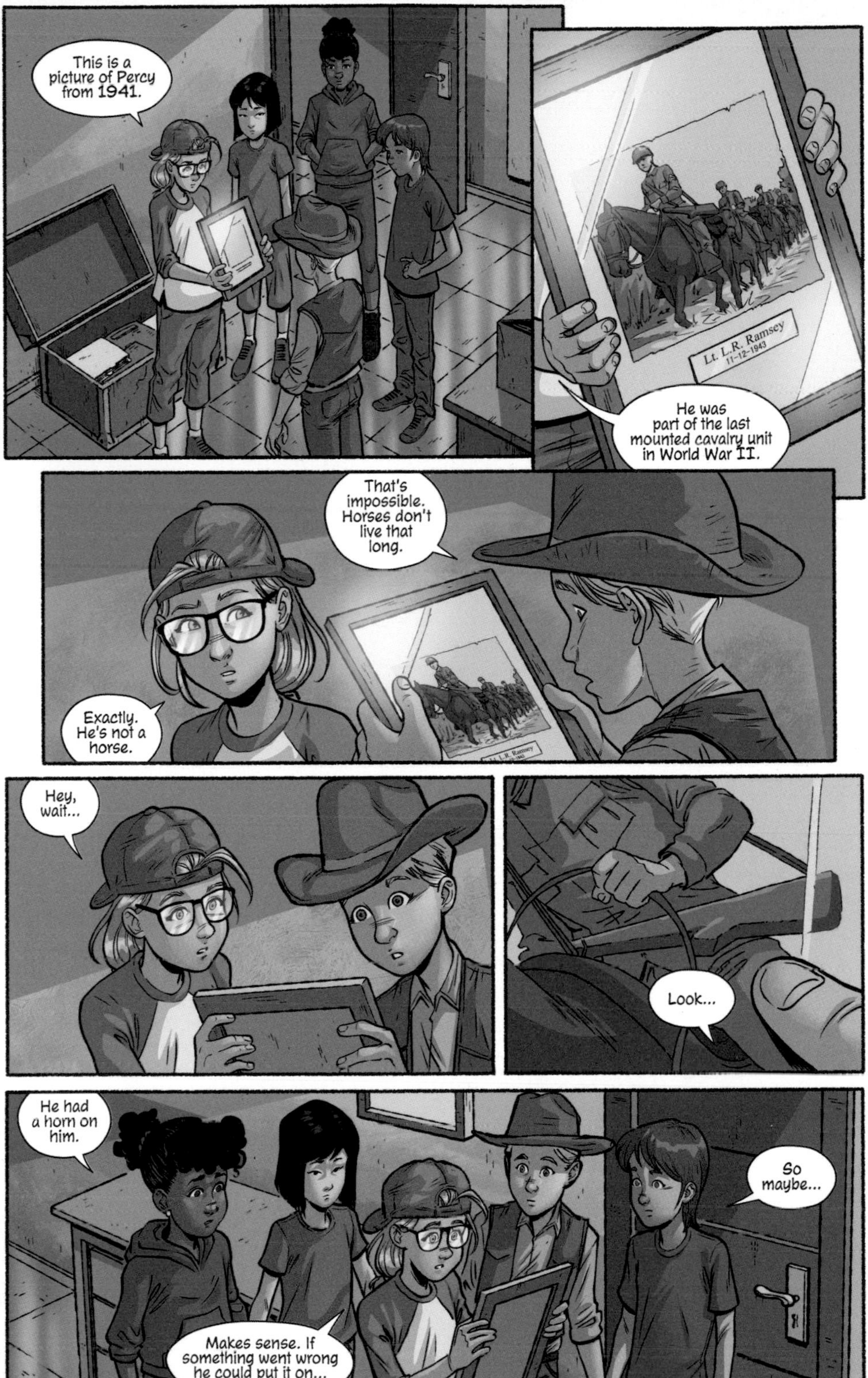
This is a picture of Percy from 1941.
Lt. L.R. Ramsey 11-12-1943
He was part of the last mounted cavalry unit in World War II.
That's impossible. Horses don't live that long.
Exactly. He's not a horse.
Hey, wait...
Look...
He had a horn on him.
So maybe...
Makes sense. If something went wrong he could put it on...

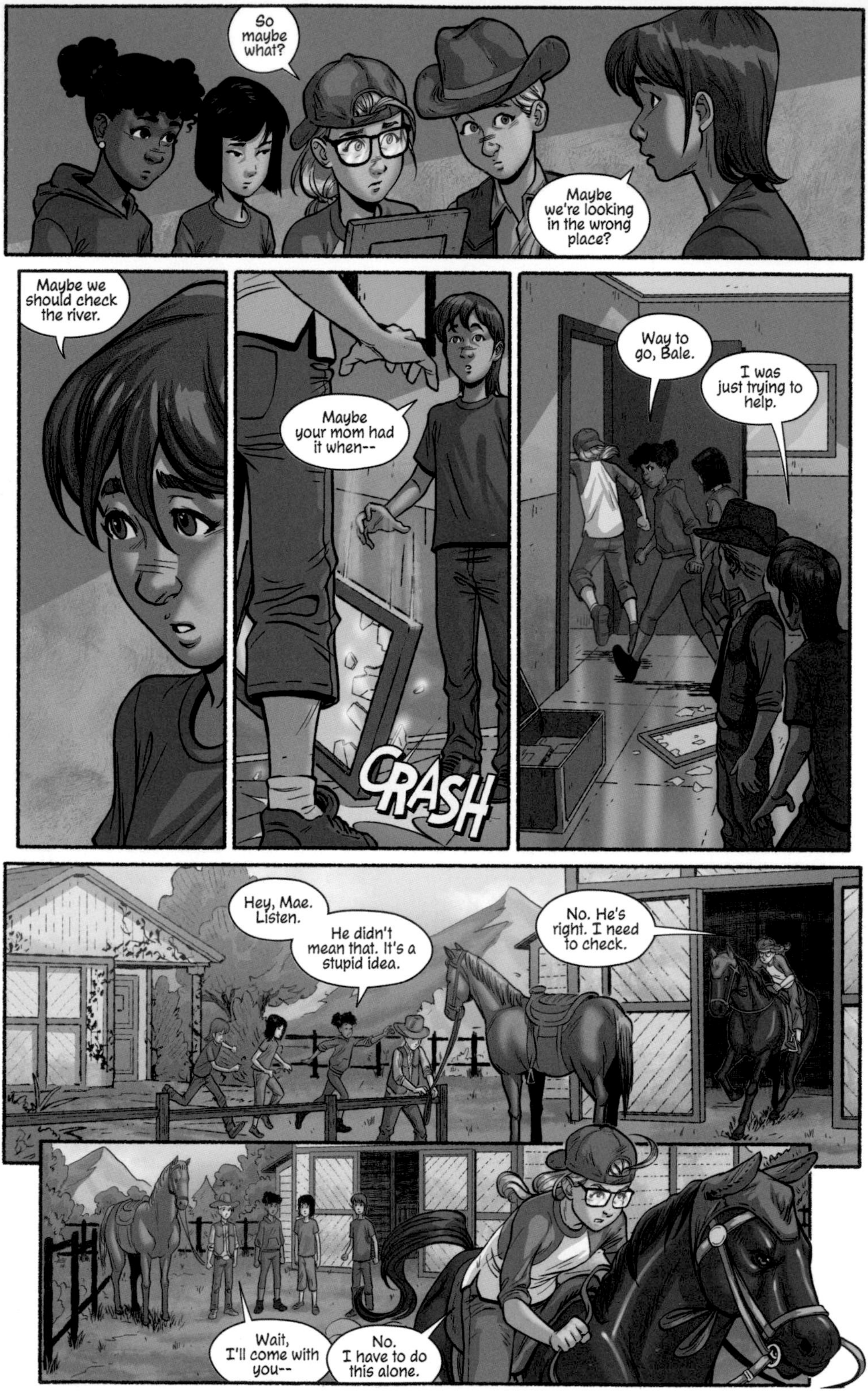
So maybe what?
Maybe we're looking in the wrong place?
Maybe we should check the river.
Maybe your mom had it when--
CRASH
Way to go, Bale.
I was just trying to help.
Hey, Mae. Listen.
He didn't mean that. It's a stupid idea.
No. He's right. I need to check.
Wait, I'll come with you--
No. I have to do this alone.

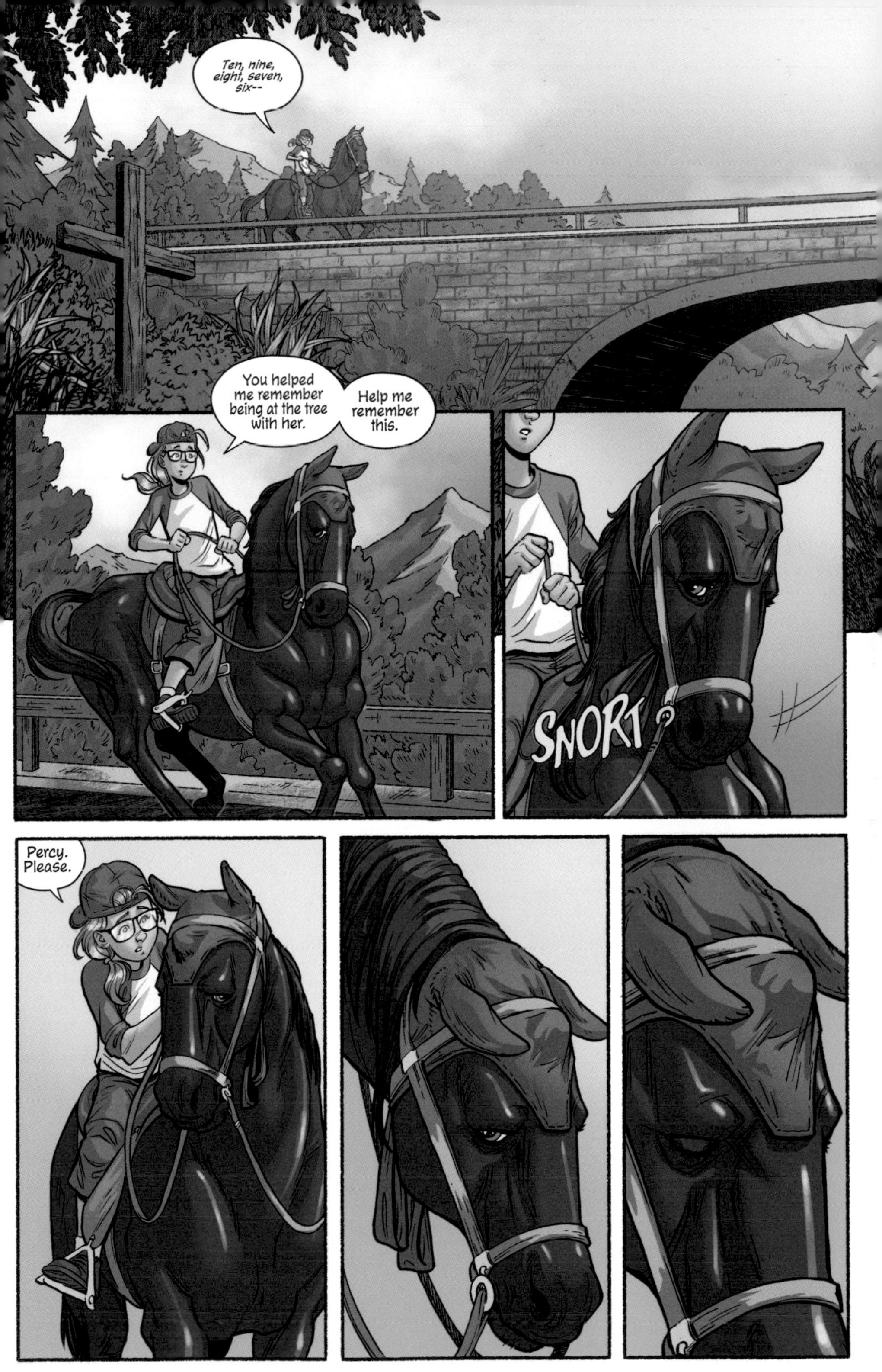
Ten, nine, eight, seven, six--
You helped me remember being at the tree with her.
Help me remember this.
SNORT
Percy. Please.

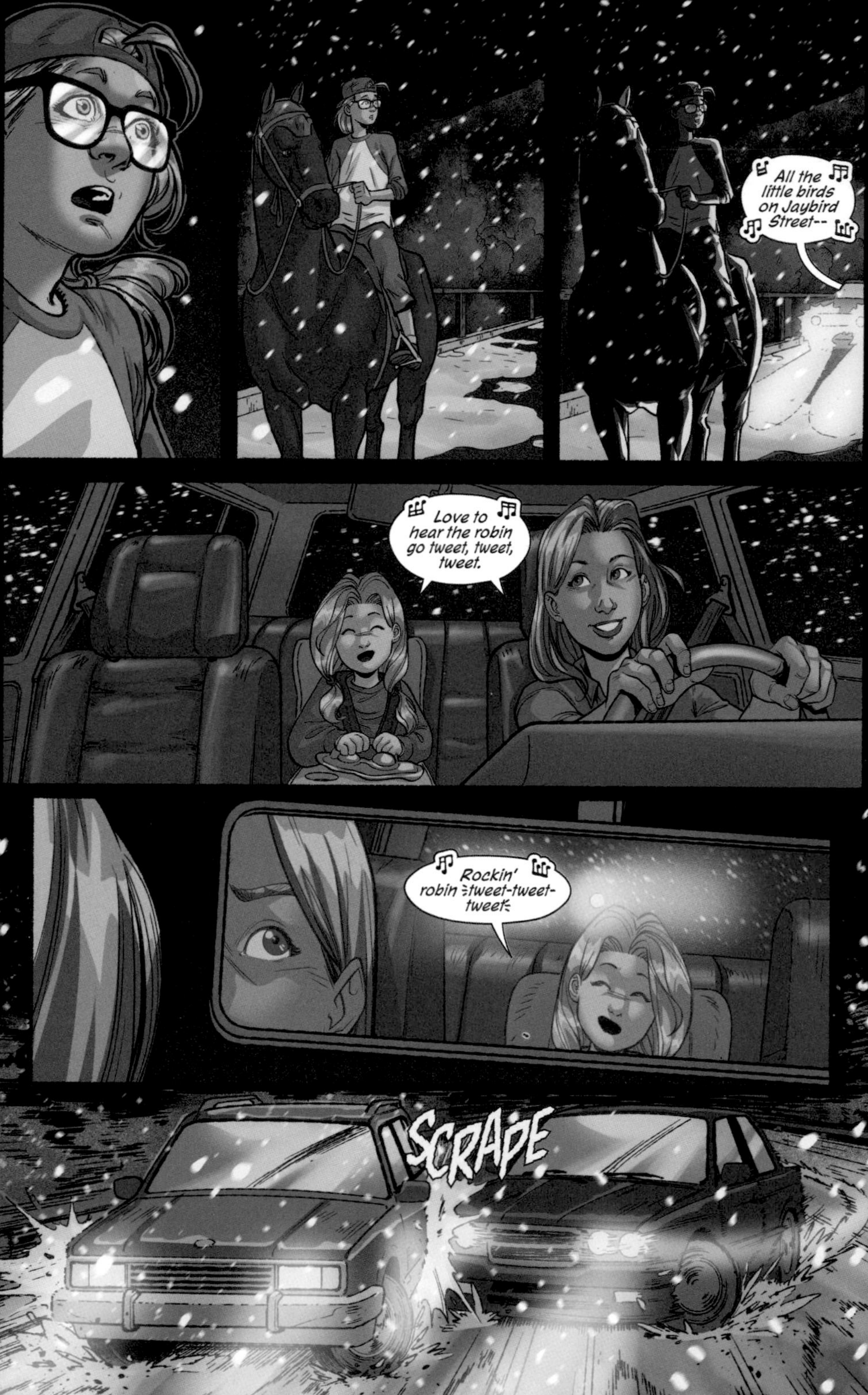
All the little birds on Jaybird Street--
Love to hear the robin go tweet, tweet, tweet.
Rockin' robin tweet-tweet-tweet
SCRAPE

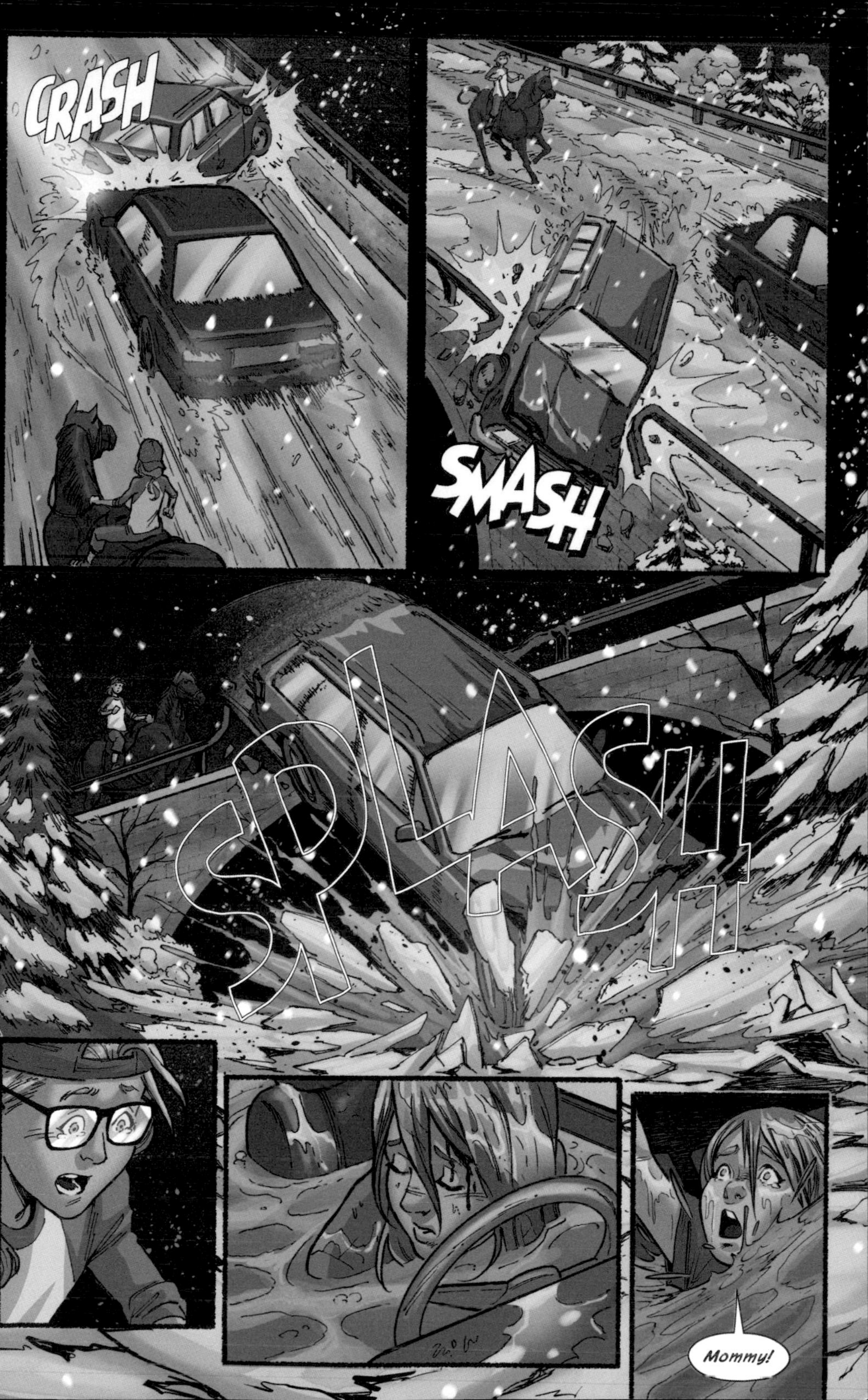
CRASH
SMASH
SPLASH
Mommy!

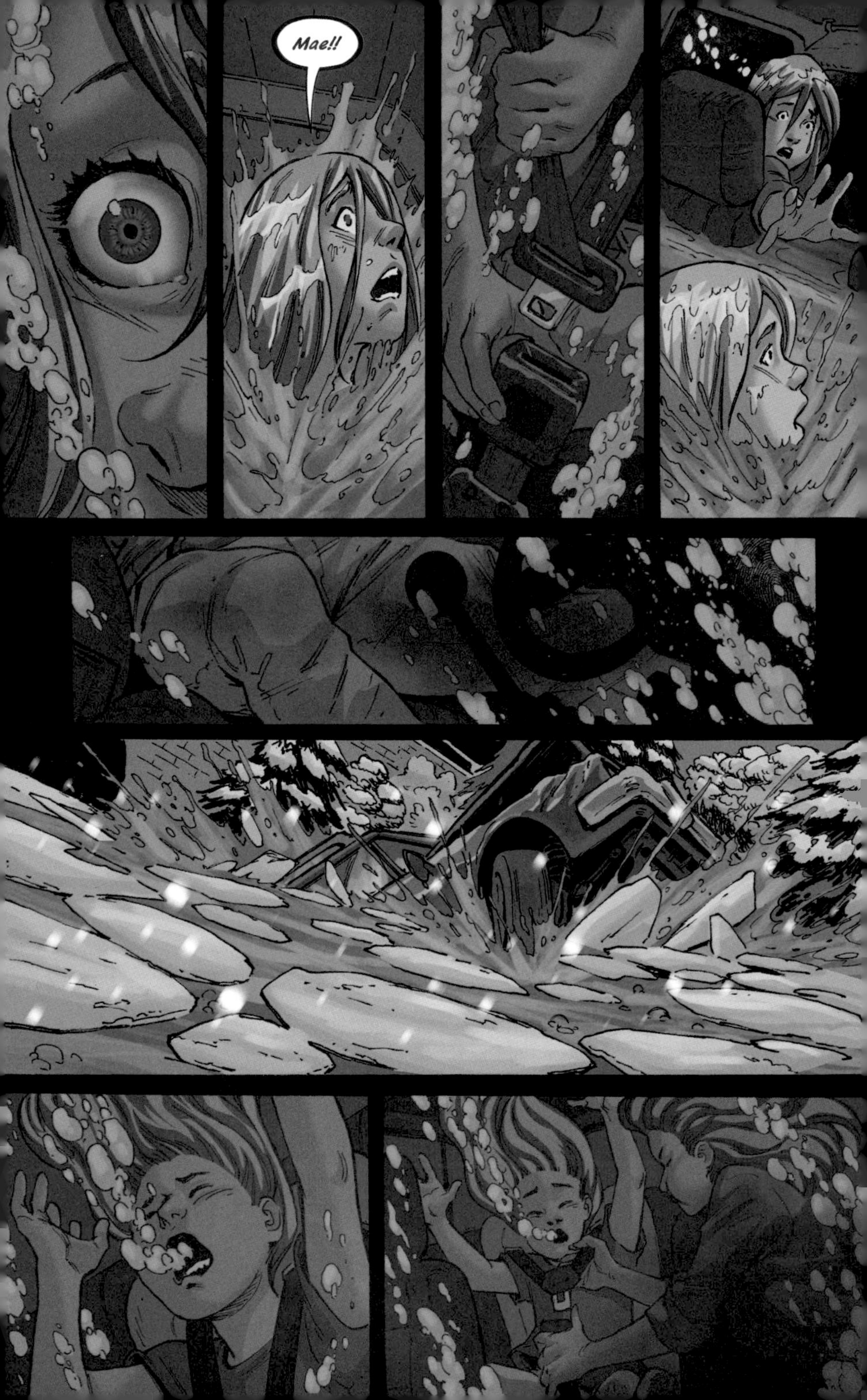
Mae!!

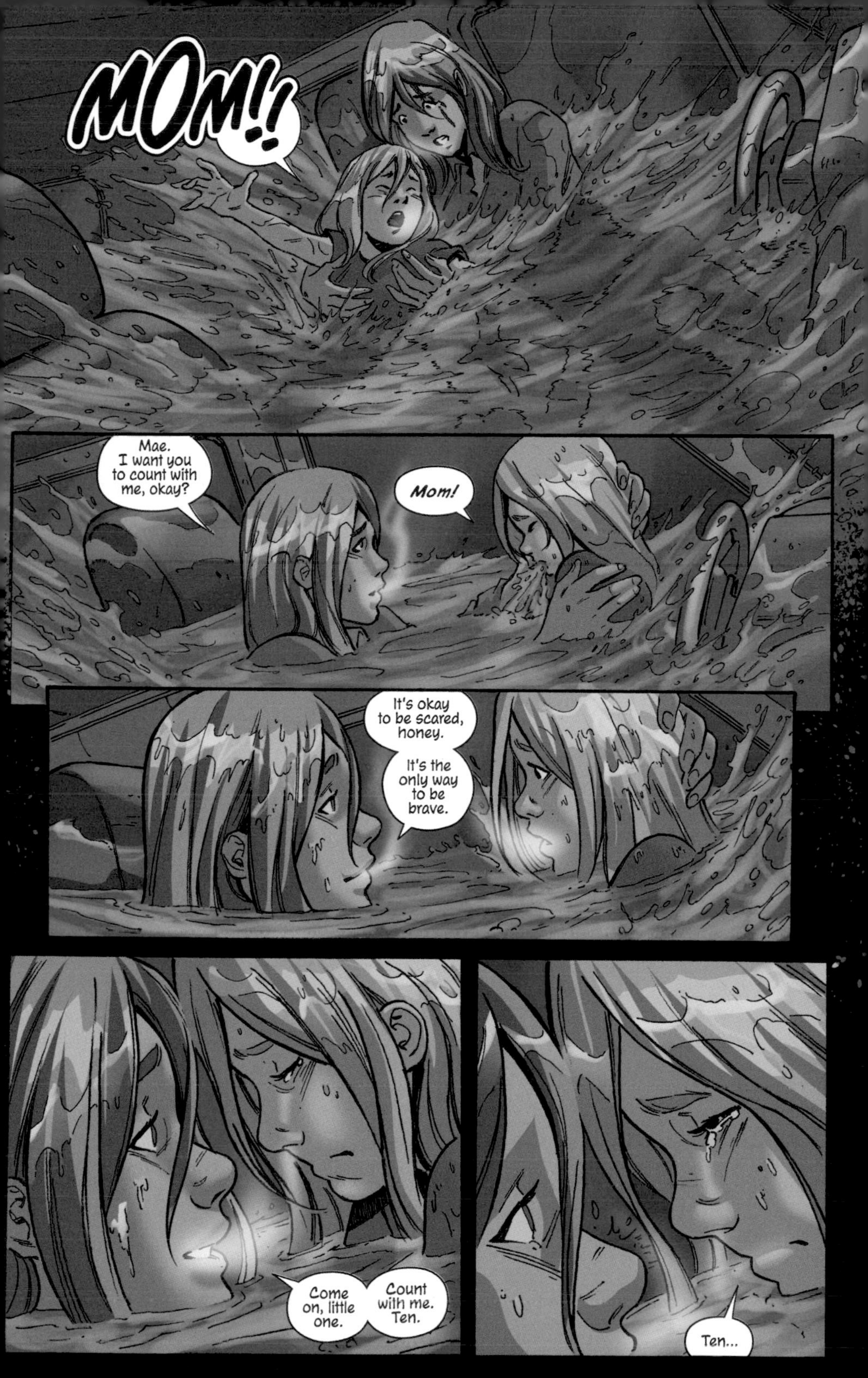
MOM!!
Mae. I want you to count with me, okay?
Mom!
It's okay to be scared, honey.
It's the only way to be brave.
Come on, little one.
Count with me. Ten.
Ten...

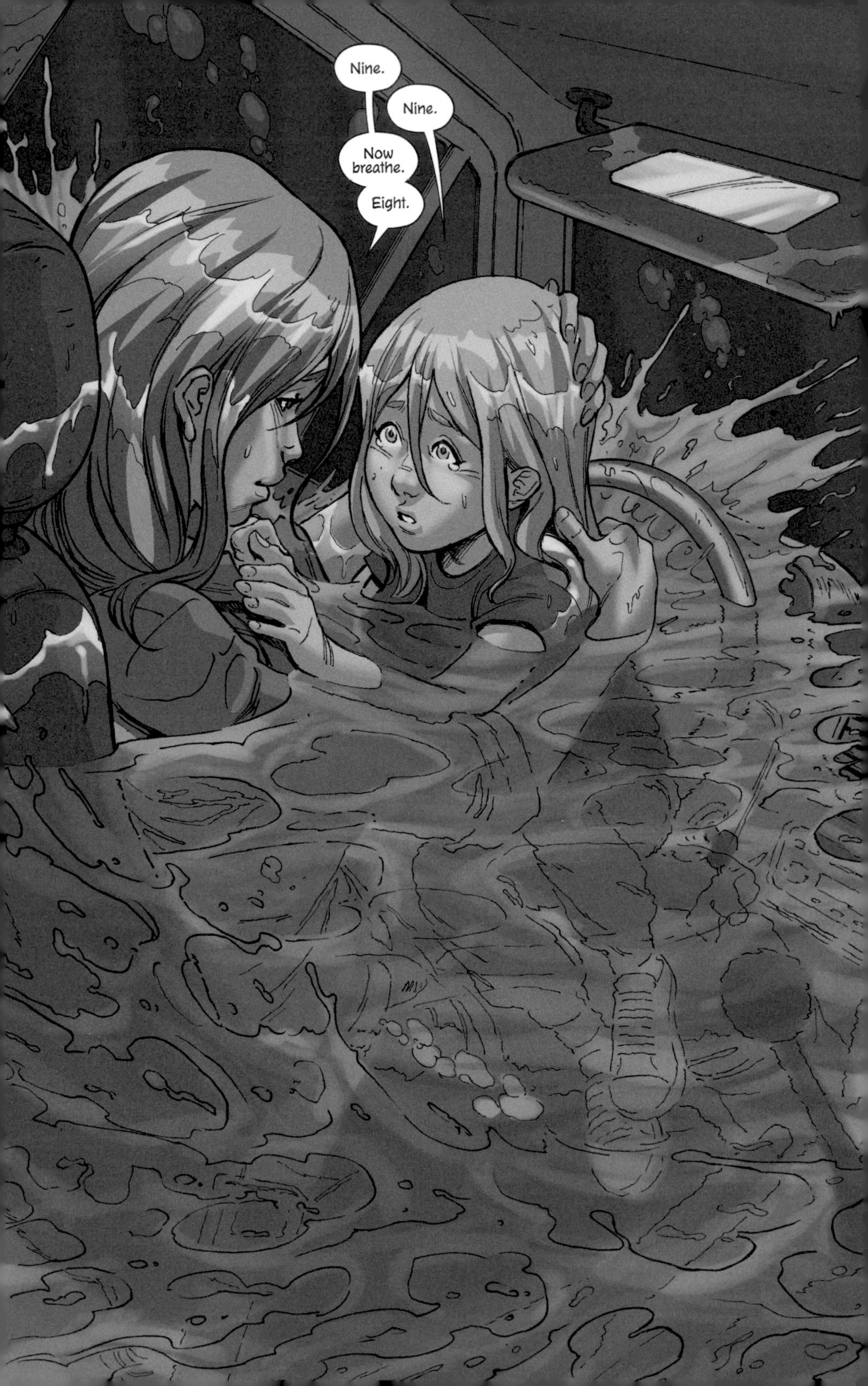
Nine.
Nine.
Now breathe.
Eight.

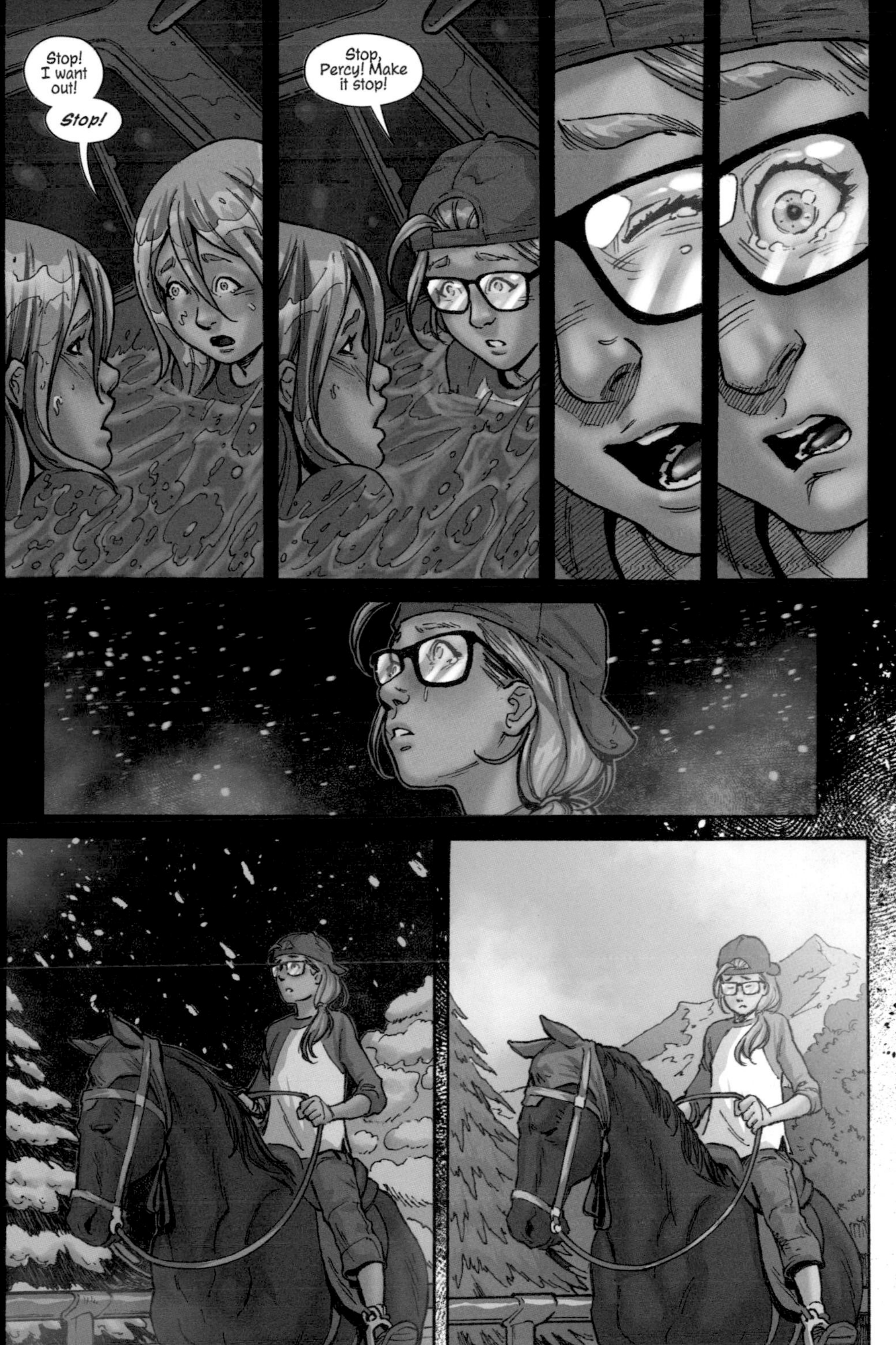
Stop! I want out!
Stop!
Stop, Percy! Make it stop!

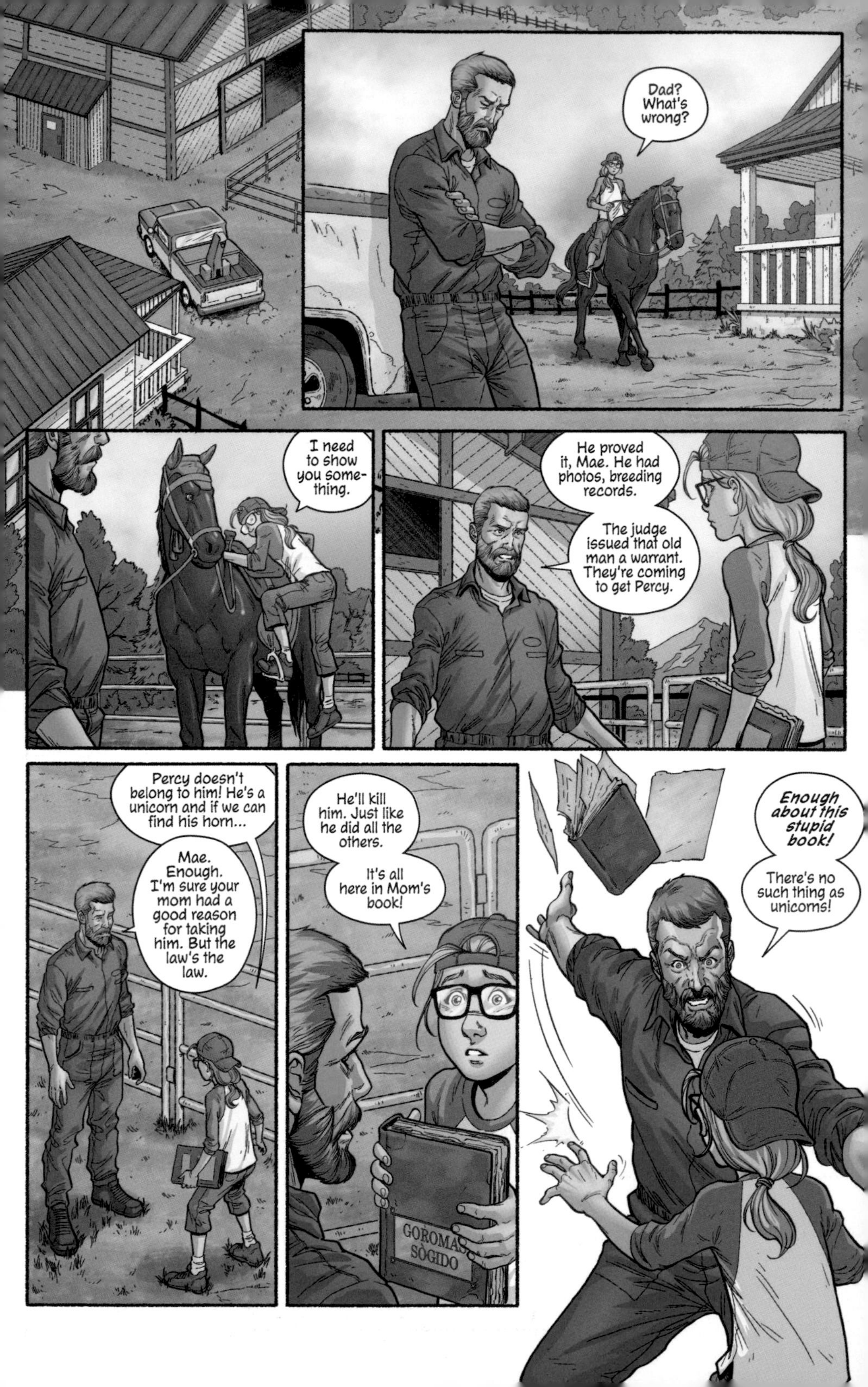
Dad? What's wrong?
I need to show you some-thing.
He proved it, Mae. He had photos, breeding records.
The judge issued that old man a warrant. They're coming to get Percy.
Percy doesn't belong to him! He's a unicorn and if we can find his horn...
Mae. Enough. I'm sure your mom had a good reason for taking him. But the law's the law.
He'll kill him. Just like he did all the others.
It's all here in Mom's book!
GOROMAS SÒGIDO
Enough about this stupid book!
There's no such thing as unicorns!

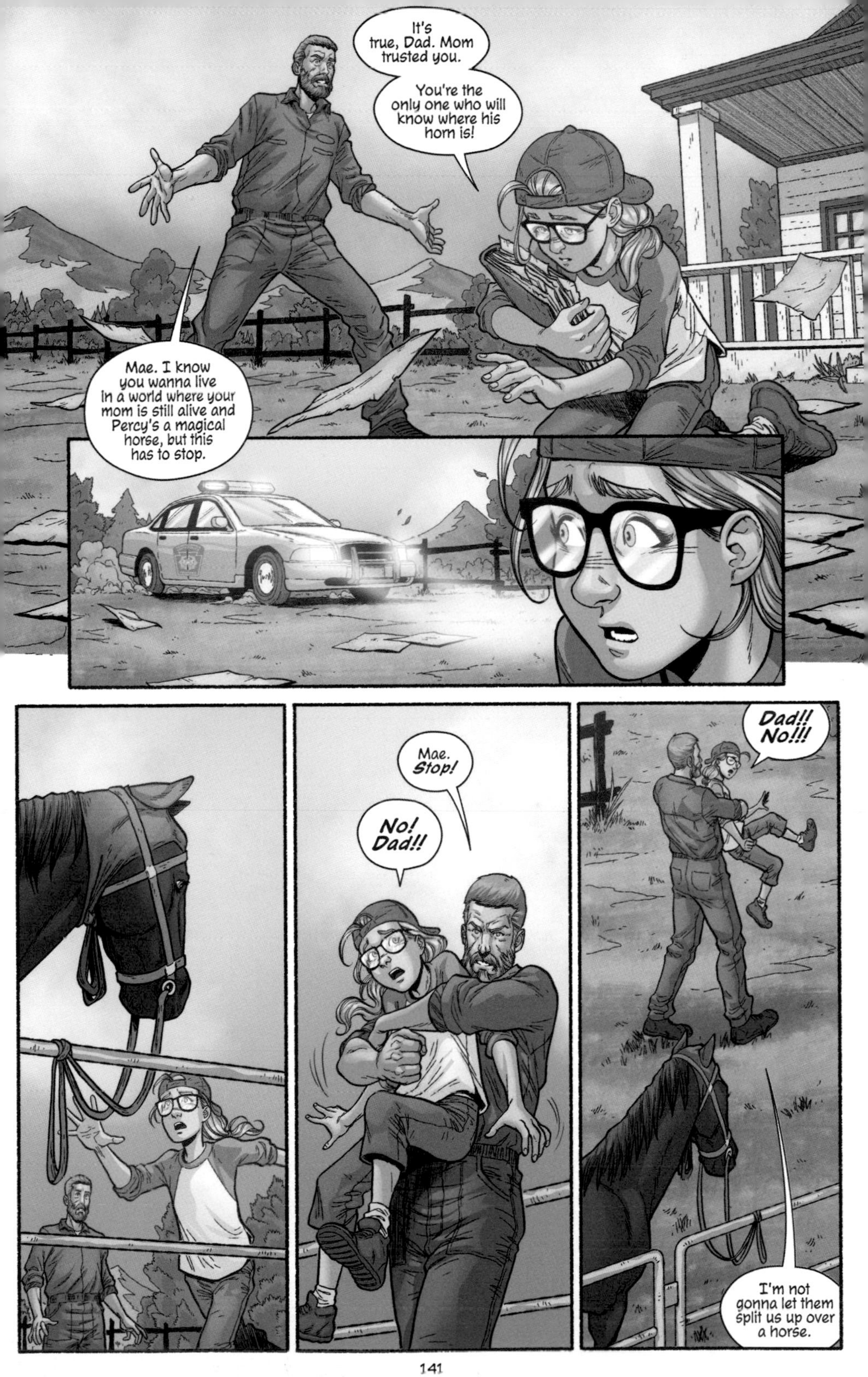
It's true, Dad. Mom trusted you.
You're the only one who will know where his horn is!
Mae. I know you wanna live in a world where your mom is still alive and Percy's a magical horse, but this has to stop.
No! Dad!!
Mae. Stop!
Dad!! No!!!
I'm not gonna let them split us up over a horse.

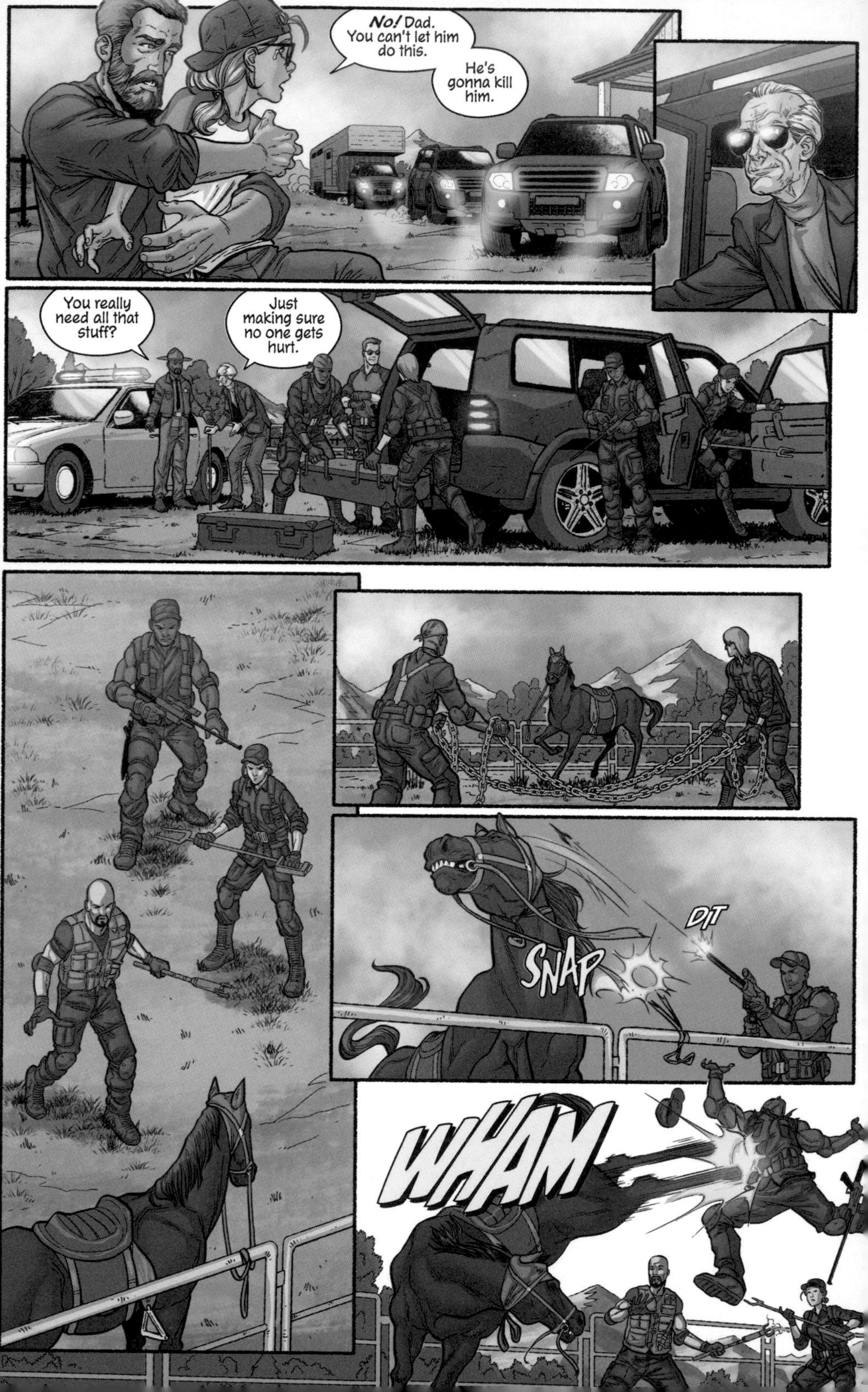
No! Dad. You can't let him do this.
He's gonna kill him.
You really need all that stuff?
Just making sure no one gets hurt.
DIT
SNAP
WHAM

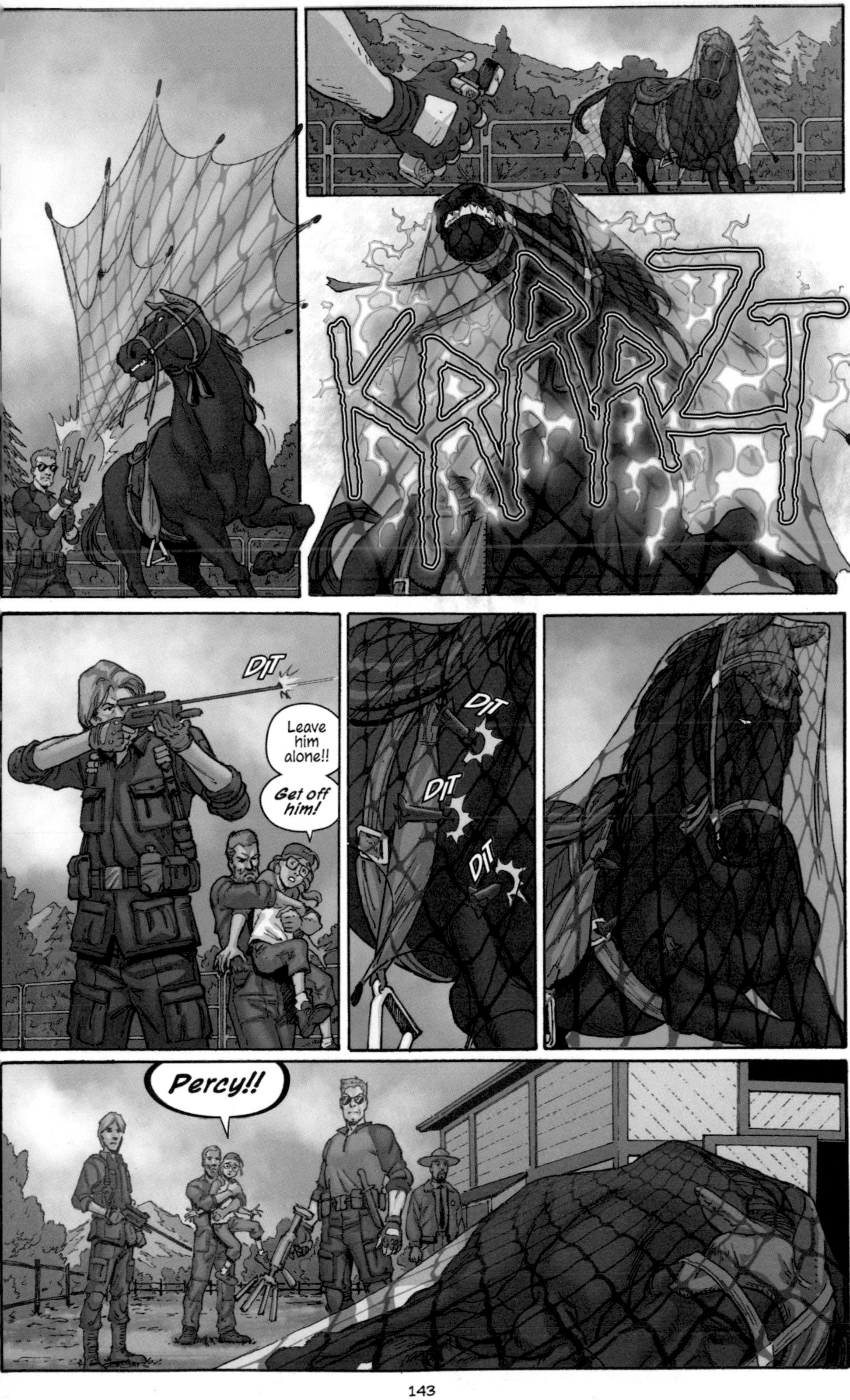
KRRZT
DIT
Leave him alone!!
Get off him!
DIT
DIT
DIT
Percy!!

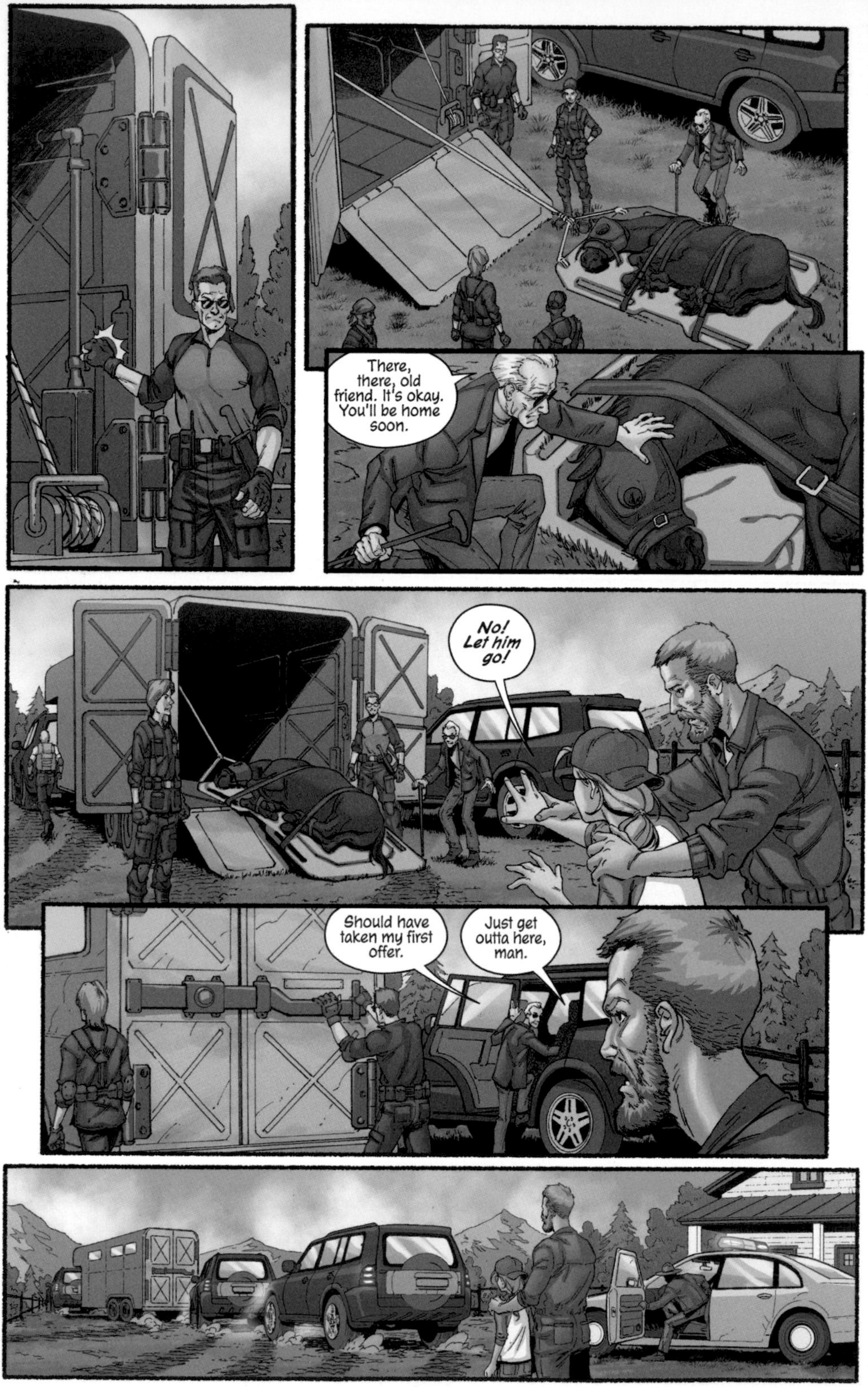
There, there, old friend. It's okay. You'll be home soon.
No! Let him go!
Should have taken my first offer.
Just get outta here, man.

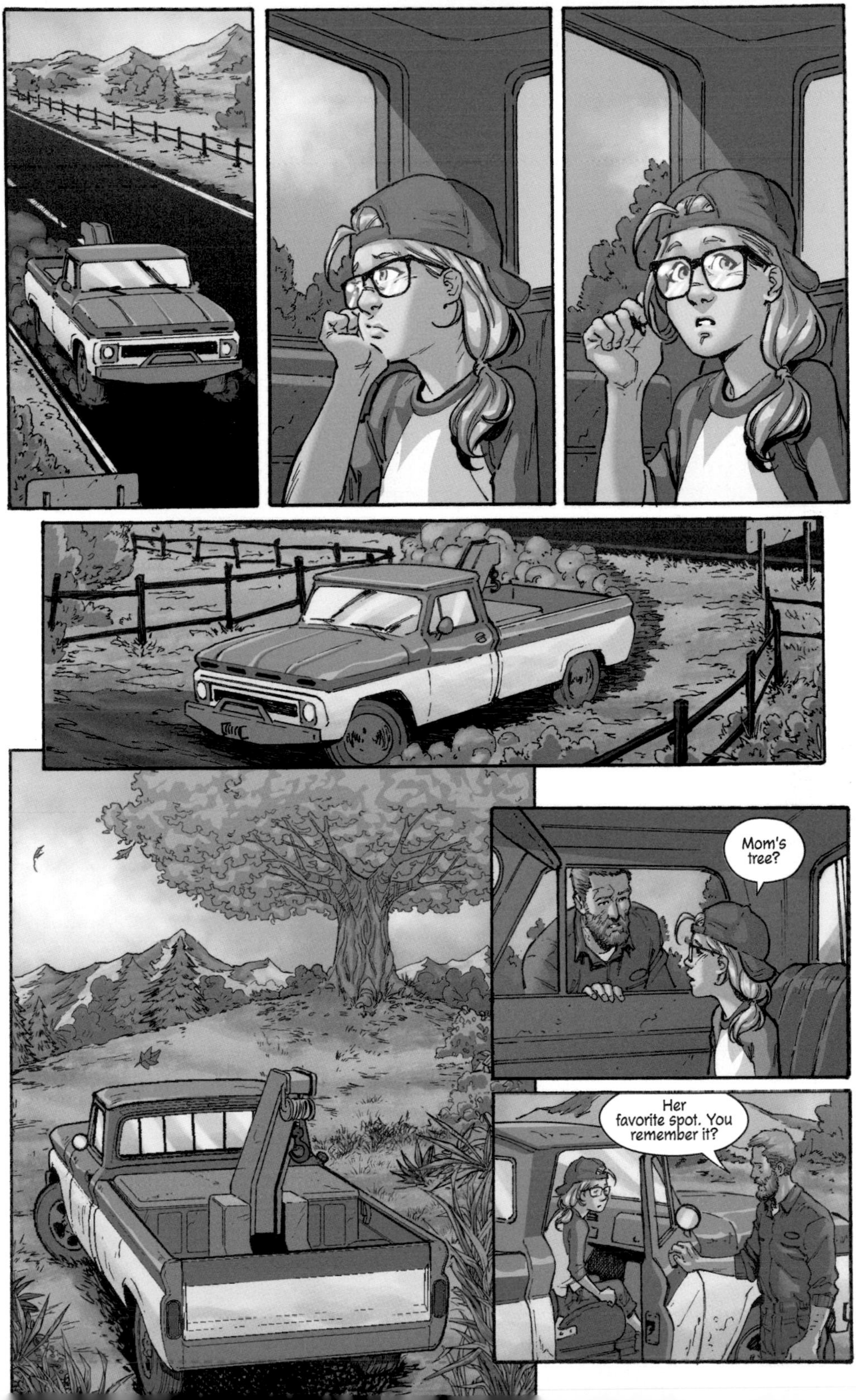
Mom's tree?
Her favorite spot. You remember it?

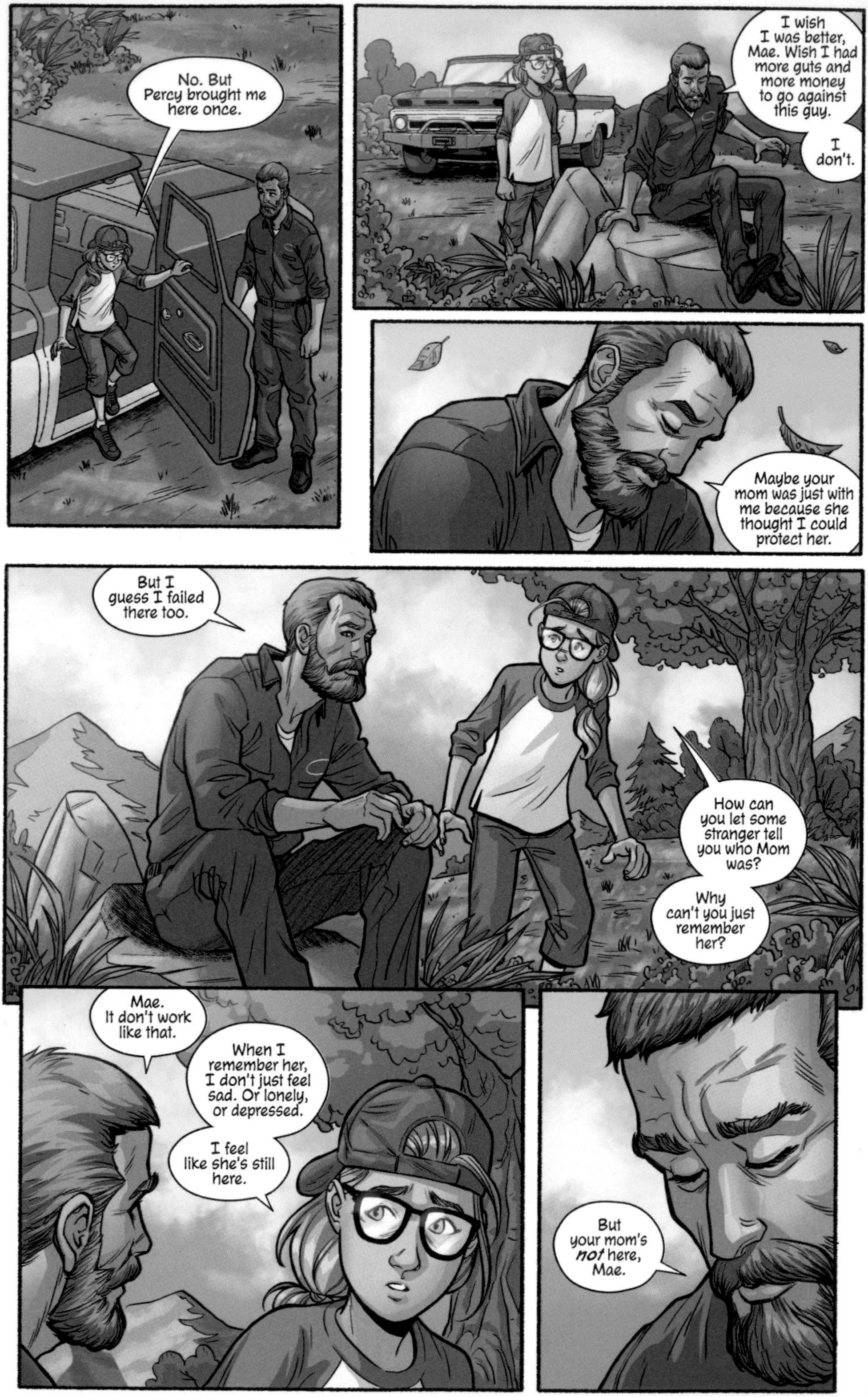
No. But Percy brought me here once.
I wish I was better, Mae. Wish I had more guts and more money to go against this guy.
I don't.
Maybe your mom was just with me because she thought I could protect her.
But I guess I failed there too.
How can you let some stranger tell you who Mom was?
Why can't you just remember her?
Mae. It don't work like that.
When I remember her, I don't just feel sad. Or lonely, or depressed.
I feel like she's still here.
But your mom's *not* here, Mae.

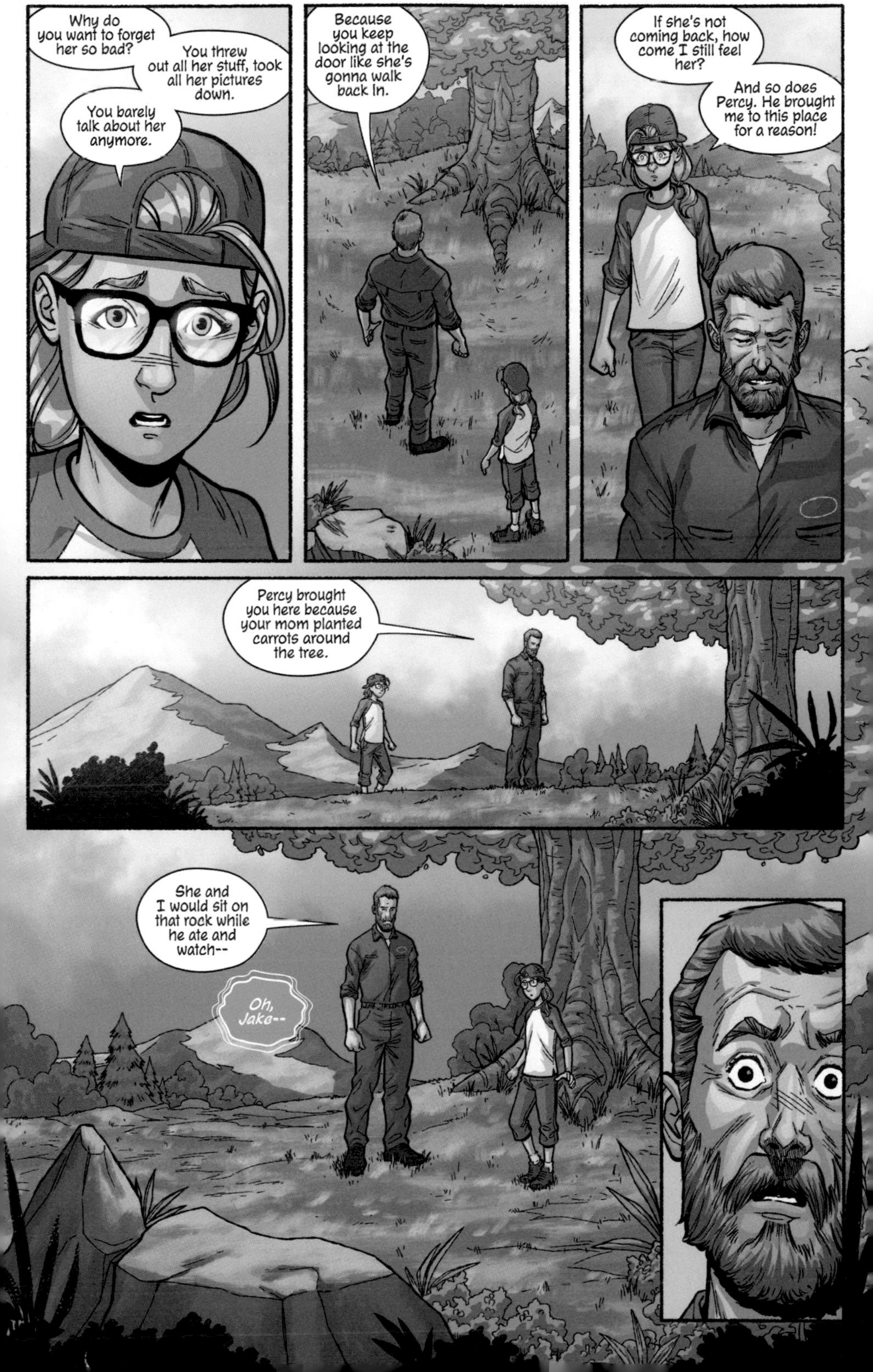
Why do you want to forget her so bad?
You threw out all her stuff, took all her pictures down.
You barely talk about her anymore.
Because you keep looking at the door like she's gonna walk back in.
If she's not coming back, how come I still feel her?
And so does Percy. He brought me to this place for a reason!
Percy brought you here because your mom planted carrots around the tree.
She and I would sit on that rock while he ate and watch--
Oh, Jake--

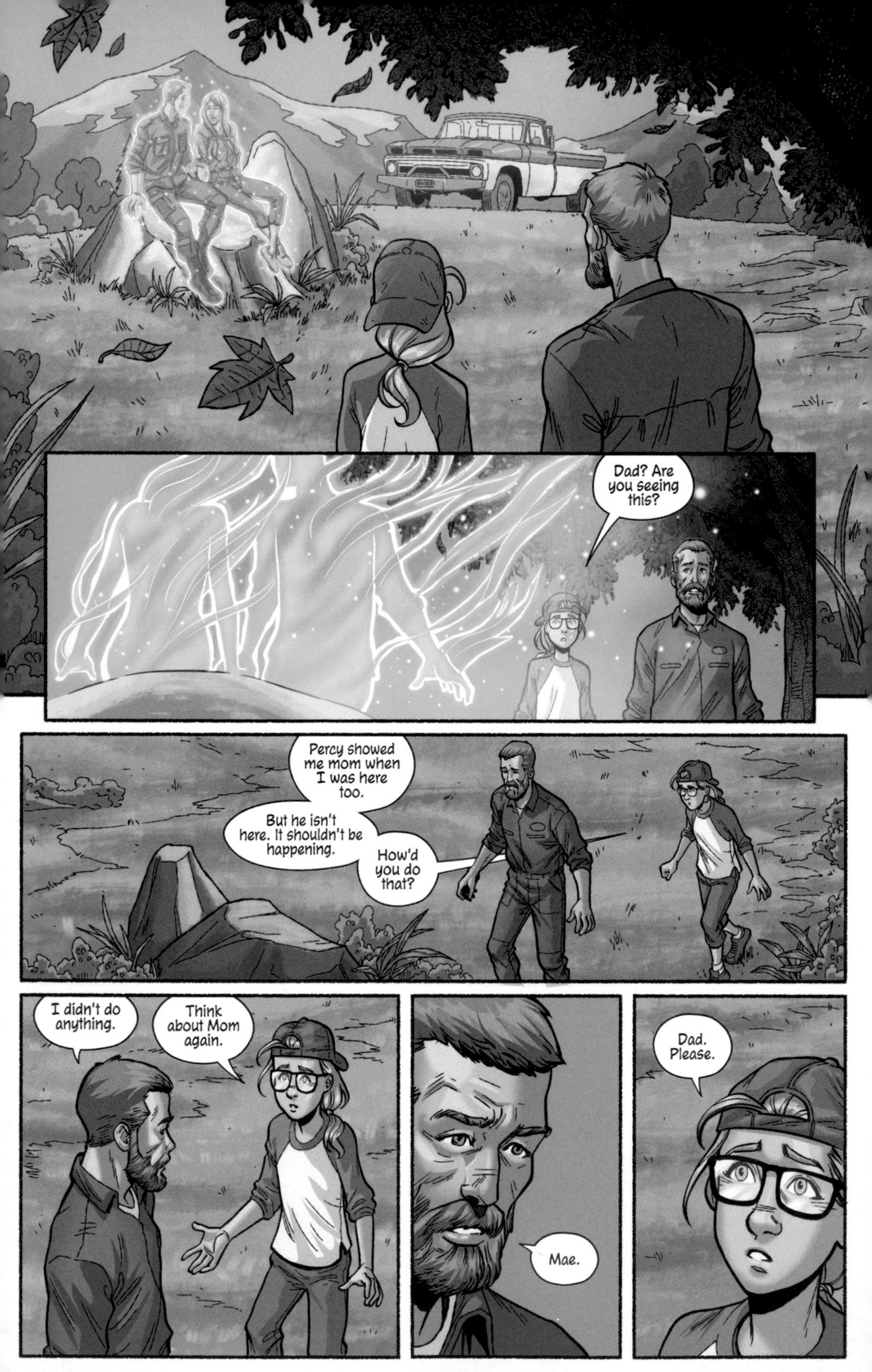

Dad? Are you seeing this?
Percy showed me mom when I was here too.
But he isn't here. It shouldn't be happening.
How'd you do that?
I didn't do anything.
Think about Mom again.
Mae.
Dad. Please.

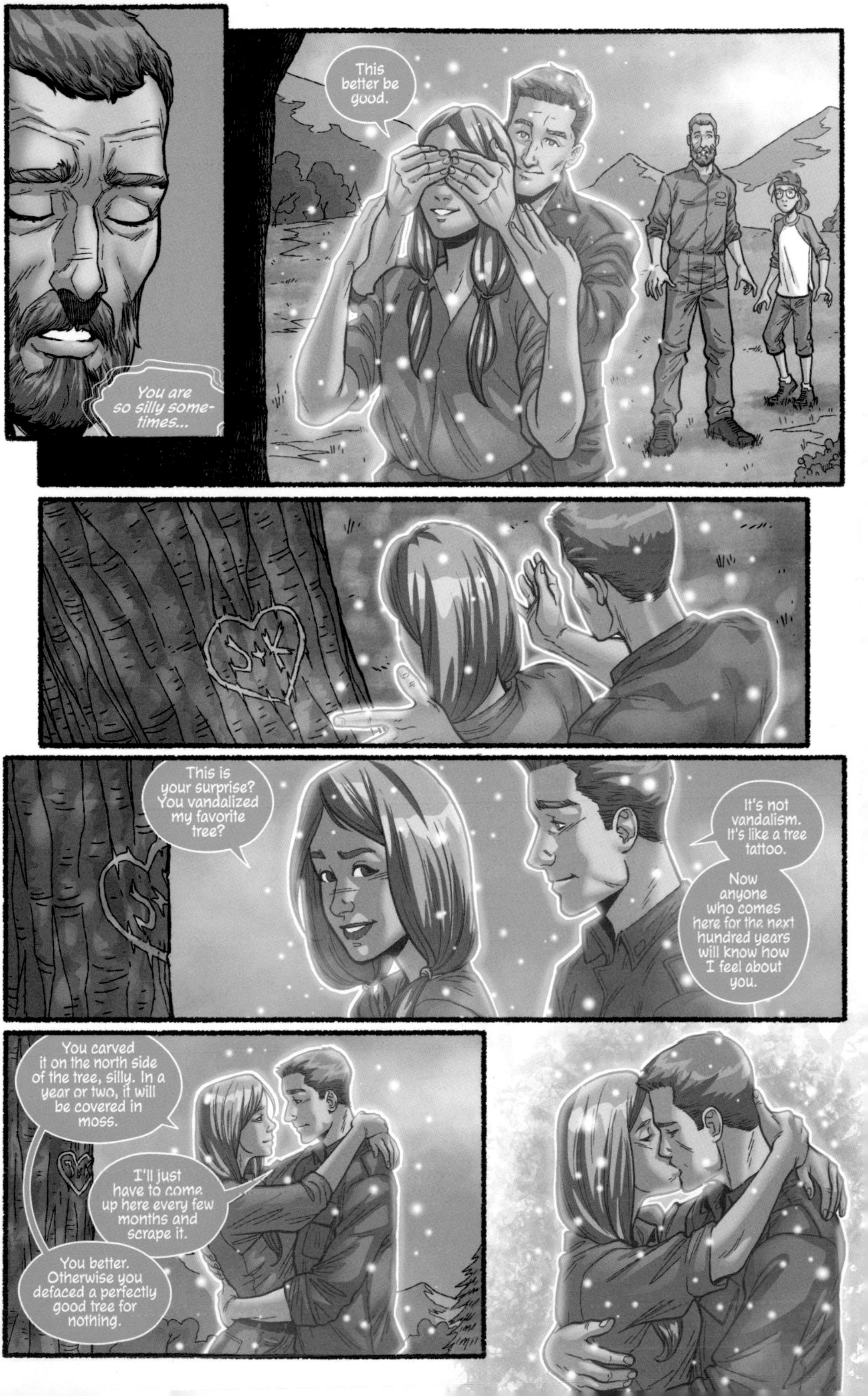
You are so silly sometimes...
This better be good.
This is your surprise? You vandalized my favorite tree?
It's not vandalism. It's like a tree tattoo.
Now anyone who comes here for the next hundred years will know how I feel about you.
You carved it on the north side of the tree, silly. In a year or two, it will be covered in moss.
I'll just have to come up here every few months and scrape it.
You better. Otherwise you defaced a perfectly good tree for nothing.

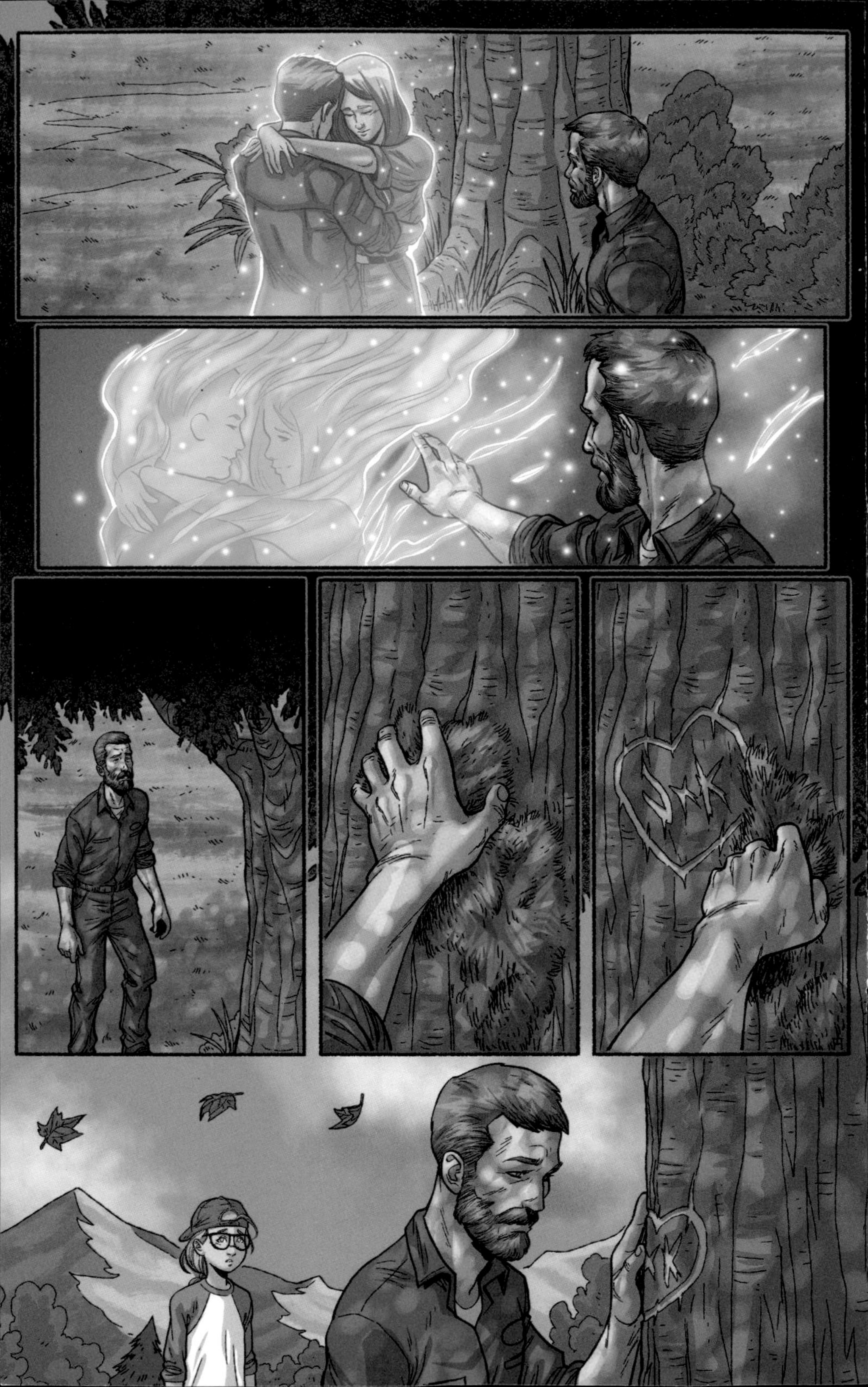

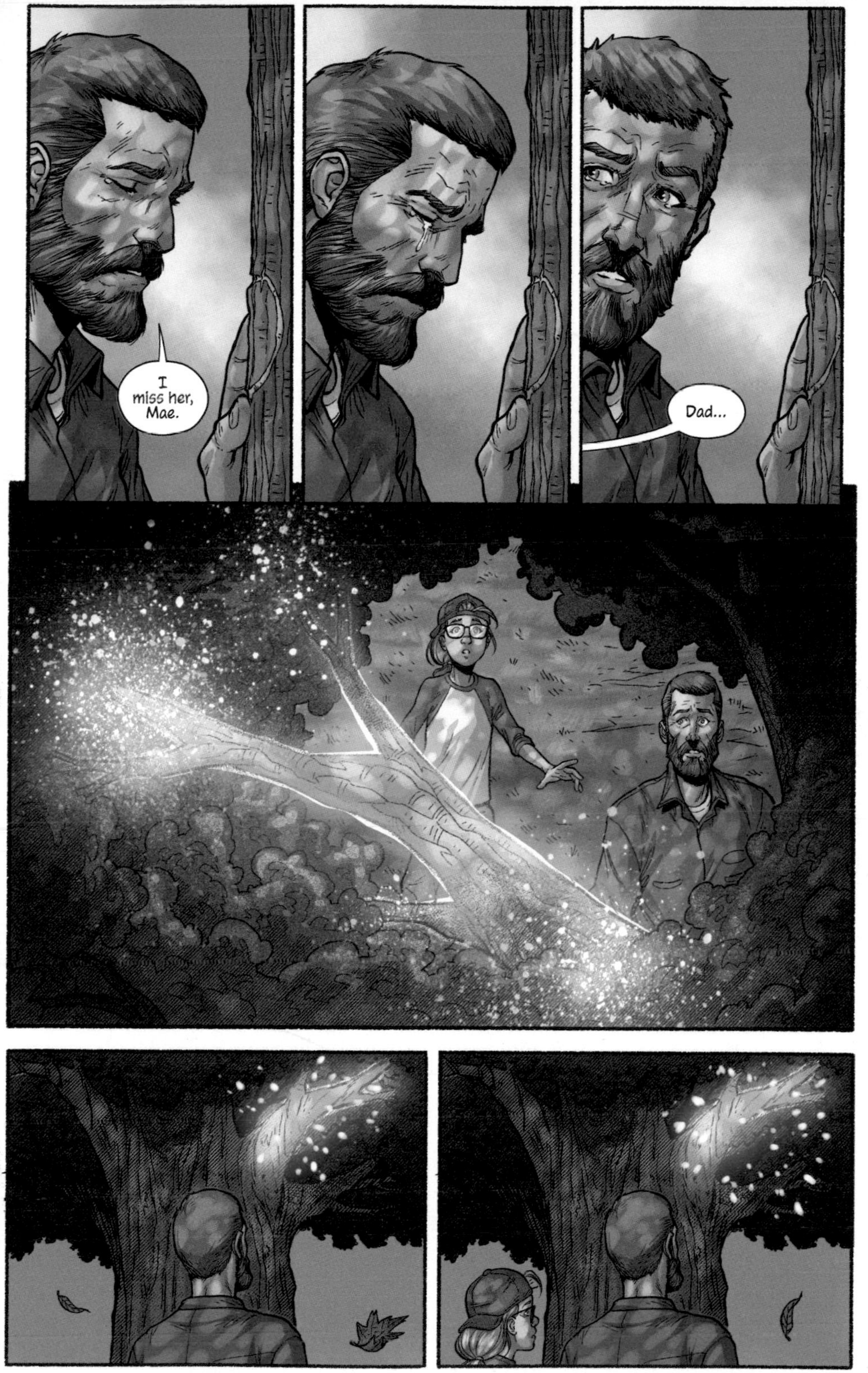
I miss her, Mae.
Dad...

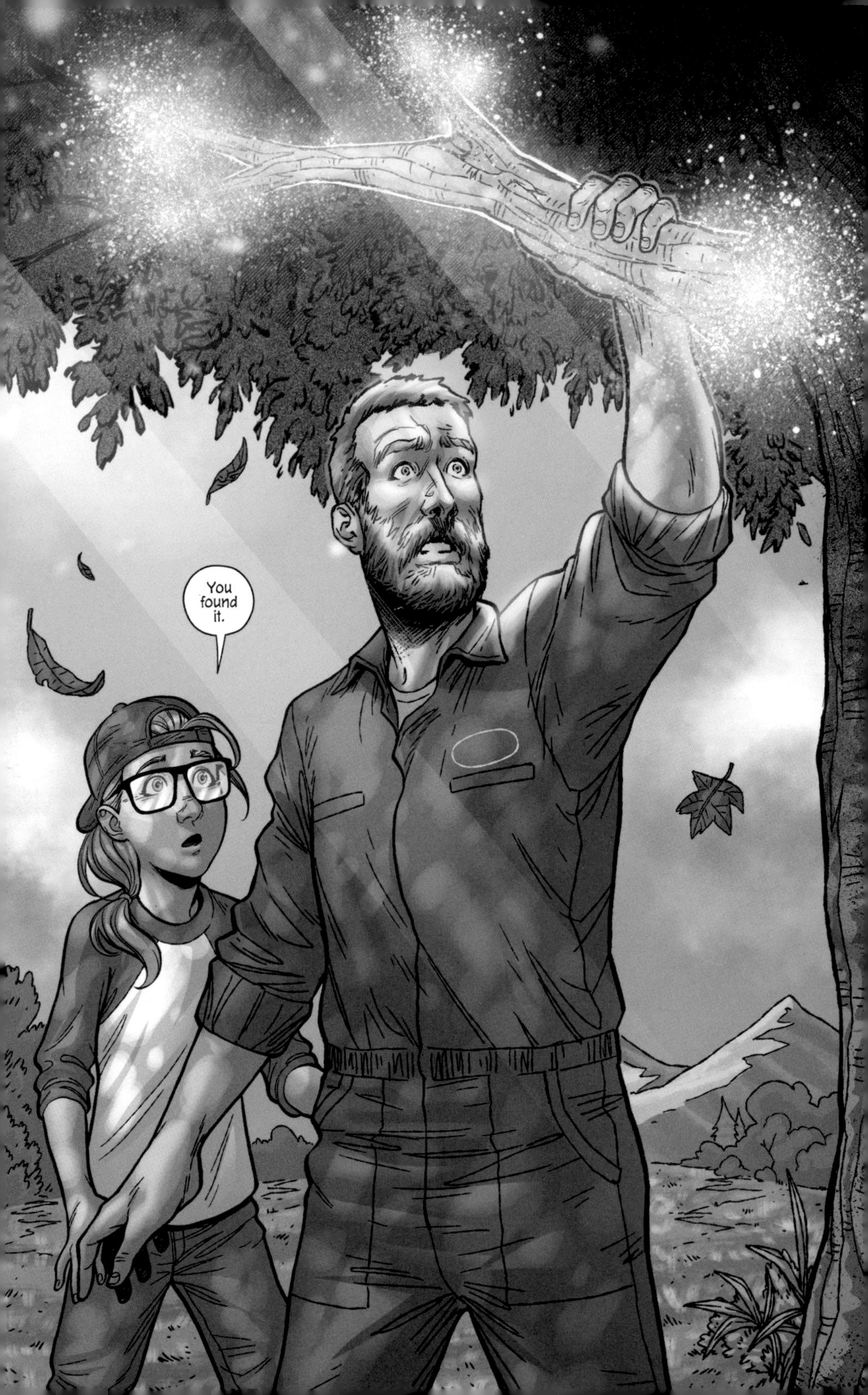
You found it.

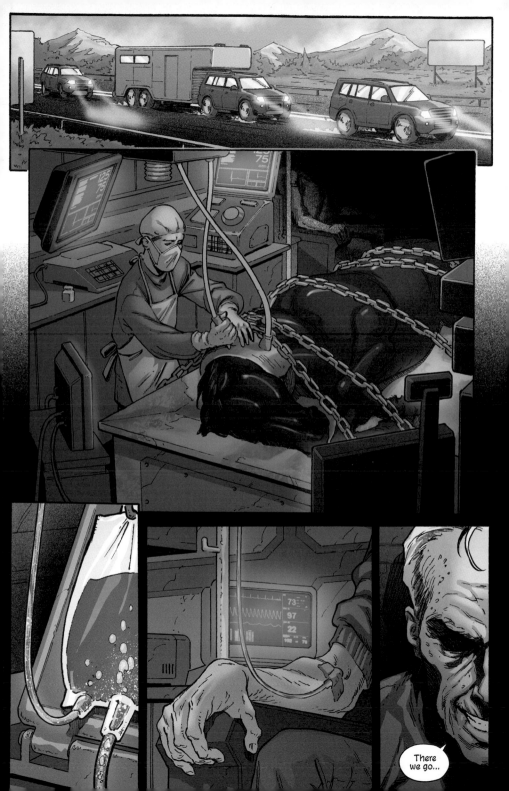

There we go...

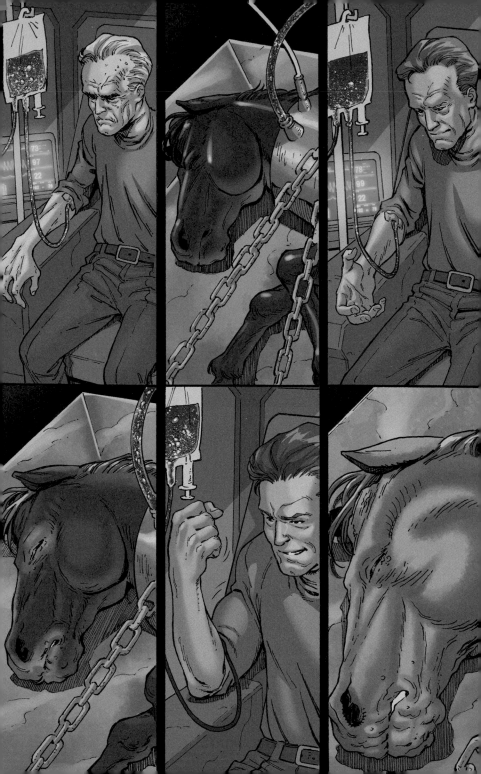

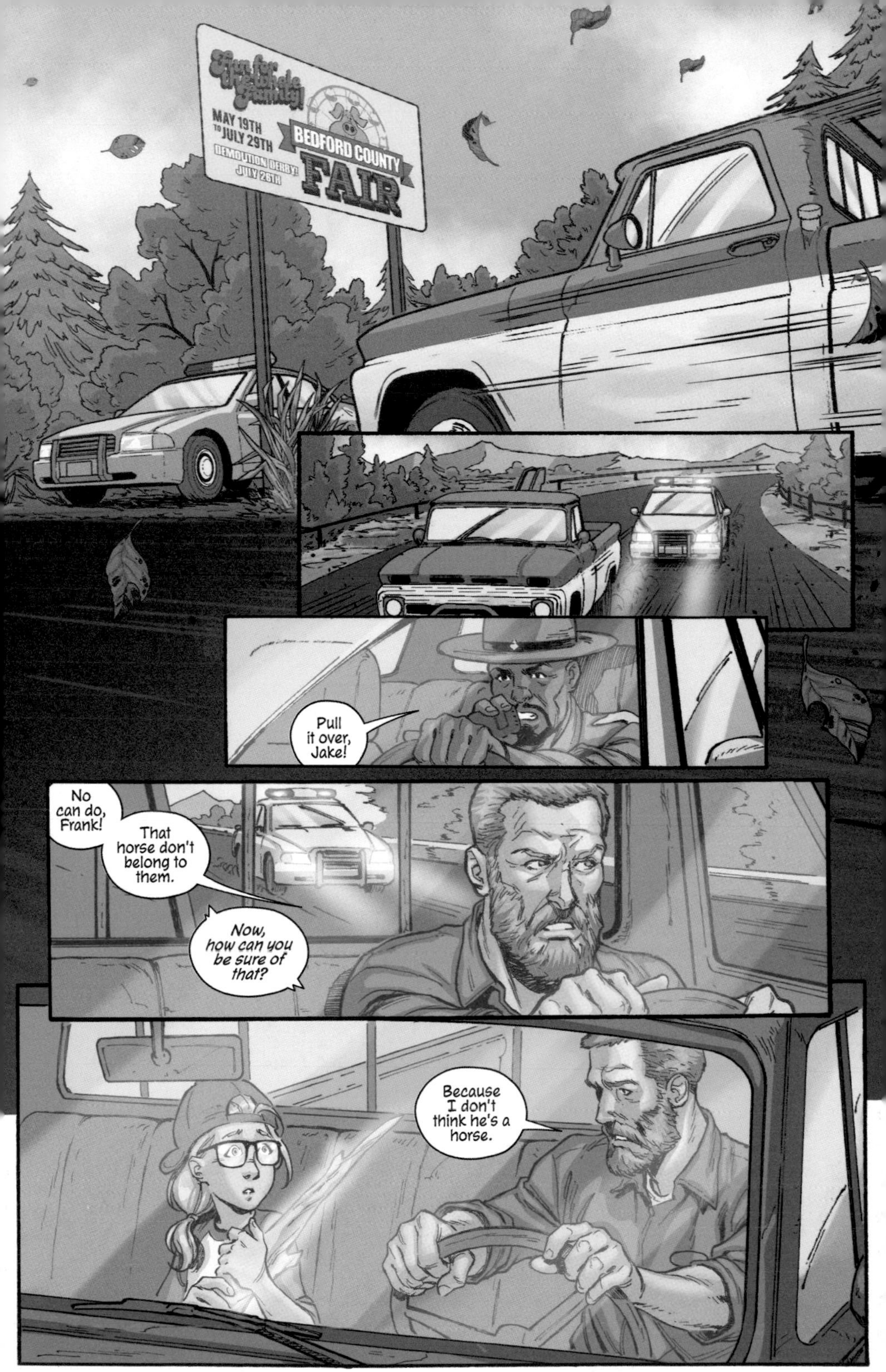
Fun for the whole family!
MAY 19TH TO JULY 29TH
DEMOLITION DERBY! JULY 26TH
BEDFORD COUNTY FAIR
Pull it over, Jake!
No can do, Frank!
That horse don't belong to them.
Now, how can you be sure of that?
Because I don't think he's a horse.

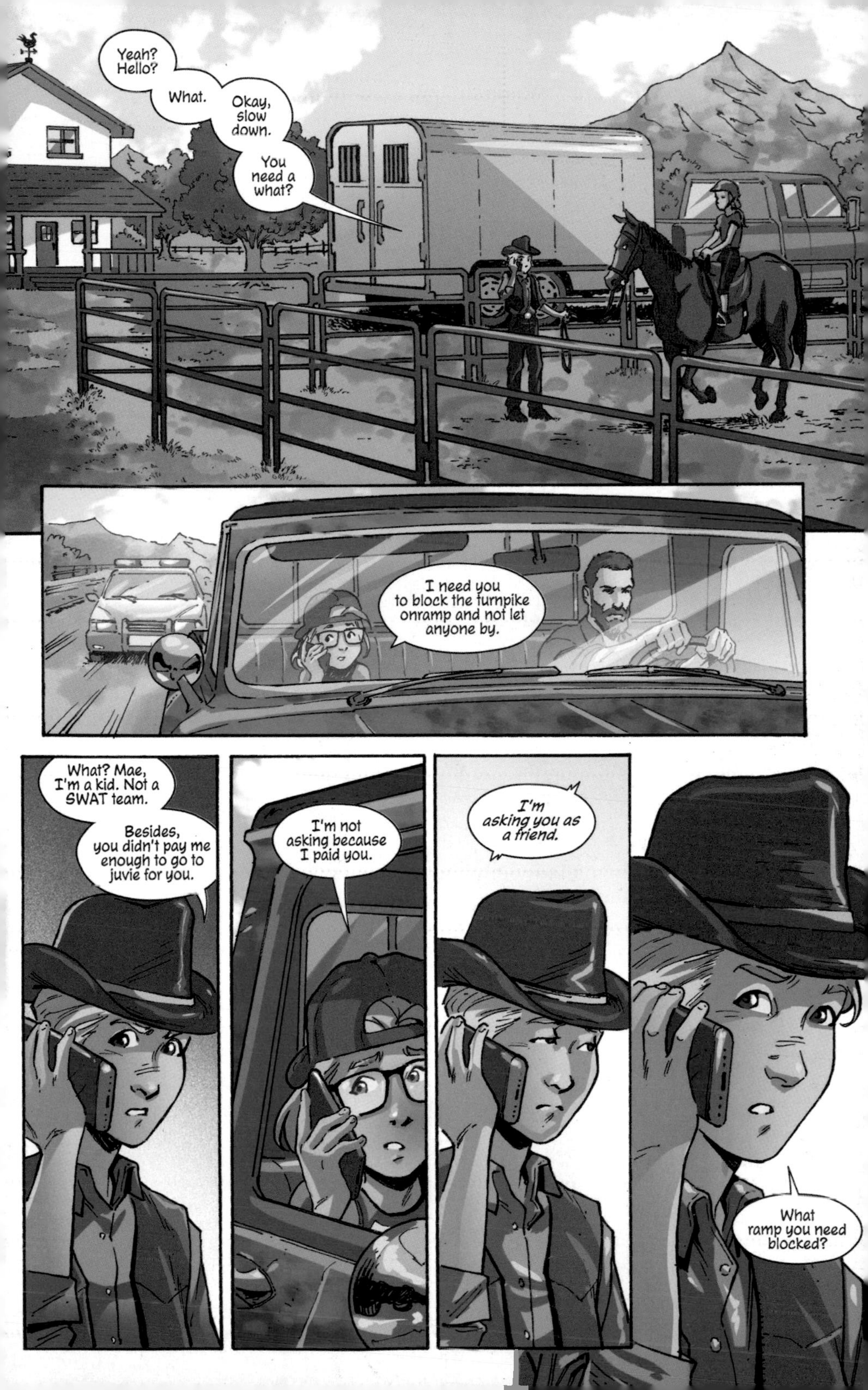
Yeah? Hello?
What.
Okay, slow down.
You need a what?
I need you to block the turnpike onramp and not let anyone by.
What? Mae, I'm a kid. Not a SWAT team.
Besides, you didn't pay me enough to go to juvie for you.
I'm not asking because I paid you.
I'm asking you as a friend.
What ramp you need blocked?

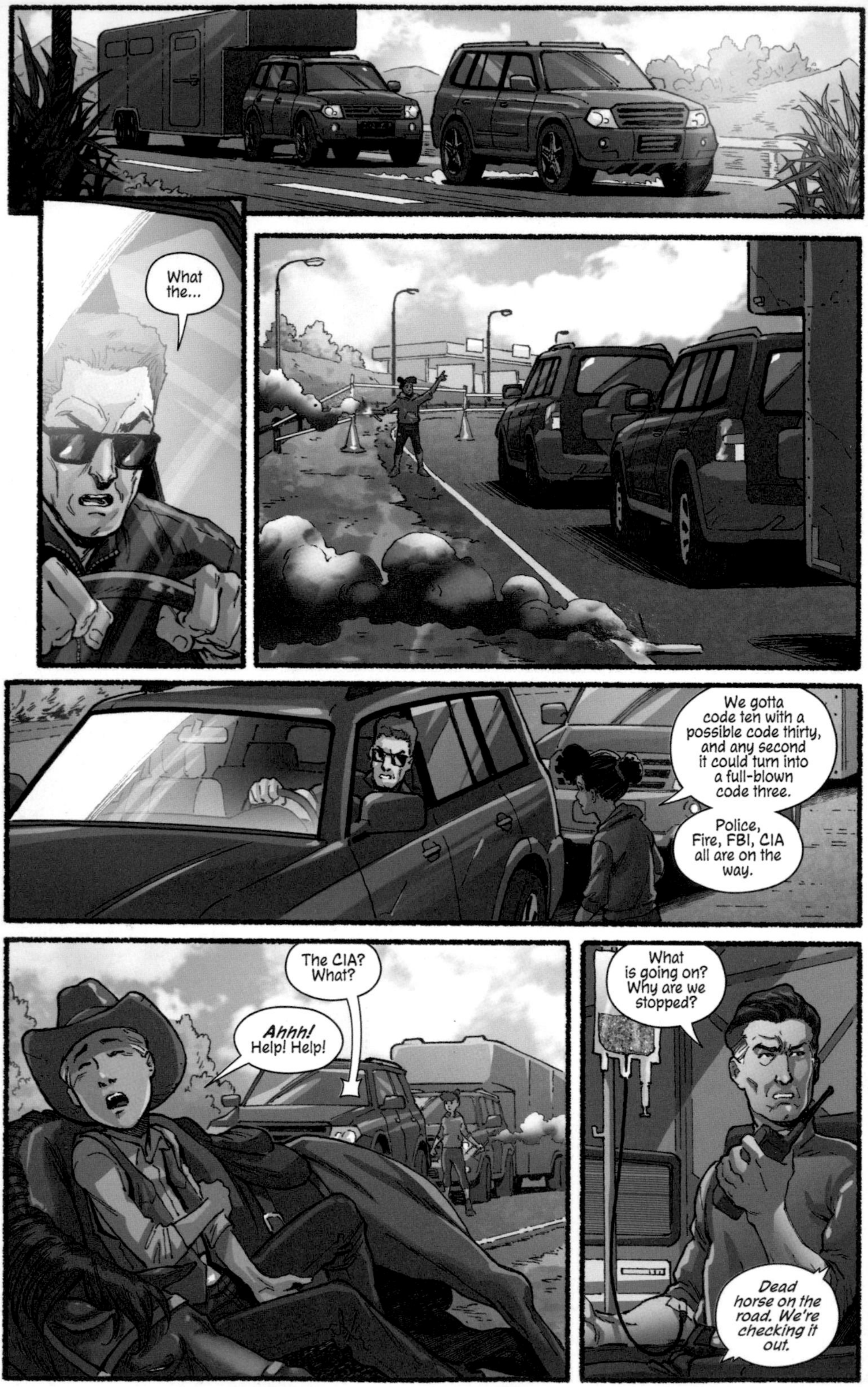
What the...
We gotta code ten with a possible code thirty, and any second it could turn into a full-blown code three.
Police, Fire, FBI, CIA all are on the way.
The CIA? What?
Ahhh! Help! Help!
What is going on? Why are we stopped?
Dead horse on the road. We're checking it out.

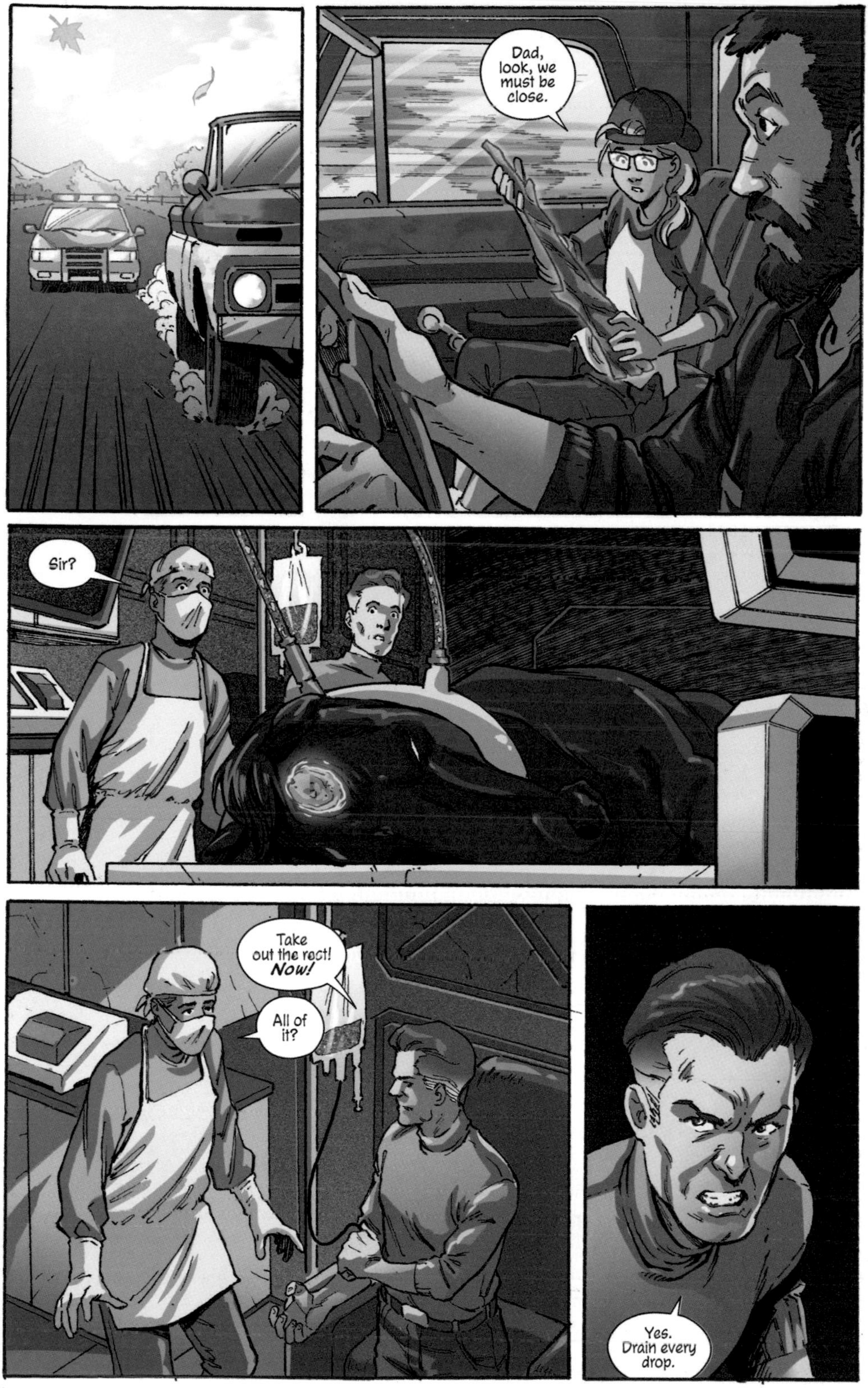
Dad, look, we must be close.
Sir?
Take out the rest! ***Now!***
All of it?
Yes. Drain every drop.

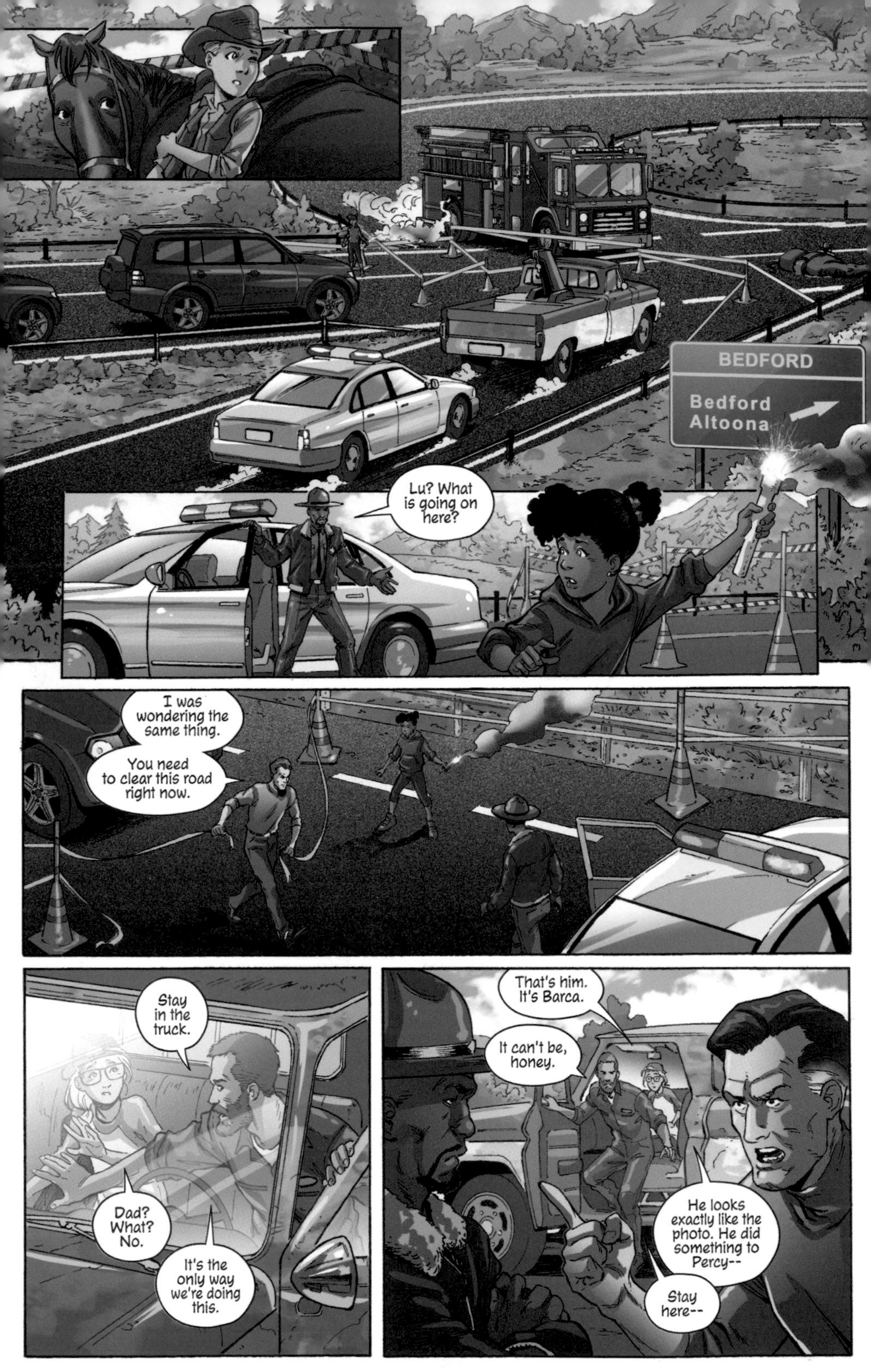
BEDFORD
Bedford
Altoona
Lu? What is going on here?
I was wondering the same thing.
You need to clear this road right now.
Stay in the truck.
Dad? What? No.
It's the only way we're doing this.
That's him. It's Barca.
It can't be, honey.
He looks exactly like the photo. He did something to Percy--
Stay here--

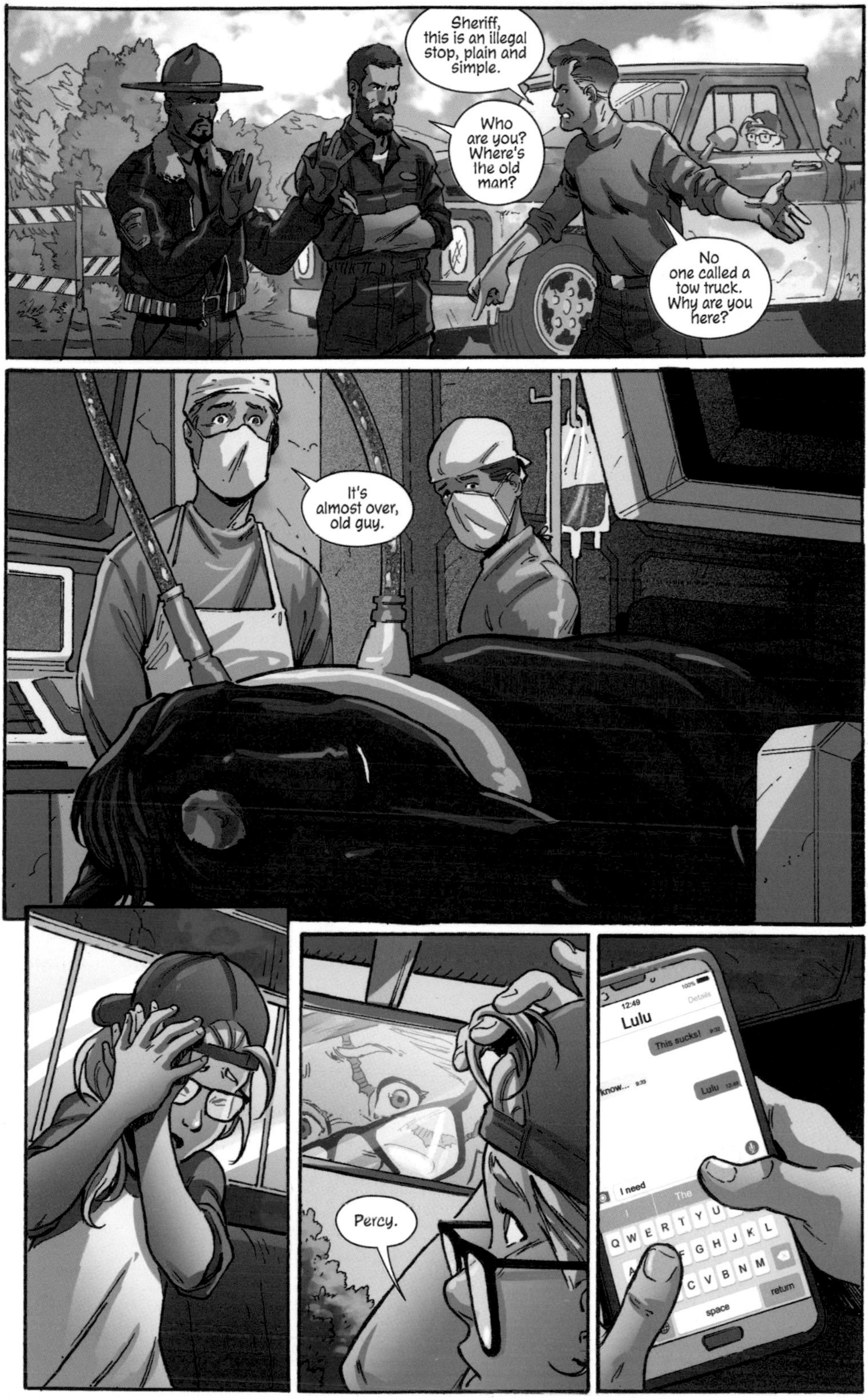
Sheriff, this is an illegal stop, plain and simple.
Who are you? Where's the old man?
No one called a tow truck. Why are you here?
It's almost over, old guy.
Percy.
Lulu
This sucks!
I need

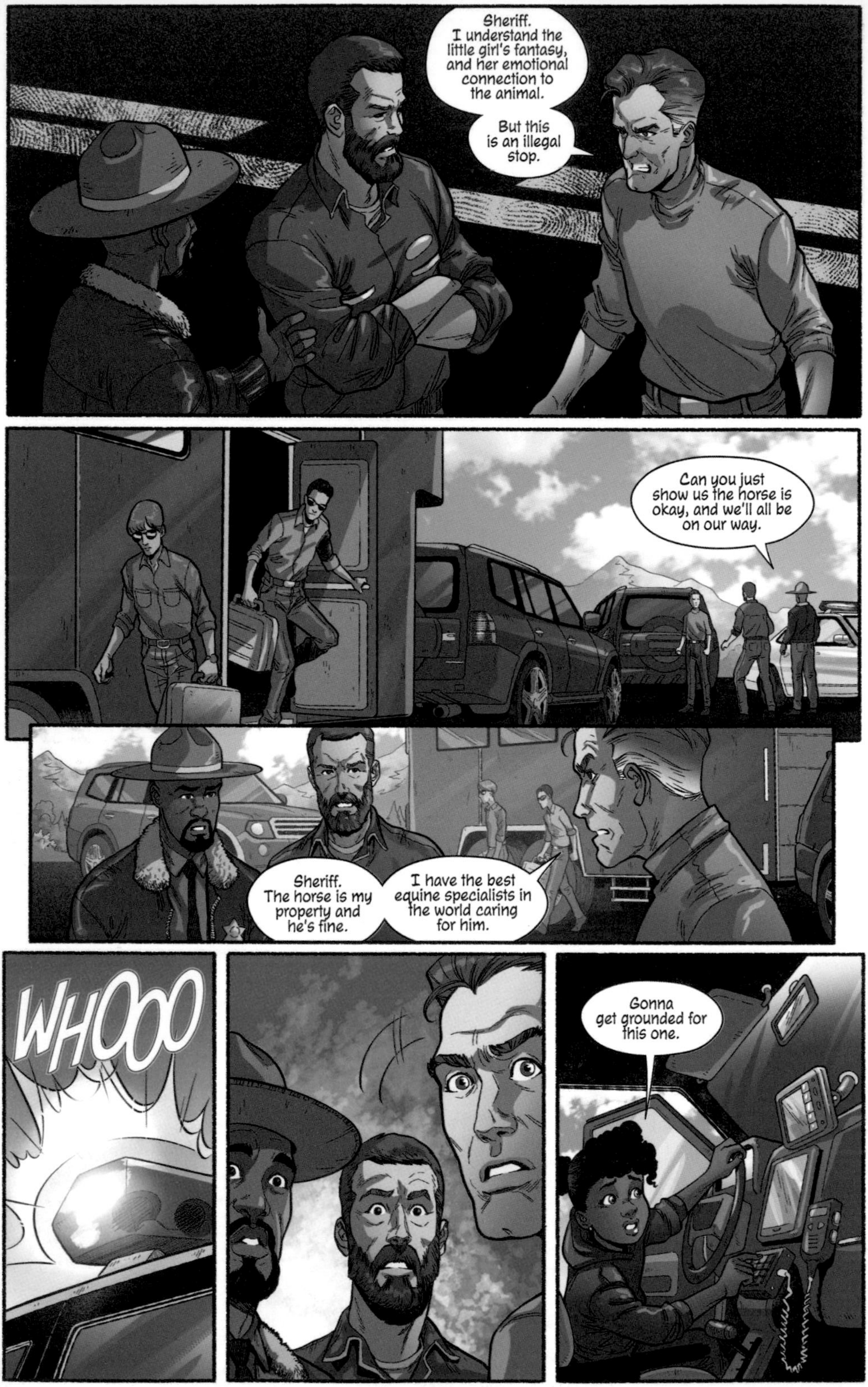
Sheriff. I understand the little girl's fantasy, and her emotional connection to the animal.
But this is an illegal stop.
Can you just show us the horse is okay, and we'll all be on our way.
Sheriff. The horse is my property and he's fine.
I have the best equine specialists in the world caring for him.
WHOOO
Gonna get grounded for this one.

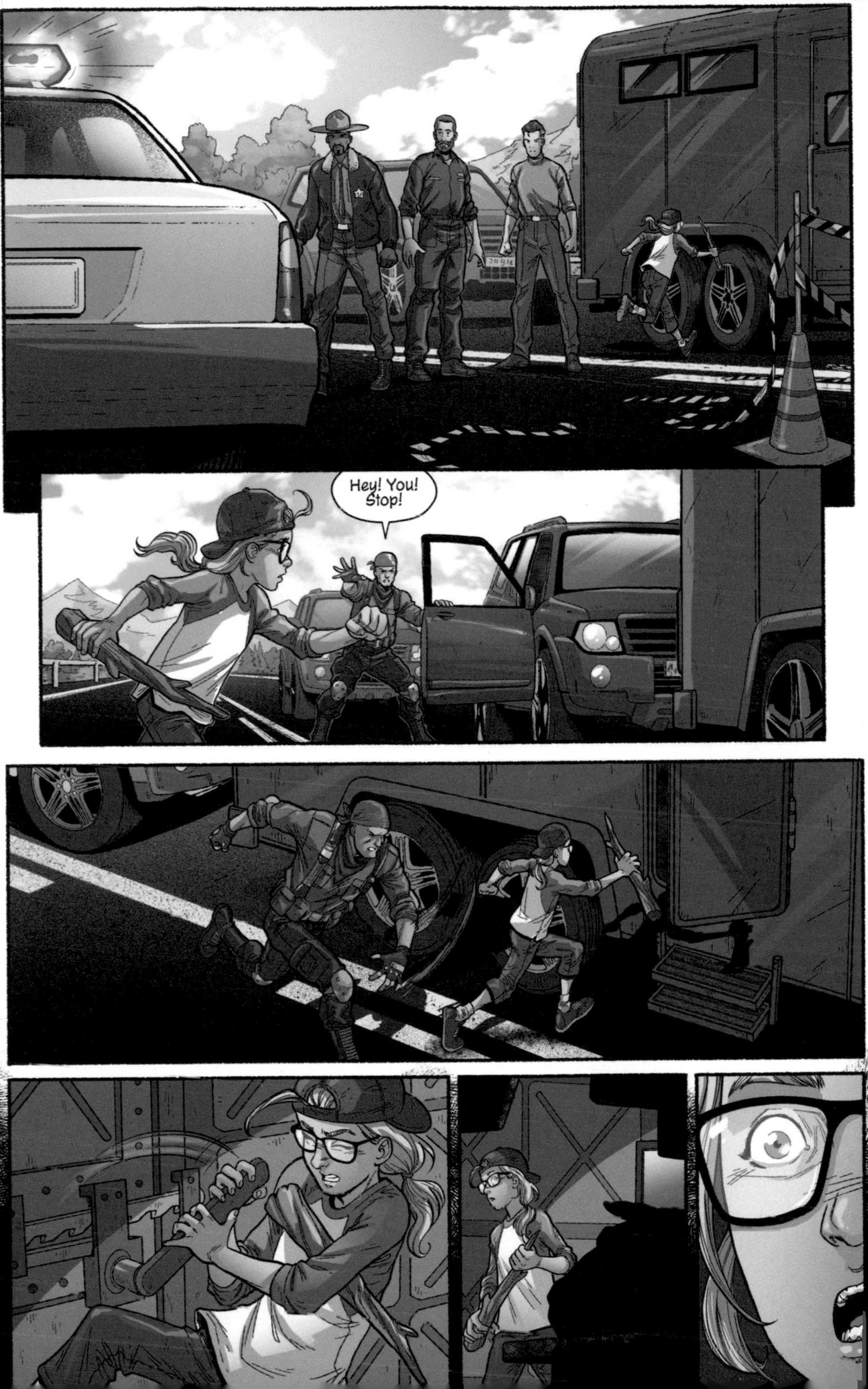
Hey! You! Stop!

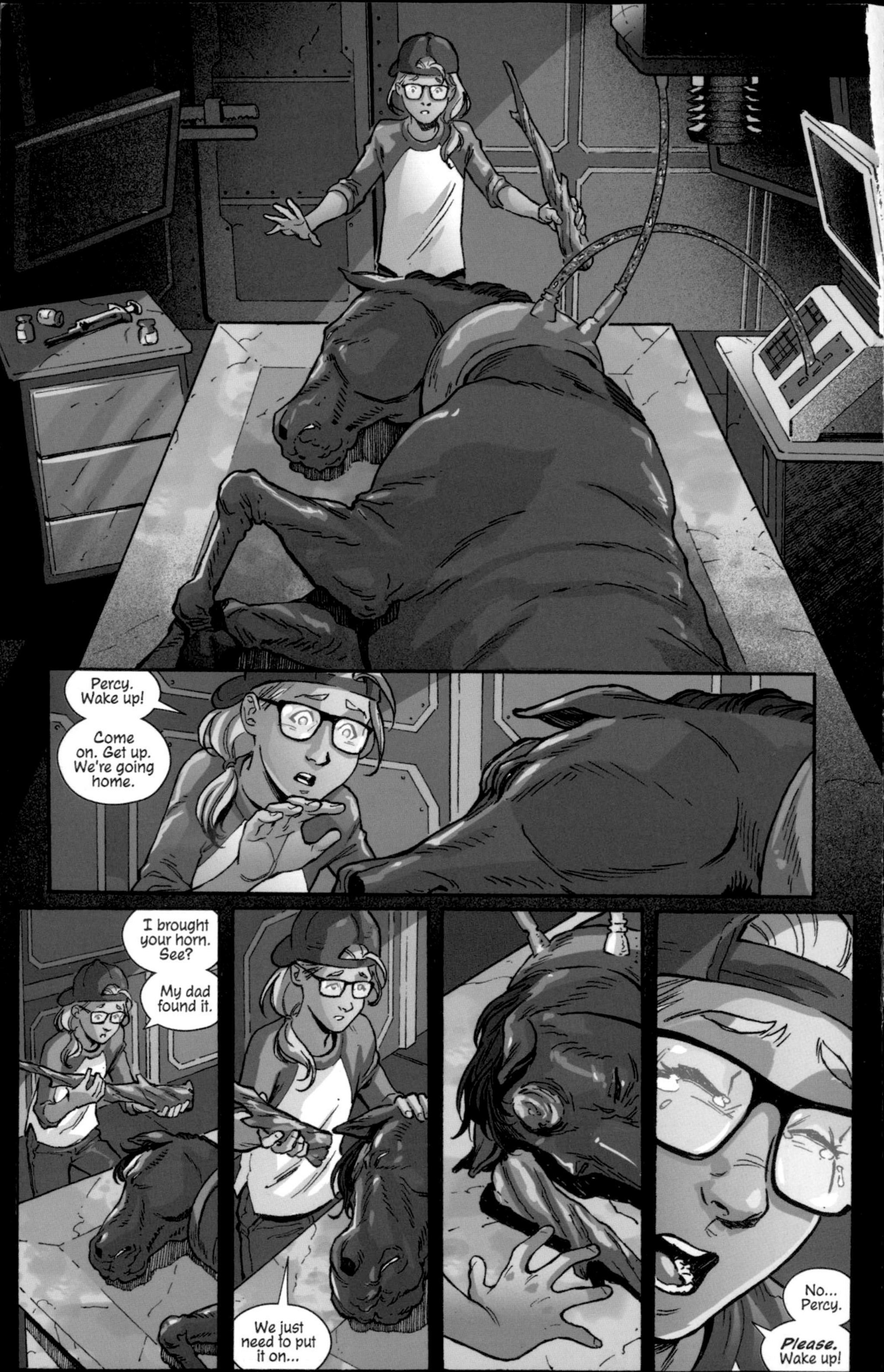
Percy. Wake up!
Come on. Get up. We're going home.
I brought your horn. See?
My dad found it.
We just need to put it on...
No... Percy.
Please. Wake up!

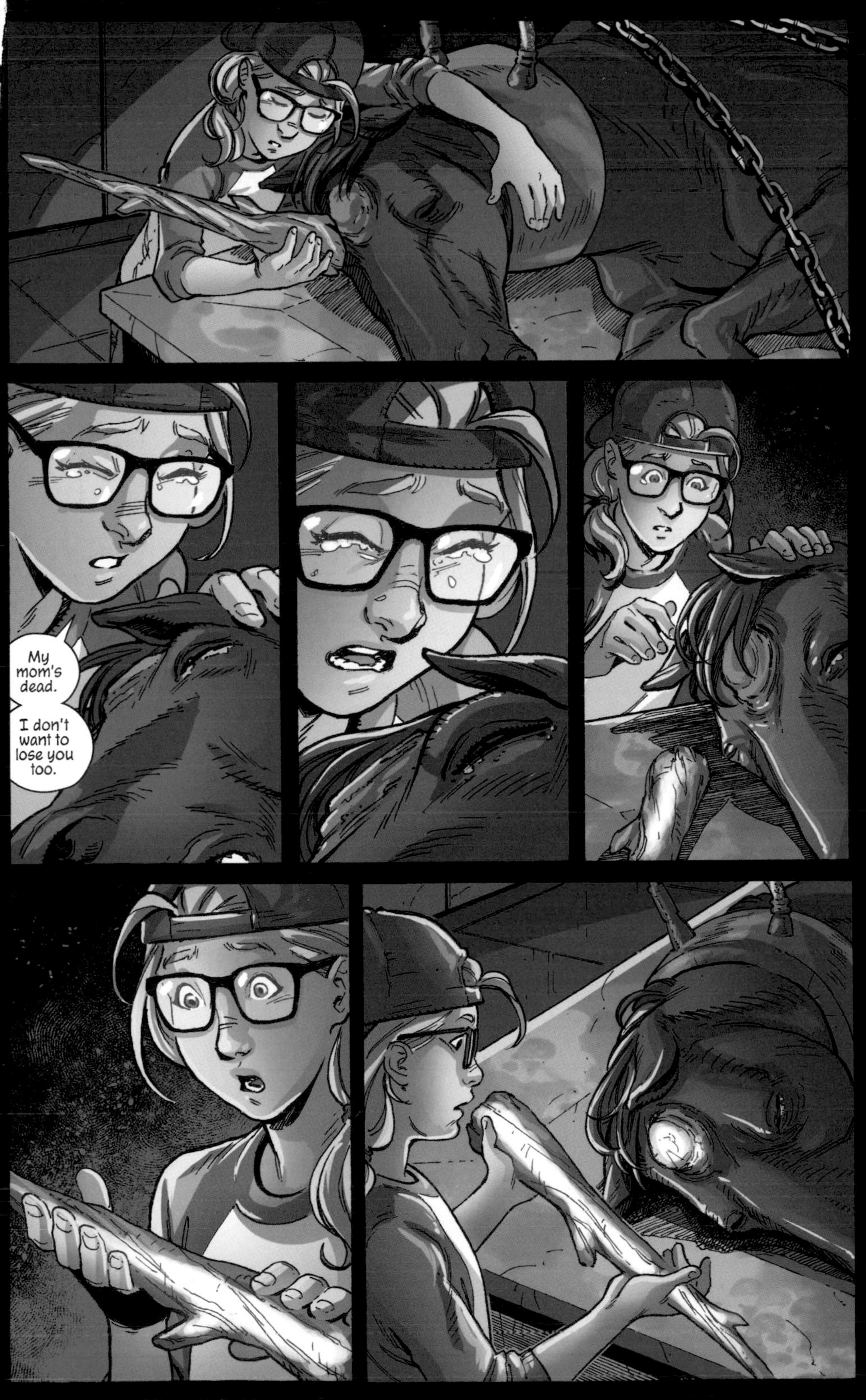
My mom's dead.
I don't want to lose you too.

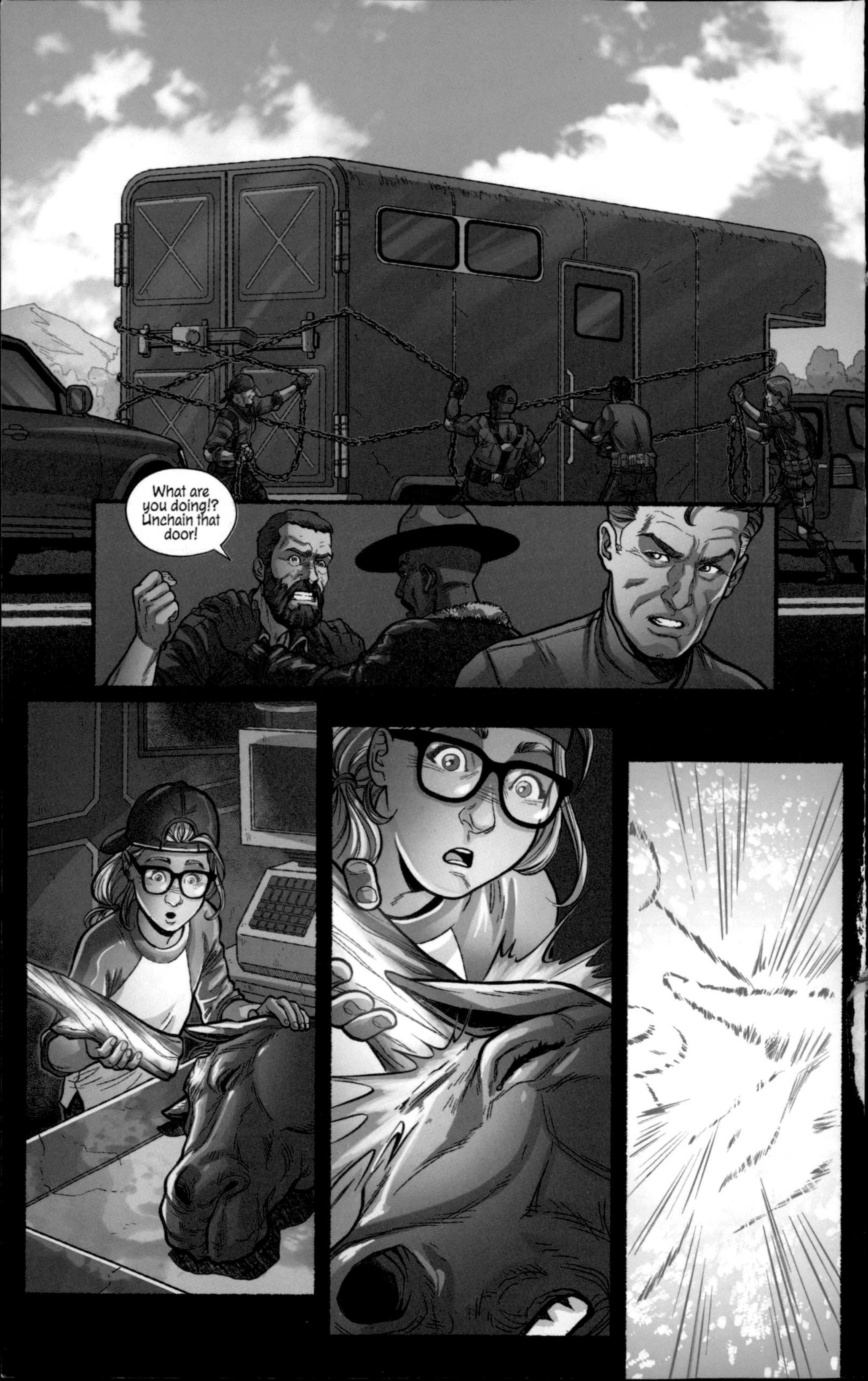
What are you doing!? Unchain that door!

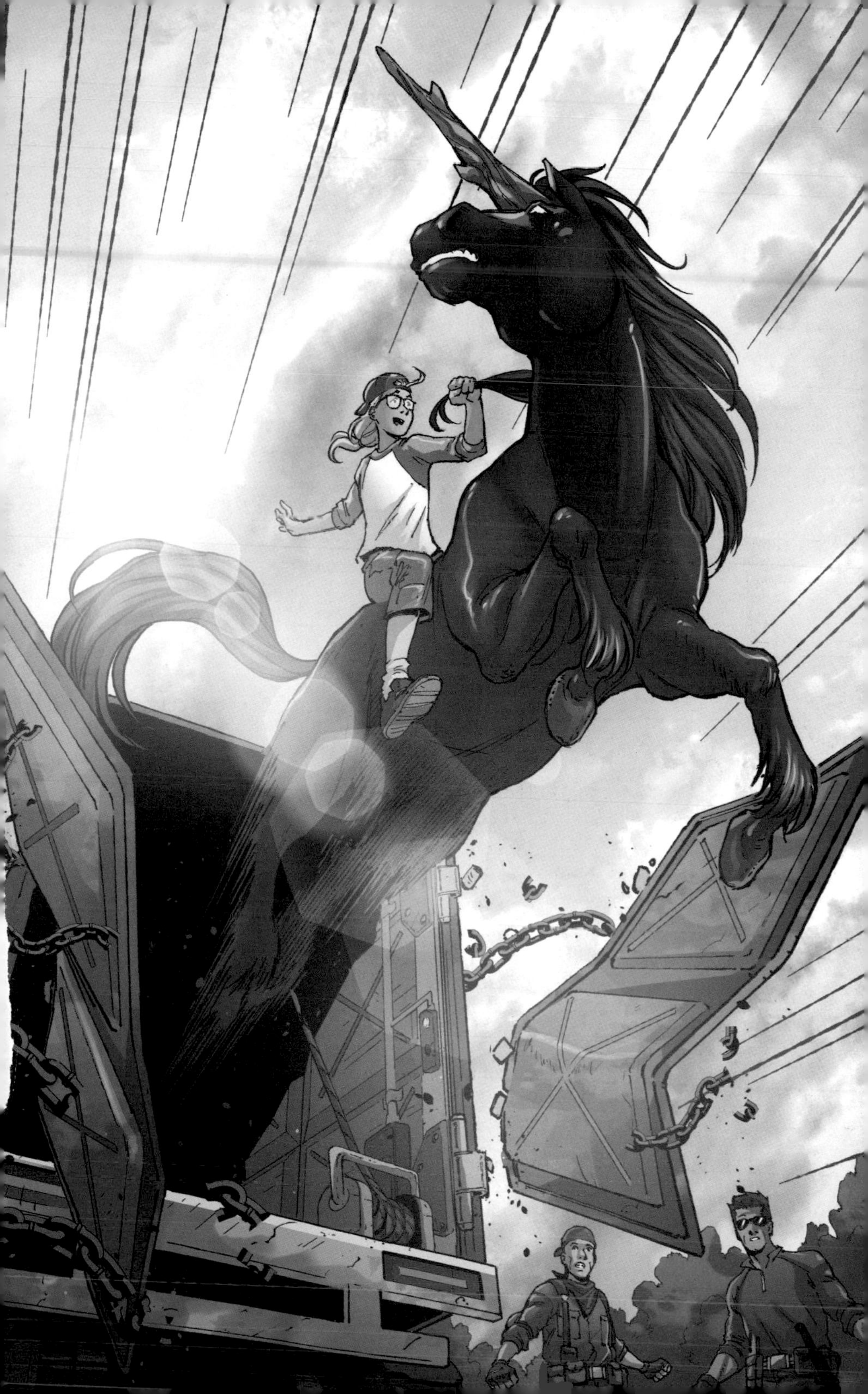

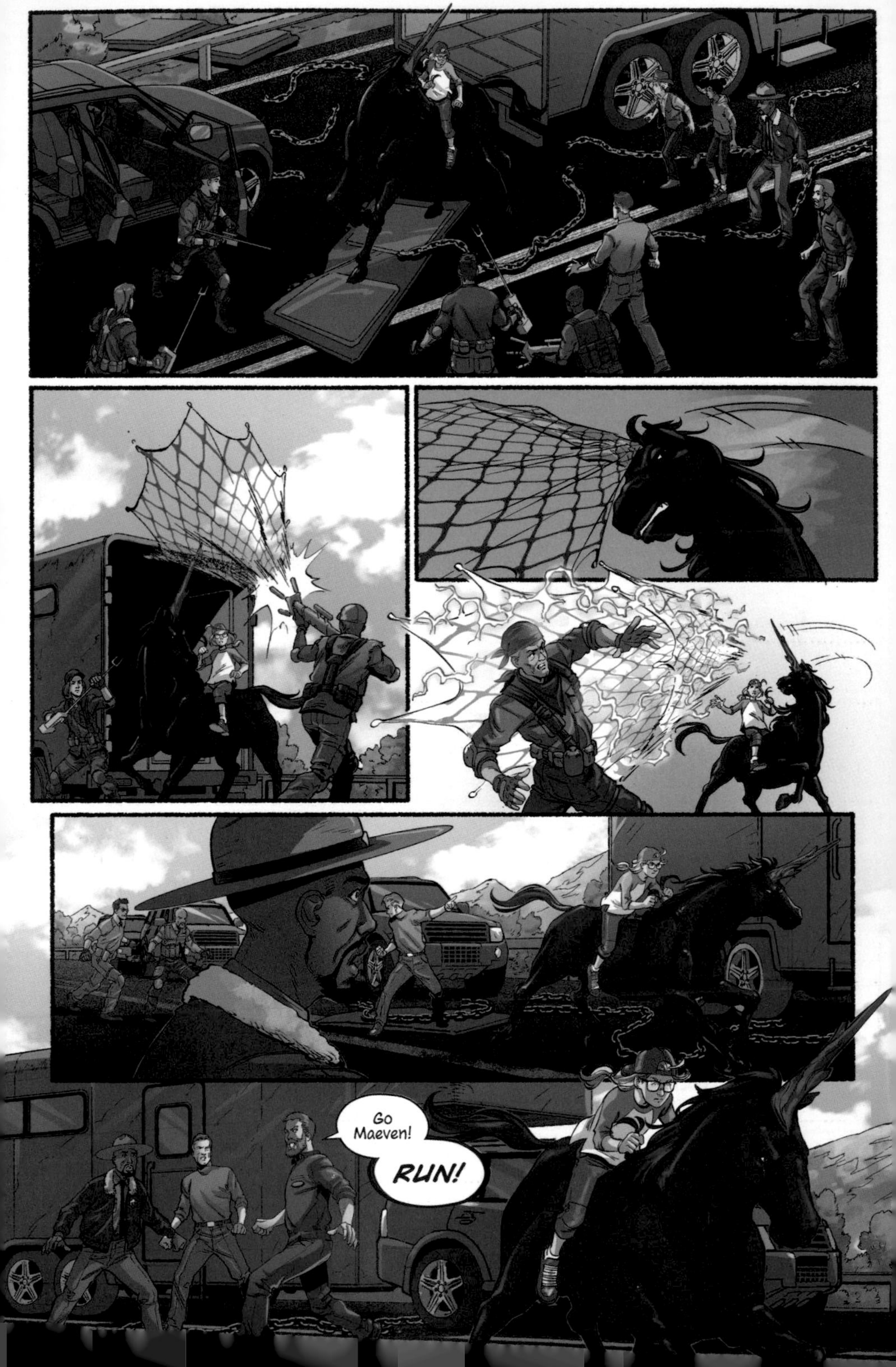
Go Maeven!
RUN!

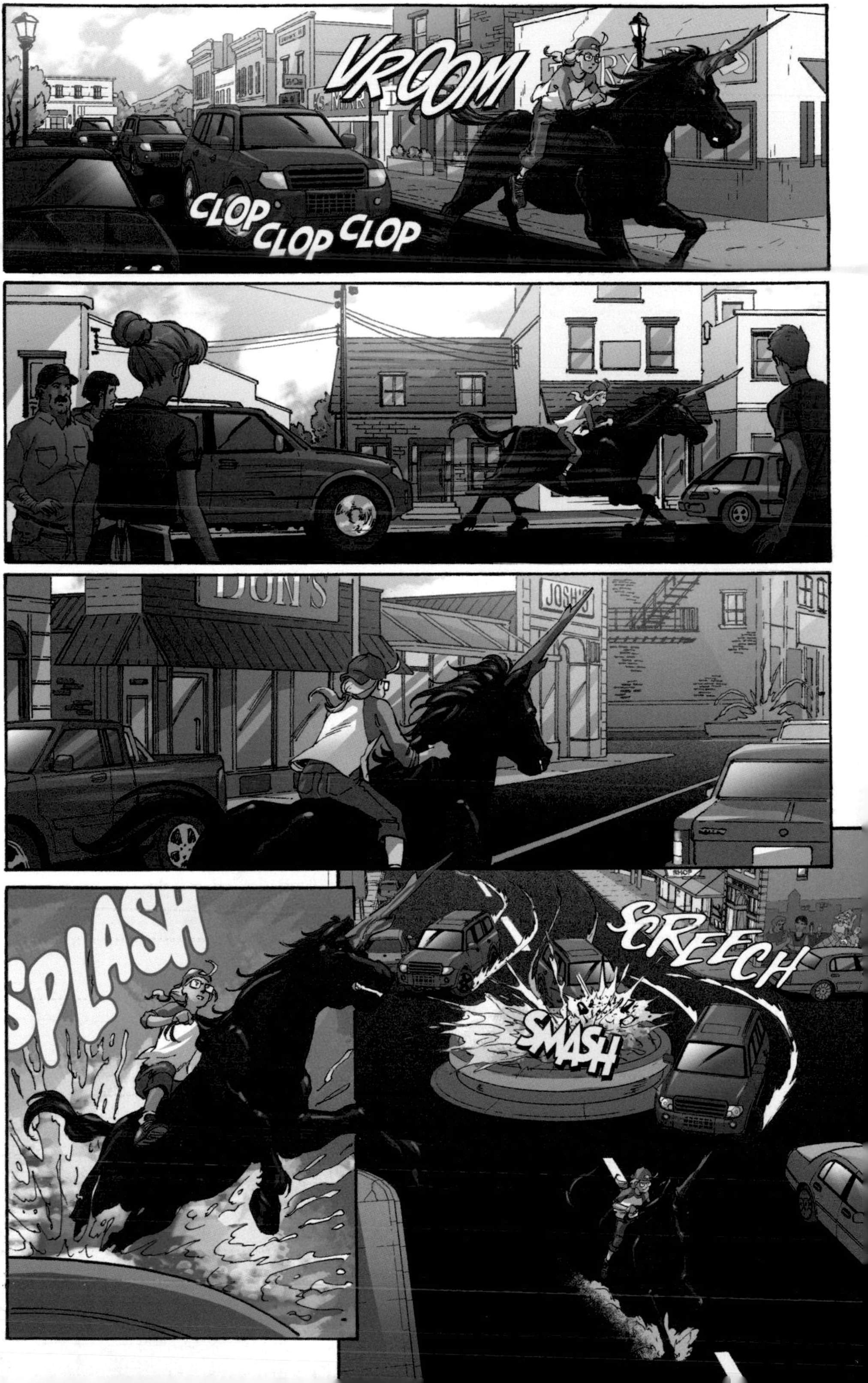
VROOM
CLOP CLOP CLOP
DON'S
JOSH'S
SPLASH
SCREECH
SMASH

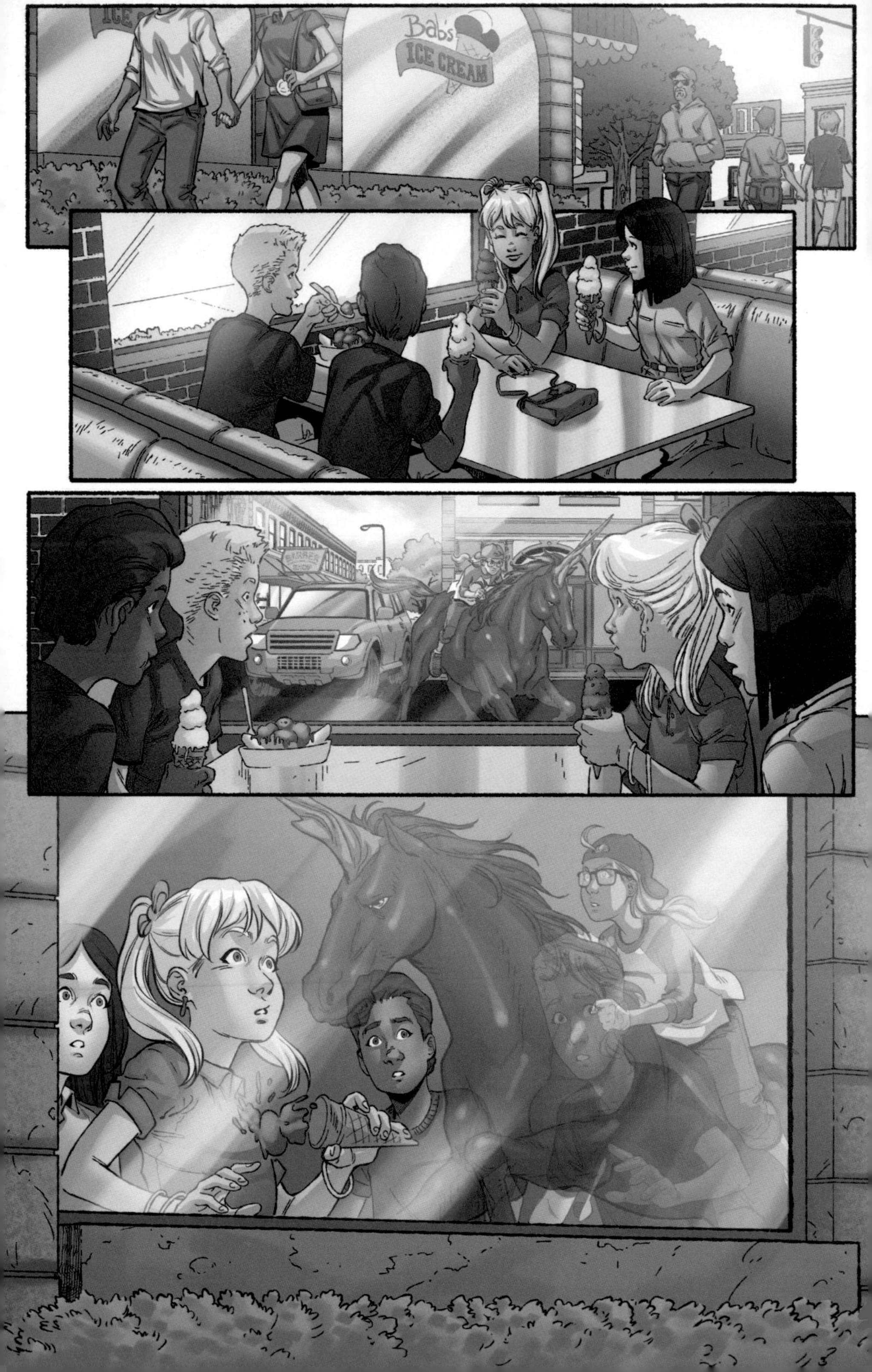
Bab's
ICE CREAM

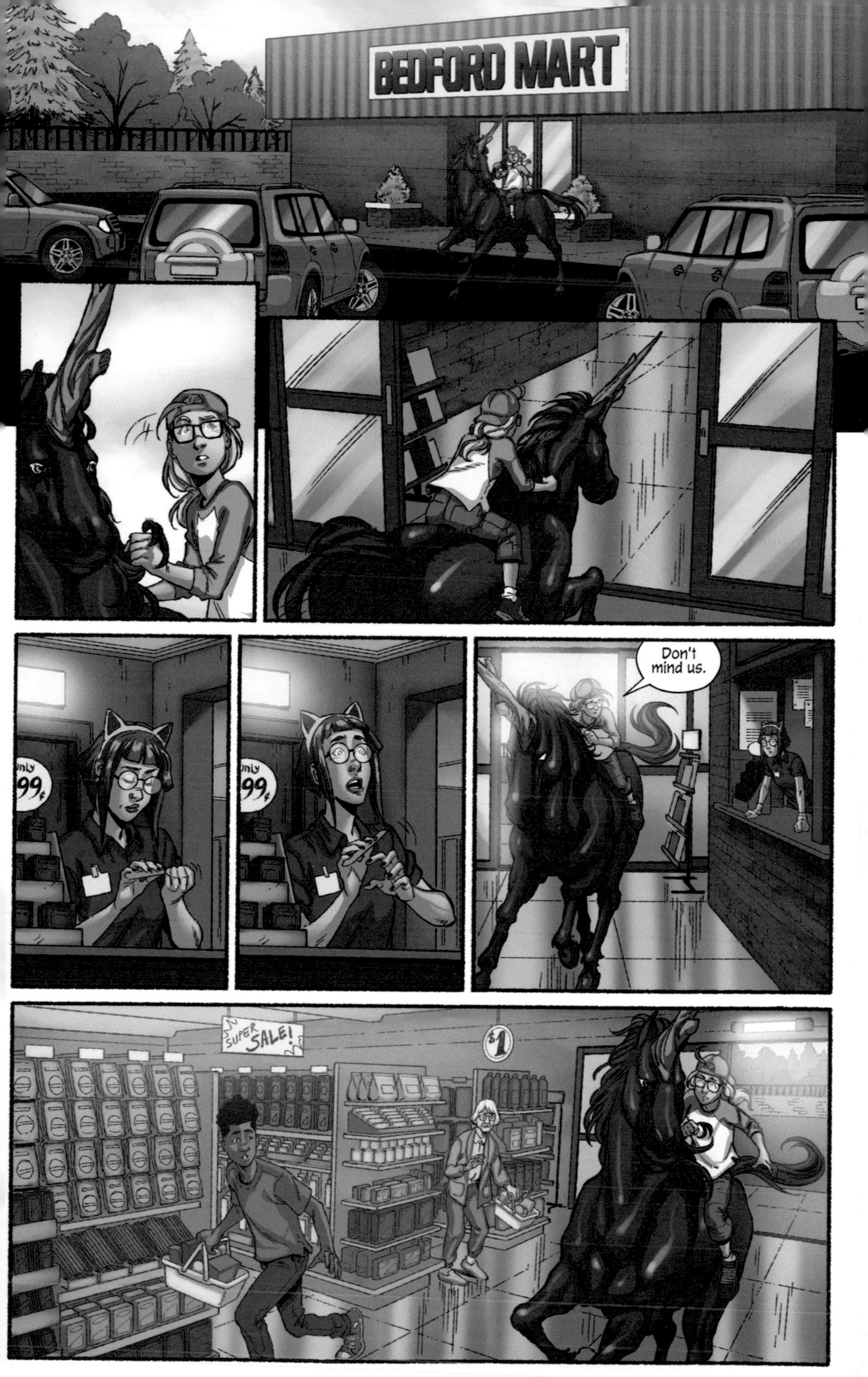
BEDFORD MART
only
99¢
Don't mind us.
SUPER SALE!
$1

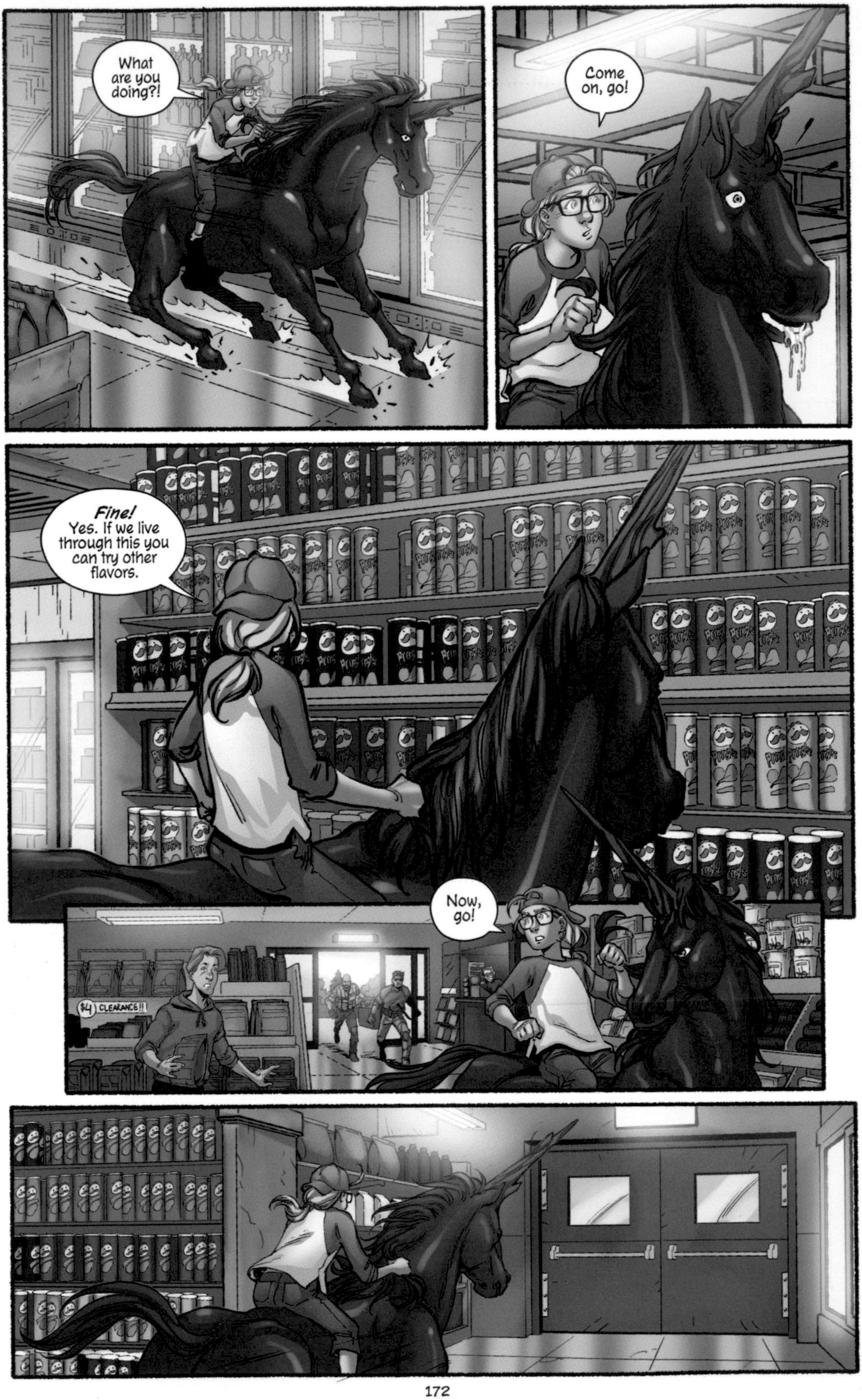
What are you doing?!
Come on, go!
Fine! Yes. If we live through this you can try other flavors.
Now, go!
$4 CLEARANCE!!

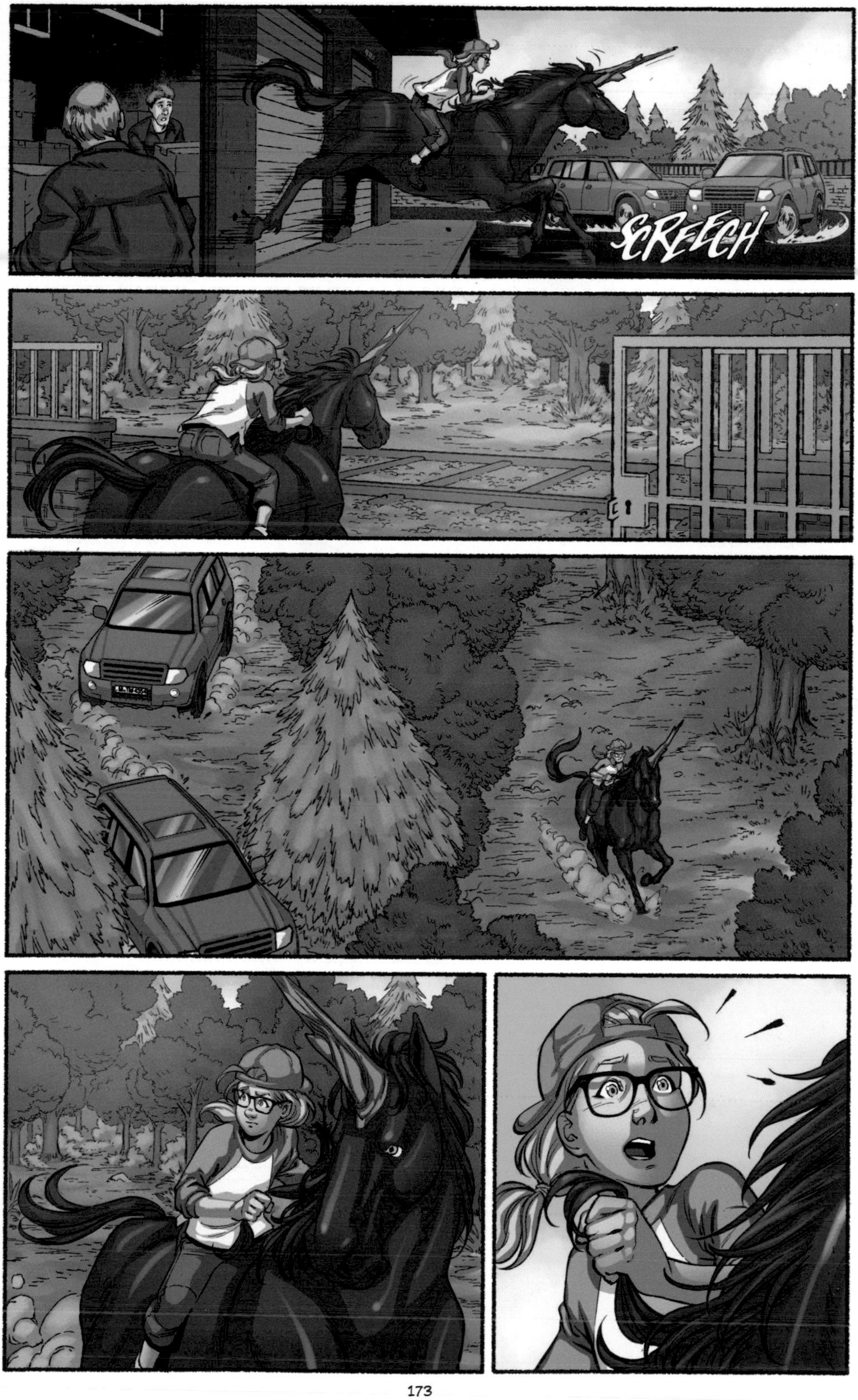
SCREECH

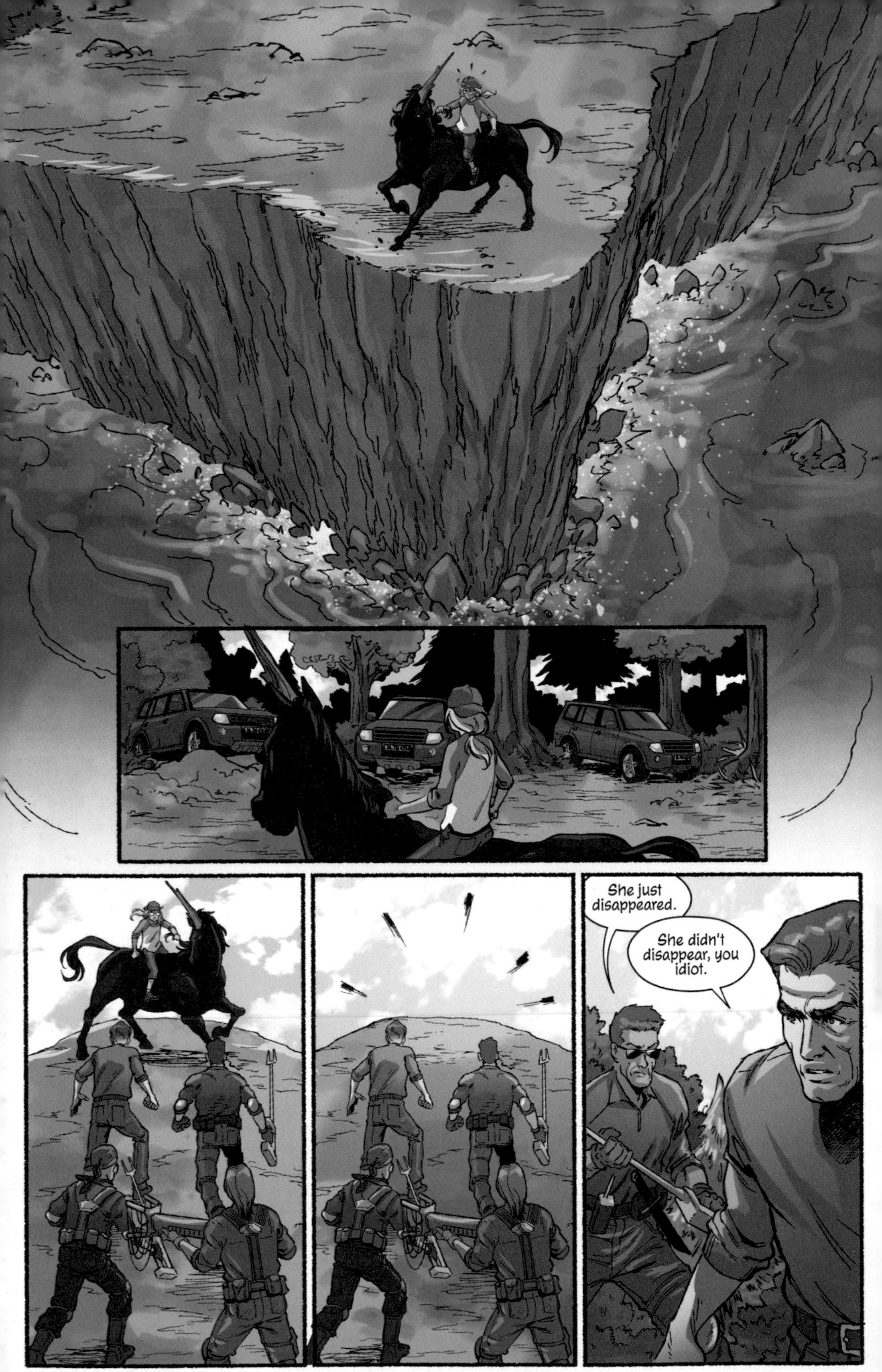
She just disappeared.
She didn't disappear, you idiot.

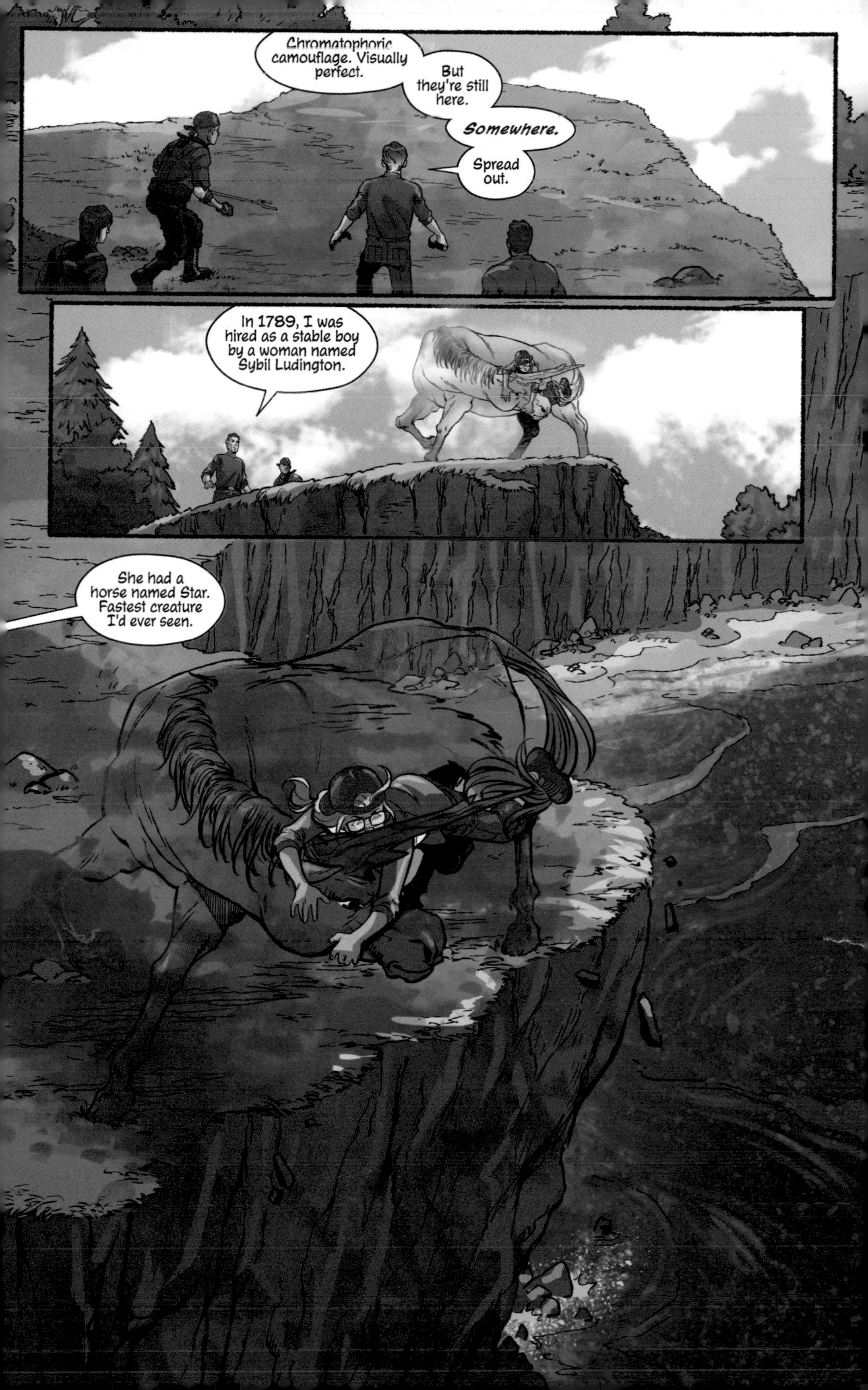
Chromatophoric camouflage. Visually perfect.
But they're still here.
Somewhere.
Spread out.
In 1789, I was hired as a stable boy by a woman named Sybil Ludington.
She had a horse named Star. Fastest creature I'd ever seen.

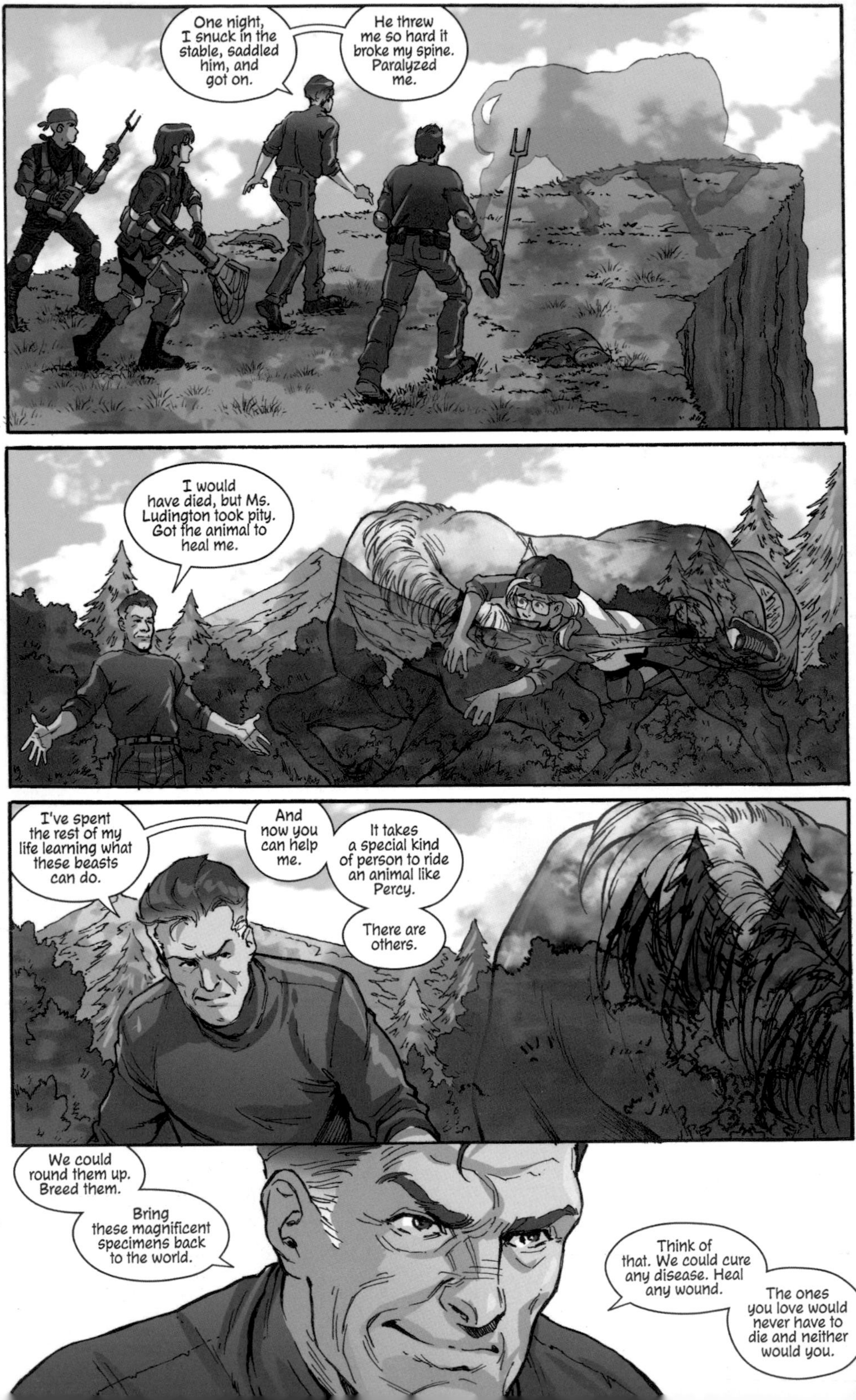
One night, I snuck in the stable, saddled him, and got on.
He threw me so hard it broke my spine. Paralyzed me.
I would have died, but Ms. Ludington took pity. Got the animal to heal me.
I've spent the rest of my life learning what these beasts can do.
And now you can help me.
It takes a special kind of person to ride an animal like Percy.
There are others.
We could round them up. Breed them.
Bring these magnificent specimens back to the world.
Think of that. We could cure any disease. Heal any wound.
The ones you love would never have to die and neither would you.

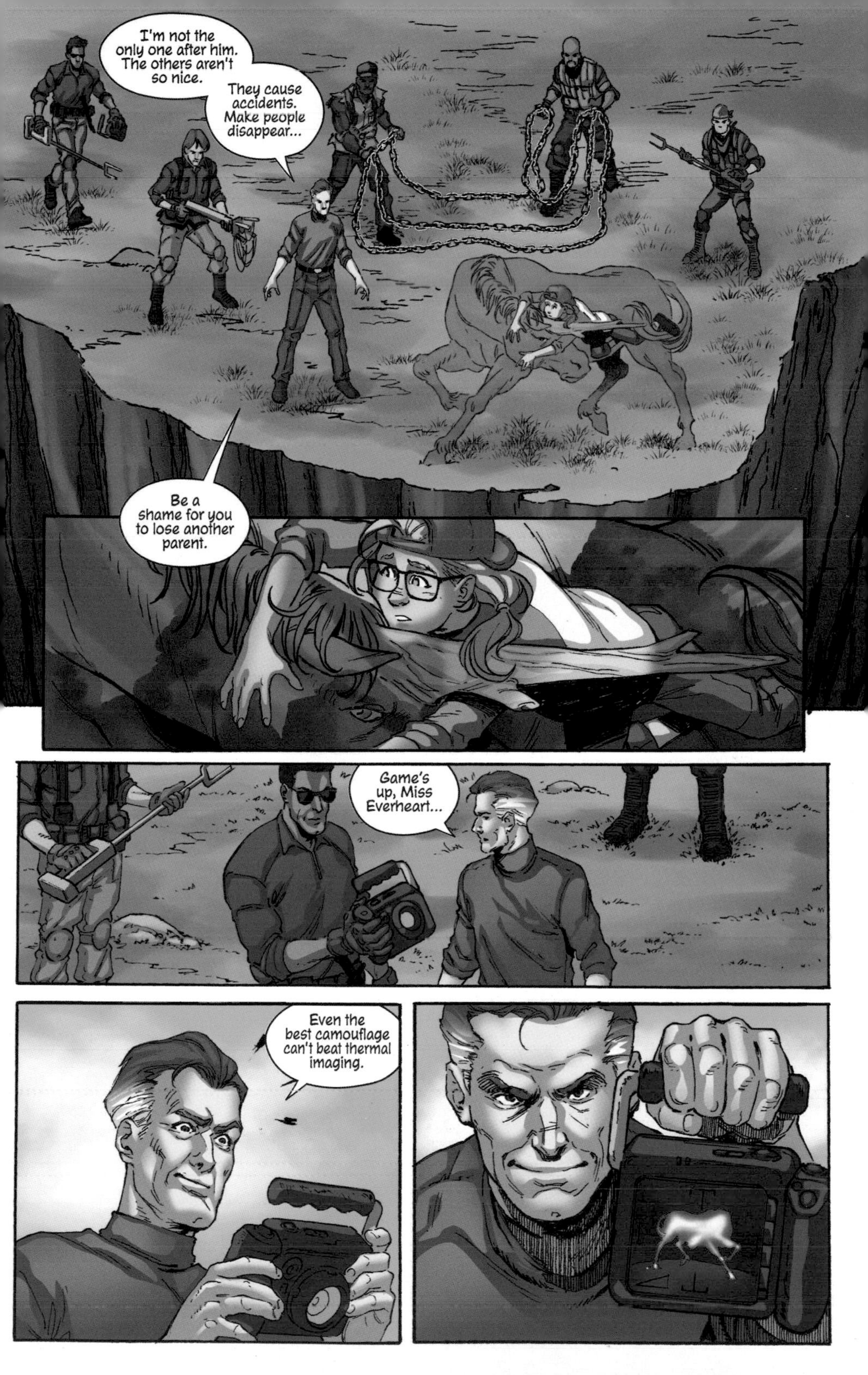
I'm not the only one after him. The others aren't so nice.
They cause accidents. Make people disappear...
Be a shame for you to lose another parent.
Game's up, Miss Everheart...
Even the best camouflage can't beat thermal imaging.

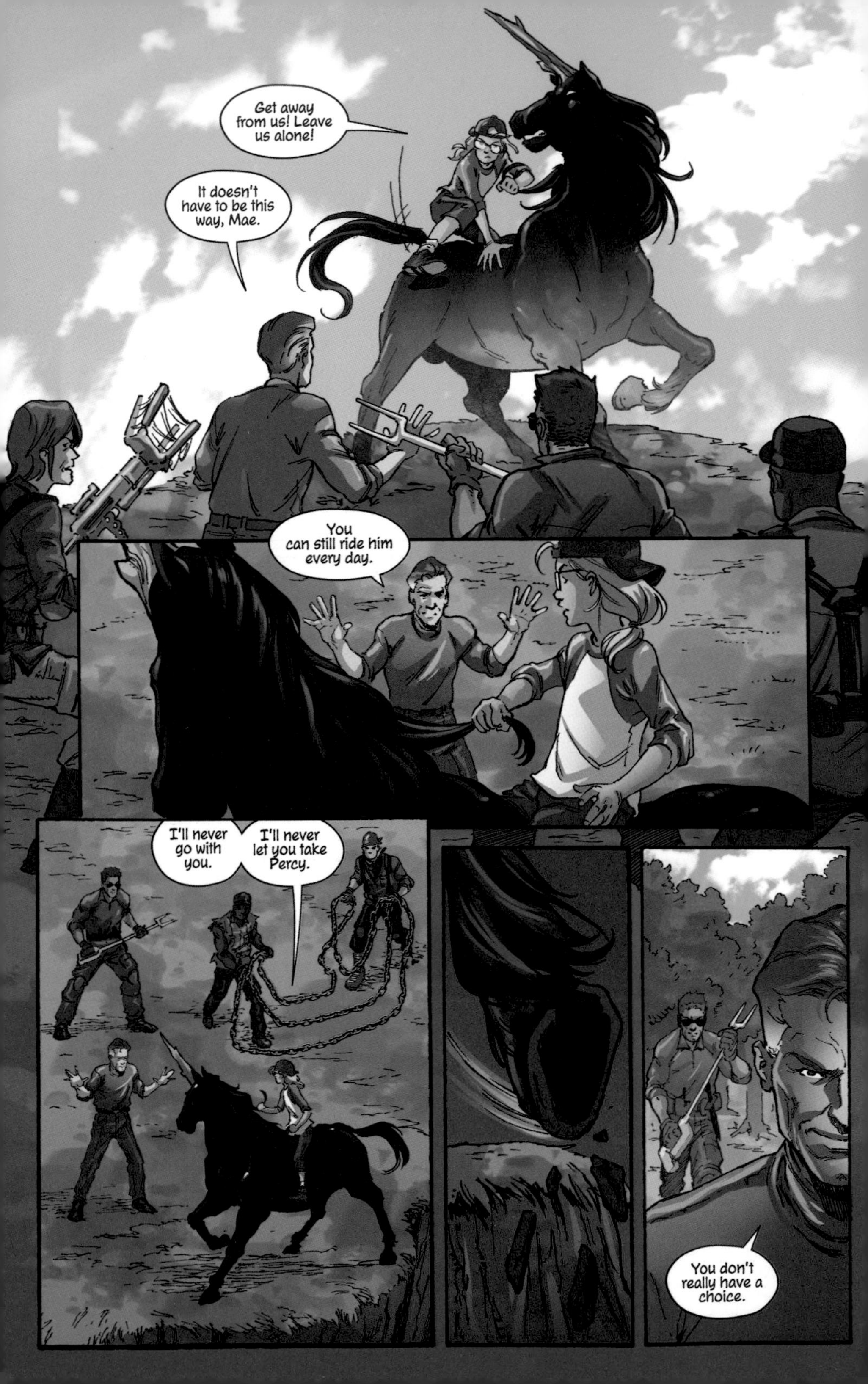
Get away from us! Leave us alone!
It doesn't have to be this way, Mae.
You can still ride him every day.
I'll never go with you.
I'll never let you take Percy.
You don't really have a choice.

It's okay, boy. It's okay to be scared.

It's the only way we can be brave.

Ten. Nine. Eight. Seven.

Nowhere left to run, Mae.

Six. Five, four...

Three, two--

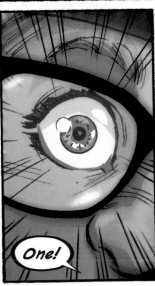

One!

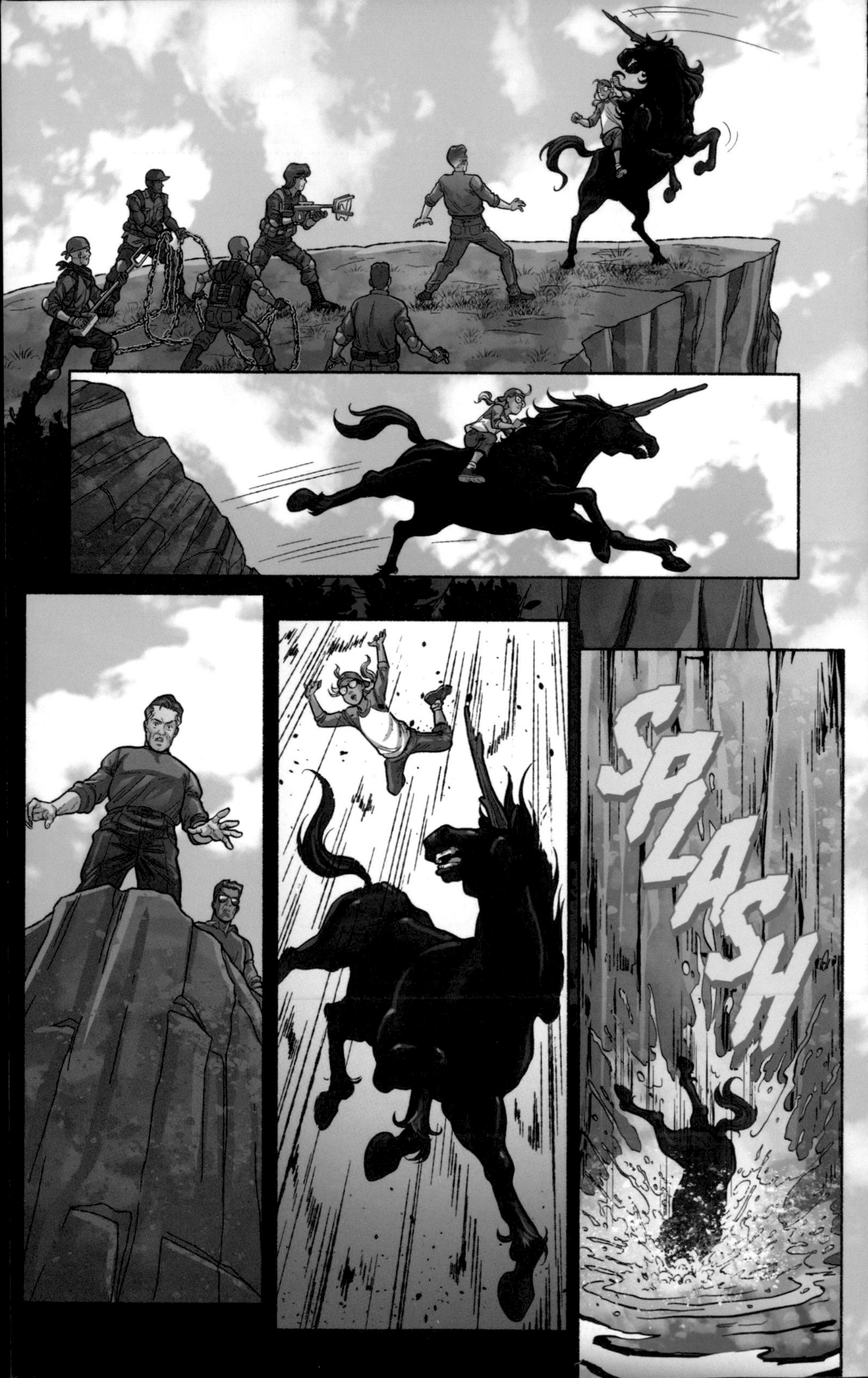
SPLASH

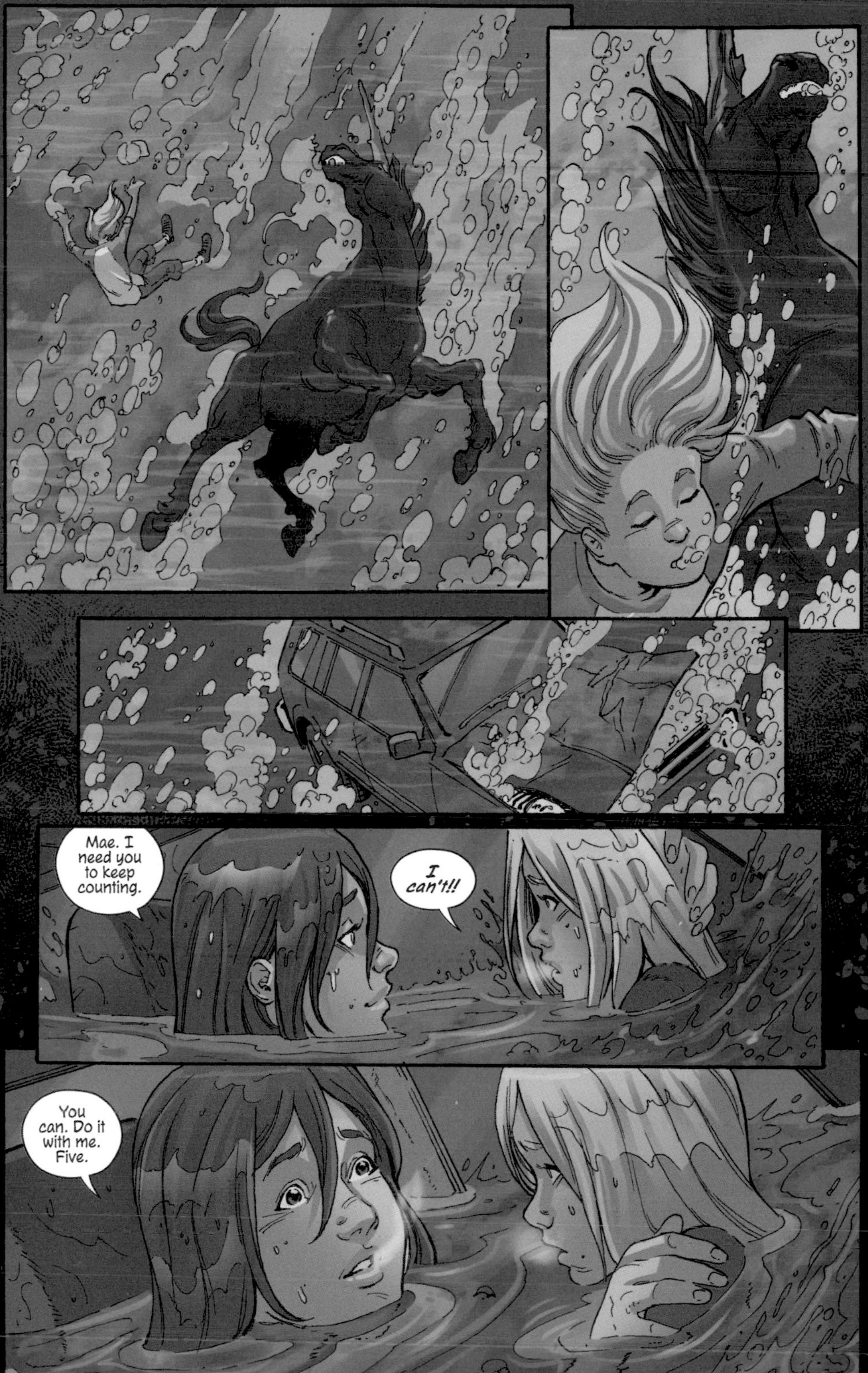
Mae. I need you to keep counting.
I can't!!
You can. Do it with me. Five.

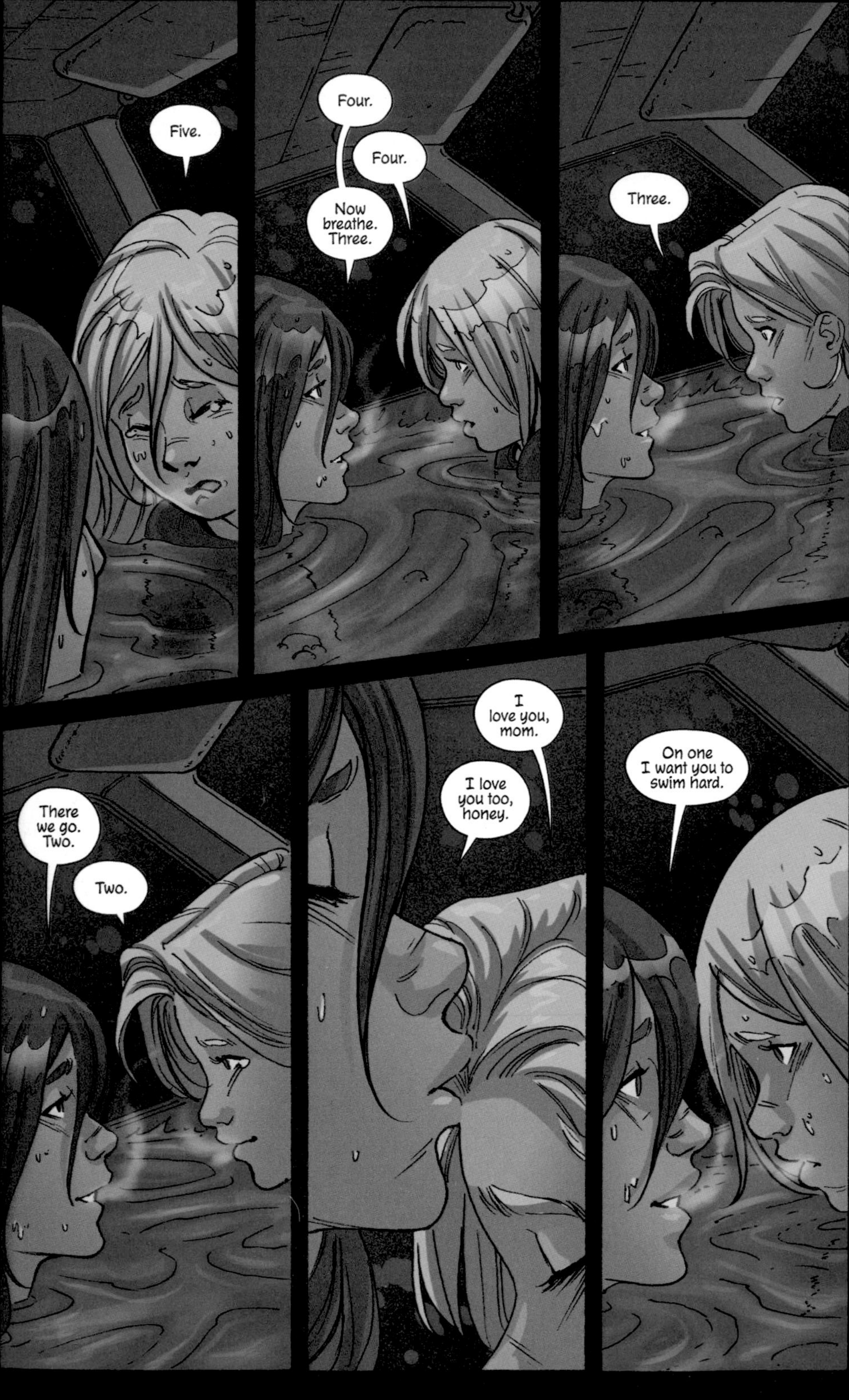
Five.
Four.
Four.
Now breathe. Three.
Three.
There we go. Two.
Two.
I love you, mom.
I love you too, honey.
On one I want you to swim hard.

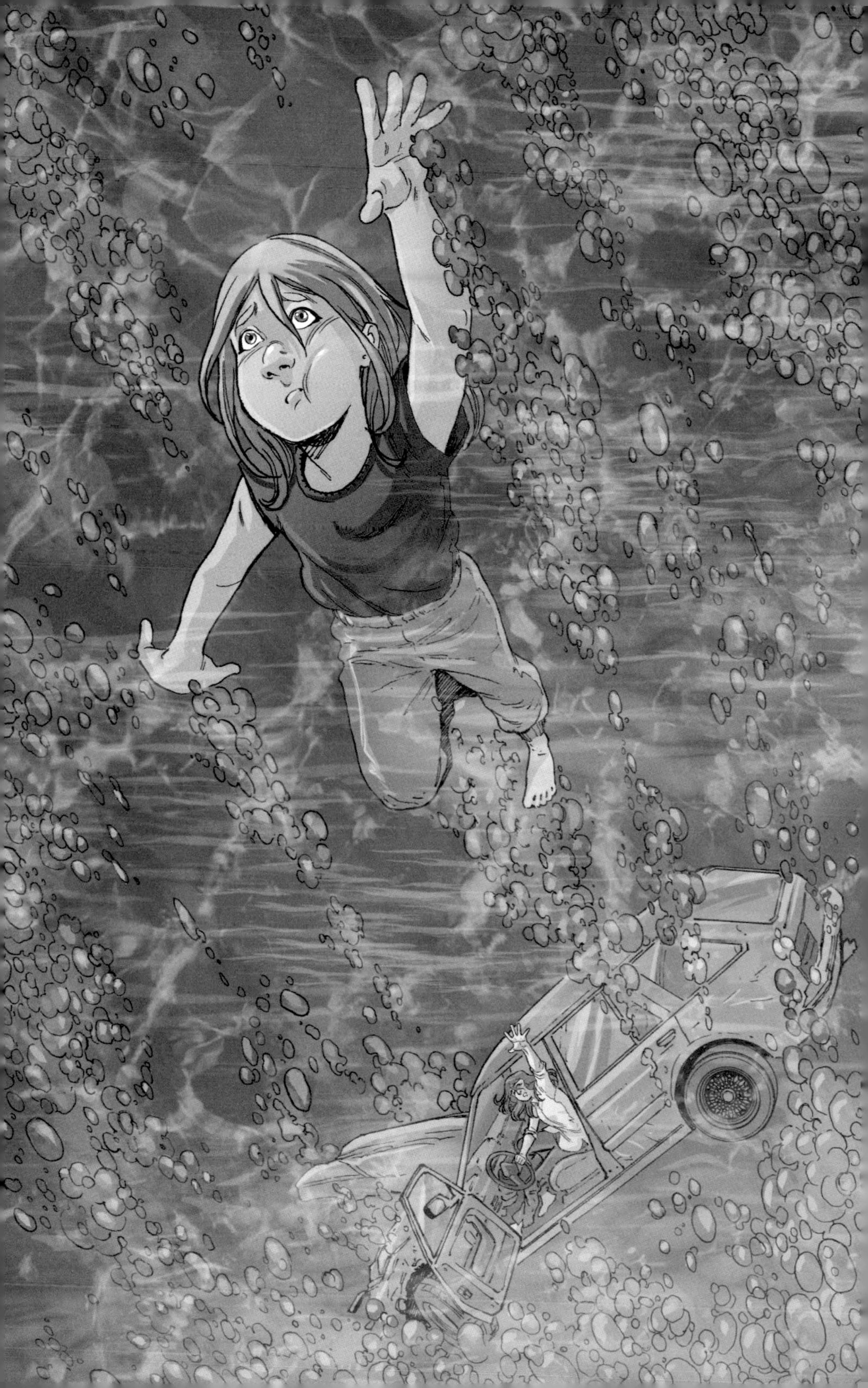

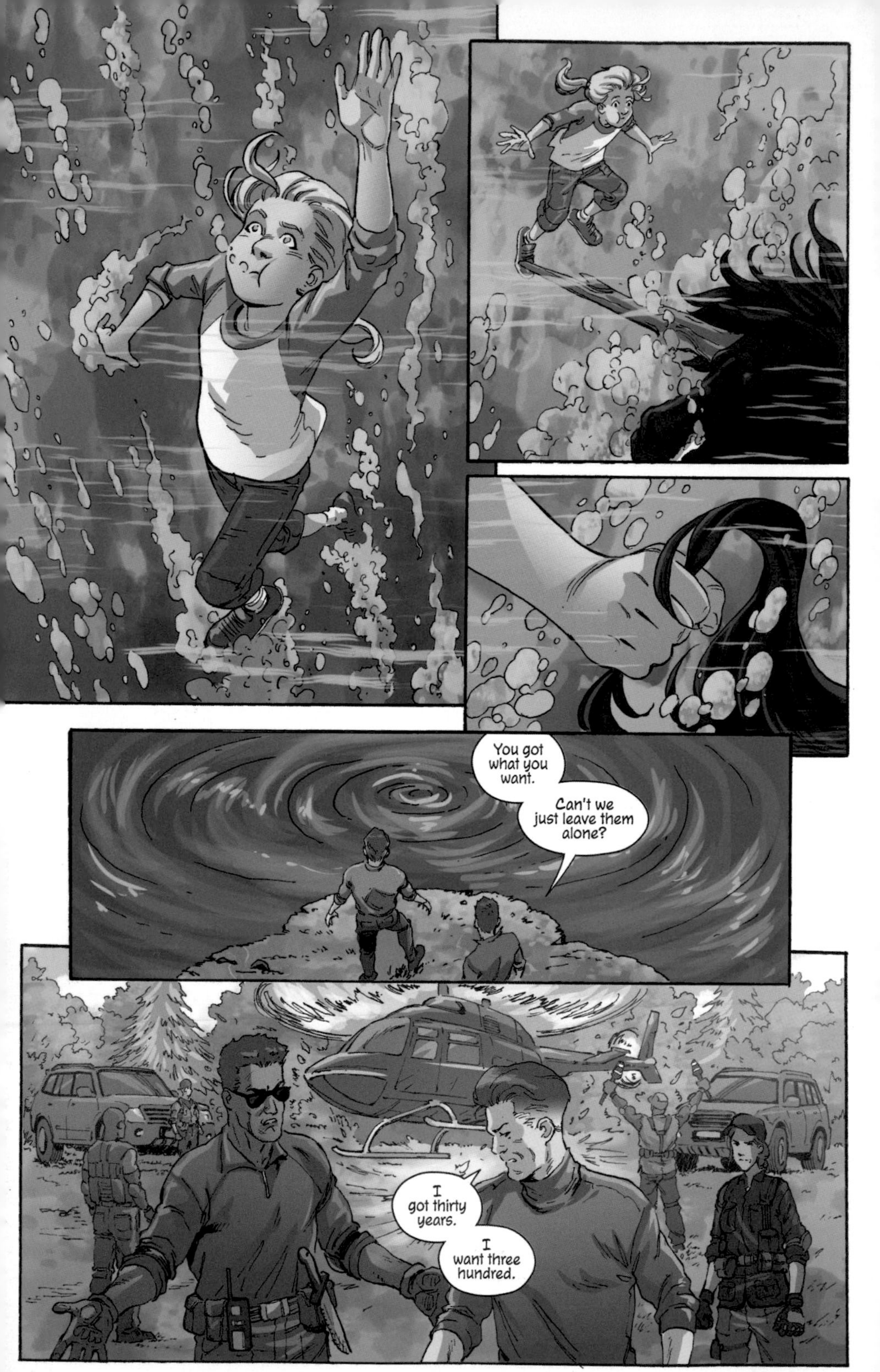
You got what you want.
Can't we just leave them alone?
I got thirty years.
I want three hundred.

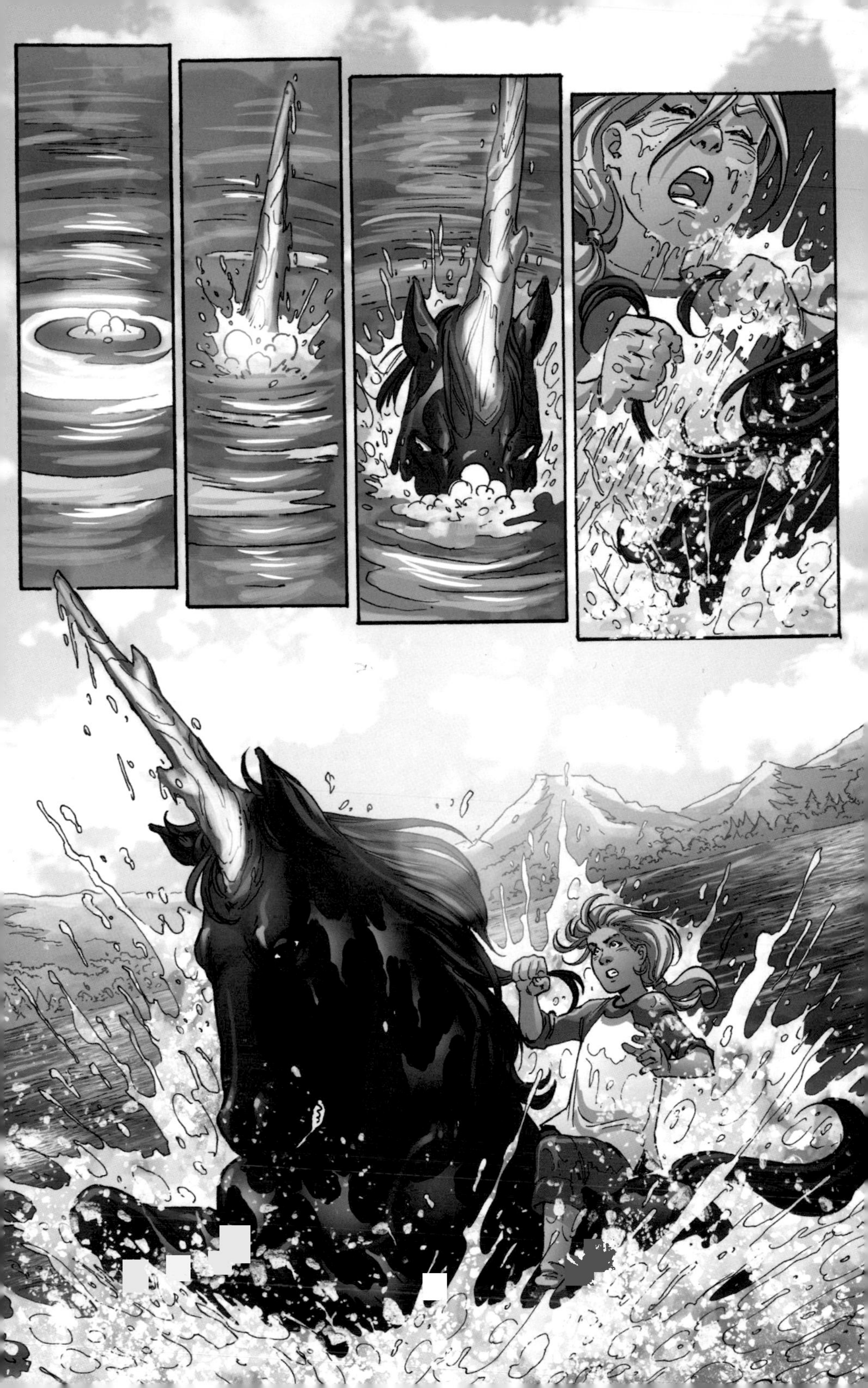

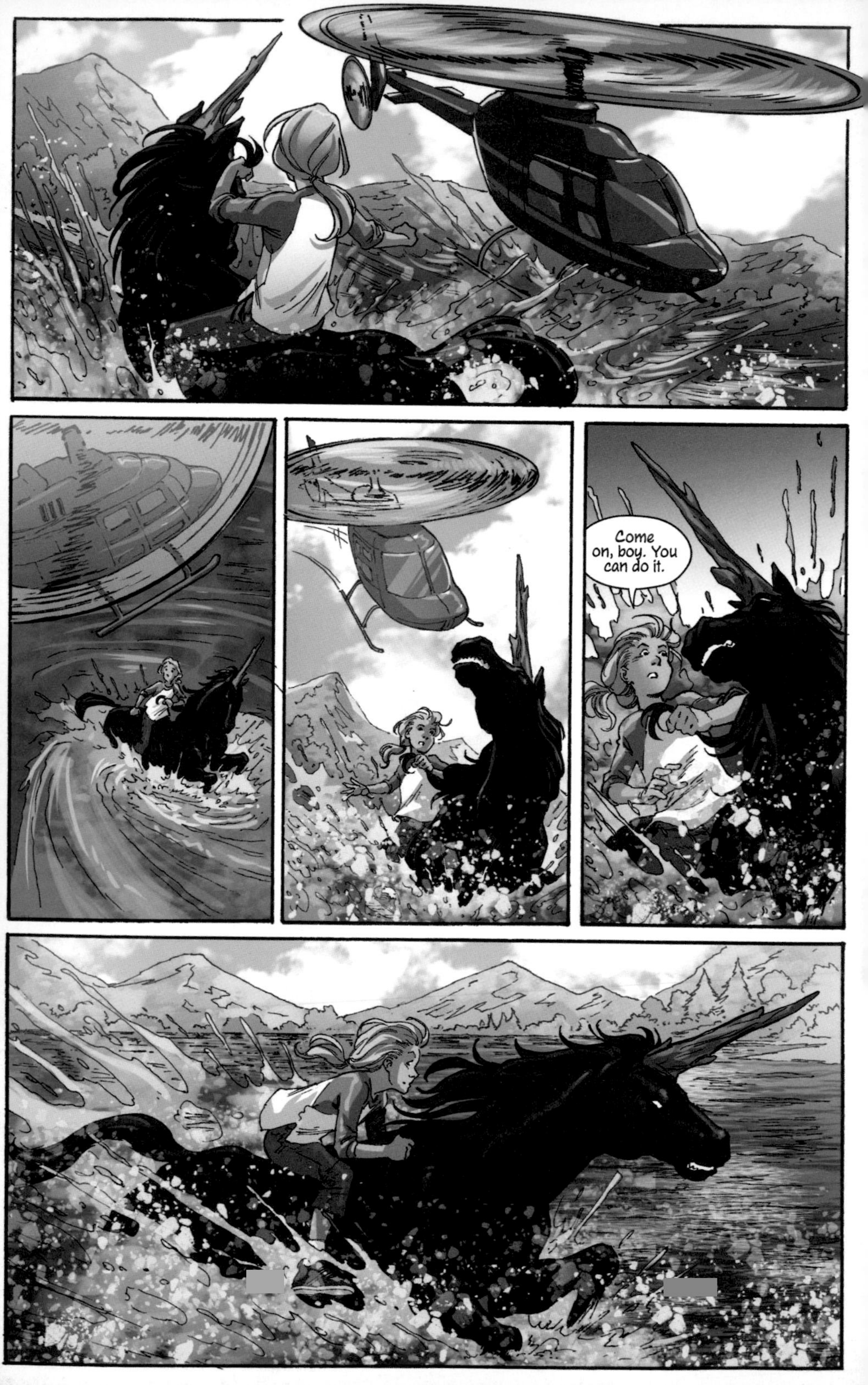
Come on, boy. You can do it.

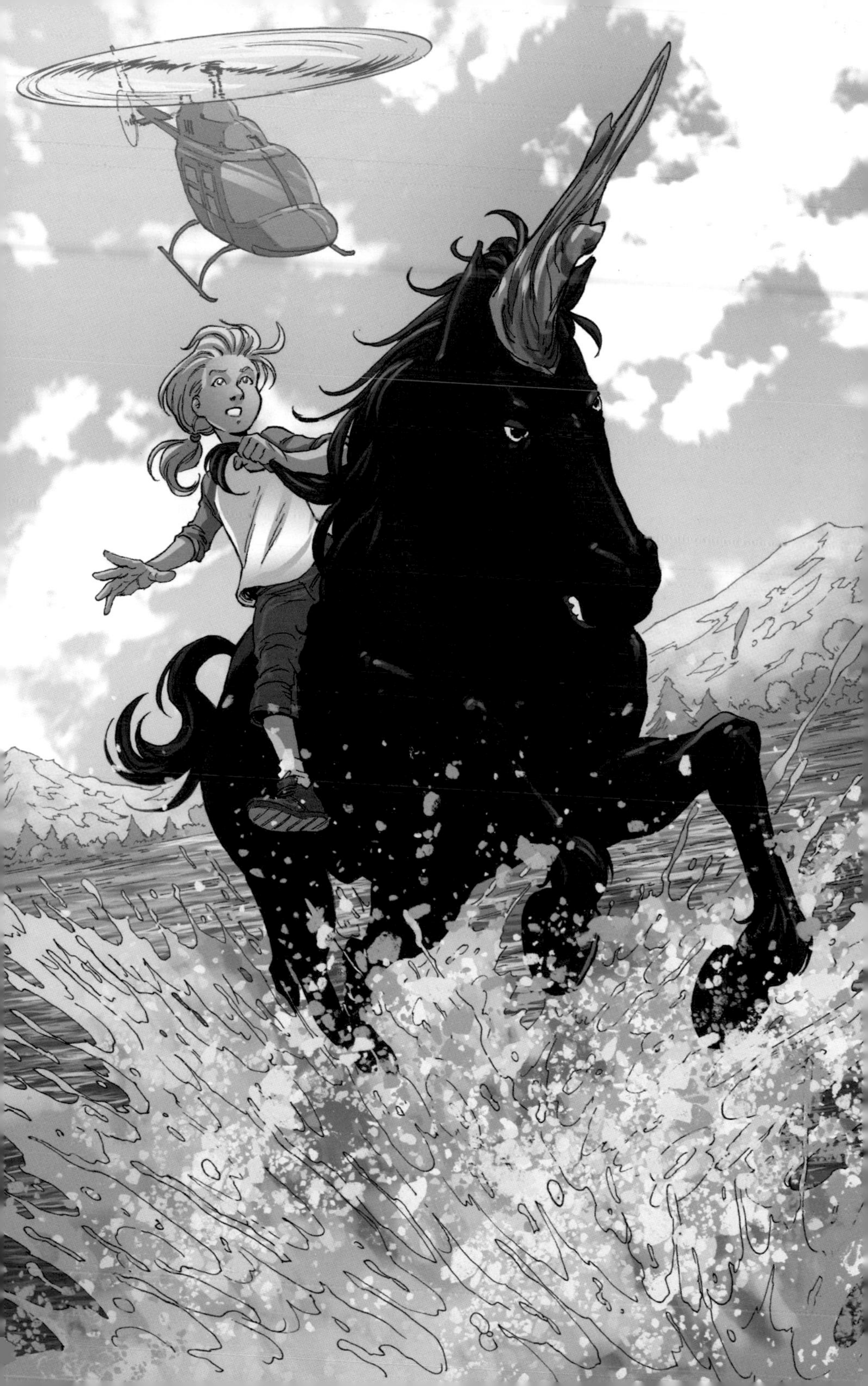

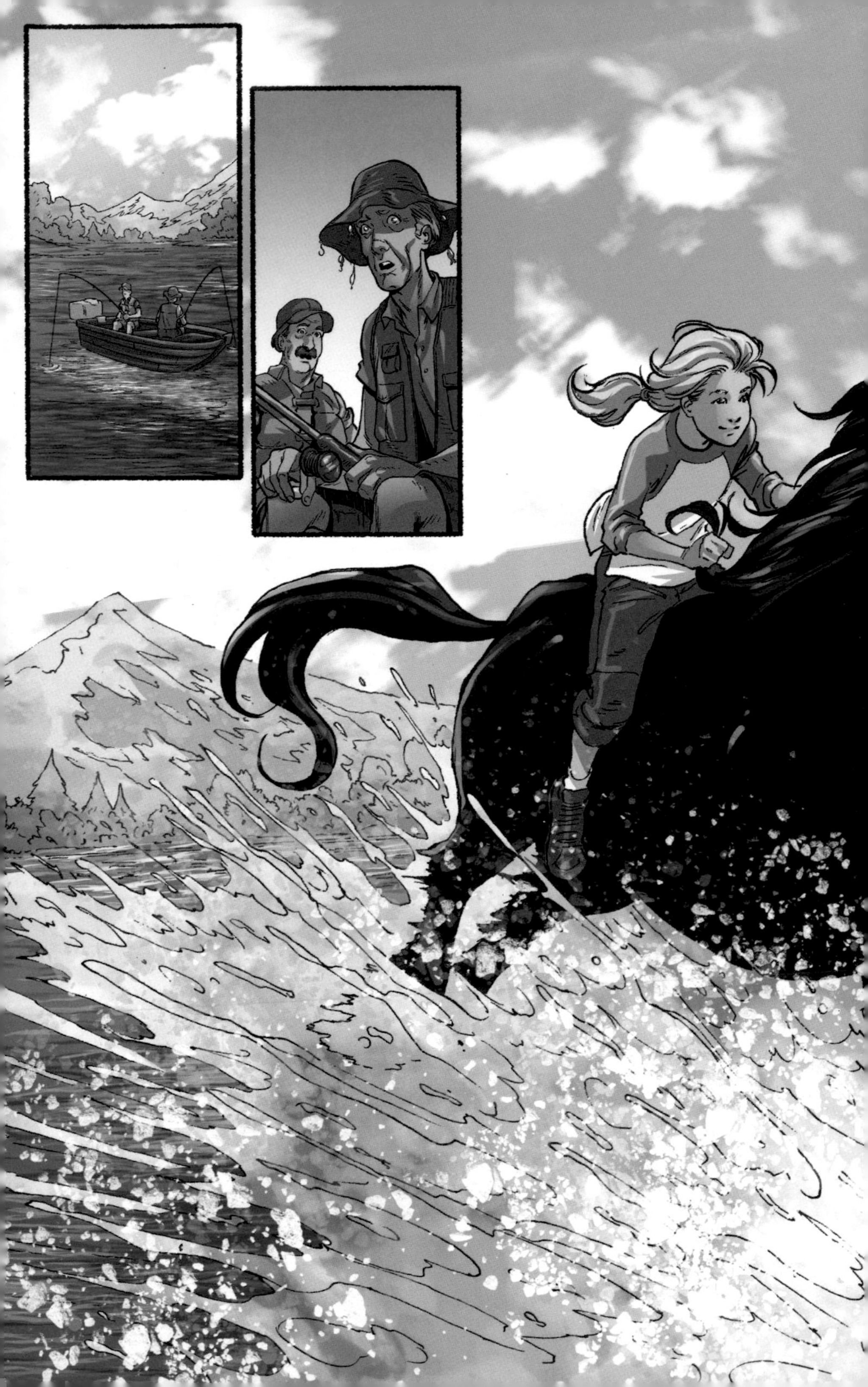

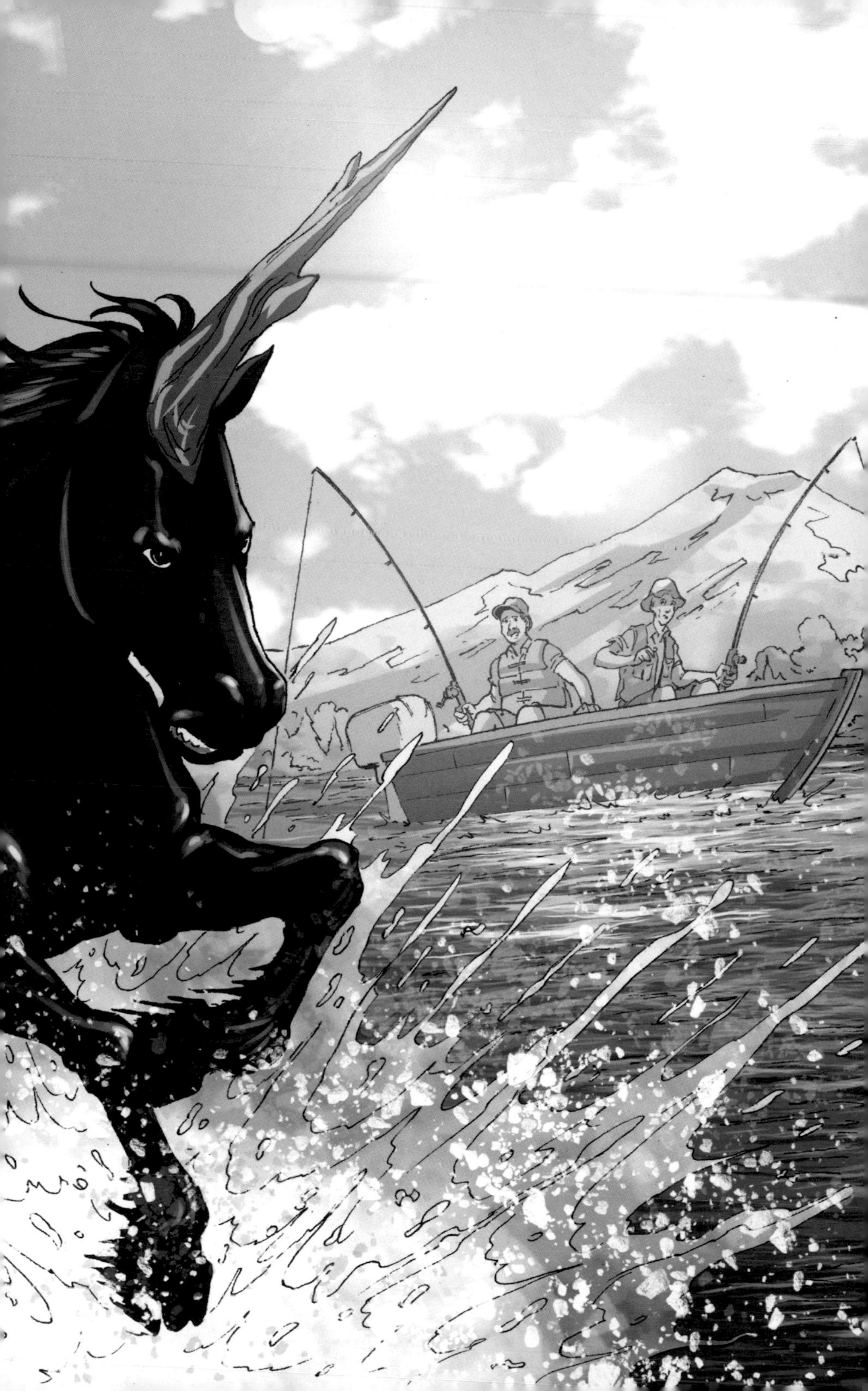

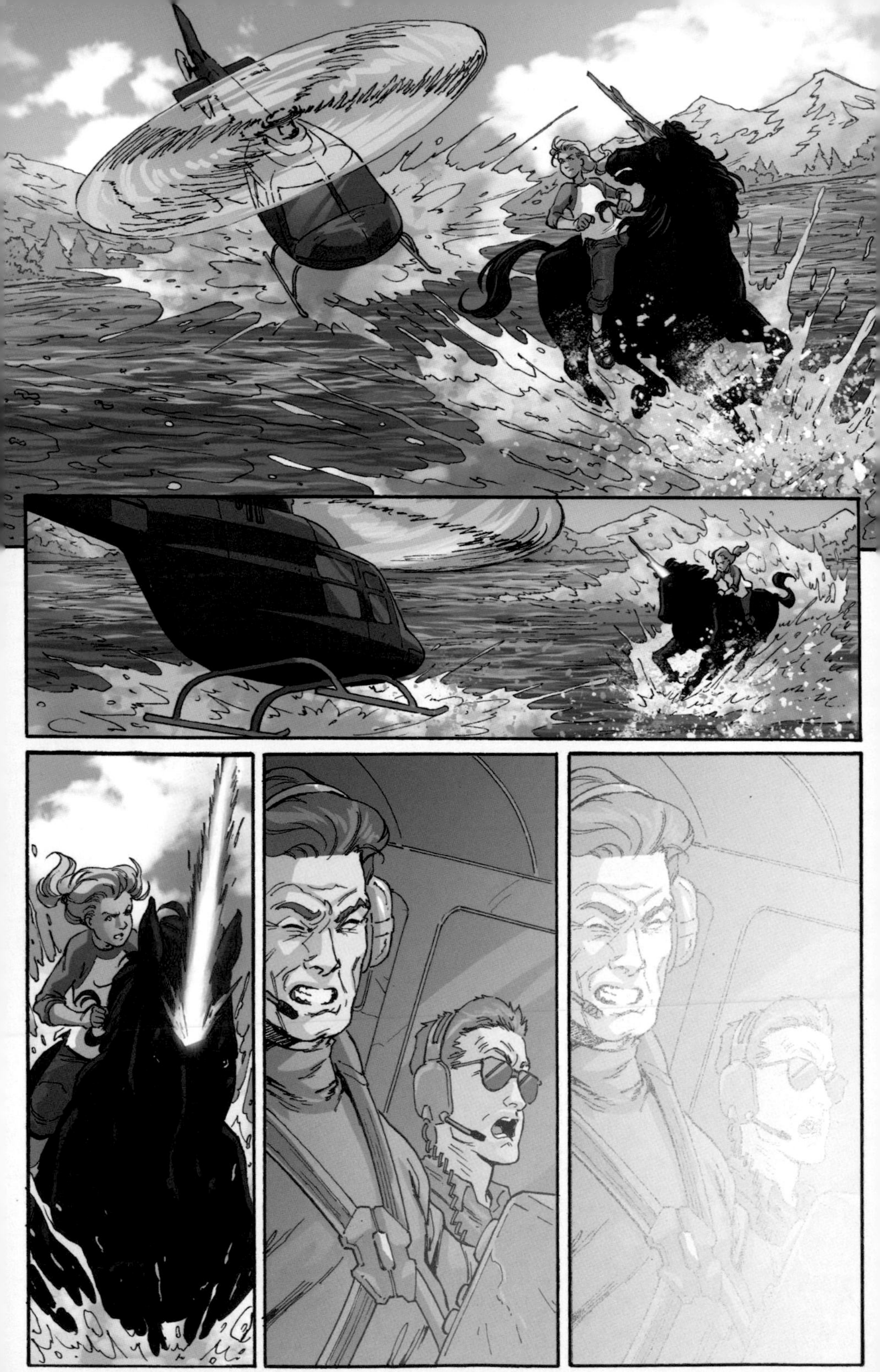

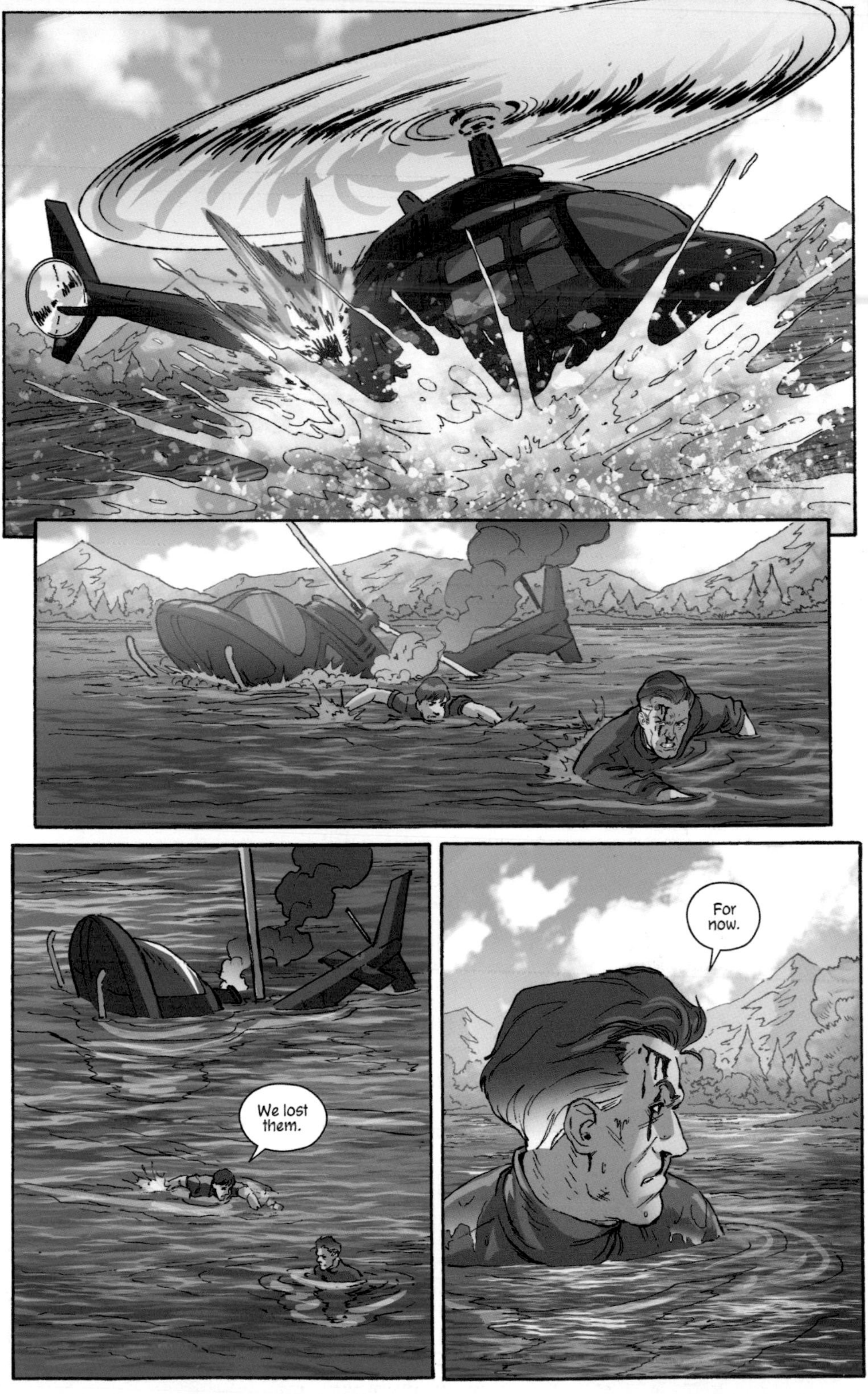
We lost them.
For now.

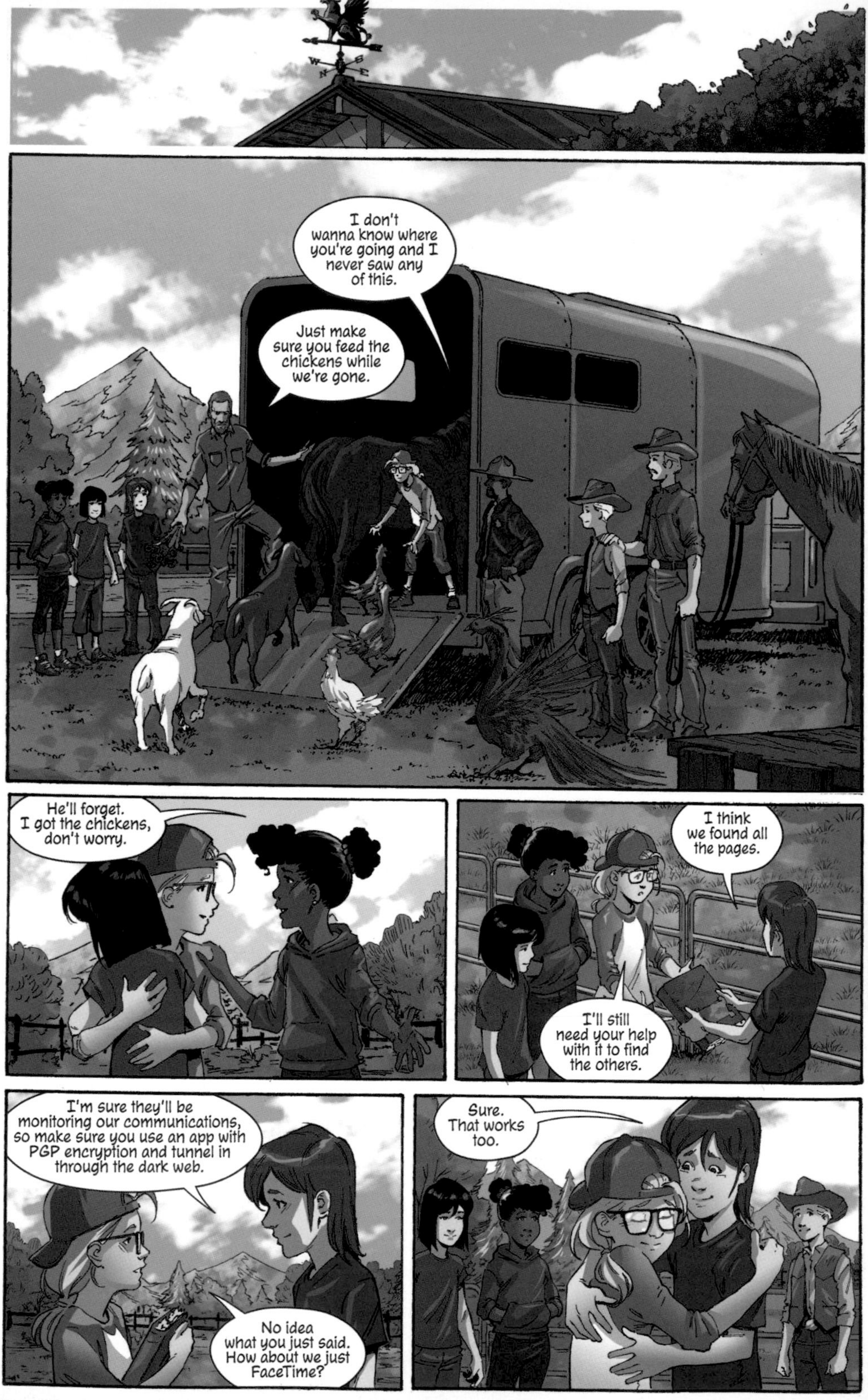
I don't wanna know where you're going and I never saw any of this.
Just make sure you feed the chickens while we're gone.
He'll forget. I got the chickens, don't worry.
I think we found all the pages.
I'll still need your help with it to find the others.
I'm sure they'll be monitoring our communications, so make sure you use an app with PGP encryption and tunnel in through the dark web.
No idea what you just said. How about we just FaceTime?
Sure. That works too.

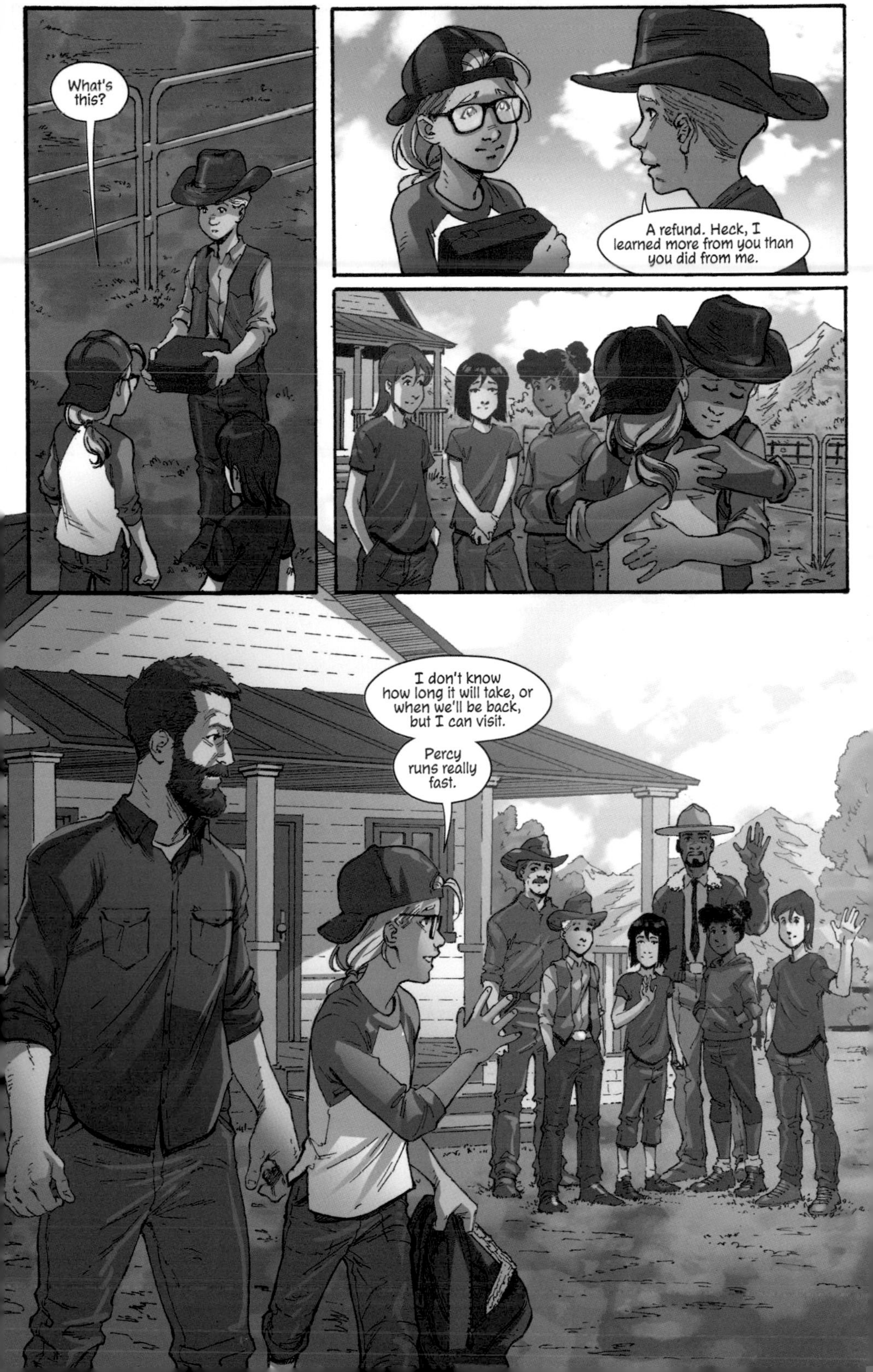
What's this?
A refund. Heck, I learned more from you than you did from me.
I don't know how long it will take, or when we'll be back, but I can visit.
Percy runs really fast.

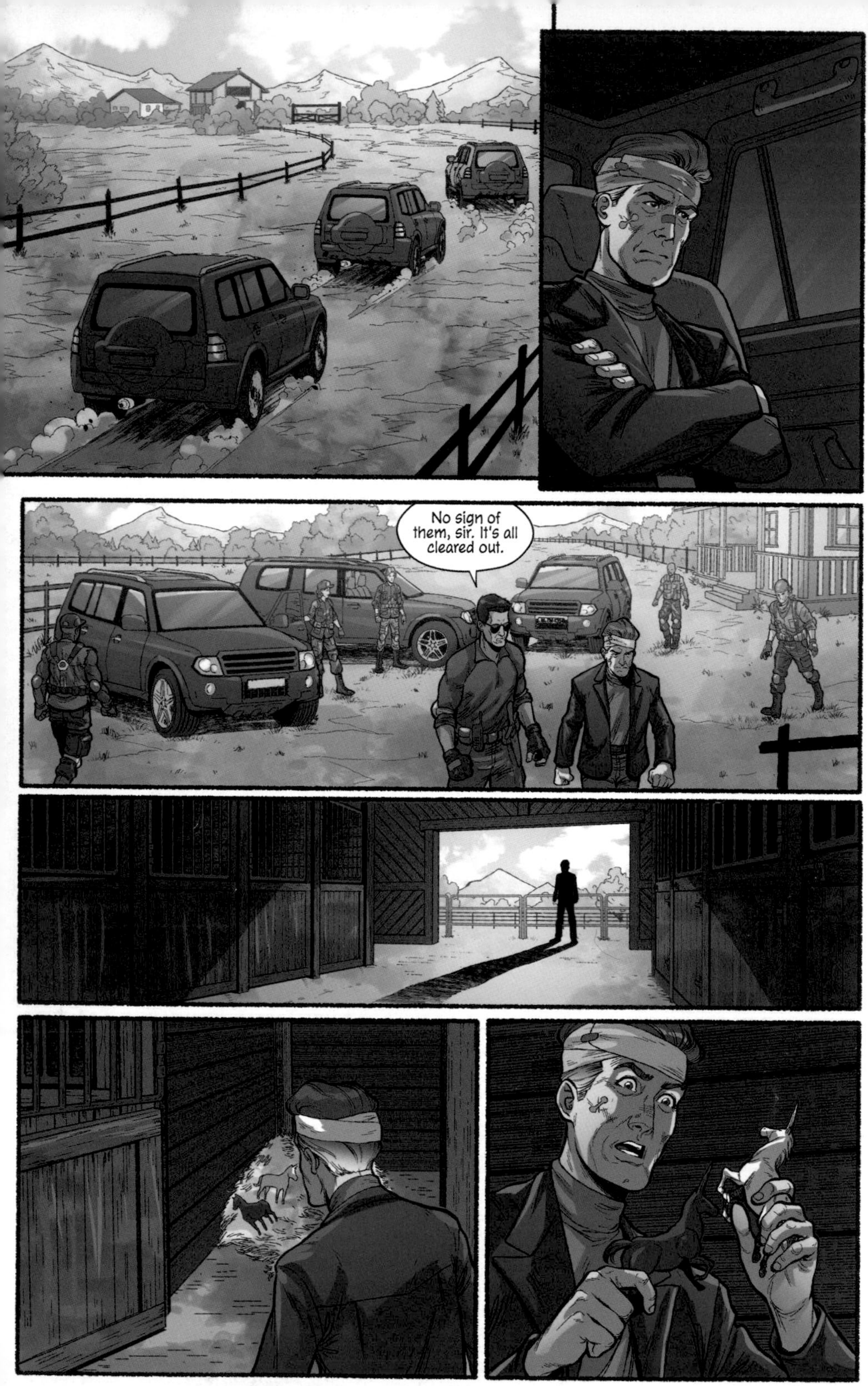
No sign of them, sir. It's all cleared out.

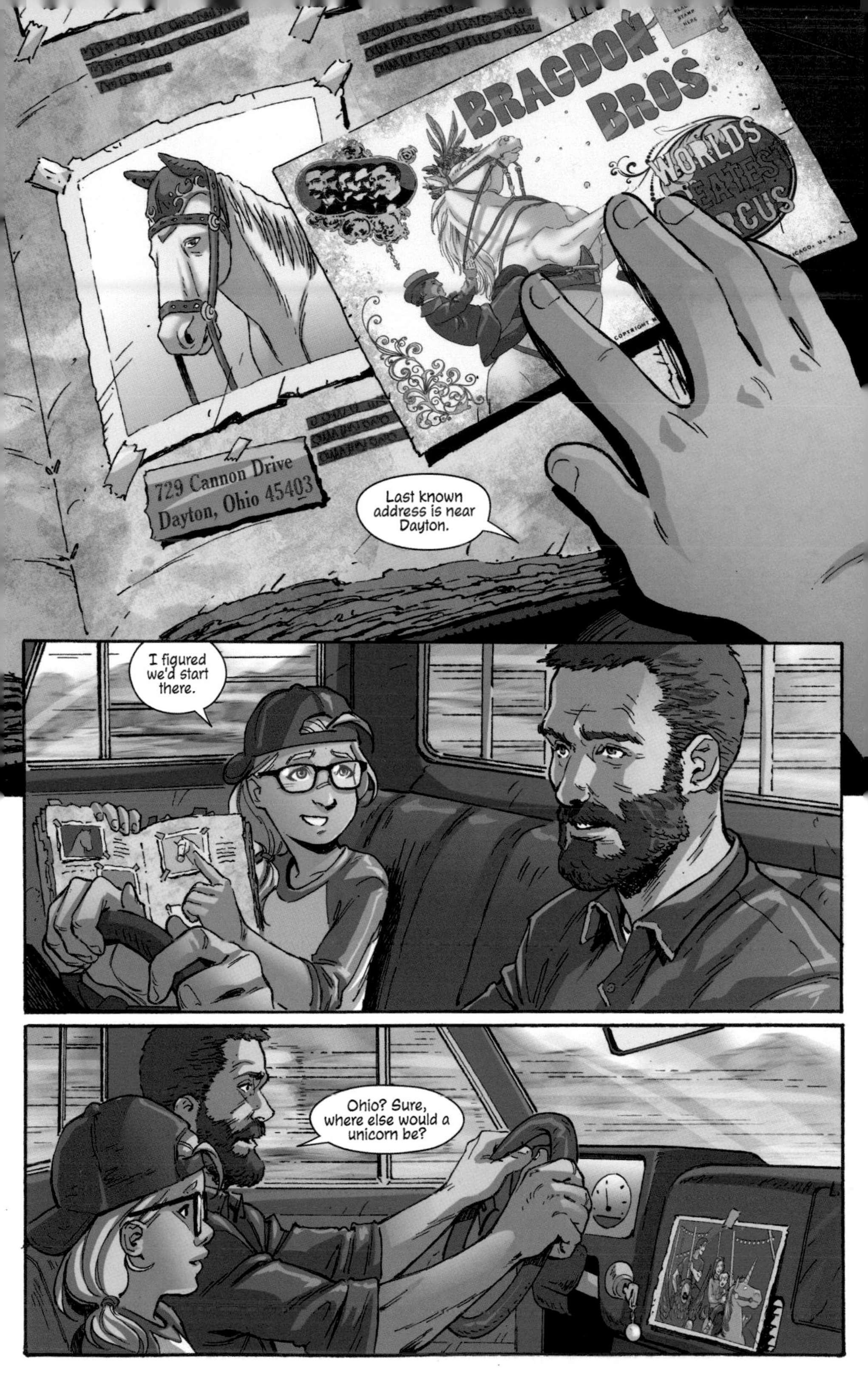
BRAGDON BROS
WORLDS
729 Cannon Drive
Dayton, Ohio 45403
Last known address is near Dayton.
I figured we'd start there.
Ohio? Sure, where else would a unicorn be?

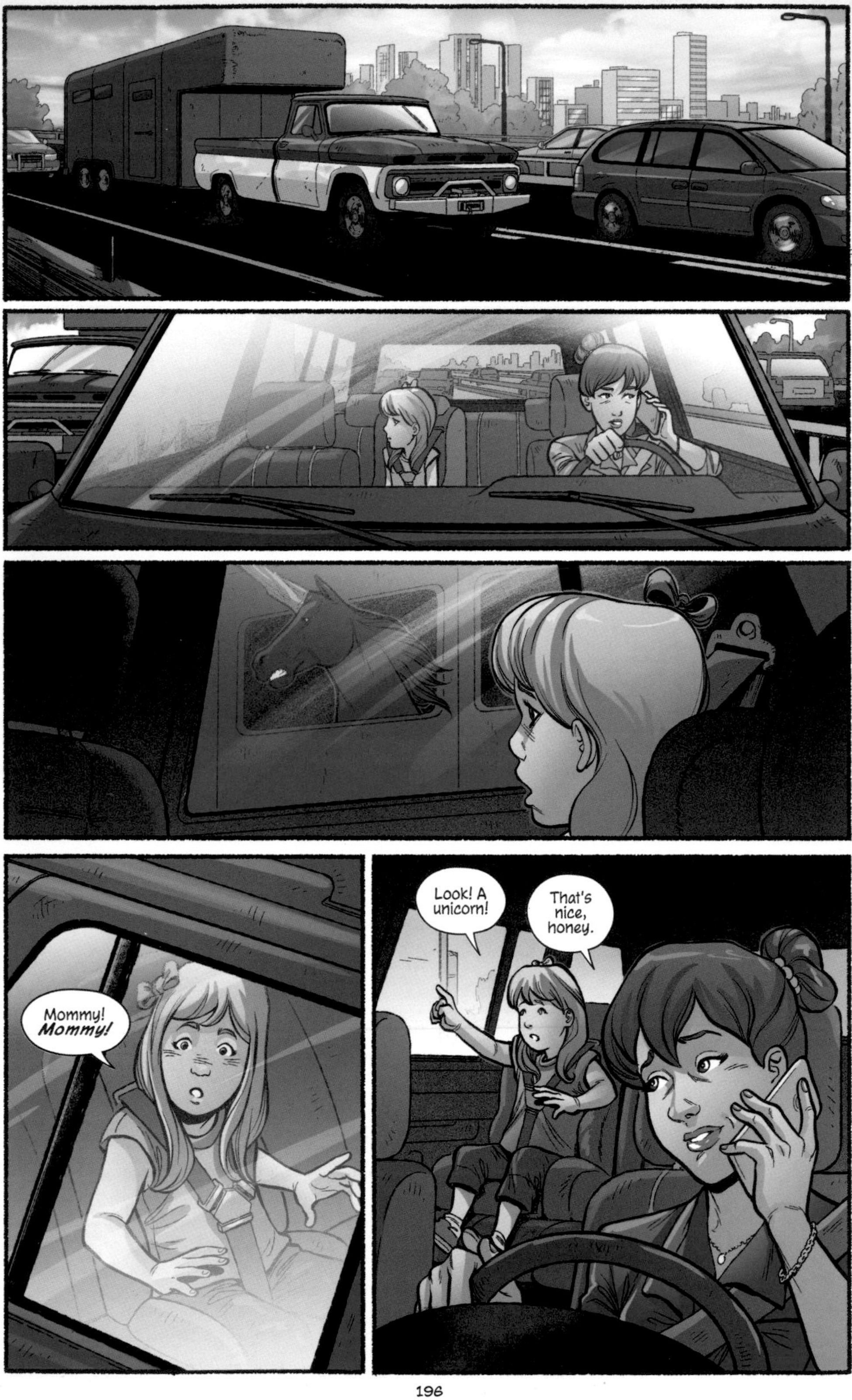
Mommy!
Mommy!
Look! A unicorn!
That's nice, honey.

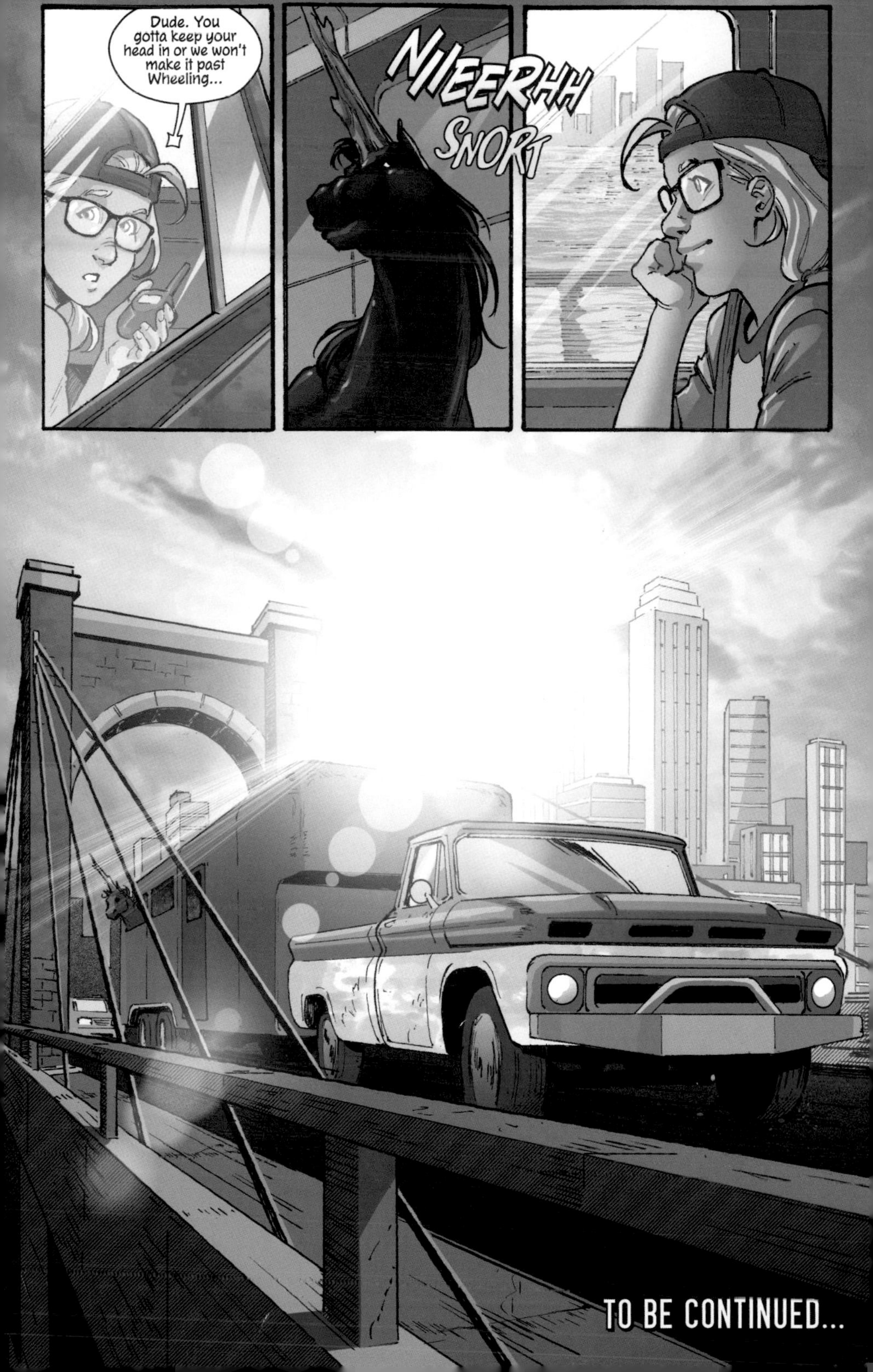
Dude. You gotta keep your head in or we won't make it past Wheeling...
NIIEERHH
SNORT
TO BE CONTINUED...

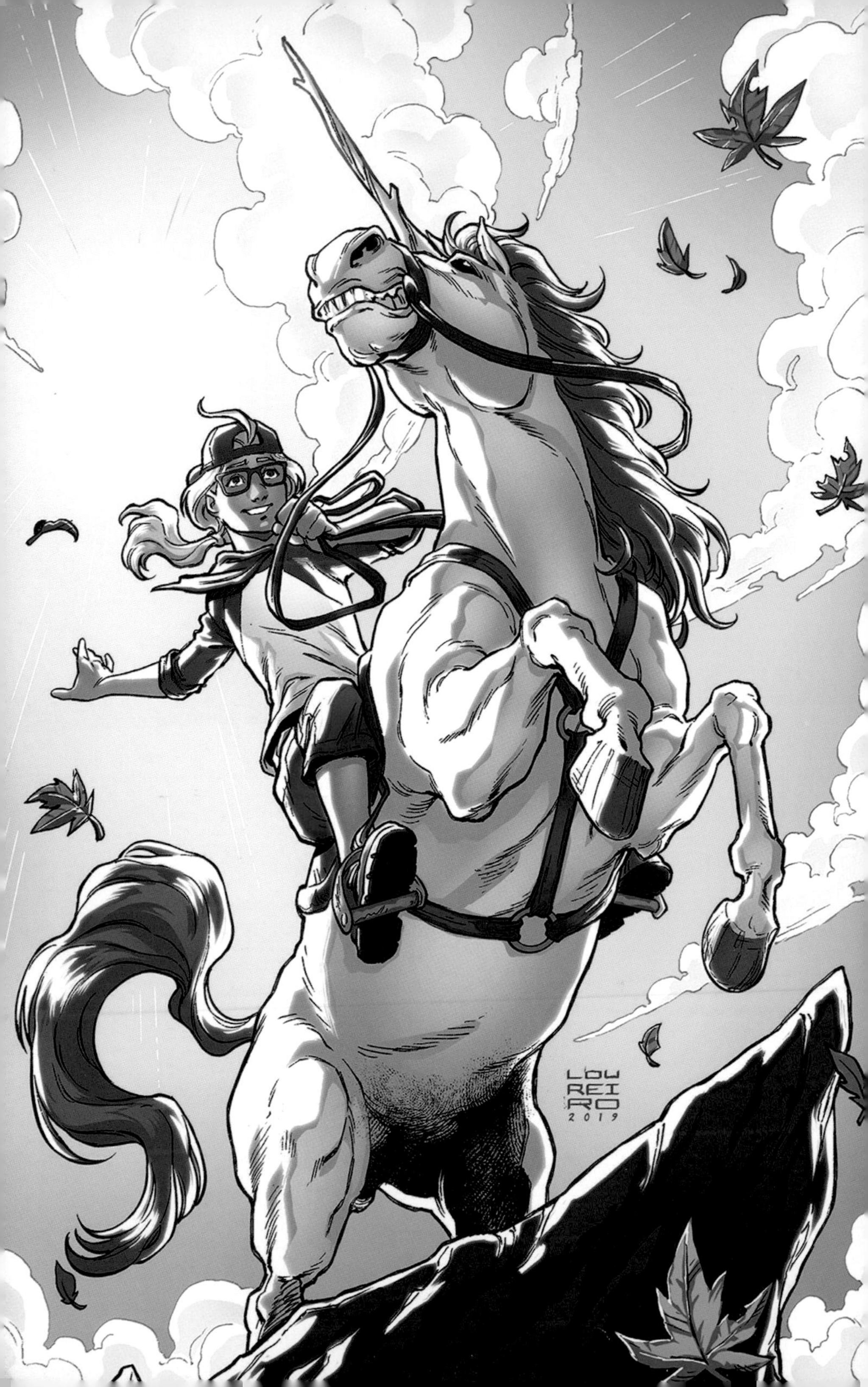
LOU
REI
RO
2019

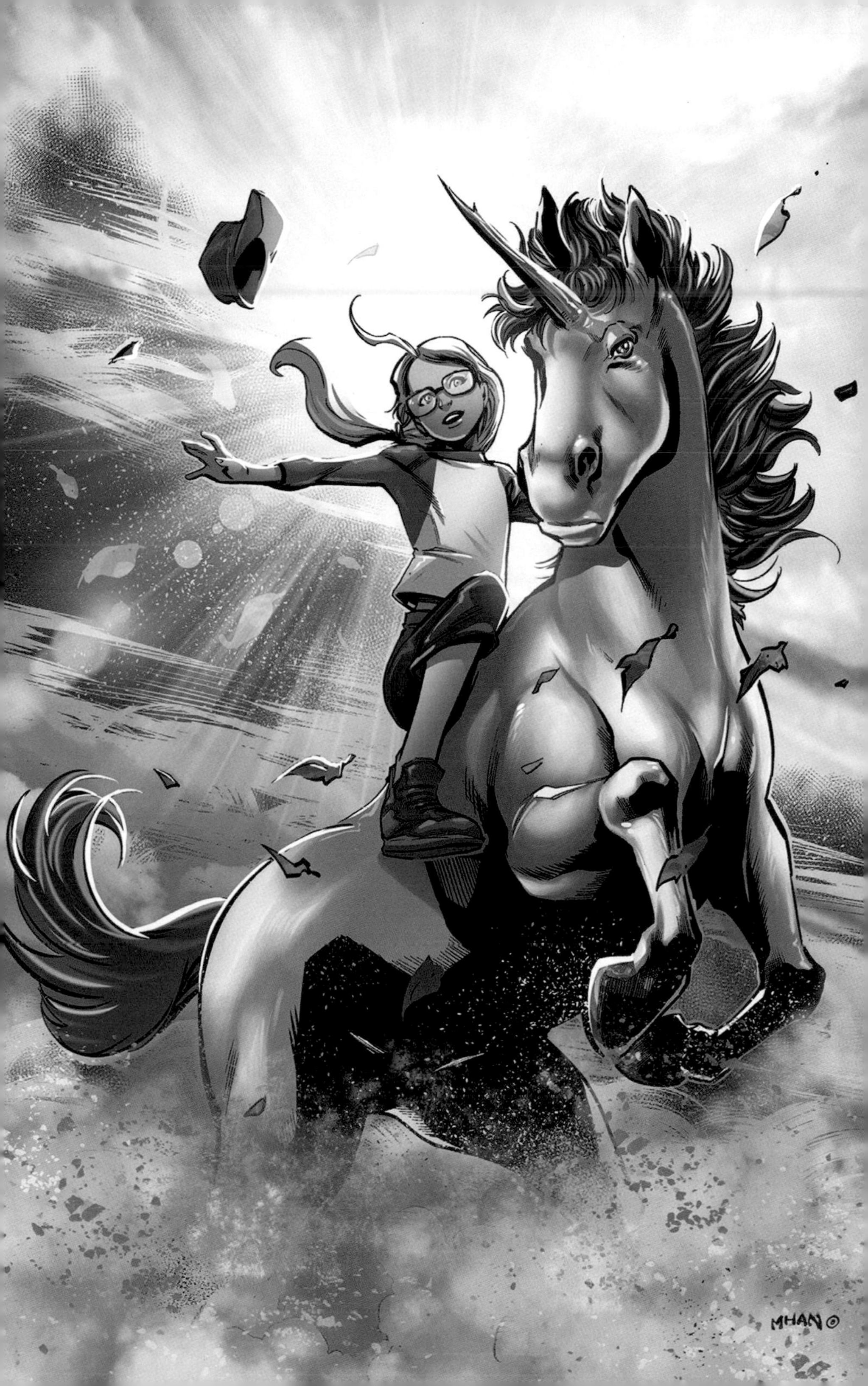
MHAN

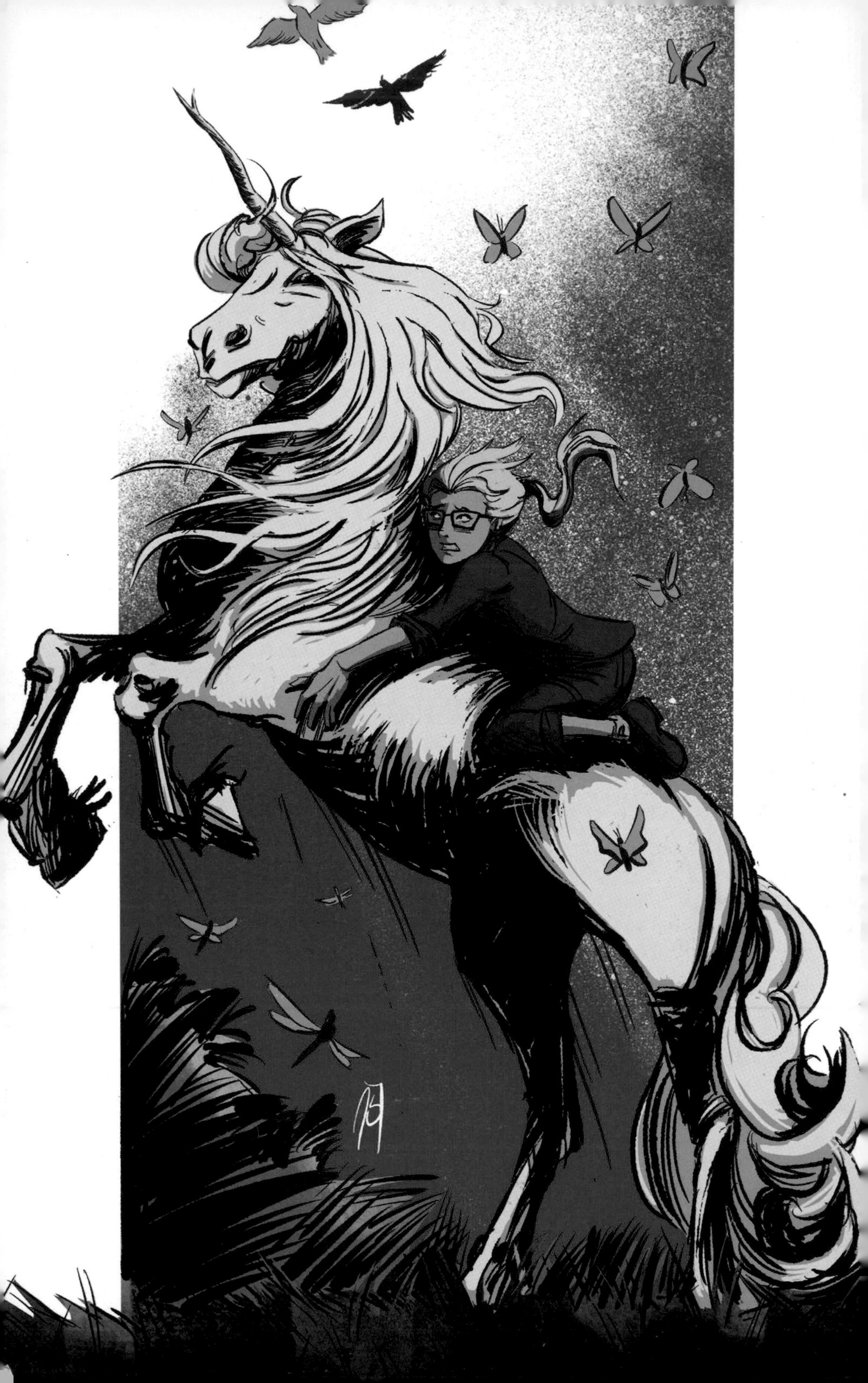

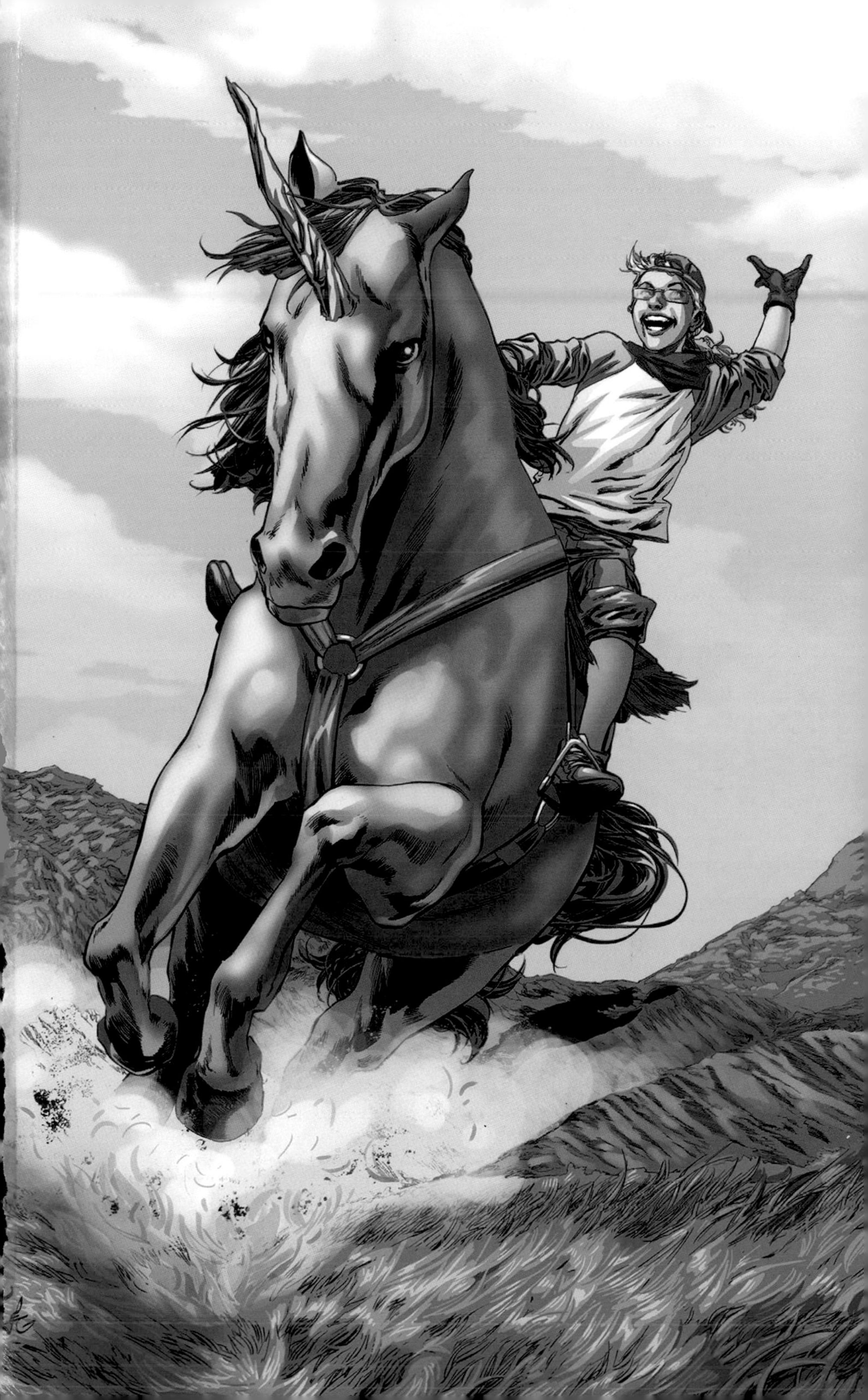

Published by SCOOT!
SCOOT! is an imprint of Scout Comics & Entertainment
12541 Metro Parkway Unit 20
Fort Myers, FL 33966

Library of Congress Control Number: 2021937433

Hardcover ISBN: 978-1-949514-92-6
Paperback ISBN: 978-1-949514-72-8

3 1901 06213 7197

SCOUT COMICS

First Edition 2021
Cover art and book design by Nicholas Ely
Printed in the USA